... e ...

"I'm [illegible] ryone will know how rich he is."

"I don't think so. He's just the assistant. It sounds like he lives in some ordinary apartment in a not-great part of Santa Monica."

"You saw it?"

"No! I told you, we just had dinner. I drove myself." It was just a tiny lie. And F. X.'s car hadn't indicated huge success, either—an ancient, salt-pocked BMW he'd probably driven out from the East Coast. "I'm sure he's fine, well off, whatever. His family probably is—he's from Darien." Lynn realized she was going on too long about F. X. "Anyway, what makes you say he's rich?"

"When you're a billionaire like Richard Plante, how much of a sacrifice is it to toss your bag carrier a couple million? It's what they do. It's like a tip."

"Oh, Jamie. You're crazy."

"I can't blame you," he said.

"For what?"

"For wanting to go out and have fun with rich, handsome men. I know I've been boring. I'm never here."

"You're not boring. And I don't find F. X. handsome." *You're* handsome, she thought, looking into his dark eyes.

"Then why do you simper every time you mention him?"

Lynn laughed. "Okay, maybe I was simpering, I don't know why. I knew you'd act jealous. But he's awful. I have no interest in seeing him again. I was even thinking that during dinner." Lynn tugged on Jamie's arm. "How can you think I'd ever want to be with anyone else? It's insulting."

"But you do know," he said, "if you ever slept with another man, that would be the end, right?"

"You're making me mad," she said, raising her lips to his.

I'll bet he does. Because men are

Prosper in Love

Deborah Michel

BERKLEY BOOKS, NEW YORK

THE BERKLEY PUBLISHING GROUP
Published by the Penguin Group
Penguin Group (USA) Inc.
375 Hudson Street, New York, New York 10014, USA

Penguin Group (Canada), 90 Eglinton Avenue East, Suite 700, Toronto, Ontario M4P 2Y3, Canada
(a division of Pearson Penguin Canada Inc.) • Penguin Books Ltd., 80 Strand, London WC2R 0RL,
England • Penguin Group Ireland, 25 St. Stephen's Green, Dublin 2, Ireland (a division of Penguin
Books Ltd.) • Penguin Group (Australia), 250 Camberwell Road, Camberwell, Victoria 3124, Australia
(a division of Pearson Australia Group Pty. Ltd.) • Penguin Books India Pvt. Ltd., 11 Community
Centre, Panchsheel Park, New Delhi—110 017, India • Penguin Group (NZ), 67 Apollo Drive,
Rosedale, Auckland 0632, New Zealand (a division of Pearson New Zealand Ltd.) • Penguin Books
(South Africa) (Pty.) Ltd., 24 Sturdee Avenue, Rosebank, Johannesburg 2196, South Africa

Penguin Books Ltd., Registered Offices: 80 Strand, London WC2R 0RL, England

This book is an original publication of The Berkley Publishing Group.

This is a work of fiction. Names, characters, places, and incidents either are the product of the author's
imagination or are used fictitiously, and any resemblance to actual persons, living or dead, business
establishments, events, or locales is entirely coincidental. The publisher does not have any control over
and does not assume any responsibility for author or third-party websites or their content.

PUBLISHING HISTORY
Berkley trade paperback edition / May 2012

Library of Congress Cataloging-in-Publication Data

Michel, Deborah, [date]
Prosper in love / Deborah Michel.—Berkley trade pbk. ed.
p. cm.
ISBN 978-0-425-24727-3 (pbk.)
I. Title.
PS3613.I34495P76 2012
813'.6—dc23
2011051568

PRINTED IN THE UNITED STATES OF AMERICA

10 9 8 7 6 5 4 3 2 1

For Tom, of course

Upon my word, I believe there is nothing he likes so much as going about and making mischief between men and their wives.

—ANTHONY TROLLOPE, *He Knew He Was Right*

Young people should think of their families in marrying.

—GEORGE ELIOT, *Middlemarch*

One

Lynn and Jamie Prosper were hardly one of those couples that seemed doomed from the start. On the contrary, they'd been happily married for two and a half years when F. X. Donahue reentered Lynn's life.

It was at one of the museum's cocktail parties. Lynn was chatting up an important collector when she happened to let her eyes stray around the edges of the large, stark gallery, part of the new addition—and there he was. She hadn't seen F. X. since college. At first she thought she must be mistaken. It had been, what, seven years? No, eight since he graduated—he'd been a year ahead of her. The last she'd heard, he was in sales for some company in Connecticut. She could see him only in profile, but really, there was no mistaking the handsome, too-large head, the blunted nose. And though he was not short, he had that bantam stance of men used to getting their way with women.

The elderly collector was busy regaling her with tales of having flirted with Françoise Gilot on the beach the very day that famous photograph was taken—Picasso marching behind his mistress in the sand with an oversized parasol. But at last he wound down. His glass was empty. Lynn of course offered to get him another drink, but he turned her down with a great show of chivalry. In his worldview, midlevel female curators in their late twenties were barely distinguishable from pert secretaries.

F. X. spun around when Lynn tapped him on the shoulder. "Why, Lynnie Kovak," he said, his face creasing into a grin, but in such a way as to make her wonder if he'd known all along that she was there.

"It's not Kovak anymore," she said.

"No!"

"Yes." Lynn couldn't help beaming.

"I guess I shouldn't be surprised. Is he as good-looking as I am?"

If only Lynn had never met F. X.

But is that fair? Just as easy to say a jealous man should never marry a flirt, or that sometimes differences in background can be too great to overcome. Those are the sorts of comments made in hindsight, as if one should have known all along and in fact seen disaster coming. But Lynn and Jamie's decision to wed had seemed obvious and inevitable and *right* to anyone who knew them. They even looked like a matched set, both slender, with glossy brown hair and dark, intelligent eyes, Jamie three inches taller, Lynn four months older. In their living room, in front of a pretty bay window, was a long, comfortable sofa—one of their first purchases as a married couple—and their favorite thing to do on weekends was curl up there, one at each end with a book, their feet touching in the middle.

"Is he nice?" F. X. smirked. "Rich? Successful?"

"Of course," said Lynn. She was as yet unaware of how the intervening years had treated F. X. "Well, not *rich*. But

very smart. And funny. He's a lawyer with Gerhardt, Lyons."
It was one of the best firms in Los Angeles. "But what are you
doing here? Visiting?"

"I live here now." He was watching her closely, as if this
were a trick question.

"Did you just move?"

"In November."

It was June. It was irrational to feel hurt that he hadn't
called; there was no reason for him to know she was in Los
Angeles, except that it was where she was from. Lynn wouldn't
say that she and F. X. had been close back in college, but
they'd often gravitated toward each other at parties, leaning
against walls and joking about what was going on around
them. Niceness wasn't one of F. X.'s stronger attributes, but
he did have a sharp sense of humor. He was so critical, so
unforgiving in his assessment of people, particularly women,
that it was flattering to be deemed acceptable, if only for light
conversation. Lynn had made the rather self-congratulatory
assumption that he put women worth talking to somewhere
above women worth sleeping with. And F. X. had made no
bones about sleeping with lots of women. The fact that he
had a girlfriend, a very pretty Southern blonde, didn't seem
to stop him. Lynn had taken a perverse pride in her friendship
with F. X., especially when the sweet guy down the hall in
her dorm took her aside to tell her she really shouldn't be
hanging around with him, that he'd hurt her. "But we're just
friends," she'd protested. "Still," he'd said, clearly not believing her, "it's not good for your reputation." Having always
been a nice girl, Lynn had liked this, too.

"I'm working for Richard Plante," F. X. said.

Richard Plante—one of the four famous Plante brothers,
the second generation of one of the largest, most profitable
family-owned businesses in the country. They'd been written

about again and again—how the company had started off in livestock feed but was now so diversified as to defy description. Its base was still Oklahoma, but the brothers were spread out all over the United States, each responsible for a different arm of the business. Richard was the youngest brother and was widely acknowledged to be the least talented.

"Yeah, I know," said F. X. "You thought I had some lame job in Stamford. I did, but Plante Brothers bought out the company."

"F. X., I never thought—"

He waved this away. "Don't worry, I knew you never thought I was that smart. Got by on animal cunning, right? And the fraternity term-paper files. It's okay. I always knew you were a snob."

"Me? You're the one from Darien."

But F. X. was right, and the fact that he was from an affluent Connecticut suburb only played into Lynn's dismissal of him. His mother had been a housewife, his father an insurance company executive. When F. X. went home he'd take his dirty laundry with him, and his mother would mail back his boxer shorts the next week, washed and ironed. Still, to Lynn, the product of West Coast Jewish intellectuals, there was something exotic in all this. Once, F. X. had mentioned that as a good Catholic (Lynn had needed to be told that his initials stood for Francis Xavier) he was saving himself for marriage. Knowing his dating history, she'd scoffed. F. X. had seemed genuinely offended.

"I'm serious," he'd said.

"You've slept with tons of women."

"But I've never gone down on any of them. That's what I'm saving for marriage."

If F. X. had been a typical frat boy on the East Coast, there was something refreshing in the sight of him in his (surprisingly well-cut) khakis amid all the slick, dark, Italian, L.A. suits. "So, how did you end up in L.A.?" she asked.

"Richard got it into his head that he wanted to try his hand at the entertainment business. So here I am. I'm just his assistant—his yes-man, bag carrier. But I like it here. L.A.'s all right. You should have invited me out when we were in college."

"We weren't that good friends."

"Hmm. Are you sure we didn't . . ."

"Positive."

"Because I could have sworn . . ."

"That's only because you did with everyone else."

"*Now* I remember why I always liked you."

"What about you?" she asked, pleased despite herself. "Are you married?"

"Me? No, free as a bird. Hey," he said, "you look great. Really great. So, are you a donor?" A devilish eyebrow lifted. "I was told this party was for heavy hitters."

"I work here. In the education department. So I know *you're* not a donor. You'd be on my list."

"Your list to educate?" There was a curl to his lips, which were sensuous looking and mobile to begin with. Suddenly Lynn was not quite at ease.

"Actually," he said, as if he realized he'd gone too far, "I'm here under false pretenses. Someone Richard knows invited him, but he had to go back to Tulsa at the last minute and passed the invitation on to me. In fact," he added, "you'll probably have my boss on your list soon."

"Really?" None of the Plante brothers was known as an art collector.

"Hey, want to grab a bite? Or do you have to go home to make dinner for hubby? What's his name, anyway?"

"Jamie. And he's on a business trip, so I don't have to go

home and make dinner. I mean, not that I have to go home and make dinner any night."

F. X. looked amused.

"Oh, you know what I mean." But Lynn felt flustered, as if somehow, by accident, she'd been disloyal.

Why shouldn't Lynn have dinner with an old college friend, one she hadn't seen or even thought of in years? Anyone would be curious, and Jamie was out of town. She probably would have ended up just stopping at the market for a salad bar dinner otherwise. And it seemed graceless and childish to keep insisting on driving herself to the restaurant when she could leave her car in the museum employee lot. F. X. had to pass back that way anyhow on his way home.

He surprised her by choosing a new restaurant she'd heard of but hadn't been to yet. She had to remind herself that F. X. had already been in Los Angeles for months and didn't need her to play tour guide. Even more disconcerting, the hostess seemed to know him, and although the place was packed and Lynn had heard it was impossible to get reservations even on weeknights, they were shown to a table right away. The hostess was ravishing in that typical L.A. restaurant hostess way, sloe-eyed with a perfect figure. But F. X. didn't eye her in his usual predatory manner. He had either changed or grown subtler.

The room was beautifully, expertly lit; the whole place seemed to glow. Lynn settled back in her chair. She loved restaurants; she'd practically been raised in them. Her mother, a feminist scholar, didn't cook. Oh, she'd opened cans now and then when Lynn and her two sisters were little, poured cereal, washed strawberries—never grapes, not during grape-picker strikes—but for the most part the Kovaks dined out.

Jamie, on the other hand, had grown up in St. Louis, with home-cooked meals every night. Lingering for hours over dinner and coffee in the latest restaurant was not his favorite way to spend an evening in the best of times, and lately he'd been working so hard that all he wanted at the end of the day—when he was in town to begin with—was to come home and rest.

Lynn realized that F. X. was watching her. He smiled—an indulgent smile. That's fine, she thought; let him think he was indulging her. For whatever reason, he was content to entertain the young wife while her adored husband was away. Lynn rather liked that role, for both of them. At the same time, she couldn't help but wonder what was in it for him. The F. X. of old rarely acted outside his own self-interest.

Lynn eyed the hostess again as she led new arrivals to their seats. She really was astonishingly attractive. Everyone in the restaurant was. Lynn took in the profiles of the gazelle-like women seated around her. It was very possible she was the least attractive woman in the room—except for one frizzy-haired woman in a suit jacket. But she looked important, a studio executive or a big agent.

"Do you want wine?" F. X. said, distracted by the menu, not at all flirtatious. "Or to start with a drink?"

It suddenly occurred to Lynn what she was for F. X.: a break from beauty and pulchritude. A rest, a relief even. It was probably what he had seen in her back in college, and she didn't mind that, either.

He snapped his fingers. "I know, let's have champagne. Didn't you always like champagne?"

"Sure," she said, flattered that he remembered. "I'd love a glass."

"A glass? Let's have a bottle. Come on, live a little. Anyway, I'm driving."

This was accurate only up to a point. Lynn would have to drive home from the museum.

"Same Lynnie," F. X. said, "never out of control, never straying remotely close to the edge." He laughed at the look on her face. "It's okay—a sweet, nice girl is a good thing to be. When I decide to get married it'll be to someone like you."

"Right, then have affairs with the exciting, dangerous ones."

"Maybe." But he met her eyes with his own gray-blue ones. "Seriously, when I get married it'll be for good."

"Your wife won't mind the philandering?"

"She won't know about it."

"You've got to be kidding."

"Not that I'm saying I will. I just don't believe in divorce, that's all. I'm going to marry someone who feels the same way."

"Do you really not believe in divorce?"

"Not for myself. It's not that I disapprove on principle. Others can do what they like."

"But what if you realized you'd made the wrong choice and were miserable?"

"That's part of being a grown-up. You live with your choices. In the Catholic Church," he said, "marriage is a sacrament."

It had always been a favorite game of F. X.'s to lead people on, then laugh at them for not realizing he'd been joking all along. "Well," said Lynn, "I guess I childishly went into marriage without giving it as much thought as you have."

"Nah, I'm sure you guys are perfectly happy. You look happy. You look great."

They happened to reach for their waters at the same time and accidentally clinked glasses. F. X. grinned at her across the table.

"Are you seeing anybody?" she asked.

"As a matter of fact, I am."

But Lynn had just remembered his comment about being free as a bird. She felt sorry for the woman, whoever she was. "Is she here in L.A.?"

F. X. nodded. "She's from Brazil."

She had imagined him with a preppy blonde like his old college girlfriend. "How did you meet?"

"A strip club."

"A stripper? Or another customer?"

"Nice, Lynn, you're getting better. I thought I had you there."

"You didn't really meet her in a strip club, did you?"

"What do *you* think?"

Lynn realized that her phone was vibrating in her purse. Probably Jamie. He'd probably called home first and was wondering where she was. She couldn't answer—she hated when people answered phones in restaurants, and anyway she wouldn't want F. X. listening in. Another beautiful girl, very young, but with a sommelier's cup on a heavy chain dangling into her cleavage, arrived with the champagne. Lynn had the feeling F. X. knew her, too. She was gratified to see him leer after her when she turned to go. He saw Lynn watching, and winked.

He hadn't changed at all. Lynn was sure that Jamie, who was an excellent judge of character, would detest F. X. on sight. She missed Jamie. How lucky she was.

"What?" said F. X.

Lynn looked back at him. "What, what?"

"You were smiling. You don't believe in my Brazilian girl-friend?"

God, Lynn thought, he couldn't stand not being the center of attention for even one minute. It hadn't occurred to her to question the existence of the Brazilian girlfriend, but now of course she had to. That was how it worked with F. X. If you were quick enough to catch his hints, he'd give you that private, congratulatory smile. You didn't even have to say anything— he'd catch the look in your eye. And it was exhilarating, that feeling of operating on all cylinders. Suddenly, though, the idea of it made her tired. Why was she here with him? If she'd been home, she could have talked to Jamie.

Lynn looked more closely at F. X. across the table. He had the same cheekbones, the piercing light eyes, the cleft chin, but his face was also rounded, almost babyish. He was still very good looking, but in the years since she had last seen him his brow had thickened. His features seemed less finely drawn, the skin over his nose coarser. She was twenty-nine; he was only a year or so older. Was this what it meant to lose one's looks with age? She had never doubted that it happened, but it was the first time she'd noticed it in someone she knew.

F. X.'s shoulders rose and fell infinitesimally, a small sigh escaping his lips. One thing about F. X., he had an instinct for where he stood with a woman. He was alert to the subtlest changes in chemistry or emotion. Lynn reached for her glass of champagne. It's okay, she told herself. No danger here.

Two

J ust tell me," said Jamie, "did you ever sleep with the guy?"

"Of course not! I told you, F. X. was just a friend. Not even a friend exactly. I was just . . . amused by him."

"He doesn't sound amusing. He sounds like a jerk."

"Oh, he is! He's so transparent. I think that's what I liked—being the one who hadn't slept with him."

There was something off in the calibration of this conversation. Lynn could hear it and knew Jamie must, too. She had told him all about running into F. X. as soon as he got back from New York. Jamie had actually called twice from his hotel while she was out to dinner, but it was late, New York time, when she was finally alone in her car, and she knew he wouldn't have wanted to be woken. Still, she'd imagined him going to bed not knowing where she was, and how much she would have hated that herself.

Lynn looked over at him. He was standing at the counter of the funny little living room wet bar, riffling angrily—no, not angrily, really—through the stack of mail she'd left there for his return. She'd known he wouldn't like it, about F. X., but she had to smile at the sight of him—a deep, genuine smile, one he couldn't fail to recognize. He looked up and met her eyes.

Lynn and Jamie had met in a bar. (Lynn would quickly add that it wasn't what it sounded, that they had each been brought by different friends to a birthday party that happened to be taking place in a bar.) The point was that their eyes met, and they both felt it. Lynn had wanted to look away, embarrassed with so many people watching, but the force field of Jamie's gaze held her. During the evening, she talked, laughed, and even flirted with others, but eventually, inevitably, she ended up next to Jamie leaning against a jukebox in the corner of the loud bar. Their hands, resting on the glass over the song choices, accidentally brushed, and when they bowed their dark heads together for the first time, the better to hear each other, it was as if time paused with them. When it started up again a heartbeat later, all seemed right in the world.

On their fourth date (four nights later), they drove up to Mulholland after dinner. It was a cliché—they both knew it. They stood together on the shoulder of the road, the sparkling spread of the city below them. Jamie turned to Lynn and he took a deep breath. She waited, but he didn't say anything. She gave him one of her sweetest, most encouraging smiles, and he smiled back and took another breath but still didn't speak. He just stared into her eyes as though amazed by the wonder of her. Which was lovely, but eventually it became clear to Lynn that she could help. "Sometimes . . ." she began, her eyes soft. "I love you," he blurted, and she'd been gratified that she'd understood just what he needed. Later, as they scrambled back up the dirt slope to where his car waited, she'd stumbled and wrecked the heel of one of her favorite pairs of shoes, which somehow made the whole thing perfect.

"Well, I'm sure F. X. *wanted* to sleep with you," Jamie

said, and sure enough his tone had shifted. He came over to her on the sofa. "That's how guys are, especially in college. He wouldn't have bothered talking to you otherwise."

"That's not a very nice thing to say about men. Wait, are you saying that's the only reason you talked to me when we met?"

Jamie just grinned—and drew closer.

"Anyway," she said, pleasantly flustered even after two years of marriage, "the girls he went out with were much prettier." *Oh, Lynn!* Jamie's face darkened; she hurried on. "You know Richard Plante? The Plante brothers? That's who he's working for. He's his assistant or something."

This was supposed to placate, but Jamie was still frowning. "You're kidding."

"No, why?"

"His assistant?"

"His yes-man, F. X. said." Lynn was relieved that Jamie had picked up on that belittling word, just as he was supposed to. "He's not that bad, Jamie. See, he says things like that about himself."

"I'll bet he does. Because then everyone will know how rich he is."

"I don't think so. He's just the assistant. It sounds like he lives in some ordinary apartment in a not-great part of Santa Monica."

"You saw it?"

"No! I told you, we just had dinner. I drove myself." It was just a tiny lie. And F. X.'s car hadn't indicated huge success, either—an ancient, salt-pocked BMW he'd probably driven out from the East Coast. "I'm sure he's fine, well off, whatever. His family probably is—he's from Darien." Lynn realized she was going on too long about F. X. "Anyway, what makes you say he's rich?"

"When you're a billionaire like Richard Plante, how much of a sacrifice is it to toss your bag carrier a couple million? It's what they do. It's like a tip."

"Oh, Jamie. You're crazy."

"I can't blame you," he said.

"For what?"

"For wanting to go out and have fun with rich, handsome men. I know I've been boring. I'm never here."

"You're not boring. And I don't find F. X. handsome." *You're* handsome, she thought, looking into his dark eyes.

"Then why do you simper every time you mention him?"

Lynn laughed. "Okay, maybe I was simpering, I don't know why. I knew you'd act jealous. But he's awful. I have no interest in seeing him again. I was even thinking that during dinner." Lynn tugged on Jamie's arm. "How can you think I'd ever want to be with anyone else? It's insulting."

"But you do know," he said, "if you ever slept with another man, that would be the end, right?"

"You're making me mad," she said, raising her lips to his.

Three

Near the end of the first day back after July Fourth week-end, Lynn picked up the ringing phone on her desk, expecting Jamie. When another man's voice said, "Hey," she recognized it right away.

"F. X.?"

"You never called to thank me for dinner. Was hubby mad?"

"Of course not. Why would he be mad?"

"I don't know. You tell me, Mrs. Prosper."

Lynn had in fact meant to call, but Jamie's reaction had stayed her hand. She'd thought about a note, but that seemed ridiculously formal, and then she and Jamie had gone out of town for the long weekend, to Tahoe. Now Lynn felt abashed by her lapse of manners and the tiniest, tiniest bit annoyed with Jamie for being behind it.

"Why?" she said. "Was your stripper mad?"

"My stripper?" F. X. gave a bark of laughter. "Not at all, she showed me a great time this weekend in Venezuela."

"Venezuela?"

"It's where her parents live."

Hadn't he said Brazil? But Lynn didn't care—she just wanted to get off the phone. Jamie was right about F. X.—he was awful.

"I was just calling," he said, "to invite you and Jamie to something Wednesday night. A Mona Frumpke opening. You've heard of her, right?"

Of course Lynn had heard of her. Mona Frumpke was famous in the art world for the—not gallery exactly, but the sort of floating salon she ran. She threw party-cum-openings every now and then in different, quasi-secret locales, invitation only. Lynn had never come close to being invited.

"I thought you'd be interested. Then maybe we could all grab a bite somewhere. I'll see if Chaka can join us."

"Is this through Richard Plante?" It sounded as though the billionaire really was getting involved in the art world.

"No, I wrangled this invitation on my lonesome." F. X. sounded amused rather than offended. "I happened to sit next to Mona on a long plane trip. Two different delays, so we sort of . . . bonded."

I'll bet you did, Lynn thought. *Mona*. Chaka.

"So, we're on?" he said. "Is Jamie a big art fan, too?"

"Oh. No."

"He's not?"

"No—I mean, yes. He is. But I just remembered, Jamie has to go out of town again tonight. He won't be back until Thursday."

"That's too bad. This sounds like it's going to be fun."

Lynn didn't say anything.

"Listen," said F. X., "if Jamie's out of town, why don't you join Chaka and me? It sounds like he's out of town a lot."

"He is. There's this big deal he's on in New York right now. He has to be there practically every week." Lynn chewed her lip. A Mona Frumpke opening. At least F. X. was calling Jamie by name now.

"I'd love for you to meet Chaka. It'll be fun."

"I don't know . . ."

"Come on, don't be a baby. Aren't you allowed out on your own?"

"Of course I am. I mean . . ."

F. X. laughed.

Professionally, of course, it would be great for Lynn to see a Mona Frumpke party—Jamie would understand that. Plus, F. X.'s girlfriend would be there. "Okay," Lynn said, "it does sound like fun. I'd love to. And thank you. Thanks for inviting me—for inviting both of us, even though Jamie can't come."

"Hey, Lynnie," said F. X., sounding amused, "no problem."

But when Wednesday evening came, F. X. showed up at Lynn's door alone. Lynn peered around him to his car parked in front of her house, but there was no South American beauty in the passenger seat.

"Isn't Chaka coming?"

F. X. turned to look, too, as if surprised his girlfriend wasn't there. "Oh, Chaka's not able to make it. She had to fly up to San Francisco at the last minute for some modeling work."

"Oh," said Lynn. How was she going to explain it to Jamie? But no, that was ridiculous, she had done nothing wrong. "Let me just grab my purse," she said.

The opening or party or whatever it was, was held in a house up on Mulholland Drive at the top of a street called Outpost. Outpost was a small canyon not far from where Lynn and Jamie lived in Hollywood, but Lynn had never been up it before. The densely treed road switchbacked sharply, and the houses practically embedded in the steep hillsides weren't particularly large but they had an enviable air of bohemian richesse. Even though Lynn knew these events weren't traditional art shows, she had imagined they'd be going to a gallery or at least some sort of public space, an airplane hangar, maybe.

"Is this Mona Frumpke's house?" she asked F. X., once he'd handed his car over to a red-jacketed valet. They were following a stream of people up a long, straight gravel walk to an enormous, saffron-colored, walled, Moorish-looking mansion that seemed to exist in a different sphere altogether from the houses they'd passed on the way up. The cars had entered through a massively paneled oak gate, each coffer embellished with an iron rosette, reminding Lynn of a drawbridge.

"Mona's?" F. X. laughed. "Hardly. Mona lives in Beverly Hills. You'd never catch her out here. She must have borrowed this from someone. Or, knowing her, it's on the market and she'll get a commission when it sells next week thanks to tonight."

The house, Lynn thought, would have been very beautiful had it been old. It seemed, at least from the outside, to have all the details and workmanship and solidity that people always say you can't find anymore, but the effect was ruined by the fact it looked like it had been finished last Tuesday. But Lynn stopped herself. Why should it be less appealing just because it was new if it was well done? What sort of snobbery was that? Houses like the older ones she'd admired on the way up had been, she knew for a fact, mocked as pastiches when they were new in the 1920s or 1930s. She wished Jamie were here to see it. She felt the heels of her shoes slide in the gravel as they crossed the vast expanse of square courtyard to the front door. A butler stood waiting just outside, and behind him a line of tall, serious-looking men in white gloves offering flutes

of champagne on silver trays—a step up from the usual cater-
ing staff.

In the foyer, which had archways leading in all directions,
Lynn and F. X. were about to fall in step behind the previous
arrivals who were heading through an archway to the right,
to where the installation apparently began. Ahead of them, a
cluster of other guests had stopped in front of the first piece,
although from where Lynn stood it appeared to be just a sheet
of yellow legal pad paper stuck on the wall. Lynn glanced
around for some sign or plaque giving the name of the evening's artist.

"Effie," cried a voice, high and gravelly at the same time,
and a platinum-haired woman with white skin and vermilion
lips glided up to them. Her hair was bobbed, shiny, and close
to her head. *Marcelled*, Lynn thought, never having seen anything like it in the flesh. The woman was wearing a white
Grecian-style dress that came only to her knees, and high-
heeled shoes that were, in contrast to the rest of her, very
contemporary looking: sandals with rhinestones covering the
narrow straps. There was nothing youthful about her, but
nothing old, either. "Effie, darling," she said, enfolding F. X.
in a hug with her hands splayed out as if her nails, also vermilion, were still wet. "Mmmwah," she said, and winked at
Lynn. "And this must be the elusive Chaka." She was unabashedly looking Lynn up and down. If she'd been expecting a
South American beauty plucked from a strip joint, Lynn was
probably not what she'd imagined. The pleased, rather smug
expression on the older woman's face bore this out. Lynn
wondered if F. X. had ever slept with her and guessed yes.

"Mona," said F. X., "I'd like to introduce you to an old
friend of mine, Lynn Kovak. No, make that Lynn Prosper.
Lynnie got married since I first knew her—very, very happily,
she keeps telling me."

"Oh?" Mona eyed her speculatively. Lynn wanted to kick F. X.

"And now Lynn's a big muckety-muck at the museum."

"No, I'm not," Lynn said. "Not at all. Just an associate curator."

"Oh? Who do you work with? Anyone I might know?"

"Right now I mainly answer to Earl Smithson."

"Smitty?" cried Mona. Earl Smithson was the museum's deputy director, and normally Lynn, a mere associate curator in the education department, wouldn't have had much to do with anyone so exalted. But recently he had handpicked Lynn to play an additional role—informal liaison between the curatorial staff and the development department, the two of which had taken on the aspect of separate duchies forever in covert internecine battle. Lynn turned out to be adept at making sure the labels for exhibition works were properly handled, particularly the way donors were listed. Typeface, size, and even punctuation could be telling—and disputed. "Oh, fabulous," said Mona. "We love Smitty! Now, why haven't I seen you before at my little 'dos?"

"I'm sorry to say I've never been invited."

"What? Well, we'll have to rectify that, now that I see what a delightful girl you are. Lynn Prosper, did you say? I'll have to scold Smitty for not having introduced you before. He knows I love young blood." She gave an alarming smile and turned to F. X., who lifted her limp white hand and kissed the air above it. It figured. That was exactly the sort of thing F. X. would know—that you're not actually supposed to touch your lips to the woman's hand.

Mona turned away to greet the next guest, and Lynn was about to move on when behind her she heard their hostess's voice harden. "Excuse me," Lynn heard her say, "I'm Mona Frumpke. I don't believe I have the pleasure of your acquaintance. May I see your invitation?" Lynn knew there were no printed invitations to these events. She couldn't help glancing back, and saw the horrified expression on a young woman's face, about her own age.

"I . . . I'm afraid I don't have mine with me. But I'm with Blum Gallery. I understood that . . . since I'm in the art world . . ."

Lynn couldn't listen anymore, it was too painful. She kept moving down the hallway where the installation began. "Boy," she said to F. X., "I'm glad I never had enough information to crash one of these."

"Oh, Mona just likes to have her fun. She really is harmless."

"Does she really keep track of everyone she invites? There must be hundreds."

"You probably get your routine down after a while."

Mona had been on the art scene forever, since the eighties. How old must she be? Early fifties? Late forties, at least. Knowing F. X., he knew, but Lynn didn't like to ask. She focused instead on the artwork. The first piece was, indeed, a page from a yellow legal pad, standard size and tacked to the wall with a common thumbtack, red in color. What made it clear that it was to be considered art was that it was outlined on the wall by a black border. There was a small black numeral three at the bottom and a red dot sticker next to that, indicating, just as in a regular gallery, that the piece had been sold. Lynn automatically looked around for numbers one and two.

"What's that?" F. X. said, and Lynn looked down on the floor where he was pointing, just beneath the tacked sheet of paper. There was a small pile of what appeared to be fine white sand or dust on the floor close to the wall. Lynn looked up at the ceiling, at the wall, then back down, bending to look more closely.

"I think it's supposed to be the plaster from the hole the tack made."

F. X. bent over it, too, frowning.

"Of course there's way too much of it for that," Lynn said. "I think it's part of the piece. Look, it draws attention to the fact that the piece of paper, the artwork, has been hung in this manner. And maybe also even to the fact that the walls of this house are plaster or stucco, not drywall, making the house itself part of the piece."

"So the pile of dust is art, too?"

"Look at it, its shape. It's basically an arrow pointing up at the sheet of paper. Or maybe you look at it and the thought pops into your mind, 'Mountains out of molehills.'"

F. X. stared at her. "You're kidding, right?" He looked from the tacked-up piece of paper to the mound of plaster dust. "Where do you get all that? From *that*?"

Lynn laughed. "I'm just talking. It's what you learn to do in art history classes. Sort of stream of consciousness. That's the thing about art: Everyone's reactions are valid. But if you've looked at a lot of art from different periods, you start to see references to works that came before." She leaned in to read what was written on the yellow sheet. It was a list in messy but easily legible handwriting, in pencil. (*Impermanence, erasability*, Lynn noted to herself, getting into the swing of it.)

It was a list of names, men's names, with numbers, dates, and sometimes question marks in parentheses:

Brian the Kisser, 4 (?)
Leo Spiegel, 1989
Mark Yablons, 1989
Cole Foster, 15, 1992

And so on. There were some skipped lines that just had question marks. The list had three columns: the second in the middle of the sheet; the third, with only three names, squeezed into the right margin.

They moved along the wall to the next piece, which turned out to be an old black-and-white photograph, the kind with a white border and deckle edges. At the forefront of the photograph were two children on tricycles, a little boy and a little girl. The girl, who had short, dark, curly hair, looked directly at the camera with a grimace. The boy, blond, with thick bangs and a bowl cut, faced the little girl, leaning over his handlebars toward her, a determined expression on his face. This photograph, too, was surrounded by a black border. There was the number four under the bottom right corner but no red dot.

A few feet farther down the hallway a Moorish arch opened into a small room where the exhibit continued. Lynn and F. X. had been pretty much alone in the hallway, but this room was full of people moving slowly around the walls to look at what appeared to be more traditional artworks, oil paintings maybe. There was no furniture in the room, nothing to give any indication of its purpose in the house, yet it did not feel like a gallery space with its big, paned windows and doors leading to other rooms.

"Wait," said F. X., taking a step back into the hallway. "What's this?"

A wooden lectern stood on the far side of the archway. Lynn hadn't noticed it. On its slanted top lay a stained and worn spiral notebook. F. X. tried to pick it up and Lynn saw that it was attached to the podium by the kind of plastic-covered wire cord used to secure expensive leather or fur coats to clothing racks in department stores. Nudging him aside, Lynn flipped through the notebook and started to read from the beginning. It looked like the same slanted handwriting as on the legal sheet, but neater. Lynn could feel F. X.'s breath on her neck as he leaned over her, reading, too.

The notebook held the explanation of the exhibit. The artist had decided, after running into an old boyfriend unexpectedly on the streets of London, to find out what had happened to everyone she had ever kissed. She had not, she wrote in her introduction, been successful in finding or even remembering them all, but the exhibit was the documentation of her process and experiences.

F. X. waggled his eyebrows at Lynn. "Maybe some of it will be pornographic. Can you imagine having to track down everyone you kissed? Who can remember?"

Lynn thought about it. She had kissed more than a few men in her dating days. She'd been one of those people who actually enjoyed the whole dating ritual. But would you have to include all of the random, end-of-date good-night kisses bestowed merely out of politeness? She didn't really count those, but if she had to she could probably track down most of even those half-forgotten men. She kept pretty good records in her daily calendar, which she tended to use as an ad hoc phone book as well. "I could do it," she said. "Not that there have been that many," she felt compelled to add.

F. X. made a scoffing sound. "We're talking about kissing, not sex. Although it's usually pretty much the same list, isn't it?"

"You sleep with every woman you kiss?"

F. X. narrowed his eyes at her. "You say we never slept together?"

She sighed.

"You're sure?" he insisted.

"Would you be happier if I said, yes, you're right, it's just that it was completely forgettable?"

"Fine, fine. Then that makes you one of the few women I kissed but didn't sleep with. There. Happy?"

"F. X.," said Lynn, "we never kissed."

"Sure we did."

"In your dreams, apparently."

He looked puzzled.

"We didn't!"

"Okay," he said, "so I'd have a tough time making a list like that. Not that I ever would—it would be the height of ungentlemanly behavior."

"As opposed to sleeping with hordes of women."

"Lynnie," said F. X., with something akin to pity, "I never sleep with anyone who's not willing." He grinned. "It's not like I have to force myself on women."

Lynn went back to flipping through the notebook. It said that the sheet of paper tacked to the wall had been the artist's initial attempt to make a list. Half forgetting F. X., Lynn moved back to the yellow sheet. This time she looked at the last entries first:

Charles Croft, 28, 2003–06
Fra. Dona., 2006
Mark Y., 29, 2006

Wait a minute, was Mark Y. the same Mark Yablons at the beginning of the list? Had she gotten back together with a high school boyfriend? Lynn was assuming the numbers were age and year kissed. But whose age? Hers? His? And what about "Brian the Kisser, 4 (?)"? Lynn moved back to the old photograph. Could the little boy be Brian the Kisser? She studied the photograph more closely. The boy and girl were at the bottom of what appeared to be a long cement driveway with a chain-link fence on the left and a sandbox filled with lots of toys on the right. You could see the edge of a swing set at the right-hand corner of the photograph. Lynn had the impression of a preschool rather than a backyard. There were too many toys, and the sand area seemed too big. Had Brian the Kisser been in nursery school with the artist? Had he made a habit of chasing little girls down to the end of the driveway and having his four-year-old way with them?

F. X. was waiting for her back at the lectern. "So, you're one of those people who drift off by themselves in museums. I hate that. I didn't come here to look at this stuff by myself!"

"I'm sorry," Lynn said, startled by his outburst. "Actually, I like to look at art with other people, although . . ." F. X. didn't appear to be listening. "Why?" she said. "Bad date at a museum?" She hadn't imagined F. X. spending lots of time in museums, although of course he'd been at that party at hers.

"Not just one date. I wouldn't complain if that's all it was. It's you sensitive, intellectual types mooning in front of the brilliant masterpiece. Although I guess some weenie men do that sort of thing, too. You know, like Rilke. What did he say? About spending two hours looking at a few Cézannes? God."

He was talking about the poet's letters to his wife, famous letters, at least to anyone in art history. But how improbable for F. X. to know anything about Rilke, let alone be able to quote him.

"And you're standing there, feeling like a philistine, fighting the impulse to start counting the seconds out loud or check your watch. They all do it—you, Chaka, Melissa—"

"Melissa?" Lynn realized almost immediately from F. X.'s face that this was what she was supposed to have asked. "Okay," she said, "so who's Melissa?"

F. X. switched to a shocked and, in Lynn's estimation, completely put-on expression. "Boy, Lynn. Sometimes I wonder if you're listening to anything I'm saying. Melissa is the mother of my child."

"Your child?"

"You know—my son."

"F. X., I had absolutely no idea you have a son. You never mentioned it. You do remember that until we ran into each other we hadn't spoken since college?"

"I'm sure I mentioned Michael. I talk about him all the time. I love the kid. Michael Joseph."

Lynn was getting tired of this. "Yeah, well I guess you told me sometime after we kissed and had sex because I remember it about as well."

F. X. regarded Lynn for a moment, then pulled her by the arm back down the hallway, through the entry vestibule to the other side. He paused at a half-closed door, peered inside, then opened the door and led her in. He kicked the door shut behind them with the edge of his foot. And took Lynn by the shoulders in the empty room and kissed her.

It was over almost as soon as it began. He'd already let her go by the time she realized what was happening and shoved him away. "What—"

He put a finger to his lips. "There, it's done. We've kissed. End of story. I was tired of arguing about whether we had or hadn't."

Lynn took a deep breath, trying to think of a withering reply. It hadn't been a real kiss, hardly more than a peck, almost too quick to notice that his lips were dry and soft. There had been no lingering, not even the hint of wanting to linger. She lifted her chin, glancing around. The room F. X. had pulled her into was a large one, almost ballroom sized. It was empty except for several clusters of identical chairs—

Louis XVI–style gilt armchairs upholstered in a rose-colored silk brocade. In fact, the whole arrangement of the room was so odd that Lynn wondered if it wasn't another art installation. There was even a drop cloth in one corner.

"Now," he said, "can we get back to my son?"

Lynn should have turned on her heel and walked out.

F. X. was dragging two of the gilt chairs closer together. With a glance at Lynn, he sat. "He's three," he said. "Michael just turned three."

Lynn remained standing, but uncertainly. "Does he live here?" she said.

"Oh for God's sake, will you sit down, I'm not going to eat you. No, his mother lives back in Connecticut."

Lynn sank into the chair.

F. X. leaned in toward her, his hands on his knees. "Do you want to hear the whole story?"

"Sure." She steeled herself against gullibility.

F. X. had been seeing this woman, Melissa. She was living in New York at the time and was older than he was—five years older—a successful PR woman who (the way F. X. described it) enjoyed playing older wicked city woman to F. X.'s boy from Connecticut. At the time, he had not yet started working for Richard Plante. He and Melissa had been dating for about six months—not exclusively, certainly not on F. X.'s part—when she got pregnant.

"So I asked her to marry me," he said.

"You did?" Lynn remembered what F. X. had said about marriage and Catholicism.

"What do you take me for? I certainly wasn't going to ask her to have an abortion. She's Catholic, too."

Lynn just shook her head.

"I was thinking of the baby. But we were actually pretty

good together. She was sharp. Funny. Until she turned into a psycho."

Melissa wanted to postpone any talk of weddings until after the baby was born. Lynn would have thought that F. X.'s mother, she of the laundered boxer shorts, would be horrified by all this, but F. X. claimed she had been relatively unfazed. He was, after all, the third of four boys. All she wanted was her son's happiness.

The child was born. F. X. offered to move to Manhattan. Melissa demurred. He offered to find a place so that she could move to Connecticut. She turned down this offer, too.

Lynn couldn't help being impressed by F. X.'s flexibility, his desire to be with his son.

But things turned ugly—without F. X. even realizing it at first. After Michael Joseph was born, his parents gradually drifted out of their romantic—or rather, sexual—relationship. Around the child's first birthday, F. X. noticed that Melissa wasn't returning his calls as quickly, then sometimes not at all. First she canceled one afternoon F. X. was supposed to spend in the city with Michael, then a weekend. She professed to be very busy and became progressively cagier about her schedule. F. X. was no fool. He called a lawyer and initiated a suit for paternity rights. It was only then that he discovered that Melissa had legally changed the baby's name from Michael Joseph Donahue to Michael James Spector, her own last name. He decided to sue for at least partial custody. She claimed she wasn't sure the child was his. A paternity test settled that question. Next she requested that the court deny F. X. unsupervised visits, claiming that he'd behaved inappropriately and even violently toward his son, then almost two years old.

"He was acting up," F. X. told Lynn, outraged at the memory. "He was two, behaving badly on purpose, and, yes,

I raised my voice. What parent hasn't done that? Yes, I said he'd get a spanking if he didn't stop. But I wasn't going to hit him. I just said it. I never spanked him in his life."

"That's ridiculous," said Lynn. "You can't deny someone visitation rights for something like that."

But evidently you could. Melissa might have been vindictive and crazy but she was also savvy and well connected. She knew a number of judges and people in child protective services and had made large political contributions at the local level, where it counted. Lynn wasn't convinced you could suborn the justice system like that, but however she did it, Melissa convinced enough people that F. X. was not only in the wrong, but possibly an unfit parent and a potential danger to her child and herself.

"I guess some people heard me yelling at her when I found out about some of the stuff she was pulling," F. X. admitted. "Sure I yelled. It's my son she's playing games with. But it was in her apartment in New York where she's on the co-op board, and part of the time we were out in the hall—so Michael wouldn't hear." He gave a bitter laugh. "She got her neighbors to testify, and then this woman who lives on another floor comes and talks about how I'd had an affair with her, too, while I was seeing Melissa, and there was even a third woman who used to live in the building." F. X. leaned his head in his hands, rubbed his eyes.

"But didn't you say she moved to Connecticut? That was good, wasn't it?"

F. X. raised his head. "Yeah, that was after I moved to L.A. Part of why I moved here was that she up and moved to San Diego without telling me first. Why should she have to inform me? I have no rights. So then I arranged this stuff in L.A., and two months after I get here, she moves back—to Connecticut, this time, to my hometown. She's sucking up to my family now. My parents get to see my son and I don't. But it looks good in court, that she doesn't have anything against the grandparents having a relationship with him. She's such a vicious bitch."

"How often do you get to see your son?" Lynn asked. She felt chastened. "When was the last time?"

"Last weekend." He gave another harsh laugh. "It had been planned for ages. I flew all the way back there and at the last minute she changed her mind and only let me have forty-five minutes with him, supervised by some social worker. I was supposed to get four hours!"

Last weekend? Hadn't he said he was in Venezuela with his stripper girlfriend? But this story about his son was so awful, how could Lynn stop to press him on inconsistencies?

He was watching her now, a half smile on his face. "Pretty pathetic, right? Finally brought down low. I was going to move back, but she only lets me see Michael once a month and I can usually take one of the company jets. Plus, my lawyer found out she's still holding on to her San Diego condo, so if I did move back there she'd probably move again, too. Her firm has a San Diego office."

And hadn't Mona Frumpke called Chaka elusive? Was there a girlfriend at all?

"F. X.," Lynn said, "it just sounds crazy."

"You're telling me." He stood. "Listen, now that I've depressed myself, do you mind if we just go? You don't mind, do you?"

"No, of course not," said Lynn, rising, too. "No, I totally understand."

The truth was, as startling as F. X.'s revelations had been and as genuinely sorry as Lynn felt for him, she did not want to leave. She felt like a bad, selfish, superficial person, but she wanted to see more of the party, not to mention the installation. What about those paintings in the room they hadn't gotten to? But F. X. was waiting in the doorway. Lynn let her fingers trail across the arm of her chair as she moved reluctantly away from it, tracing the indentation in the carved, scrolled arm.

In the entry vestibule Lynn noticed what she hadn't on the way in: a Lucite pedestal with a moundlike white object on it, also encased in a Lucite box. It looked soft, changing shape in gradation, like a ghostly 3-D map of a sedimentary mountain. Two other partygoers were leaning over it, peering and pointing. Lynn wanted more than anything to go over and see what it was. But F. X. gave her an impatient frown, and she had no choice but to follow him out.

Four

Lynn shared an office at work. It was a decent-sized cubicle on a corridor of like cubicles, the corridor-side wall made of glass for an open, airy feel. You could see everyone coming and going, and they could see you. The woman she shared it with—it was mainly women in the education department, in the museum as a whole, actually, until you got to the highest levels—was another associate curator, slightly senior to Lynn and a couple of years older. That is, Glynnis Bastien was senior in their department, but the more Lynn was called upon to take on other work by the lofty Earl Smithson, the more she was told to set aside her normal responsibilities, which then fell to Glynnis.

They each had a long, built-in desk on opposite walls, so that when they sat in their rolling office chairs they were back to back with five or six feet between them. They would often swivel and talk, friendly with each other without being friends. They never socialized, unless it was in a group from the museum. They never even had lunch together since they always seemed to be eating at different times. The acoustics in the

office were such that when they were both on the phone they
didn't bother each other in the least. The office was stark and
modern: glass and white walls, white desktops that were wiped
down by the custodial staff every night, graphite-colored
ergonomic desk chairs. Above the desks was corkboard where
people could hang personal photos or whatever they liked.
Glynnis had tacked up some photographs of her family and
her cat. Lynn used hers for clippings and notes for whatever
she was working on. On the wall between them, the one
opposite the glass wall and the door, hung a small, lesser, but
beautiful Corot from the museum's permanent collection. A
landscape. All the offices were lent paintings from the ware-
houses. They were changed at intervals in the same way that,
in other offices, a new potted plant might show up in the
corner every now and then.

Lynn was on the phone when Earl Smithson came striding
down the hall, his long, gray-clad legs moving back and forth
in the deputy director's own particular purposeful yet languorous stride. She was ordering some books she hoped would
prove interesting, in preparation for an exhibit scheduled for
the following October. Glynnis was also on the phone, but
she swiveled around to watch their boss walk past. A moment
later he was back. He stopped in their doorway and peered
in as though he had never before seen the sort of offices his
associate curators inhabited and thought them a rather cunning arrangement for the little people. Earl Smithson was
either a Boston Brahmin or one of those Midwesterners born
into some bleak, blue-collar existence who transforms himself
into a transatlantic Cary Grant or Noel Coward type in hopes
of being taken for something like a Boston Brahmin. Regarding Earl, rumor went both ways.

"Lovely Corot," he said. "Positively verdant. How did you
young women nab that one? All I've got in my office this

month is a nasty de Kooning. One of his 'Women.' Wonderful painting, I mean, but not very restful. That reminds me," he said, turning to Lynn, who by now had managed to get herself off her call, "I had a jangle from Mona Frumpke this morning. Were your ears burning, Miss Prosper? She was singing your praises."

Earl Smithson called all the young women at the museum "Miss" and all older women "Mrs." regardless of their marital status. His longtime secretary, for example, an iron-haired woman somewhere in her fifties who had never married, seemed perfectly happy to be Mrs. Hatch to the whole museum. Whenever the subject came up among the junior curators, someone would nod wisely and say, "You know, in the old days that's how it was. 'Mrs.' was a term of respect and age. It had nothing to do with marriage." The quirk, or affectation—however you wanted to look at it—was chalked up to Smithson's ancien régime manners.

"Hello, Miss Bastien," he said, turning to her now. "Have you heard of Miss Prosper's succès d'estime?"

"Not a word of it. I'm sure she's far too modest for that." Earl Smithson got everyone talking like a nineteenth-century novel.

"Mona will be outside in twenty minutes," Earl said to Lynn. "She drives a green Jaguar. She wants to take you to see some young artist of hers, a young woman, I believe."

"Twenty minutes?" Lynn stood. "But"—she looked helplessly around at her desk—"I have a meeting with the Costume Council."

"Ah, let Miss Bastien take that. The Costume Council is right up your alley, isn't it, Miss Bastien?"

"Absolutely." The Costume Council was one of the more prestigious fund-raising arms of the museum.

"It's a pity we didn't have advance notice," Earl said, "or

that Mona didn't want to do this on the weekend. Then perhaps you could have gotten that charming husband of yours to go along. Mona seemed very, very interested in him! But she's away for the whole month of August, so this might be the only time. It's a real honor, you know, Mona coming to get you like this. Usually we curators go to her. But time's a-wasting and"—he peered into Lynn's face—"you probably want to repair to the powder room to freshen up."

L ynn slid into the glove-leather and tortoiseshell interior of Mona's bottle-green Jaguar, already feeling the prickings of misgiving.

"Liberated from those dreary halls at last, eh?" Mona lifted a dark eyebrow that did not match her platinum bob. "I guess you owe me, then." She laughed musically and stamped on the accelerator. The car screeched away from the curb.

Lynn braced herself for the long ride to the Valley.

"I'm so glad you're interested in Jessica's work," Mona said. "Don't you think it worked perfectly in that house? Jessica did the installation herself, really a marvelous job, as though the work were designed for the site, don't you think? A very talented girl, Jessica Klein."

Jessica Klein, Lynn silently repeated to herself, to remember the name.

Mona looked at her sharply. "You knew that was the artist's name?"

"I . . ." Lynn began. It felt like a trick question, and she recalled the unfortunate gallery girl at the party. "No, I didn't."

"Well, it would be funny if you did," Mona said with a self-satisfied smile. "It wasn't listed anywhere. My little joke, considering how autobiographical her work is."

"I hardly got to look at the art," Lynn said. "F. X. . . . we . . . unfortunately we had to leave almost right away."

"I know. F. X. told me. Isn't that tragic about his not being able to see his own son? Have you met her? The mother?"

Lynn shook her head, relieved to have some indication that he hadn't been making it up.

"A real bitch, if you'll excuse my saying so, and frankly not at all what I'd have thought F. X.'s type." Mona touched her lacquered waves. "Speaking of types, I hear your husband's a doll."

From whom had she heard? F. X. had never met Jamie.

"It sounds like he's interested in everything," said Mona. "Not like those dull hedge-fund managers everyone's married to."

Ah, from Earl Smithson. Lynn's boss had always liked Jamie. They'd first met at one of the museum Christmas parties when Earl had come over to congratulate them on their then-new engagement. He was always good at knowing things like that. When Lynn was drawn away by another guest, the two men had commenced what turned into a disconcertingly long chat. The other museum husbands, not a large group, tended to fall into one of two categories. There were the arty types—struggling young painters no longer so young who taught art and even English at private schools and hoped that their wives' connections in the art world might get their work seen by the right people (in their minds, all it would take). The other group was adamantly not arty. They were businessmen, the suited bores (though never in so beautiful a specimen of suit as Smithson himself) who cast an indulgent, skeptical eye over the wife's little museum job. In general, they fared better than the artists. Earl Smithson was at least civil to them. He respected a good head for business.

"He's a lawyer?" said Mona.

"Yes—real estate deals, mainly. He studied architecture in college."

"Oh?" Mona perked up. But Jamie didn't like it when Lynn answered that way. She'd done it once in front of him in a group, and afterward he'd taken her aside. "You've got to stop," he'd said. "What I do has nothing to do with architecture."

"But you did study it," she'd protested. "It's part of who you are."

"Not anymore. You think your friends won't find me interesting enough if I'm just a lawyer?"

"You want to hang on to a man like that," Mona said. "Take it from one who knows what's out there." She drove fast and well, her hands on the Jaguar's wheel in the approved ten-and-two position. "He's interested in the arts?"

"Yes," Lynn said cautiously.

"Not a collector, though?"

"No." Lynn smiled.

"Ah, collectors. They're one's lifeblood, aren't they? But sometimes one gets so tired of them. Sometimes I wish we could all simply be interested in the art from a less selfish perspective—just sheer appreciation of beauty and creativity and the conviction that the world's a better place for it. Is that how your husband is? So romantic. Lovely. We in the business of art all get so jaded, don't we? Your husband sounds truly lovely. Lucky girl."

"I do think I'm lucky," Lynn said, then kicked herself for not responding to the art part of Mona's comment.

"But he must have some faults, no?" Mona seemed all too happy to stay on this subject. "Please tell me he does, otherwise I'll have to kill myself."

Lynn laughed. "No, he has faults."

"Like what?"

"Well . . ." Lynn knew to be careful here. "He can be a little jealous."

"Oh, please, you're like the girl who says, 'Please don't hate me because I'm beautiful.' Poor thing, your husband adores you so much he's jealous."

"No, seriously," said Lynn. "It can be extreme. One time—"

"Yes?"

Lynn was torn between caution and the awareness that she was expected to entertain. "Well, I'd gone out with this guy before Jamie and I met. Someone I worked with. He left to start a restaurant. Everyone was invited to the opening. I was supposed to go with some people in my department, and—"

"Dear girl, you didn't bring Jamie along, did you?"

Was Mona going to say it was her fault? Everyone else— well, her mother and sisters—had agreed she'd done nothing wrong. "I thought he'd like it less if I went by myself—although it was perfectly innocent. It had been ages since we'd gone out. I didn't even like the guy that much."

"Was there a scene?" Mona's eyes sparkled. "Did they fight?"

"No, of course not. Nothing like that."

The art doyenne looked disappointed, and Lynn sensed that she'd flubbed her story.

"He didn't talk to me for two days, though."

"Two days? And you hadn't done anything? Your husband didn't find your old boyfriend trying to corner you at the prep station?"

"No. Well, just a kiss—"

"Ah!" said Mona.

Lynn suddenly remembered how F. X. had pulled her into that empty room and kissed her. This had completely slipped her mind in the greater drama of his son (a story she'd reported to Jamie, thinking it made F. X. seem benign and worthy of sympathy—until Jamie said he didn't believe it for a moment. "He's playing you," he'd said).

"It was just a kiss hello," she said to Mona. "On the cheek, when we came into the restaurant. It was nothing. What was I supposed to do, shake hands?" This was, in fact, exactly what she'd said to Jamie in the car on the way home from that restaurant opening. She'd been driving, paying particular attention to the road because it was raining, so it had taken her some time—an embarrassing amount of time, in fact—to notice that he had stopped speaking to her.

"Two days!" Mona repeated.

"Not really, I'm exaggerating. It just took him a little time to get over it."

While Jamie hadn't literally remained silent for two days, he certainly had acted cool toward Lynn for that long, which had driven her crazy. She couldn't imagine staying mad like that. She kept pressing him, trying to get him to respond, unable to believe she still hadn't been forgiven. She hadn't done anything! Finally he'd faced her. She was forgiven, he said. It wasn't even a matter of forgiveness, he'd just needed time to process it, that was all.

It was funny how two people could be so in sync and yet sometimes be at cross purposes—and over the silliest things, as if Jamie were willfully deciding not to understand. Like the way she always had to dig things out of him. The first time he talked to Earl Smithson, for instance. Of course she'd been curious afterward and had asked what they'd talked about for so long. Nothing really, he'd said at first. She'd had to prod and prod.

"We talked about architecture," he admitted at last.

Then she understood his reluctance. "How did that come up?" she asked.

"I don't know."

She gave him a look.

"I guess it was the Arch," he said. "We were talking about what it means to grow up with beautiful architecture. He spent part of his childhood in Paris."

"I'll bet he did," Lynn said.

"His family didn't want him to go into art. His father was a dentist."

Earl Smithson's father was a dentist? A dentist who moved to Paris? She wondered if anyone else at the museum knew this.

"It sounds like his father was pretty successful," Jamie said. "He collected Modern art. But when Earl"—*Earl!*— "wanted to go into art history, his father refused to pay for graduate school. He said art was fine but should stay a hobby, that it wasn't a real profession for a man. So your boss worked in sales at *Institutional Investor* for a year or so."

Lynn had shaken her head in disbelief.

"He hated it, though. He went back to school, said his father didn't speak to him for years. He just kicked over the traces."

"He what?"

Jamie laughed. "That's how he put it. I admire him. He did what I didn't have the nerve to do."

"Oh, Jamie," Lynn had said.

She'd been thrilled that her boss liked Jamie, but also a little irked. Lynn thought of herself as the gregarious one, but it was Jamie in whom people seemed to confide. His quietness probably had something to do with it. He listened. It had occurred to Lynn that if she could just be like that—waiting, not pressing—Jamie would tell her things in his own time. But she never had the patience.

She'd pressed him, too, early in their relationship, about

why he'd abandoned architecture, which he clearly loved. He'd been in an accelerated program at Harvard where undergraduate courses counted toward a graduate degree, but had decided to switch to law school after the death of his father, a lawyer himself. Lynn had been shocked to learn that he'd died while Jamie was still in college; she hadn't known anyone their age who'd lost a parent. "Did your father always want you to be a lawyer?" she'd asked. "He never said," was Jamie's terse reply. Jamie's mother, at any rate, had been thrilled by the switch. Lawyers made a far better living than architects.

"How can you not know these things?" Lynn's married sister Sasha had asked her. "I know everything about Kam."

Lynn knew that Sasha assumed she'd failed to ask the questions—that Lynn was afraid to ask, or worse, that Jamie refused outright to answer. But Sasha didn't understand how slippery those conversations could be. When Lynn kept pushing about his father, what their relationship had been like, what his father might have thought about Jamie's career choices, Jamie had finally cried out as if in pain that he was sorry, he didn't know, how could he tell her what he didn't know himself?

At last Mona pulled up in front of a shabby little cottage on a steep, almost cockeyed street God knew where in the Valley at eleven A.M. on the nose. Mona followed Lynn's eyes to the dashboard clock and smiled her barracuda smile. "Promptness is the courtesy of kings."

The door to the house opened and a young woman wearing a tan-colored paisley sundress stepped out. The dress was the first thing Lynn noticed because it reminded her of a sundress she'd once had. But that had been when she was thirteen, and here was Jessica Klein wearing what looked like its twin—the same wide shoulder straps and shirring at the chest, the muted brown-on-tan paisley pattern with swirls of white and turquoise dots. Lynn remembered the dress vividly. It had been the one summer she'd gone to sleepaway camp. The camp had dances every Friday night, and the uniform for girls had been sundresses and tennis shoes.

"Come in," said Jessica, who wore her dress barefoot, "but it's a mess." Mona and Lynn stepped into a large, long room. A long wood counter running across the back wall appeared to be the kitchen. There wasn't much furniture: a sheet-covered mound for a sofa, a plywood "coffee table," a couple of wooden desk chairs. Dirty dishes were everywhere, and stacks of papers, jars of paint and dirty water, paintbrushes, bottles of turpentine, sheets of construction and origami paper. So Lynn was a little surprised when Jessica said, "Or probably we should just go down to the studio."

A thin black-and-white cat wound its way around Lynn's legs.

"Jessica," said Mona, "you know I can't abide pets."

"Sorry, sorry. We'd better go right down. This way." The young woman reached past Lynn's shoulder and took a key on a grimy string off a large nail next to the front door.

The studio was down a rickety staircase at the back of the house and faced a tiny brown patch of grass. Jessica saw Lynn looking. "I'm thinking of incorporating something about gardening next," she said.

Jessica Klein didn't look like most people's idea of an artist. What she looked like, Lynn realized, was someone she might have gone to high school with—a dark-haired Jewish girl whose naturally frizzy hair had been blow-dried straight. She had a largish nose and high cheekbones. Her eyes were lined all the way around with kohl pencil and she was wearing pale, sparkly lip gloss. Lynn could imagine her trotting off on all those dates chronicled in her installation.

The studio was like the house, but worse. Lynn noticed

the notebook itself tossed casually on a shelf. At least she assumed it was the notebook from the party. Leaning against the wall to the left was a large painting of a shoe, boldly and loosely executed, its scarlet heel facing the viewer. Then she saw a smaller canvas propped up on a table, the same shoe but from a different angle. This one, only about ten inches by ten inches, was done in a completely different style. The red heel looked shiny, like patent leather perhaps, while the shoe itself looked like glossy black silk, the rendering of the fabric worthy of a Dutch master. The whole painting glowed with an old-fashioned sort of beauty. Lynn felt a ripple of surprise. This was not at all what she'd been expecting from what little she'd seen of the installation, which had looked amusing but gimmicky.

"Ah, that's my self-portrait," Jessica said behind her. "On my way to a party."

"Proust?" Lynn said without thinking.

"What did I tell you?" Mona said to the artist. "Didn't I say she was a gem?"

"There are actually two party scenes in Proust with shoes," Jessica said mildly.

Lynn thought for a moment. She could only think of one. "When the Duc de Guermantes insists on going to the party even though he just found out his cousin has died? He pretends he hasn't heard yet? And the narrator sees the Duchesse's red heels as she gets into the carriage?"

"Now you've conflated the two episodes. And my painting to boot, ha ha. See, there's one scene where the Duc and Duchesse are getting ready to go to a dinner, and Swann and the narrator are there, and Swann tells the Duchesse he's dying. But the Duc's hurrying her because they're late. Then, as they're getting into the carriage he notices she's wearing black shoes with her red dress, and makes her go upstairs to change into red ones—after making such a fuss about how late they were that she couldn't stop to console her dying friend. The scene with the cousin dying is later. The Duc and Duchesse come home to change for a costume ball, and that's when they hear, but they hurry to change, anyway. There's a discussion of some pointy-toed shoes, and the Duc isn't sure if they're meant for his costume or his wife's."

"Imagine not being able to tell," said Mona, glancing down at her own impeccably shod foot. A pointed tan leather toe peeped out from under her cream-colored slacks.

Lynn happened to have long, narrow feet, while Jamie, not that much taller than she, had small, compact ones. Lynn secretly feared they wore the same size but had always made a point of not finding out.

"It's interesting," said Jessica, "how both scenes associate shoes with death."

Carried out feetfirst, Lynn thought but did not say.

"Now, Jessica," said Mona, "does that mean your self-portraits have to do with death?"

"Don't all self-portraits?"

Lynn wandered over to a pile of canvases that had been stacked face down against some low cabinets. "May I?" she said over her shoulder.

"Oh, sure," said Jessica. "Those are the ones that were hanging in the first room, right after the stand with my spiral notebook. I hear you didn't get to see much of the installation."

The first painting had the look of a blurry, grisaille photograph. It had been done in oils, the paint very thinly, or at least very smoothly, applied. It was the scene from the photograph in the hallway at the party, the one of the two children on bicycles, but in the painting the children were gone. It was just the chain-link fence, the cement driveway, and the sandbox, all closer up than Lynn remembered from the photograph.

And yet the presence of the two children was palpable if you had seen the photograph. It was like a painting of ghosts. Lynn found it very beautiful and slightly eerie, and tried to imagine what it would be like to come across it in a museum or gallery without knowing anything else about it.

There was a knock on the door, which had been left ajar behind them and now swung all the way open with a loud, long creak.

"F. X.!" said Mona, moving quickly to his side. Jessica's eyes lit up.

"Sorry I'm late."

"Not at all, not at all," said Mona. "We're just getting started. We haven't even gotten to *you* yet."

"We're like your harem in here." Jessica giggled in a girly way that didn't go at all with her accomplished paintings.

"Hello, Lynn," he said, meeting her eyes with leisurely amusement. He turned back to Jessica and Mona, rubbing his hands together. "Ladies, I'm dying to see everything."

"Did you talk to Richard about Jessica?" Mona asked him.

"Uh-huh." F. X. moved to the frayed notebook that chronicled Jessica Klein's search for old loves. He started flipping through it. It was just the notebook, no security cord or lectern.

"Well?" said Mona.

"I told him about your things. He seemed interested. Said he'd love to be invited."

Mona gave a low laugh. "Of course for him we'd mainly want to focus on blue-chip stuff."

"Yeah, but I think he likes the idea of emerging young artists—discovering them, being the first. He likes to think of himself that way."

Lynn turned away. It felt obscene to be listening to a conversation like this. She found herself facing some drawings that were tacked on the dirty wall, much the way the sheet from the legal pad had been tacked up at Mona's party. She even glanced down at the floor to see if there were the same little piles of plaster, but of course there were not. The drawing on the left was a line drawing of a man in profile, almost Daumier-like, with an oversized, leonine head and bandy legs. Suddenly Lynn realized: It was supposed to be F. X. Was it? She peered closer, then turned to look at F. X. It was definitely his nose, his whole body's profile captured in a single squiggle of line.

F. X. caught her looking. "Oh," he said, "is that the one of me?" He joined her in front of the drawing, still holding the notebook.

"You two know each other from before?"

F. X. grinned. "How else would I have gotten on the list?"

She stared at him, bewildered, and when he started flipping through the notebook, she thought she was being dismissed. But he held a page open to her. It was a copy of the list that had been tacked up at Mona's party. F. X. was holding his finger at the second-to-last entry, "Fra. Dona. 2006." He eyed her expectantly.

"How?" she began, but even before he said anything the pieces began to fall into place.

"What's my first name, Lynnie?" F. X. prompted.

Lynn had noticed that abbreviated entry the first time she saw it. At first she'd wondered if it were a woman. Dona. But her mind had almost instantaneously made another association: *Fra*, or Friar, like Fra Lippo Lippi, that Browning poem from high school she had never understood. Donahue.

As if on cue Jessica called over, "Francis Xavier, did you see your portrait?"

"What kind of shoe is he?" drawled Mona.

"A brrr-rogue," said Jessica.

"With a long tongue," Mona said, and the two women tittered.

"Do you know what they're talking about?" F. X. asked Lynn, still grinning.

"No." She didn't meet his eye.

"Seriously, though," said Mona, "did you do it from life, Jessica dear? It's very like."

"Nope," said the artist. "From memory."

"Astonishing," said Mona. Now she went to Lynn's side, giving her a significant look. "Really astonishing."

It was true; Jessica Klein was a remarkably accomplished draftsperson. It made Lynn wonder why she'd chosen that gimmicky installation, the tracking down of old boyfriends. It was the sort of thing those with much less technical talent usually fell back on. "So," she asked, looking back down at the list, which F. X. still held open, "Mark Y. Is he the same as Mark Yablons?"

"Yes!" said Jessica, delighted.

"You knew him in . . . high school? And then he came back into your life?"

"This is exactly what you're supposed to do: make up a story to explain the information. That's how I got the idea. I read about this study that showed that even when we're given information that makes no sense, the brain works hard to make a story—that's one explanation for dreams. But yes, Mark was someone I grew up with. I kissed him one time— it was just at a party actually, we didn't even go out, but I counted it because I'd had a crush on him for so long, so it meant a lot to me. But the next year he switched schools. And then years later, last year, as you can see from the date, I ran into him and we dated for a little while." Jessica smiled. "And no, I'm not still seeing him. That's just where the list ends. Once I started working on this, I didn't keep adding on."

"Oh," said Lynn.

"Okay, I'll tell you the truth, I didn't just run into Marky. I was driving by his parents' house one day. I'd just been thinking about him and felt like it. I didn't see him that day, but then I kept driving by until one day he was visiting. I was there when he was getting out of his car. Like it was meant to be. It didn't last long, though. Too weird. For him, I mean." She shrugged.

Jessica walked Lynn through the rest of the pieces that had been part of the one-night installation. Each represented a person on her list, although few were actual portraits. They covered various styles, but most were unequivocally beautiful in a rich, emotional way. There was no time to dwell on each, and Lynn moved from one to the other with a sense of frustration—but contented frustration, as if the knowledge that each had a story she'd want to hear was enough. Jessica had taken a mundane life of trite encounters and transformed it into something riveting.

Mona glanced at her watch—for the second or third time, Lynn realized. "Look, kids," she said, "I really must run. I have to get downtown. F. X.?" She and he seemed to exchange a look. "Would you mind driving Lynn back to work, there's a dear?"

"Oh," said Lynn, "I don't mind leaving now."

"Yes, but you see, I have to go in the opposite direction. You don't mind, do you?" She gave Lynn a winning smile.

D on't mind Mona's little joke," F. X. said, breaking the silence. They were already back over the hill. "She guessed my showing up would make you uncomfortable. She knows the whole story. You can't pay any attention to her, it's just how she is—not mean, but she does like to stir things up."

What whole story, Lynn wanted to ask, thinking uneasily of how F. X. seemed to keep forgetting they'd never gone out—a euphemism that in itself would have made him laugh.

F. X. kept turning his head to look at her. "You don't seem happy to see me, Lynnie. Are you mad about that little dance back there? You figured it out, right? That I slept with both of them, Jessica *and* Mona?"

"Am I mad?"

"You never call. I always have to call you. That's not like you, Lynn. Aren't we friends?"

She thought of Jamie. "No."

"Ouch. Wait, let me guess, it's hubby who's not happy, right? Not thrilled about an old college friend coming back into the picture? About you going to Mona's thing with me? See, Mona was right. She has a sixth sense about stuff like that. Never mind, I'd be worried, too, if I were your husband."

"F. X."—Lynn's voice was cold—"Jamie has absolutely nothing to worry about."

"Of course not," he said. "Nothing personal, just a comment on men in general and husbands in particular. If Jamie were thrilled about you running around town with me, then I'd say you'd have something to worry about. So you can tell me—is he?"

"Is he what?"

"Bothered by it."

"Yes," Lynn spat out. "He's never even met you and he dislikes you intensely."

"Intensely," said F. X.

"No, not intensely. That's my word."

"Oh? Even more interesting."

Lynn could have kicked herself. She wondered when she'd ever learn to keep her mouth shut.

"How long did you say you guys have been married?"

"I didn't, but two and a half years."

"Love at first sight?"

"As a matter of fact."

"Uh-oh."

"Of course," said Lynn. "You wouldn't believe in something so maudlin."

"Oh, I believe it happens. Eyes meet, sparks, electricity, wow I'm in love, the real deal, who ever thought?"

"What can I say?"

"But tell me," said F. X., "how do you know it's not going to fizzle out?"

"It hasn't yet."

"So your happy marriage isn't getting old yet? Not suffocated by routine? Hubby working too hard, trying to get ahead, make partner, maybe not putting you first anymore?"

Lynn shifted in her seat—then, realizing what she'd done, kept shifting until she was looking F. X. dispassionately in the eye.

He cocked his head. "You're not starting to feel neglected? Wondering where all the romance went?"

"Not at all."

"Glad to hear it."

Lynn crossed her arms across her chest.

"Look," he said, "I may not be married, but I've seen a lot of marriages. Hey, maybe that's why I'm not married." He looked to her for a smile, but she did not oblige. "Anyway, it's this outsider's observation that you need to work at a marriage."

"Of course you do, you have to—"

"God, no, not that boring, temperature-taking crap. I'm talking about shaking things up. *Épater le bourgeois!*"

This was too much like F. X.'s unsettling reference to Rilke.

"I look at you, Lynn, and it frightens me how complacent you are—so smug, so happy. You're the one who should be frightened. You can't take what you have for granted like that. What you think you have. So here I come, concerned about an old friend, a nice girl, and yeah, maybe I was trying to shake things up for you. Give your husband a little shake so he appreciates what he has. You haven't done anything wrong, I haven't done anything—although, hey, I'm a willing volunteer if you change your mind."

Lynn rolled her eyes.

"You just watch," he said. "Jamie's paying attention now, isn't he? I bet you're going to thank me some day for this little *épater*. That's me, Lynnie, just here to help."

Five

By rights, Lynn and Jamie should never have been invited to the Jacquemets' baby shower for the Scovilles. From start to finish, it was a lesson in the perils of socializing. Jamie had known George Jacquemet and Bruce Scoville in college but hadn't counted himself in their set of friends. He still didn't, but living in Los Angeles they all ran into each other now and then. The shower invitation stemmed from a brief stretch earlier that fall during which the three couples crossed paths so many times in so short a period that it became embarrassing: a mutual friend's party, a Harvard classmate's wedding, and, finally, a black-tie benefit at which Jamie's firm had taken a table. It came out that the Scovilles had themselves taken their whole table for ten. And the Jacquemets were full of the new house they'd just bought in Pacific Palisades, a trade up from their first, although that one, too, had been in the Palisades and therefore way out of Lynn and Jamie's price range.

Jamie had the impression that one or maybe both of the wives were heiresses, which would explain a lot about the marriages, particularly the Jacquemets'. George Jacquemet was exceedingly good looking, with dark, bedroom eyes and liquid Southern charm. His tall, thin wife, Libbet, had something of a hatchet face. She and Bruce's wife, Kerry, had, as Lynn understood it, been on the tennis team together at some women's college. Stocky, good-natured Bruce Scoville worked for what was evidently a very profitable family company, something to do with frozen vegetables.

"I wouldn't mind seeing the house," Lynn said, when Jamie handed her the invitation. "After hearing so much about it."

It turned out to be in one of those new, gated developments farther back from the ocean, which to Lynn defeated the purpose of living in the Palisades. Although it was already dark out and therefore impossible to tell, the location even seemed to preclude any kind of view. Their car was stopped at a white clapboard guardhouse by a uniformed guard who made a show of checking a list that Jamie had to initial before they were allowed to drive on. They drove down silent streets, lot after bare lot waiting for spanking new mansions to rise from the dust and join their fellows in Palladian-windowed glory. It was hard to say exactly what period or style the Jacquemets' peach stucco fortress was supposed to represent. The entry had a Spanish-style archway, but it rested on two white Doric columns. The highly shellacked, oaken front door boasted elaborate etched glass.

"Shh, it's not that bad," Jamie said, at the look on Lynn's face as they got out of the car.

"What are you talking about?" She came to a stop in the middle of the dark street. "It's awful."

Jamie looked stern for a moment, then sighed. "I know. But we shouldn't be snobs. It probably cost a fortune—we could never afford it." Their own house was in a modest neighborhood on the outskirts of Hancock Park: street after street of look-alike bungalows and side-by-side duplexes originally built to house lower-echelon studio employees like costumers or grips when the movie industry exploded in the 1920s. Lynn and Jamie liked that history, just as they liked that the windows in the living room still had their original, painfully thin, wavy glass. They had bought the house the year after they were married—a sort of anniversary present to each other, Lynn thought of it.

"Doesn't it make you feel better," she said, "how tacky their house is?"

"No." But seeing the abashed, disappointed look on Lynn's face, he laughed and put an arm around her as they crossed over to the house. As it turned out, Jamie did not prove immune to the temptations of one-upmanship.

Lynn wasn't sure whether to be relieved or disappointed that the furnishings weren't as bad as the house itself. They were merely pedestrian, and practically wearing price tags: scroll-armed sofas, probably George Smith, covered in showroom-fresh scratchy kilim; a large tufted leather ottoman instead of a coffee table, with the requisite tray on top. The rug, however, was truly beautiful—Oushak, probably late nineteenth, early twentieth century. Lynn's field wasn't textiles, but you did pick up things working in museums. She had the idea in her head that the Jacquemets were more old money than new, and the rug was a tantalizing hint that this might be true.

George Jacquemet had a fluid, sexual saunter. He approached, margarita glass in hand, with an ironic smile and a glance around his own high-ceilinged room that to Lynn seemed to say, *Not my doing.*

"Lynn," he said while still shaking Jamie's hand, "I saw you the other day. You were shopping. In Beverly Hills."

Confused, Lynn accepted a kiss hello.

"You saw me, didn't you? I was in my car. When you were crossing the street in front of Barney's?"

"What?" she said. "I wasn't— Which day?"

"It's a dark blue Beemer and . . . which day? I think it was Friday. Yeah, Friday afternoon, around three. What'd you do, sneak out to go shopping? By the way, the woman I was with was—"

"George, I don't think that was me. I wasn't in Beverly Hills that day."

"No kidding. I could have sworn it was you. Same hair. Same cute figure. Hey, Libbet." His long-faced wife had come up behind him, but Lynn would have bet that her eye had been on him for some time. Kerry and Bruce Scoville drifted over as well to greet the new arrivals. Even at their own party, the two couples stuck together—the Jacquemet-Scovilles, was how Lynn and Jamie privately referred to them.

"How's work going for you, guy?" said Bruce, switching a shrimp skewer to the pudgy fist already holding an oversized margarita glass, so he could pump Jamie's arm. "Crazy, right? This economy? It's like you can't not make money." He sucked the last shrimp off the skewer. His mouth had a greasy look— he was like a big, self-satisfied toddler.

"Actually," said Jamie, "my work's pretty boring. Just a lot of three-hundred-page contracts to go over."

Bruce and George both laughed as though Jamie had made a good joke.

"Hey, you should give Bruce a call," George said. "His company's going nuts. He might be able to throw some work your way."

Jamie was holding himself very still. "I'm really just doing real estate law at the moment. But I'd be happy to put you in touch with the right partner for whatever you need."

Everyone fell quiet. The basketball-sized mound under

Kerry's floaty maternity dress was the first thing that caught Lynn's eye. "You look great," she said, turning to her. "I hope I look that good when I'm pregnant."

Kerry, a petite blonde, just smiled.

Lynn and Jamie were able to escape into the party as new guests arrived. Moving from room to room, they ran into one or two people Jamie knew, but none with whom he had more than a few words to exchange. There was lots of joking and hilarity over the number of margaritas "imbibed," the drinkers batting that word around as if they'd just learned it, the way second graders get a thrill saying, "Your epidermis is showing." After about twenty minutes Lynn and Jamie felt their duty done and began to move back toward the front door. The coast looked clear, but when they were partway across the room, the Jacquemet-Scovilles swooped down on them again from out of nowhere, en masse as usual.

"Not going yet?" Libbet said brightly. She clearly would be making no attempt to persuade them to tarry.

"I have an early day tomorrow," Jamie said. (Don't bother, they don't care, Lynn thought.)

"Any interesting plans for the holidays?" said Bruce, and Lynn saw Libbet shoot George an exasperated glance.

"Just Tahoe," Lynn said. "We always go—after Christmas with Jamie's family." She tried to catch Jamie's eye. Far be it from the Jacquemet-Scovilles to know what Tahoe in December meant to them.

"Tahoe?" said Kerry. "That's where we'll be! The four of us have a time-share there," she added, just a little too proudly. "Where do you guys stay?"

"Oh," said Jamie, "we have a house there."

Lynn had never before heard Jamie refer to the Tahoe house as his, let alone with the sort of casual finality that begs further questions.

"Parents' place?" said George.

"Nope," said Jamie. "Ours."

Lynn saw Libbet Jacquemet raise an eyebrow at her husband.

Jamie's father had bought the turn-of-the-century stone cabin out of the blue on a one-time fishing trip out West the year before he died. Lake Tahoe, California, was hardly an obvious or convenient vacation destination when you live in St. Louis, and Jamie's mother had been less than pleased— quite vocally so—by an acquisition in which she'd played no role. The house had been left directly to Jamie and his siblings in their father's will.

"What part of the lake?" said Kerry.

"West Shore."

"Ooh, that's the nicest part, isn't it? We'd love to see it. Hey, why don't we all get together when we're there?"

"That would be great," Jamie said, too heartily.

As if she couldn't bear this any longer, Libbet turned to Lynn. "How's the museum business going?"

"It's great, thanks. I love it. Actually, we have a really interesting show coming up. It's—"

"How nice," Libbet said. She turned her head to survey the room.

"I don't believe in art," Bruce announced.

"Oh?" said Lynn, in as neutral a tone as she could manage. Not neutral enough; she saw Jamie bite his lip. One of the things she loved most about him was his decency, the fact that he had strict standards of behavior that included not mocking one's hosts to their face. He was such a good influence that when she asked her next question she was genuinely ready to listen to Bruce's answer. "What about art do you not believe in?"

"Don't get me wrong, I believe in the creative urge. That's

part of being human. That's my point. What I don't believe in is some faggot bluestocking in a museum deciding what's art and what isn't."

"Art with a capital *A*," said George Jacquemet.

"Exactly," said Bruce. "Museums—who are they to tell us what we should like?"

Faggot bluestocking? Museums as "who"? Yet there was something Lynn liked in what Bruce said about believing in the creative urge. "Actually," she told him, "you're right. There's a whole school of thought—and even museum shows— that question exactly that."

"There is?"

"See, hon," said Kerry, "you're a trendy thinker."

"Whaddya mean?" he said to Lynn, ignoring his wife.

"Just that there's debate even within the art world about what museums are there for. Actually, I was just at this symposium where—"

"God," drawled George, "I just knew we'd end up having some kind of intellectual conversation here with Lynn. Didn't I tell you that, Lib?"

They had just come in the front door, and Lynn was saying over her shoulder, "So, do you think George Jacquemet is having an—" when the phone rang. She hurried to the kitchen to get it.

"Lynn, is that you?"

"Andy?" There was a lot of static on the line. "Where are you?"

Jamie's younger brother laughed. "On a cloud. Walking on air. I have some news, but I can't tell you until I tell my brother. You understand?"

"Of course. He's right here." Jamie had reached her side. She held out the phone.

"My mom?" he mouthed, backing away.

"Andy," she whispered back, her hand over the mouthpiece. She handed him the phone and went to wait at the dining room table, where the paper still lay from that morning.

Andy was the member of Jamie's family with whom Lynn felt the most attuned. There was a looseness about him, an openness. Jamie also had a sister, Julie, who was actually eighteen months older—she just seemed like the younger sibling. (To say that Jamie was the middle child did not begin to capture his position in the Prosper family. He was the oldest son.) Lynn had met Julie first, less than a month after she and Jamie met, dispatched to L.A. by their mother, Lynn suspected, to check her out. Pretty, sweet Julie had just become engaged at the time: the son of an English viscount, an "Honorable," whom she'd met while doing a garden design course and working as an au pair in London. "You know," she'd explained, rolling her eyes, "if you're addressing a letter or something you're supposed to write 'the Honorable Mr. Piers Monkham.' It's just a courtesy title." But she clearly enjoyed it, and it would have been churlish to deny that there was something exciting and glamorous about marrying into the British aristocracy.

After Julie, Andy had been a surprise. In the first place, Lynn had assumed that Andy would share his older brother and sister's sleek, dark, good looks, but Andy was a redhead, with pale freckles and green eyes. Although six years younger than Jamie, he was taller and more substantially built. She didn't realize it then, but in looks he took after their mother, who, surprisingly enough, had been a field hockey player in her youth, and was still one of the top women golfers at her club. Andy turned out to be a good sport in the other sense.

His end-of-summer trip, planned before Lynn and Jamie met, was supposed to be a bit of brotherly bonding before his sophomore year of college. But Andy seemed perfectly content to hang out with his brother and new girlfriend in the first throes of love—or go off on his own, to take surfing lessons or get his hair cut in Venice by a girl with extensive body tattoos. Andy made them all go to Olvera Street together, an "authentic historic Mexico" tourist trap Lynn hadn't been to since she was six. "Jumping beans for everyone," he'd insisted. Before leaving he had confided to Lynn that he thought she was the best thing that ever happened to his brother, that he'd never seen Jamie like this before.

After about three minutes at the dining room table, Lynn could stand the suspense no longer. "No way," Jamie said as she walked back into the kitchen. "That's amazing!"

After graduating from college, Andy had taken the summer off to backpack around the world. He was still on the road a year later. The last Lynn had heard, he was in Chile for the summer, working at some luxe resort as a ski instructor.

Jamie was still listening, nodding. He really was a good listener. "No way," he said again, then more silence on his end. Lynn wondered if her own conversations ever sounded like that. Probably not. "Listen, Andy," Jamie said, "I'm so— You'll see, it's the best. Congratulations." He held the phone out to Lynn. "Andy wants to talk to you."

Lynn gave him a questioning look, but Jamie just grinned.

"Did he tell you?" Andy said.

"No, he just handed me the phone."

"He knew I wanted to tell you. I'm engaged!"

"What? Oh, Andy, that's wonderful!" She did some quick math: he was only twenty-three. "How exciting." But then she had to ask a rather awkward question. "Andy," she said, "to whom?"

He laughed, and Jamie, listening by the refrigerator, laughed, too.

"Jamie never tells me anything," she apologized. "Nothing interesting. We got a baby announcement from another associate, and he never even mentioned she was pregnant." But there she was, talking about herself. "So who is it? Have I met her? Heard of her?"

"I didn't know, either," Jamie said.

"She's amazing, we met skiing," said Andy, but there was a beep. "Is that your call waiting?"

"Yes, but never mind. Go on, tell me about it."

"No, you go ahead and pick up. I'll let Jamie tell you all the details. It's late here and I've got to run, anyway. But I'll talk to you guys soon."

So Lynn clicked over to the other call. It was Jamie's mother, Philippa.

"Lynn! Have you heard the news? The wonderful news? Has Jamie heard?"

"We just got off the phone with Andy. It's so exciting. Do you want to talk to—"

"She sounds like such a lovely girl. From a lovely family. The Peales. Now, Lynn, have you ever heard of the Peale family? From Rhode Island? They're a wonderful old Rhode Island family."

"No, I don't think so," said Lynn, a chill falling over her.

"No? I'm surprised. They are a very big family."

"Lots of children?"

"No, Lynn," said Philippa, and Lynn could practically hear her gritting her teeth. "Not big in that way. *Prominent* is what I meant. A very *prominent* family. And fabulous skiers, Andy says."

"Oh," said Lynn, "that's nice, then." She glanced up and

saw Jamie looking at her with . . . was it concern? Disappointment? She felt sorry, and mean.

"It is nice," Philippa said evenly, "because Annika Peale is such a nice girl. Truly refined. I'm so happy for Andy. I don't mind telling you, I've been a little worried about him. He's been drifting ever since he graduated, no direction, although of course he's still very young. Not too young to marry, though. Not at all. I think this fashion you young people have for staying single so long is downright silly. And shortsighted. Why, Lynn"—if Lynn thought her transgression was going to go unremarked or unpunished by Philippa, she should have known better—"can you imagine that when I was your age, Julie was eight and Jamie almost seven?"

"I know," Lynn said, and for some reason this fact always did chasten her.

"And how is your family, dear?" Philippa said brightly. "Your sister Dee? Still in New York, working as hard as ever?"

Dee, the oldest of the three girls, was an investment banker. Her real name was Diana. Their mother had always detested the nickname. Dee had instituted it for herself the second she was on her own at college. "Dee," Ella Kovak had repeated scathingly. "It sounds like a perky sorority girl. And Diana is such a strong, beautiful name." On the surface this appeared to be Dee's only rebellion. She had gone to Princeton and Harvard Business School, then on to a job that paid more than her parents made put together, even the year Ella's second book, the one on the sexist treatment of black women by black men during the civil rights movement, made the *New York Times* "And Bear in Mind" list. Their father, Harold Kovak, was famous (or infamous, depending on how you looked at it) for his psychedelic drug research at Berkeley, but he had never made as much as people thought, having refused to have anything to do with the big pharmaceutical companies. Dee had always given every appearance of being the classic eager-to-please, successful first child. But anyone who knew and understood the Kovaks could see that Dee had been thumbing her nose at her parents the whole time. Business school! A corporate banking job!

"And has she met anyone yet?" Philippa asked, her voice earnest, urgent, with that small throb of sympathy.

"Oh, yes, she's meeting lots of people," Lynn said, "just no one she likes quite enough." This had become her stock reply. Dee was thirty-four.

"And how is dear Sasha in Hawaii?" asked Philippa. "And Kam? The boat shop doing well, I hope?"

Lynn remembered the first time she'd told Jamie's mother about her sisters, about how Sasha, the middle sister and beauty of the family, had married one of her father's graduate students. While still in college. (Each daughter, it seemed, had her own brand of rebellion.) Philippa had seemed so friendly, so interested in everything, and Lynn had answered her questions happily, although even back then she'd quickly realized that she and Jamie's mother might have different ideas about some things. "It must have been hard for your eldest sister," Philippa had said the first time she'd heard this family lore, "to have a younger sister get married first." Sasha had only been twenty at the time, Dee barely twenty-three. (The three sisters were each two and a half years apart.) After they married, Sasha's husband had turned down a promising postdoc position to go home and help out with his family's charter boat business.

"They're all great, thanks," Lynn said. "Congratulations on the wonderful news about Andy." And thrust the phone at Jamie.

Jamie joined her in the bedroom almost twenty minutes later, flopping down on the bed where she'd been trying to concentrate on Thomas Mann's *Doctor Faustus*. "Leave it to Andy," he said.

"What?" Lynn wasn't sure she wanted to hear, but she closed the pages of impenetrable philosophical student debates with relief. They made her feel glum about the lack of intellectual discourse in her own life. Even in college, look at what she'd had—F. X.! "I'm so stupid and awful!" she cried out. "I don't know why you married me."

"What are you talking about? Because of this stupid Peale heiress?" Jamie snuggled closer to Lynn on the bed, or tried to. She pushed him away.

"Heiress? She's an heiress?"

He looked at her in surprise. "I thought my mom told you. You knew she had to be rich."

"I'm so sorry I'm not an heiress! Sorry I've deprived you when everyone else you know managed to land one." She clambered over him and positioned herself on the edge of the bed, her back to him. It was a comfortable, low-slung bed—just the mattress and box spring; they had dispensed with the frame. The box spring was covered with a beautifully tailored white linen skirt with taupe linen flange, carefully tucked up by Lynn so as not to be too long. A down comforter inside a pure white, soft-as-silk duvet cover topped the whole thing. Jamie always said he loved the bed, that it was like a cloud. The ceiling was painted a peaceful sky blue. The Jacquemets' master bedroom—everyone had gotten a tour of the house—had a massive four-poster, complete with matelasse coverlets and pillow shams and silk jacquard draperies, all coordinated by the Jacquemets' decorator. There had even been what looked like a cashmere throw draped on the bench at the foot of the bed. Lynn hadn't cared for any of it, but it haunted her none-theless. In the end, wasn't their own beautiful bed just a mattress on the floor?

"Lynn," Jamie said again, and there was so much love and good humor and knowledge of her in his voice, but also concern, that Lynn turned around and smiled a little sadly at him.

"I don't deserve you," she said.

"I'm the one who doesn't deserve you! I just thought . . . well, I thought you'd think it was funny about the Peales. Do you know who they are?" He was clearly trying to cheer her up. "The cardboard Peales." When Lynn looked blank, he said, "They make pretty much every cardboard box we have in the house."

"You mean shipping boxes? Like packages come in?"

"It's even worse," Jamie said, drawing closer and kissing her nose. "Every thin cardboard box. Cereal boxes. Cracker boxes. Any box with that insert-the-flap closure. That's theirs. Someone else does the tear-strip boxes, like the ones butter comes in."

"Or Tampax," said Lynn. Jamie gave a small frown, as men often do at the mention of such things, and Lynn felt the opposite of refined. Suddenly she saw herself through Philippa's eyes: *I have a daughter married to the son of a viscount, a son set to marry the heiress to an old East Coast paper goods fortune. But my other son married into a family where the absentee father's a drug-taking hippie, the mother's one of those loud-mouth women's lib man-haters, and one of the sisters is married to a Hawaiian who works at a boat rental shop.* The irony of it all was that Lynn's family looked down on Jamie's.

"You're going to wake up one day and be sorry you married me," she said.

"I'll never be sorry. I love you. It's as simple as that."

"That art party of Mona Frumpke's," she blurted out. "The one thing I didn't tell you, F. X.'s girlfriend didn't come."

Jamie pulled back, confused.

"And I went to see one of Mona's artists a little while ago, and F. X. was there! He's slept with Mona. And the artist. He's awful—I don't know if it was before his girlfriend or during. I wish I'd never gone to dinner with him in the first place. You were absolutely right about him. Although I do think it's true about his son. Mona said—"

"Okay," Jamie said slowly.

"I should have told you at the time, it was nothing, but you're always so jealous." She'd meant to tell about that stupid innocent kiss, too, but there'd been something in the slowness of that "okay." "I told you you'd be sorry you married me," she said.

"Of course I'm not sorry." He rubbed his eyes.

"You still love me?"

"Of course I do." He dropped his hands and looked at her. "Why? Have you stopped loving me? Now that you're gallivanting around with other men?"

"Idiot."

"You're sure?"

"That you're an idiot? Yes."

"Seriously." To her surprise, he did look serious.

"Of course I haven't. I can't believe you even have to ask. You know I love you more than anything."

"Okay then," he said. They settled back into each other's arms in their heavenly cloud of a bed. "That's all that matters."

Six

"Business school?" said Dee.

Lynn had waited until she was at work the next morning to call. "I know! The ski trip to the Andes was a present from her parents for getting in."

Jamie's siblings had always held a fascination for Lynn's sisters, who followed the Prosper family fortunes with gusto, like a favorite soap opera. Andy's last serious girlfriend, in college, had been a Deadhead. No wonder Philippa was pleased.

"And they're already engaged?" asked Dee. "Isn't that awfully fast?"

"You think that's fast? They already have a date. In March, can you believe it?"

"In the middle of her first year of business school?" (Their mother, whom Lynn had reached first, had said the same thing, her academic soul scandalized.)

"She didn't want to wait until summer," said Lynn. "The wedding might get in the way of her summer job."

"How'd Philippa take *that*?" According to Jamie's mother, a good wife always put the man first. And was eager to give up her career in favor of marriage.

"Oh, she said wasn't it wonderful how unspoiled Annika was, and what a good work ethic she had despite how much she's grown up with."

Dee laughed. "Poor Lynn. Poor Andy."

A flurry of motion caught Lynn's eye. One of the department receptionists was on the other side of the glass wall, waving her hands excitedly. Lynn turned to her, a hand over the mouthpiece, and the woman stuck her head in the door. "I have Richard Plante on the phone. He's on hold. Line two."

Lynn's heart gave a funny thud. "I've got to go," she said to Dee, and pressed the flashing button for the other line.

"Lynn Proper?" came a man's voice, hoarse yet oddly high.

"Yes, this is Lynn Prosper," she said, making as diplomatic a correction as she could.

"Prosper, Prosper—right. Won't make that mistake again. Fool me once, shame on you, fool me twice, shame on me." He had a twang, too. "But I'll cut to the chase. Here's the lowdown. I want to get involved with the museum. F. X. Donahue gave me your number.

"As you know," he went on after a pause—at which Lynn realized that perhaps she should have said something—"I'm fairly new to Los Angeles." He pronounced *Los Angeles* with a hard *g*. There was a strange whistling in the background—a bad connection? She imagined a man in cowboy boots.

"This town has quite a number of museums, I've discovered—a whole lot of good causes in general. But art—well, the world just can't get enough of it, not in my book. So what do I do to start?"

"Well . . ."

"As it happens, I was invited to one of your shindigs by a business acquaintance, but I was out of town. How do I get one of those invitations myself the next time round?"

"I can certainly put you on our list." She was relieved to find something concrete to offer. "It would be a pleasure. I'm in the education department, but I'd be more than happy to put you in touch with someone in development."

"I have a better idea. Why don't I hop on over and you can give me the grand tour. We'll sort it all out then."

"Well, I . . ."

"I'll be there in ten minutes. No time like the present! I'm in my car as we speak. In sic transit. Or, hey, are you tied up right now?"

Ten minutes? What was with these people? Mona in twenty minutes, Richard Plante in ten? "Well, it's just that the museum's closed today, so . . ." Lynn recovered herself just in time. "So, yes, this is the perfect time for a private tour. But I'm not really . . . Perhaps you'd like to meet our director, Earl Smithson. I can see if—"

"Nope, just you for starters. Don't want to make a fool of myself in front of too many of you good people with my ignorance."

"Oh, I'm sure you'd never . . . That will be perfect, then," she could do little else but conclude. "Ten minutes. I look forward to it."

"Me, too," said Richard Plante. "We both do."

Both? F. X., again? When security called up fifteen minutes later to say that a Mr. Plante and guest were downstairs, Lynn sighed.

There were two people standing on the polished white granite floor of the great foyer when she got downstairs: a tall, gangly man with a scraggly goatee, in a tacky-looking summer-weight khaki suit; and a pocket Venus of a woman with shiny black hair halfway down her back, wearing a tight, bright yellow straight skirt, a sheer floral blouse, and patent-leather green stilettos that laced up her ankles. Lynn suddenly felt dowdy in her favorite black cropped pants and ballet flats.

The gangly man was striding toward her, his hand extended. "Richard Plante," he said. "And this is my fiancée, Chaka Vela."

Lynn blinked.

"The splendiferous Chaka Vela!" Plante crowed.

Chaka shot him a glance from under heavy-lashed, almond-shaped eyes and extended a hand to Lynn. It was a small, tanned hand, with a muscular vigor that was a far cry from the bird bones Lynn often encountered. No, Chaka's lean brown hand was more like an alert prairie dog.

"So glad to meet you," Lynn said. Chaka eyed her coolly.

Lynn realized she'd been wrong about Richard Plante's suit as well. It was clearly expensive, made of an extremely thin fabric with a light sheen, and beautifully tailored. The jacket was oversized, the pants on the short side, but that had been the intention. Still, the overall effect when you looked at it objectively was slightly ridiculous, harking back to the Talking Heads and *Miami Vice*, although the billionaire wore a white polo shirt under the baggy khaki jacket instead of a black T-shirt.

"Well," said Lynn, clapping her hands together like the tour guide she was supposed to be. "We're so glad you could make it." As soon as she'd hung up the phone with Richard Plante, she'd sped over to Earl Smithson's office to see what she should do. He'd been surprisingly unperturbed by the thought of a young associate curator with no experience at reeling in big donors showing an interested billionaire around. At least Earl would be joining them later. Despite what Richard had said, Lynn and her boss had agreed that the tour would end at his office. "Have you been here before?" she asked Chaka, afraid of offending the real quarry.

"No, never," said the woman, tossing her perfect shiny hair. "I never even knew it was here, although I've driven by many, many times." She had an accent, a funny lilting lisp that made Lynn think of a native Spaniard saying the word *Castilian*. Had Richard Plante really said she was his fiancée? Lynn's eyes flickered to the woman's left hand, neatly folded around an acid-green patent leather clutch, and sure enough, there on the ring finger was an enormous emerald-cut diamond that reached almost to her knuckle. Lynn quickly raised her eyes again—in time to see Chaka give a small, tucked-in smile.

"Have you worked here many, many years?" the woman asked.

Bitch, Lynn thought. "About three." Lynn, who was twenty-nine, guessed Chaka's age at twenty-five or so, in part because of how she was dressed. She could have been twenty-one or even nineteen, and Lynn wouldn't have been terribly surprised. "Should we begin?" she asked.

"Why not?" said Richard.

Why not, indeed? Lynn led them up the grand staircase, Chaka's heels clicking behind her, to the old wing that had, when Lynn was a child and used to come with her mother, been all there was to the museum. The museum had undergone a massive building phase in the nineties, and the new addition, which included the entire entrance atrium and two other wings of large white galleries, had pleased none of the critics, but had coincided with a significant jump in attendance.

The old wing still housed the permanent collection. Here the walls were pale sueded gray and the light diffused. This suited the paintings just fine, as they were not necessarily the finest examples of artist or period. But it was the art collection Lynn had grown up with, and she regarded it with fondness.

Self-consciously, she pointed out its highlights: a nice Modigliani, a Vermeer, a minor Blue Period Picasso Harlequin.

Richard Plante turned out to be more informed about art than Lynn expected. She realized she'd been thinking of him as F. X.'s dupe. But he had clearly done his homework. He conversed intelligently about the various other art museums, including the sudden profusion of vanity museums housing private collections that had popped up in Los Angeles, especially in the past two decades. Lynn's museum, the city's oldest, had lost out on those collections thanks to a combination of unreasonably demanding donors and the imperious high-handedness of Earl Smithson's predecessor. Richard seemed to know not just about the art but also the inner workings of the museums' boards, their comparative financial viability, their plans for the future. Lynn had to remind herself that he was a businessman and understood these things.

The bottom line was that the cachet of the museum she worked for had ebbed in the face of competition. "I love an underdog," said Richard Plante.

"Where does that leave me?" Chaka murmured, as she wandered back for another look at a spectacular collection of silver chalices and Crusades-era jewelry recently bequeathed by an eccentric real estate tycoon who while alive had stored the precious pieces in several suits of armor in his Bel Air mansion.

Richard Plante strode through the galleries at Lynn's side. She'd guessed right—he was wearing cowboy boots: two-toned, tan snakeskin boots under his breezy linen suit. As he walked he stamped them down on the polished marble floors, heel-toe, heel-toe, with a determined carelessness that gave him unexpected weight. He wanted to hear what Lynn was currently working on and had elicited from her—not easily, for she knew she should be talking about other things, his interests, for instance—detailed information about the teacher-education packets for a small, secondary show on the brushstroke and the physical qualities of paint that was scheduled for the week after the big opening in late January.

"How big a part of the budget goes to those packets?"

"Oh, tiny," she said.

"Because it's all you need? Or could you use more?"

Lynn laughed. "We can always use more."

"Okay, what would you do with it if you had it?"

Lynn thought for a minute. "Well, we'd love to get more children coming through—you know, school field trips, that kind of thing. But that's an issue for the schools, too—paying for the buses and all that."

Richard stopped abruptly and turned to Lynn. "I'd love to tag along on one of the tours with schoolchildren. I don't remember ever going to an art museum in school. I went to public school, not some fancy prep school, but you've probably read about all that. It's the sort of thing they love to write about. That was my parents' theory, that since we had to run companies in the real world, might as well be educated there, too. All the way through high school. Hey, look, do you think you could let me know when one of those school tours is going? Would that be okay? Or would they worry I'm some kind of kiddie pervert?"

Chaka, who had wandered back, gave a snort of laughter.

"No, I don't think they'd think that," Lynn said. "I think it would be fine. If that's what you'd like. I can certainly look into it."

She was relieved when it was time to lead Richard and Chaka to the deputy director's office, and she quickly excused herself, as had been arranged beforehand, saying she had some documents to get to the printer's. This was, in fact, true, because the tour had gone on almost an hour longer than she'd expected.

A mere ten minutes later Earl Smithson came by her office, having seen Richard Plante and his fiancée off. He stood in her doorway, practically quivering with glee, waving a small strip of paper in the air.

"Look at this, Miss Prosper, look at this!" he cried, still waving what Lynn saw was a check. He didn't venture any farther into the office, and for the first time it occurred to Lynn that he never did—never actually went into anyone's office, at least not as far as she'd seen, but rather stayed just outside the doorway while he talked. This time she rose and joined him in the corridor. He handed the check to her, but kept his fingers close, as if he might need to snatch it back. Of course she immediately noticed the figure, scrawled in a childish hand: $1,000,000.00. It was made out to the museum, and the name printed on the top left hand corner was Richard Plante. It was a personal check.

"One million?"

"For you!"

"What?"

"Not personally, of course not. It's to be used specifically for the education department, to get more schoolchildren here, he says. He mentioned that perhaps some of it could go to special docent training for children's tours, some to grants to schools to cover bus costs, et cetera. But he made no actual specifications. It's to be used at our discretion, in the coming fiscal year. He is trusting us in this. No documents drawn up, no qualifications, although he did ask that not too far into the new year we give him an informal report on how the museum is proceeding. And then, listen to this, he will assess future needs and make long-term arrangements! That's some friend you've got there, Miss Prosper." Earl Smithson glanced at his watch, a slim gold Patek Philippe. "Say, it's late. Have you had lunch yet?"

When Lynn got home, Jamie was waiting for her in the living room, ramrod straight in the middle of the sofa.

"Jamie!" Lynn dropped her purse and hurried in. "You got back early! You're not going to believe what happened at work today."

"You have a message," he said.

"What?" She leaned over to plant a kiss on his cheek. His face was stony.

"You have a message. On the phone."

She looked at him, wondering what was wrong. "Was your flight okay? Are you exhausted? You haven't eaten yet, have you?"

He stood abruptly. "Your friend F. X. called."

Lynn froze. Jamie was watching, and his lip curled.

"What did he say? Jamie, at work today—"

"Why don't you just go listen to the message."

"Fine," she said, and headed for the bedrooms. But in the door to the kitchen she turned back to him. "I really don't appreciate your suspicion," she said.

The phone in the second, smaller bedroom, which they used as an office, had a button for voice mail and their retrieval code programmed in, so that was where they usually picked up messages, rather than from the kitchen phone. Plus there was a desk and paper and pencil for writing things down. Lynn pressed the voice mail button. There was one saved message.

"Hey," came F. X.'s voice, full of innuendo as always, "I know hubby doesn't want you talking to me—you should tell me how much you tell him so I don't make mistakes—but call me, there's something we need to discuss."

Lynn hit erase, then turned on her heel and marched back into the living room. Jamie was back on the couch, but sprawled out now, as if this no longer had anything to do with him.

"Look," she said, "I have no idea what he's doing. I mean, I think I know what it's about, because . . ."

"Yes?" Jamie looked up at her as if he couldn't wait to hear what she'd come up with next.

"Oh, I hate you!" she cried, at which he sprung to his feet.

"You hate *me*?"

"It's about work," she said.

Jamie crossed his arms over his chest with a nasty, skeptical smile.

"It is! Richard Plante gave—"

"'*Did you tell hubby about us?*'" Jamie mimicked.

"I can't control him—he did that on purpose! He's the devil!" Jamie couldn't help a spurt of laughter, and Lynn's heart slowed a little—that is, she became aware of how fast it had been beating. "He *is* the devil," she said. "He's a troublemaker. But Richard Plante donated a million dollars to the museum today." As she calmed down, though, there was room for other thoughts. Her eyes narrowed. "Just exactly what do you suspect me of?"

"You're saying your friend got his boss to donate?"

"No!" But Lynn felt queasily unsure.

Jamie dropped back onto the sofa, all stiffness gone. He slumped forward, his head in his hands, rubbing his temples. "I'm just tired," he said. "I just got off a plane."

She sank down next to him. "Oh, Jamie, I'm sorry, too. I'm sorry you're tired."

When he spoke it was in a monotone. "I was on a plane

today, I was on a plane two days ago, and last week, and next week, and forever."

Lynn looked at him. His jaw was still tight. "Is something wrong?" Tentatively, she brushed the hair from his brow.

Eyes closed, he lifted his cheek toward her, as if toward warmth—and also an invitation to caress, which she did. But it came to her that there was something forced about this, as if he were trying to distract her. "No, it's fine," he said. After a moment he added, "They're extending the deal."

"Oh Jamie, I thought this was going to be the last month."

He sat up straight, pulled away from her. "It's a good thing for me. It's because they like my work. You'd think you could be more supportive."

"I'm sorry," she faltered. "I . . . I just miss you when you're gone, that's all."

"You act as though you don't think I hate it, too."

"But if you hate it, why not quit?" Lynn rose to this idea eagerly. "You could do something else, it isn't worth it."

Jamie rounded on her—for an insane second she thought he was going to strike her. "Why not quit? I'll tell you why not. Who'd pay for all this? This house, this life. Why not quit! Right, like I can. Can you please join the rest of us here in the real world, Lynn?"

She was up in a flash. "Don't blame me. You already had this job when we met. You wanted this house, too. I didn't force you into anything."

"You're right. You're right. But if I ever had any notion of quitting, it's impossible now."

She stared at him. "Are you saying you're sorry we got married?"

"No," he said—quieter. He looked down at floor, shaking his head. "I just hate it when you say you hate me." Lynn's shoulders relaxed. "It scares me," he said.

"You know I don't mean it."

"Then why would you say it?"

"I don't know." She'd never thought about it. "It's just something I say. When I'm mad. I say it to everyone—my mother, my sisters. The people I feel comfortable with."

He just shrugged.

But where was this coming from? Of course Jamie complained about work sometimes, the way anyone does: "I hate my job, I'll never make partner." Lynn had written it off as those avowals of failure you make—"I failed the test"—to appease the gods. It never occurred to her that he could actually dislike a job that much and still stay in it. In her family, if you didn't love your work you made a change. "Look," she said, "this isn't impossible. We can sell the house if we need to, I don't care about it. We should definitely make a change if you're unhappy."

"Unhappy!" The scorn in his voice chilled her.

"Jamie—"

He turned to her, and she was shocked at how lean and sunken his face looked. "Just tell me you won't see that guy again."

"What?"

"I don't like the idea of you spending time with him, I'm sorry, I just don't. You said before you didn't want to."

"Okay, it's just . . ."

But his face was already closed.

"Wait," she said, "this is about my work. That million-dollar thing, that's his boss."

"Never mind." Jamie flopped back down on the sofa, stretched out with his feet up. "Do what you want."

"What are you doing?" she cried, throwing herself on him. He made an *oomph* sound. "This is so silly. I love you—you know that. This has nothing to do with us. I love you more than anything. This whole conversation—we just need to start it over."

His dark eyes were sad. "I'm happy about your work, really I am," he said.

"But yours! I had no idea. We need to talk more about that."

"Oh, God," he said, "it's nothing. It's just something I said—we were having a fight." He looked up at her. "I'm so tired, I just want to rest." Lynn shimmied in so that she was next to him on the sofa, and he drew her close. "Please, please don't make me talk about it anymore right now."

Seven

At work the next morning, Lynn debated long and hard whether to call F. X. back. She didn't want to. She didn't think she should—Jamie would certainly not want her to. On the other hand, she feared escalation. F. X. was clearly amusing himself. She picked up the phone and dialed.

"How are you, darling?" Ella Kovak asked, delighted as always to hear from one of her daughters.

"Oh," said Lynn, "just, Jamie's been traveling so much these days."

"It's just awful—these corporate law firms!"

"Well, that's his job," Lynn said, some might say perversely. "It's lucky Jamie's so smart. You should see, he doesn't work nearly as late as others."

"Yes, but what about billable hours? I'm sure they expect him to keep billing. Finishing your work quickly is no advantage at a place like that. The system—"

"Mother! I didn't call you to discuss the ills of capitalism."

"Oh. What, then?"

Lynn sighed. "Nothing, really. I'm just in a bad mood. Or, not bad, just . . . weird."

Her mother waited.

"I ran into this old friend from school whom Jamie doesn't like."

"Why doesn't he like her?"

"Him."

"Oh."

"Why do you say it like that? Aren't I allowed to have a male friend?"

"Why, of cour—"

"No, evidently not. Jamie doesn't want me to see him, either."

There was a momentary silence on the line between the two women.

"It's not a big deal," Lynn said. "I wouldn't care. He wasn't a close friend or anything. It's just awkward, because, you see, his boss—"

"Wait a minute," said her mother. "Jamie made you stop seeing a friend of yours because he's male?"

"He didn't *make* me do anything. He just said—"

"What did he say?"

"First of all, I wouldn't even call F. X. a friend."

"Oh, Lynn, this is exactly the sort of thing I worry about. That's how it starts: little by little, small encroachments on a woman's self-determination. So by the time something big happens you can't even say how you got there. Just that chipping away—"

"Mother, we're not talking about totalitarian governments."

"Now, I think you should tell Jamie—"

"You're completely misreading the situation. It's my fault, I described it badly."

"Why are you assuming all the blame? This is just what I'm talking about. I don't hold it against Jamie personally. You know we all adore Jamie, but any man—"

"You know what," said Lynn, "I'm sorry I brought it up."

"—or woman, to be fair—although women tend not to be in that position of power—"

"Mom, can we please just drop it? You're not understanding the situation at all. Look," she said, "I'm at work. I've got to go."

The whole thing was ridiculous. Lynn had to call F. X. The last thing she should be was afraid of him. Oh, she was sick of them all.

"What the hell do you think you were doing?" she said, no preliminaries, no niceties, when he answered his phone.

To give F. X. credit, he didn't bother playing dumb. He laughed. "Calm down. Boy, doesn't Jamie have a sense of humor?"

"Do you tell the truth about anything?"

"I told you, Lynnie, *épater les* husbands. I'm not your husband's keeper. That would be your job."

"I mean the truth about yourself."

"What do you mean?"

Lynn heard the sudden uneasiness in his voice. That was new. She wondered how many other lies he'd told. "You tell me your 'girlfriend' is coming to Mona's opening and that you went to Venezuela with her, but neither of those things turns out to be true. Then it turns out she's engaged to your boss!"

"Wait," said F. X. "What are you talking about?

"I met Chaka yesterday. She came to the museum with Richard." *Hah*, Lynn thought. He wasn't expecting to get caught. But why lie in the first place?

"Engaged?" he said.

"Did you ever even go out with her?" In her triumph at having caught F. X. out, Lynn failed to register the blank surprise in his voice.

"Of course I did," he snapped. "You must have misunderstood."

"Misunderstood the diamond the size of a matchbox she was waving around on her left hand?" Lynn was still crowing. "And Richard introduced her as his fiancée." There was such a long stretch of dead air on the phone that Lynn said, "F. X.?"

"I introduced them! I knew they'd gone out a few times. Chaka said . . ."

F. X.'s pauses and his tone throughout the conversation finally sank in. "Are you saying you didn't know they were engaged?"

"Yeah, well, can I help it if my good looks, intelligence, and modest financial success weren't enough for her?" His voice was jaunty again, yet there was something shaky about it. "Guess she was after bigger fish. All along, maybe. That would be poetic justice, right?"

"F. X., I . . ."

"You didn't say anything about me and her in front of Richard, did you? I haven't exactly let on to Richard about us. I doubt Chaka has, either. No," he said bitterly, "that wouldn't help either of our positions any."

It was Lynn's turn to be silent.

"So you have your revenge on me after all. Nice, dropping the news on me like that. You couldn't have planned it better. I guess it's hard to imagine that I have feelings."

"F. X., I had no idea."

"I've got to go. I'm at work here."

"Wait," she said, but he had hung up.

On her way home from work that day, Lynn turned on the radio, and the familiar, raspy voice of Dr. Darla filled the car. Dr. Darla Healey—the Love Doctor, as her call-in show was known—was a guilty addiction for Lynn. It was on weekdays, from four to six P.M., so she only got to hear it when she got out of the office on the early side. Dr. Darla (Lynn had read somewhere that her doctorate was in communications or physical therapy or something) had a rigorously retrograde outlook on what women should and should not do in relationships. If a caller mentioned that she was engaged, Dr. Darla would demand, "Is there a ring on your finger? When's the date?" There was a thrill to how brutal Dr. Darla could be with callers whose boyfriends clearly weren't smitten enough. Yet she had also once confided to her listeners that she sometimes met her husband at the door in nothing but a frilly white apron. "You don't just want to get married, ladies," she explained. "You want to stay married."

The call she was in the middle of was a woman indignant at some perceived misstep of her fiancé (a solitaire, next May) and clearly assuming that Dr. Darla would share her indignation. It came out that she had called an old college boyfriend to wish him happy birthday.

Dr. Darla went into attack mode right away. "Now why would you do something like that?"

"I . . . uh . . . We just stay in touch. We always call each other on our birthdays."

"Tell me, this old boyfriend, he always calls you on your birthday, too?"

The woman's hesitation said it all. "Well, men are never as good at that sort of thing."

"Oh? Does your fiancé neglect you on your birthday?"

"No, of course not, he's wonderful."

"Then why in God's name are you calling some other guy? Are you already bored with your fiancé? Isn't he man enough for you?"

"No—I mean, yes."

"Then what's getting you off with this other guy? Did you sleep with him?"

"No, I just called. Oh, you mean . . . yes, in college—yes." Silence.

"He was my boyfriend for two years."

"You weren't married, were you? No ring? No date? And now you're mad at your fiancé because he has concerns that you might be reverting back to that sort of slutty behavior?"

"I . . ."

"Tell me, Amanda—you haven't answered my question yet—what were you thinking, calling your old boyfriend? Did you want to make sure he was still hot for you?"

"No, of course not. I . . . Just to stay in touch, I guess. We're just friends."

"No, you're not. Unless I'm misunderstanding and the two of you see each other all the time, have lunch, complain about work, support each other in your troubles, then no, you're not friends. Am I misunderstanding?"

"No."

"Do you use that sullen-little-girl voice with your fiancé? If so, I can tell you he won't be around long—inappropriate phone calls or no. Why call this guy, then? For your own ego gratification, is that right? Because you don't care that much about your so-called fiancé but are hanging on in case nothing better comes along?"

"No, Dr. Darla. That's not it at all, I swear."

"Listeners, I would say that a woman who feels compelled to stay in touch with the men in her past—even just an annual phone call—has something wrong with her current relationship and something wrong with her. If she were satisfied she wouldn't even think about calling. She wouldn't need the attention of other men. Amanda, if your fiancé called me for advice"—it was clear that Dr. Darla had already cut off the caller and was now addressing her audience—"I'd tell the poor guy to hightail it out of there. The fact that you want to keep contact going with old boyfriends or whatever you call them means you clearly aren't ready to commit to this guy—and you probably aren't mature enough to be married at all."

Lynn slapped the dial, turning the radio off in disgust. "That's not true," she said out loud. "She could just have been curious." She turned onto her street. Before she reached her driveway she tapped the knob again, to hear what else Dr. Darla might be saying. All she heard was, "We'll be right back, after a station break."

Eight

Lynn tried on first one thing, then another, leaving them all in puddles on the floor, which was unlike her. She had come home early to change for the dinner she and Jamie were supposed to go to that night. This was unlike her, too. Usually what she'd worn to work was suitable for any art function she might have to go to afterward, and today was no exception.

The invitation had been hand-delivered to the museum a few days earlier: Could Lynn and Jamie Prosper please join Mona Frumpke for a dinner in honor of a friend visiting from England. "One of those aristo furniture-making chappies," Earl Smithson said when he came by her office, his own invitation in hand. The dinner was being held at a restaurant in Hollywood not far from Lynn and Jamie's house.

From the bed, Jamie watched with amusement as she slipped in and out of yet another outfit. "Do I need to change?" he asked. "What should I wear?"

"Oh, anything," she said distractedly.

Jamie came over and wrapped his arms around her. "You're beautiful," he said.

"Ugh," she protested, shimmying out of his hold. "You're clearly insane." Lynn hadn't talked to F. X. again and had no idea whether he'd been invited.

In the end she settled, as she'd half known she would all along, on a simple, bias-cut, black jersey skirt and a scoop-neck white top, belted with a thick tan leather belt. It was an old Hermès belt, actually, that Jamie's mother had offered her, claiming it no longer fit. Philippa could be surprisingly generous that way, but often undercut the kind gesture as she had in this case with her imperious, "It really is the only belt a well-dressed woman needs."

When Lynn caught sight of their hostess at the restaurant, her heart skipped. Had she and Jamie disastrously under-dressed? Mona had gone from pale blond to a shiny raven bob—with those same marcelled waves—and was wearing a short, jade-colored sequined jacket with what looked like a nude, scoop-necked bodysuit underneath. Earl Smithson was standing next to Mona near the table, wearing a dark suit with a gleaming silk tie, but that was what he always wore. Jamie had taken off his tie at home and hadn't even brought his suit jacket. But as Lynn moved forward to greet Mona, she saw that she was wearing her sequined jacket with skintight jeans and—this was the real shocker—Nike running shoes with a matching jade stripe. The whole thing was very odd.

"Darling!" said Mona, making her way to Lynn's side. "My new little friend! Everyone"—there were already four or five people milling around the long, narrow rectangular table set for twelve at the back of the restaurant—"I want you to meet my newest dear friend, Lynn Prosper. And her darling husband . . ."

"Jamie," Lynn supplied softly.

"Jamie!" Grabbing Lynn's wrist in a viselike grip, she whispered, "Now make sure you sit down here near me."

Earl Smithson had collared Jamie on his side of the table. Lynn already knew one of the couples, midrange collectors of twentieth-century American art. The wife was also a docent at the museum. Of the others, a woman who looked about Lynn's age, maybe a little younger, was introduced as the West Coast editor of one of the big New York decorating magazines, and her date was a famous Los Angeles hairdresser.

"Sit, sit," Mona ordered. "We're just waiting for Hugo, who's bringing some friends of his from London, and they're simply notorious." No F. X., then. Lynn felt a little guilty at how relieved she felt. Taking her seat at the head of the table, Mona kept her grip on Lynn, placing her on her left and Earl Smithson on her right, with Jamie next to Earl, across the table from Lynn. Married couples were of course separated. The hairdresser slid in next to Lynn, reluctantly she thought.

Fortunately the notoriously late Brits arrived moments later, and soon everyone was seated. Lynn wasn't much surprised when the hairdresser took this opportunity to switch seats. His place ended up being taken by one of the aristocratic furniture maker's entourage. This man was nice-looking and smiled at her as he sat. On Jamie's free side landed a woman Mona introduced to both of them sketchily as "Marie, you know, who has that great little store on Larchmont and does such fabulous houses."

Marie nodded just as sketchily to Jamie and Lynn, then turned to their hostess and placed her hands flat on the table in front of her with a dramatic flourish. "Darling, this table looks suspiciously familiar."

Mona laughed. "Yes, it's yours, that old refectory table— I still love it." She turned to Lynn. "I've been so disappointed by what you end up with in restaurants, now I bring my own things."

Lynn noticed the magazine editor farther down the table

listening hungrily, her eyes flickering with the possibilities of how she could use this juicy tidbit.

"I especially hate round tables," Mona continued. "I like a long narrow table you can talk across." She returned to Lynn, lowering her voice. "And now," she said, "we can catch up."

Sure enough, everyone seemed to be chatting away. Lynn glanced across the table at Jamie, but he was already deep in conversation with both her boss and the Larchmont decorator. About what? "Thank you so much for including us," she said to Mona.

"I wouldn't have missed it for the world. And your husband lives up to all that advance notice. So delightful, so polite, so smart." Where was she getting that from? Jamie hadn't said two words to her yet. "And not a hint of jealousy—not yet at least." Lynn glanced uneasily across the table at Jamie again, hoping he hadn't heard. "And handsome! F. X. hadn't mentioned that." *Because F. X. has never seen him.* "So, you liked Jessica's work?" Mona said, changing tack abruptly.

"Very much! I don't get out much to see young artists. I love it. It's something I wish I could do more of."

"Well, why don't you? Although it can be frustrating. There's a lot of dross out there."

"That's part of what makes it exciting when you see someone's work and just know."

Mona raised a raven eyebrow. "Let's be honest, dear. Jessica was an easy one—you came to her through me. I have quite a track record. If you'd seen her work in some crummy little gallery, or even worse in one of those street fairs—God, like those ones along Santa Monica in Beverly Hills!—would you have had the confidence to think highly of her work?"

Lynn considered this.

"Oh, I like that," said Mona. "Really thinking."

"No, it's a good question. I actually think about it a lot. It's exactly what we should be doing at the museum—somehow giving people confidence, a certain comfort level when faced with new art. People talk about the universality of the masterpiece, but that always seems like a dead-end discussion to me. Although beautiful art . . ." Lynn realized that Mona was staring at her curiously. "I guess what I mean is that, yes, I do think I would have recognized Jessica as a good artist—a very good artist. I do have confidence in my taste, but mainly because I've had a lot of education and done a lot of looking. I'm not saying I'd have the confidence to say who will be the next big thing."

"I don't know what will sell, but I know what I like?"

"Something like that. It's funny, those clichés—like, 'My kid could do that.' I was recently talking to someone who said just that type of thing, and of course sometimes they have a point. But this guy—behind it, I sensed—"

"Oh, Prosecco!" came a cry down the table—from a sharp-featured blonde in the furniture maker's British entourage. Mona answered someone else's question, and Lynn felt a little foolish, as she always did when she grew too excited about her subject. She looked around the table and Jamie, across from her, caught her eye. He smiled, and she felt the warmth of it in her chest. The waiter was pouring pale pink liquid into each place setting's champagne glass, and everyone was talking away, brightly, easily—nothing particularly scintillating, but the group as a whole had an energetic hum. Another waiter arrived with an ice bucket and a second bottle that he proceeded to open with an unassuming flourish—an oxymoron but also a mark of excellent service. No menus had been brought yet, but two other waiters were carrying around trays of finger appetizers. It felt more like a dinner in the house of someone with a staff than a restaurant. It occurred to Lynn to wonder if the china on the table also belonged to Mona. She tried to see what the plates looked like at neighboring tables; it seemed to be the same pattern.

"It's my new favorite." The shrill blonde was still going on about Prosecco. "So much more festive than champagne."

"That's because you're English," said the pretty magazine editor. "Don't the English always have a thing for Italy? What's that all about? E. M. Forster and Henry James and all that?"

"Well, James, of course, was American," said the furniture maker. He was tall and good looking and had an air about him as if he thought he could be perfectly cast in the BBC version of his own life.

"Oh, you know what I mean," cooed the magazine editor, as if she thought so, too.

"But you Americans," he said. "You, sir," he called down to Mona's end of the table. "Do I understand that your given name is Earl?"

"That's right," Lynn's boss said pleasantly.

"And Duke, that's another name you Yanks love. Now why is that? But not Marquess. Not King."

"Sometimes King," said Mona.

"Nat King Cole?" offered another of the Brits, the rabbity one who'd been introduced as a writer. He had seriously bad teeth, practically mossy, yet was clearly upper class.

"King Vidor!" someone else said. "And how about Count Basie?"

"Count isn't an English title," the furniture maker said with a frown.

"That's right," said the man sitting next to Lynn. "You don't see Brits naming their children 'President' or 'Senator,' do you?"

"But you do call people 'guv'nor,'" said Earl Smithson, and everyone, at least the Americans, laughed.

"The funny thing is," said Mona, "Hugo's right." Hugo was the furniture maker—Hugo Stanhope. "Remember, Smitty? Remember that party where Geordie kept calling you Earl, and that woman—"

"Hah hah hah!" erupted Lynn's boss.

"That's right," said Mona, "she thought that was your title. She kept calling you Lord Smithson all evening!" And then Mona collapsed into giggles as well, the two of them doubled over, holding on to each other at the end of the table. "That's," Mona choked out, "when we started calling you Smitty instead."

"What are you, dear?" the woman who owned the store on Larchmont asked the furniture maker. "Lord, of course, but what? Marquess, right?"

Lynn realized she was asking the question for the table's benefit, that she herself already knew the answer. It struck her that this woman and the furniture maker were somehow aligned, in league together, that she was playing hostess to the Englishman, although in a very different way than Mona Frumpke.

"No, that's my father," Hugo said. "I'm nothing, just a commoner. It's merely a courtesy title, sort of a placeholder until you inherit."

"Lord what?" the store owner insisted. Later Lynn was to learn that Hugo Stanhope was in town specifically for a launch party for his furniture at Marie Liddy's highly regarded, eponymous shop.

He gave a weary smile, as if aware that he was being put through his paces, that this was what was owed to the American market. But Lynn was pretty sure he didn't mind. Piers, Julie's husband, was exactly the same. "Essborough," the furniture maker admitted at last. "Earl of Essborough."

Lynn's neighbor turned to her. He had been introduced as

Peter, but she hadn't caught the rest. He said, "Here's where I'm supposed to say something about you Americans or this young democracy or something along those lines being fascinated by titles, and maybe even make those same tired references to Tocqueville or Baudrillard. But those are Frenchmen, come to think of it, and my point is that it's really the English who are fascinated by titles."

"No, we are, too. Actually," she said, not sure if she should, but this man had a nice face and was smiling at her so pleasantly, "my sister-in-law married an Englishman. His father is a viscount, so I've learned all about 'Honorables.' "

"Really?" He looked surprised. "What's his name?"

"Oh, I'm sure you won't know him," said Lynn, "but it's Piers Monkham."

"Piers? Piers James Laurence!"

"You know him?" Lynn instinctively lowered her voice. She had been told that Piers's father was famous for having once owned a Derby winner—"Darby," as Jamie's sister and mother had taken to pronouncing it. Julie had once showed Lynn the silver-framed photograph Piers had given her of himself at age fourteen in a morning suit, leading the horse from the winners' circle.

"We were up at Oxford together. All of us—Simon, too." He nodded toward the one with bad teeth. "Old Light-Fingered Larry." He shook his head.

"Who?"

Her dinner partner glanced across the table. Lynn followed his eyes. Jamie was engrossed in conversation with Marie Liddy and the elderly collectors, more animated than Lynn had seen him in a while. ". . . your dreams . . ." she thought she heard him say. "That's your husband?" said Peter. "It's his sister who's married to Piers?"

"Why?" said Lynn. "What was Piers like back then?" She

said it teasingly, but really wanted to know; something in his tone prompted curiosity.

"Ah, no, Piers is a great guy." He leaned back in his seat. "He's an old friend, that's all, of all of ours. He's funny, really a funny bloke. You've met him? Then you know. No, I was just . . . interested—that he ended up marrying an American, you know."

"What do you mean?" said Lynn.

"I always find it interesting when people marry outside their nationality, don't you? Didn't it affect your perception of your sister-in-law, that she married a Brit?"

Lynn regarded him. He was attractive, with fair, curling hair that reached just past his collar. He looked tall and slender—*reedy*, she imagined someone English would put it. "You're right," she said. "It did." But she was pretty sure there was something more about Piers that he had decided not to tell her.

"What's your sister-in-law like?" he asked.

"Oh, no," said Lynn, "none of that. Why don't you tell me what you're like?"

"Me? What could you possibly want to know about me?"

"Well . . . what are you doing in Los Angeles? Just visiting with your friend? Or do you live here?"

He looked at her searchingly, which struck her as odd, it was such a basic question. Then he gave another of his short, almost braying laughs. He seemed very English. "I do live here. Only recently, though. I like it very much—I don't care what anyone says."

Lynn had been hoping for a bit more than this, some hint, perhaps, of what he did. "You said you knew Hugo Stanhope from school?"

"Oh, we've all known each other dogs' years. When Hugo heard I'd be coming out, he gave me a call to come to this fab dinner party where I was sure to be seated next to the prettiest girl at the table, but that dash the luck she'd be married . . ."

"He said all that when he invited you?" Lynn was smiling.

"Course, or I wouldn't have bothered, would I?"

"Petey," called the blonde at the other end of the table, the one who'd been excited about Prosecco. "You took the key, didn't you? I forgot the house key."

"Yes, sweetums, got it. And that," he added sotto voce to Lynn, "is my fiancée, the beauteous Joan." He gave Joan a big smile and wriggled his fingers at her.

Lynn smiled in her direction, too, but the fiancée had already turned away, back to the other Brits.

When it was time to go, Earl Smithson ended up walking out with Lynn and Jamie. "So, what's he like?" he asked when they were outside.

"Who?" said Lynn.

"The director. Peter Fairhaven."

Lynn's face was a study of dismay. "That was . . ."

"You didn't know?" Jamie laughed, his arm around her.

"I never heard his last name!" She remembered the funny look Peter Fairhaven had given her when she asked what he was doing in L.A. God, what else had she said?

Earl Smithson clucked and shook his head, but he was laughing, too. "Probably the best thing that could have happened. Everyone always sucks up to him, whereas you . . . Anyway, I hear he's a right bastard on the set." Being around English accents had started to color his own speech. "Well, Jamie, just one more command performance left to get through now."

Jamie looked puzzled, and Lynn wasn't sure what he was talking about, either.

"Did I forget to mention? Richard Plante. He has most

generously offered to take not one but two tables in the muse-um's name at the opera gala." The gala, Lynn did know about. It was a black-tie benefit to celebrate opening night of a new production of Verdi's *Otello*. The supposedly spectacular sets had been designed by a major Los Angeles artist whose ret-rospective was coming up at the museum—an exhibit that was being underwritten by a bank whose CEO was also a longtime opera patron. In the business world it would be called synergy. "Richard specifically asked for you at his own table, so I expect you two lovebirds to be at your best and most charming. You know how important these things are."

Nine

Lynn placed one last plate, number fifteen, on the too-tall pile on their dining room table. It didn't even look like their table anymore, with a rental table at one end and the whole thing camouflaged by two tablecloths and an Indian silk sari.

"How did this happen?" she said.

Jamie chuckled, but nervously.

Lynn knew exactly how it had happened. It was her fault. It had all started with a call from her oldest sister, Dee.

"What are you guys doing for Thanksgiving?" Dee had asked. She'd sounded excited about something.

"I don't know. Why?" Lynn hadn't given Thanksgiving much thought yet. She and Jamie took turns whose family they celebrated with, and since it was their turn to stay in L.A., they hadn't had to worry about things like airline tickets.

"I may be in Los Angeles," Dee said. "I have a deal heating up in San Diego and thought maybe I'd drive up. But if you have other plans . . ."

"Of course we don't." Lynn was on the phone in the

kitchen; she rubbed her thumb across the chip in the end cabinet's thick white paint, years and years' accumulation of coats. This particular cabinet held their wedding china, a full sixteen place settings thanks to Jamie's mother's active canvassing of her guest list—despite the blowup over the wedding. Every now and then Lynn would take two plates from the bottom out of the vague fear that she was wearing out the ones on top. "You know what," Lynn said, "let's do it here, at my house. I'll cook."

"Don't be silly," said Dee. "We'll go to a hotel the way we always do. How about the Beverly Wilshire this year?" Poor Jamie, he'd been thunderstruck when he first learned that the Kovaks celebrated Thanksgiving in fancy hotel dining rooms.

"No, really," said Lynn, "I can do it. I want to. Who will it be? Just you, me, Jamie, and Mom. And Dad. He'll come down, right?"

Up until Lynn was eight, her father, like her mother, had been a university professor in Los Angeles. Already noted in his field at that time, Harold Kovak had been offered a tenured position at Berkeley. The plan was for him to go up on his own at first, to see how the position would pan out before Ella thought about leaving her highly desirable job at UCLA or worrying about the children's schools. Of course, he came down to L.A. as often as he could, especially when the children were young. That had been more than twenty years ago. There had never been a specific decision or pronouncement about their living situation, but Ella and Harold Kovak had maintained separate establishments ever since. Her father still usually came for holidays, but Lynn made a mental note to call him. "I can handle dinner for five," she said.

"We better call Sasha," said Dee, "even though she'll never come. But really, Lynn, it's too much. We should go out."

"No, it'll be fun. How hard can it be?"

The very next day, Lynn received a call from Sasha. From her crisp "Hi," Lynn could tell she was irate.

"So? You were going to invite everyone to your little Thanksgiving dinner but us?"

"No, I just thought . . . Can you come? We're going to have it at our house. Did Dee tell you?"

"Yes," Sasha said shortly.

"I was about to call!"

"I mean yes, we'll come."

Lynn was startled and didn't say anything right away.

"Why?" said Sasha. "Don't you want us to?"

"Of course I do, I'm thrilled. It's just that I thought you always have Thanksgiving with Kam's parents."

It was Sasha's turn to hesitate. "Actually, that is a bit of an issue. They haven't been to the mainland for years and"— she lowered her voice—"to tell you the truth, they were over when Dee called and they just assumed they were invited, too. It's my fault. I said it was a big family dinner and they just . . ."

"It's fine, Sasha," Lynn said. "It'll be fine. Invite them."

Sasha gave an uncharacteristic titter. "Well, like I said, they think you already did."

"Don't worry, it'll be great. I'm glad."

"Kam's mother says she'll make some poi."

Lynn laughed.

"No, really," said Sasha.

Jamie assumed it was safe to mention these plans to his own mother. Philippa had announced that she would be spending Thanksgiving in Rhode Island. Andy's fiancée's family had so graciously invited not only Andy but his mother, too, to join them for the holiday. How lovely the Peales were! It was, therefore, to Jamie's horror that his mother responded to his sheepish run-through of the members of Lynn's family who might be coming, with, "How lovely, your first Thanksgiving in your own home. I wouldn't miss it for the world!"

"But, Mom," Jamie said, "the Peales . . ."

"Oh, they'll understand. You know, dear, you really should invite your sister and Piers, too."

"They're in England."

"They've been talking about a trip to California. Why not? Lynn's whole family is coming, aren't they?"

When she heard, Lynn sighed and counted on her fingers. She and Jamie had four folding chairs in the garage and two extra leaves for the dining room table. She figured she could feed twelve. Fortunately, out of ignorance more than anything, she'd ordered the largest turkey.

Two weeks before Thanksgiving, Philippa called again: Andy was hurt that he and Annika had not been included. His poor fiancée, she must find this lack of warmth very odd.

"But they're having Thanksgiving at her parents!" Lynn protested.

No, they were not, Philippa informed her—as if wondering where in the world Lynn had picked up such an odd idea. Annika's father and stepmother had decided to take up some friends' invitation for a two-week African safari, the most natural thing in the world since they wouldn't be able to get away that winter when they usually did, because of the wedding. Oh, and Lynn should see the dress Annika had found. Beautiful. Fur trim!

"They really must be loaded," Lynn said to Jamie that night. "Can you imagine what your mother would have said if *my* family tried something like that? At the last minute? What if she'd still been planning on going to Rhode Island?"

Jamie just leaned over and kissed her.

The last call from St. Louis came as Philippa herself was supposed to be leaving for the airport. She wanted to know whether it wouldn't be possible to include Piers's mother, the Viscountess of Milborough. It was hardly a yes-or-no question. It appeared that Lady Milborough was already on a plane to Los Angeles, having decided at the last minute to accompany Piers and Julie, who were making a vacation of it.

Lynn got the sense that even Philippa was dismayed by the idea of the viscountess at Thanksgiving. "It's a good thing I'm bringing my silver," Philippa said. "It's a pity about the crystal, though. If only you'd had a real wedding you'd probably have enough of that, too. I don't know what Lady Milborough will think of rented glasses. She once showed me the butler pantries at Milborough. They have enough stemware for a banquet of a hundred."

"Too bad she's not bringing any," Jamie said. By this point both he and Lynn were apt to be tart.

"What's really too bad," Philippa countered, "and frankly rather perplexing, is that Lynn's mother doesn't have anything you can use."

But something magical happened when Lynn finished setting the table. She did this the day before Thanksgiving, having once overheard a socialite involved with the museum say she always did her tables twenty-four hours ahead of time. Dusk was just falling, and in the rosy light coming in through the rippled old panes in the living room, the spread of good bone china, rented glassware, and gleaming silver (just to see how it would look, Lynn had set every other place with her own silverware) took on an unexpected elegance. The table looked complete in a way that surprised her. It looked real— a real Thanksgiving table that a large, extended family might sit down to—and for the first time Lynn believed she could pull it off.

Jamie came over as she was lighting the candles. "Why are you doing that now?"

It was another thing she'd picked up from the socialite—that you should never have candles with unlit wicks. Lynn supposed this was because brand-new candles might indicate the shameful fact that you didn't light candles every night as a matter of course, but put them out only for company.

She and Jamie stood together at one end of the table. He put an arm around her and drew her close. "I love you," he said. "Not just because of this. But I know you hate to cook and . . ."

"Shhh. I don't *hate* to."

"You didn't have to do this for me."

"I know." Together they gave a soft, satisfied sigh. "And if it is a disaster," Lynn said, "at least it will make a good story for our children one day." She looked at him, smiling, and saw with surprise that his eyes were bright, as if about to fill with tears.

"It's beautiful," he said. "This is a real home."

Then the doorbell rang, and Philippa was on their doorstep.

Why, look at your table!" Philippa swept into the room in her Ferragamo pumps and the knit suit she deemed suitable for airline travel. Appearance over comfort was Philippa's motto. She was tall and broad shouldered, with ruddy cheeks and pale red hair she always wore in a smooth twist at the back of her head.

Jamie dragged in Philippa's venerable red Samsonite. "What's in here, Mom? You're only here for three days."

But Philippa was circling the table. "Now what is this?"

"Oh, just an old sari," Lynn said, then was annoyed with

herself for being self-conscious about it. "It was my grand-mother's. She got it when—"

"Didn't you have a large enough tablecloth? You should have told me. I would have been happy to bring one."

"We like it this way," said Jamie. "We think it looks beautiful."

"Oh, the bohemian look. That's in right now, isn't it? But are you sure—"

"Yes."

"And before you're so critical of my luggage, Jamie, you might remember that I have sixteen place settings of silver in there. I'll get them out right away, so you can put away yours, Lynn."

"I was thinking it might look nice to mix them together," Lynn said. "I love the way that can look."

Philippa raised an eyebrow. "Of course," she said. "Whatever you like, dear. It's your table."

Ten

On Thanksgiving Day itself Lynn encouraged everyone to come early. They were all family, and Jamie's mother would be there anyway, since she was staying with them. Lynn had imagined a gracious, leisurely cocktail hour during which she'd occasionally drift to the kitchen to check her browning and glorious bird, perhaps baste now and then. She was extremely proud of her advance planning. She had prepared all the side dishes except for the green beans, which had to be blanched in boiling water at the last minute, then tossed warm with toasted almonds, lemon, and butter. She'd even toasted the almonds ahead of time, storing them in Ziploc bags. The lemons were cut, the butter at the ready. The potatoes lyonnaise, the sweet-potato purée, and the creamed spinach had all been made two days before and only needed reheating. The homemade cranberry sauce was a matter of particular pride. Lynn hoped everyone didn't realize how easy it was, the recipe right on the back of the fresh cranberries bag. Even the stuffing—Philippa's recipe—had been made the evening before to ensure that the actual day was as carefree as possible.

Still, Lynn, who'd never so much as cooked a whole chicken, had to admit that she'd been thankful that morning for Philippa, who'd reminded her to take the giblets in their plastic bag out of the turkey's cavity before cooking, showed her that she needed twice as much butter patted on the outside as the recipe called for, and stood there nodding approvingly as she stuffed the bird. Lynn had read somewhere that if you put in too much stuffing the whole thing could explode, and this possibility had haunted her. And after she'd torn the skin hanging over the neck cavity in her first attempts with those little skewers, Philippa had even laced up the turkey for her.

When Lynn saw Jamie passing glasses of champagne in the living room, she untied her apron (she'd bought one especially for this occasion) and moved to join her guests.

"Oh," said Philippa, as if surprised, "is that everything?" She ran her eye over the kitchen, which Lynn was pleased to see looked remarkably neat. One of the benefits of all that prep work was the leisure to clean as she went. "How about your serving dishes? Do you have them all ready?" This was disingenuous on Philippa's part. The kitchen was not large, and anyone could see that Lynn did not. "I always," said Philippa, "like to think through my serving pieces ahead of time and have them lined up and ready to go. It makes that last-minute scramble so much less chaotic. And what about a gravy boat?"

Not only did Lynn not have a gravy boat, she had forgotten the gravy altogether. The gravy, the gravy, wasn't it just what was left in the pan after the turkey had cooked? All that nice butter and those succulent, steaming juices? Lynn did remember hearing something about having to skim the grease off the top. She had never been much of a gravy fan herself. She looked longingly through the doorway toward her mother, who was seated on the living room sofa, champagne glass in hand, leaning forward to say something to Lady Milborough and Kam's mother. There was laughter, and Jamie, bottle in hand, turned toward the kitchen. Lynn gestured frantically, but he didn't see, and moved to refill someone's glass.

"Shall I find you something to hold the gravy?" Philippa said, almost kindly.

Lynn turned back to her. "Yes, thanks, that would be great. A nice bowl? And I don't have a real gravy spoon, either."

"Everyone knows this is your first time, dear. No one expects perfection."

When Philippa's back was turned, Lynn ran to the bedroom with one of her cookbooks, frantically pawing through pages for gravy instructions. Then, shaken—her schedule already thrown off—she ran back to the kitchen, where she made bad use of the rest of the turkey's cooking time moving restlessly back and forth, opening and closing cupboards in search of the serving pieces she knew she had but now could not seem to put her hands on. And where was her own mother? Laughing and carrying on with the others, that's where, it never occurring to her that her slaving daughter might need help. Not to mention her two equally undomestic sisters who not only had not lifted a finger, but had never even made a pretense of offering. It was embarrassing to have so many female relatives in the house yet be stuck with this virago. No, not a virago. Her mother-in-law was the only one helping at all.

Then, far too abruptly, the turkey was ready. Amazingly, it came out of the oven looking perfect. Lynn felt a twinge of pleasure—until she remembered how much of the hard parts Philippa had done. Using the cooking rack, Lynn managed to maneuver the heavy, frightening turkey onto the platter herself—she was sweating all over now—and had it beautifully arranged and artistically surrounded by parsley when Philippa came back in from the living room, followed by Julie.

"Can I do anything?" Julie said.

"No, thanks," said Lynn, "I'm fine."

Philippa was studying the turkey. "Don't you want to take the stuffing out before carving?"

"Oh. Yes. Yes, of course. I . . . just wanted to see how it looked. Jamie?" she called through the doorway.

"Oh, don't go bothering Jamie," Philippa said.

"Mother!" said Julie, shooting Lynn a sympathetic look. "Come on, let's give Lynn some room."

"I was just trying to help," said Philippa.

"Please," said Lynn, turning her back on Julie, too, "both of you go have a glass of champagne. Jamie and I can handle this."

The turkey was like a squirmy, greasy baby. Lynn held it up while Jamie scooped out stuffing, dampening her desire for both dinner and childbirth. A leg started to tear off and Lynn moaned, dropping the whole bird abruptly and splattering grease everywhere.

"Don't worry," said Jamie through gritted teeth. "I'll be carving it in a minute."

"But I wanted people to see."

As if on command—Philippa's?—everyone began trooping into the kitchen to admire the bird. Lynn and Jamie got it back on the platter, and Lynn tried to push the oily, crumpled parsley around it. She lifted a hand to brush her hair off her hot forehead and instead wiped turkey fat through it. In mere minutes the kitchen had turned into a disaster zone. There were gobbets of fat, skin, and gray stuffing everywhere. The abandoned baster had dribbled a brownish stream all down the counter, which, original to the house, had shallow grooves and inclined toward the sink.

"Shall I start your gravy, dear?" Philippa said in her ear.

Lynn jumped. "Oh, no, I can handle it, thanks."

Everyone wandered back out as Lynn, with a deep sigh of self-pity, positioned the turkey pan over two burners on low flames. She stirred and stirred, adding a little more of her flour mixture, but nothing seemed to happen. Her arm grew leaden, the flour and turkey fat congealing on her. If only she could go and take a shower, or just get her hands on a clean dish towel. How much time had passed? Five minutes, she guessed. Glancing at the oven clock, she was appalled to see that the answer was almost twenty.

Philippa was back. "Are we almost done? Shall I take over? Why don't you take care of your beans?"

Lynn's heart lurched. She had forgotten to put the water on to boil.

This is absolutely delightful," Lady Milborough sang out in her soft accent as Lynn finally sank into her seat (only to be assailed by shuddery thoughts of precedence: Should Piers's mother have been seated at Jamie's right?). "I've so enjoyed meeting everyone. What a warm, lovely family you two have. I had no idea." She sounded as though she meant it.

Ella Kovak shot her daughter a triumphant look. Lynn looked away. But glancing around the table she did indeed see rows of smiling, apparently happy faces. Through the two columns that divided the dining area from the living room, she could also see that the cheese plate she'd put out on the coffee table had been demolished. Although getting dinner on the table had taken much longer than she'd expected, no one seemed bored or famished.

There was a bustle of reaching for food, passing dishes, and oohing and aahing. Wine bottles clinked as glasses were filled, and silverware—all Philippa's, Lynn hadn't had the strength to fight over it—clattered. The air felt thick and fragrant, like someone else's house altogether, someone else's table with the snowy linens and gleaming, elegant stretch of sari, which truth be told did not quite work together but looked pretty and young and festive nonetheless. Lynn wondered if ever in her life she'd be able to do something like this properly, rather than the close approximation she generally ended up with. But she wondered idly and almost objectively, as if from a great distance. And who were all these people? It really was amazing.

Jamie slid into the seat opposite her at the far end of the table (of the two tables pushed together). "Whew," he said, to the table at large. "Who knew carving was manual labor? You really work up an appetite."

"Oh, Jamie," said Philippa, "isn't it good of you to have worked so hard at this meal." The gravy sat in a pretty bowl in front of her on the table, pillowy in its creamy perfection. Her eyes glanced over it, as if it had been no trouble at all. "I don't think young women today realize how lucky they are. Your generation of men help out so much."

"You must have trained your sons well, Philippa," said Lady Milborough, who was not nearly as formidable as Lynn had expected. She was just an ordinary-looking older woman, slightly dowdy, in her sixties or maybe early seventies, with delicate, wrinkled skin like a creased rose petal, and watery eyes. She was wearing a yellow safari suit and looked like someone who might enjoy gardening and bridge.

"I never made my boys help out enough, I'm the first to admit," said Philippa. "I was brought up to believe in the old-fashioned way. Men work so hard at the office, they shouldn't have to lift a finger around the house."

"Really?" said Lynn's mother. "I would have thought that anyone who had raised three children would know which sex does the hardest work."

Philippa turned her clear blue eyes on her. "Why, Ella, that's too bad that you found being a mother so difficult. I loved every minute of it."

Everyone was listening to this exchange, and the table fell silent. Julie's husband, Piers, who had been shoveling large forkfuls of turkey and potato into his mouth, looked across at Lynn's father. "Now, Harold," he said, still munching, "if Julie's mum is staying here, where are you staying?"

His train of thought was clear, at least to Lynn: Lynn's mother thought raising children was hard work because she was divorced and had to do it herself; Lynn's father, who lived in another city, must be staying at a hotel.

Harold Kovak looked right back at him. "Why, with my wife, of course."

You could see the mashed potato still in Piers's mouth.

People always assumed that Ella and Harold Kovak were divorced—just as they assumed that Philippa had been widowed. But while Lynn's parents saw themselves as quite fortunate in their long-standing marriage, Philippa had no longer been married to Jamie's father when he died. Lynn herself had been surprised when this detail came out. She was pretty sure she'd never heard Philippa refer to Jamie's father as anything but "my husband" or "my late husband."

But one day, after twenty-plus years of marriage, Jamie's father had come home and simply announced his desire to live separately from his wife. There was no other woman as far as anyone could tell. As he explained it to his children, life was too short for him not to seek personal happiness. In a stroke of painful irony, he was diagnosed, not a month after the divorce was final, with metastasized stomach cancer. In his last weeks, Philippa had him moved back to the house (his own childhood home built by his great-grandfather, which she'd insisted on keeping in the divorce) and, quite selflessly, to be fair, took over his care. Everyone conceded that she was a tower of strength at the time.

"Why wouldn't Harold be staying in his own home?" Lady Milborough asked in her clear, carrying voice, frowning at her son.

"Lynn's father is a very well-known scientist at the University of California at Berkeley," Philippa explained. "In Northern California. The Kovaks keep a home there as well."

Lynn smiled to herself at this description of her father's faculty apartment just off Telegraph, a deception calculated to seem perfectly natural to the viscountess, who, indeed, said, "Oh, lovely. In the wine country, would that be?"

Kam's mother was raising her hand. She did it with a shy smile and barely raised her palm to shoulder height, but there was no question that it was raised. Should I call on her, Lynn wondered. But Lady Milborough evidently noticed, too. "And how are all of you down there?" she called down the table, looking right at Dorothy Fisher. "Such a big table, so far away."

"I was just wondering," Kam's mother said—and Lynn felt grateful for the subtle kindness of Piers's mother. Perhaps there was something to be said for an aristocratic upbringing. "Your son"—Mrs. Fisher gestured at Piers—"told me his last name is Monkham. But you are Lady Milborough."

"Please do call me Bess."

Kam's mother smiled what was clearly a refusal. She was a round little woman, and had beautiful, pearly, child-sized teeth. "But why aren't you Lady Monkham?" she asked.

Lady Milborough—and Piers, too—brightened at the question. Jamie caught Lynn's eye and grinned.

"Monkham is the family name," said Sasha of all people.

"Yes, exactly so," said Piers, a little put out at being beaten to the punch. "The title came later. We're not very grand, you see." He gave a squiffy laugh.

"Monkham is a very old name, though," Lady Milborough said thoughtfully. "Where we're from"—she made it sound like Timbuktu—"that can often be more important than the silly title you get for paying the Prince of Wales's debts or trifles like that."

"Now Mother's being generous," said Piers. "You see, *her* family is much the grander one. She's thought to have married down when she took up with old Dad."

Kam's mother gave an exclamation of pleasure. "My parents didn't like Jonah, either. See, we'd been good churchgoers since the missionaries, and Jonah—that's just Mr. Fisher's baptismal name, you don't want to hear the other—well, my mother was convinced he was a heathen." She glanced fondly at her husband, as compact, friendly, and roly-poly as she. Where their tall, handsome, brilliant son had sprung from was a mystery. "But now that he's retired"—at Philippa's inquiring eyebrow, she added, "from the sugarcane factory—he's a deacon of our church. Fancy that."

"You see," said Lady Milborough, tapping her plate eagerly with her knife, "you Americans—marvelous! You can take blueblood and inheritance any day. Give me a country of self-made men. Here is Mr. Fisher, doing an honest day's work in a sugarcane factory, and then his son—not that there's anything wrong with a factory, no, an honest day's work, as I said—but his son goes off to college, studies chemistry—"

"Ethnobotany, actually," said Sasha.

"Ethnobotany? You don't say? Isn't that a coincidence. We had one to dinner once, an ethnobotanist. Did something in the Amazon. Rubber, I think it was. Yes, because we all thought it so funny as the first viscount had been rather big in rubber. A deeply strange man. This ethno-fellow, I mean, not the first viscount. Although . . ." Piers's mother drifted off vaguely for a moment. "Yes, well, doesn't that make sense, then?" she said. "Ethnobotany and Hawaii."

Lynn glanced at Philippa, but to her surprise her mother-in-law avoided her eyes.

"Yes," said Sasha, "but Kam's not in that field anymore."

Lady Milborough—a good half of the table, in fact—turned to Sasha.

"We run a boat charter for tourists," she said.

"Much more difficult," Lynn's father muttered under his breath. "In the lab one doesn't have to bother with commoners."

Piers wiped his chin and pushed back his chair. "Point me in the direction of the loo?"

"It's at the end of the hall, through the kitchen," said Lynn. She wished she could get up, too, slip down the hall and maybe into the second bedroom for a little nap.

"Now, which island are you on, Cameron?" Lady Milborough asked.

"Actually, ma'am, it's short for Kamehameha. Maui. It's where I grew up."

Lynn noticed Philippa's mouth tighten. She remembered how, the first time she'd mentioned Kam's name to Philippa, her mother-in-law had brightened: "Not part of the Hawaiian royal family?" she'd asked.

"Oh, Maui is lovely," said Lady Milborough. "We do so love it there. In fact, we've had the most wonderful skipper the last two times we were there. I wonder if you know him? Jim, his name is."

There was another short silence.

"You don't happen to know his last name, do you?" said Kam.

"Oh, yes, something with an *F*."

"Farraway?"

"Yes, that's it. Lovely man. Salt of the earth. You know him?"

"I work with him. He's one of our best skippers."

"Oh, yes, we love Jim. So you're with the same outfit?"

"Actually," said Sasha, "Kam owns it. He bought out the previous owner, who wanted to retire."

"He did?" said Jamie and Lynn at the same time.

Sasha nodded proudly. "Just last week. We didn't want to say until the whole thing was final, which was Friday. Then, since we were coming, we figured we'd tell you the news in person."

There were congratulations all around, and more champagne poured for a toast. As everyone was sipping contemplatively, and Lynn started to relax a little—were things coming to a close?—Andy's fiancée, next to Jamie at the other end of the table and who up until then had barely opened her mouth, said, "So you like running a boat charter better than being a scientist?" There was something sharp about Annika, although you didn't necessarily see it at first. She was a small, generic blonde, with lightly wavy hair cropped in a neat bob. She had just started business school at Wharton.

"I loved ethnobotany, too," Kam said, "but when it came down to it, it wasn't the long-term life I wanted." He looked fondly at his parents.

"So you made the trade-off," said Piers, who had just slipped back into his seat, "between a high-prestige, high-paying career, and doing what you love. I really respect that." He nodded encouragingly at Lynn's father as though expecting his affirmation of this worthy sentiment. Lynn took in the glazed look of idolatry on Piers's face. She had seen this look before on her father's students and campus followers and found it, as always, enervating. He'd been gone awhile, too. Lynn hoped their one bathroom didn't smell now.

"Do you enjoy your work, Piers?" her mother asked.

"Me? Sure, I like the bank. A bunch of pretty good eggs. But I like my hols. I wouldn't mind being out on a boat and being paid for it. Or something even more experimental and mind-altering." Another glance Harold's way.

"We always encouraged our children to pursue what they love," said Ella. "If you love something, and you're good at it and work hard, everything else will fall into place."

"One has to be realistic, though," said Philippa. "One has to earn a living, support a family. You had three girls . . ." She trailed off, perhaps at the sight of Ella's expression. Not that Philippa was a woman to be cowed, but she probably had less of a stomach for public battle than Lynn's mother.

"It's just as important for men to feel free to make those choices," Ella said. "It's a shame—a crime—how so many men feel trapped by what they assume to be structural imperatives. They need to understand that they have more freedom than they think."

"You can work hard and earn a good living, and still love your job," said Philippa. "Jamie, for example—"

"Mom," he said.

"Jamie loves his job."

The sound of Jamie's name caught Lynn's attention, and she strained to hear what was being said without ignoring Kam's parents, who were consulting with Sasha, Kam, Harold, and Dee at their end of the table about the sights they should see in their limited amount of time in Los Angeles.

"He does?" Andy said with a laugh.

"Why shouldn't he?" said Philippa.

"Speaking of jobs," Jamie said, raising his voice a little, "I have some bad news for Lynn." At this Lynn felt justified in abandoning her own conversation. She was pretty sure it was supplication she heard in Jamie's voice. "It looks like I'm going to have to go to New York again. Notice how I'm telling Lynn in public so she can't kill me."

"Why would Lynn kill you?" said Philippa. "Of course you have to do whatever your job requires."

"It could be worse," said Jamie. "What they really want is for me to transfer there."

"You're kidding," said Lynn. She wished he weren't all the way across the table.

"What a wonderful opportunity," Philippa said. "New York!"

"Well, Mom"—Jamie glanced Lynn's way—"Lynn has a job. They're talking about months—six maybe."

"Why do they want you to transfer?" asked Annika, all business.

"I'm on this real estate deal. The client is this architect who's kind of a bigwig. He's based in New York, and right now he's making a fuss about the team being here and not there."

"Really?" said Annika. "Which architect?"

"His name is Leslie Hatchett."

"Les Hatchett? You're working with him?"

"You've heard of him?"

"I practically grew up with his daughter. They're one house over from us in Watch Hill."

Of course they were. Part of Les Hatchett's allure and fame as an architect, Lynn knew, was that he was also heir to a shipping fortune.

"Have you met Barb?" Annika asked.

"I'm just a lowly lawyer on this project," Jamie said. "I don't—"

"Oh, you should meet her. You'd love her, I just know you

would." Annika's cool eyes flicked down the table to Lynn. "Both of you. She's out here all the time, I'll have to set something up. Let's see . . ."

Lynn saw Andy pat Annika's hand on the table in a quelling gesture.

"Wait," Lynn said to Jamie. "Next week? When will you be back?"

"Sometime Friday."

"Friday? But the opera thing's Thursday night."

He had clearly forgotten. "I'm sorry, Lynn, I can't change this."

"We've known for ages." She smiled apologetically at the rest of the table, well aware that this wasn't the appropriate place for this conversation. "Can't you come back one day early?"

"I have a breakfast with Les Hatchett." He was shooting her pleas with his eyes—pleas, however, from which he couldn't keep a whiff of exasperation.

"Ooh!" said Philippa. "How wonderful."

"It's work, Mom," Jamie said.

But Lynn knew this was directed at her. Mine's work, too, she wanted to say. She noticed her mother's posture—poised to jump in. "I'm sure we'll figure it out," Lynn said.

"Anyone for coffee?" said Dee, jumping up. Perhaps she, too, had taken note of their mother. "And when you're ready, Sash and I brought pies from the best pie place in L.A."

Lynn read in Philippa's face her utter disdain for storebought pies.

It was late when everyone finally left. Lynn's family had done their best to outstay her in-laws, a fruitless gesture since Philippa was, after all, staying at the house. In the end, Lynn found herself alone in the small kitchen with her mother-in-law. Jamie had lingered anxiously before being shooed off to bed. "Please come, leave the rest of the dishes for tomorrow," he'd begged Lynn, but she found herself unequal to that challenge.

Philippa had snagged the prime position at the sink, taking the high moral ground of washing while Lynn was left to hover with a dish towel. After three or four plates had been sudsed, rinsed, and deposited in the drying rack, Philippa spun to face Lynn, her navy pumps pointing outward in strict third position. "Family is so important," she said.

"Yes, it is." Lynn wondered where this was going.

"I've always been proud of the fact," said Philippa, "that my family has married well going back at least four generations."

Now Lynn could see that her mother-in-law was furious, absolutely rigid with emotion. Rattled, she said, "I'm not sure what you mean, 'married well'?"

"I mean, of course, marrying someone who is your social match—or better."

Lynn had to look away. Through the doorway, the deserted dining room table stretched out in the shadows, denuded of its china and borrowed silver. Even the sari had been folded and put away. The rickety, rented table, though, still stood in position at the far end. "I guess," she said, "I just never thought of it that way."

"I can't imagine," said Philippa, "what other way of thinking about it there is." She gave a shrug of her meaty shoulders and turned back to the dishes, her red-blond hair a shining coil.

Lynn stood staring at her back a moment or two until she realized that this was exactly what Philippa intended. So instead she placed her folded dish towel neatly and definitively on the counter and said, "You know, after doing an entire

Thanksgiving dinner, I'm beat. I think I've earned my rest, plus Jamie hates it when I don't come to bed. But, Philippa, please, please feel free to leave this mess for tomorrow."

Lynn started down the hallway, rather pleased with herself. She should have known better. Philippa's voice came wafting after her. "You're absolutely right, Lynn dear. You did a superlative job, and frankly I'm relieved to see it at last. A wife who can't get a hot meal on the table for her husband won't be a wife for long."

Eleven

Lynn leaned forward on the jump seat toward Richard Plante, who was sitting across from her in his stretch limousine. "You really didn't need to do this," she said.

"What kind of host would I be to let a lovely young lady drive herself at night?" He looked smug against the luxe leather seat, looking more like a fat cat than usual—literally more substantial than the spare, almost scarecrowish figure in a light-colored baggy suit that had been her first sight of him. He was in black tie, and his cummerbund strained around his middle. Chaka was next to him on the seat.

"You're a wonderful host," said Lynn. "It was a wonderful evening. That Iago was amazing."

"How about you, Francis? Francis isn't as big an opera buff as the rest of us, are you?"

F. X. was on the other jump seat. "I'm embarrassed to say that was the first opera I've ever been to."

"It was?" Lynn turned to F. X. for practically the first time that evening, as if it were safe now that they were almost to her house and the evening over.

"I guess you don't know everything about me, Lynnie," he said.

They had of course sat next to each other during the opera, but Lynn had chatted more with Richard, on her other side. F. X. and Chaka had been at either end. During the dinner, F. X. had been seated across the table from her and next to Chaka. Richard Plante had been out of his seat a good deal, as if he had too much energy and too many people who wanted to talk to him to sit still. Once or twice Lynn had noticed F. X. and Chaka with their heads together when he was gone. Chaka had looked smug; F. X., tense.

"I adore the opera," Chaka purred, leaning forward a little. "I used to go all the time with my family in Sao Paulo—before our fortunes turned, that is." Lynn saw Richard take her hand on the seat between them. Yet everything she said seemed directed at F. X. "My mother trained as an opera singer, did you know that? It was a big scandal for her family at the time. They disowned her. That's how she ended up with my father." She sat back again and recrossed her slender legs, swinging the top one up and down, a few silvery strips of sandal drawing the eye down to the little foot, toes pointed hard. Up and down it moved, toward F. X. and back. He turned away to stare out the dark car window.

Out of her own window Lynn saw that they were speeding down Beverly Boulevard—the last stretch, past the mansion-lined streets of Hancock Park. A few minutes more and she'd be safe in her own bed. And tomorrow Jamie would be back.

Lynn was a little nervous about having to tell him about F. X. and the opera dinner. Lynn had begged Jamie to see if he couldn't switch his trip, but he'd refused to even look into it. "No one really cares if I'm there," he'd said. "Tell Earl it's my work. He'll understand that." And as soon as he was in New York Jamie seemed to forget the problem altogether, never bothering to ask how breaking the news to Earl—or Richard—had gone. In a million years she wouldn't have forgotten to ask him about something like that. If Jamie had thought about it for one minute, the likelihood of F. X. taking his seat would have occurred to him. In a way, he had only himself to blame.

Something brushed Lynn's left arm—F. X., leaning across her, reaching for the refrigerated compartment. He pulled out a heavy decanter and a lowball glass.

"Vodka?" she said.

"You kidding?" He sounded annoyed, tense. "This is water. I have to drive home."

F. X.'s car was at Lynn's house. That had been the arrangement: F. X. driving in from Santa Monica so that Richard and Chaka would have to make only one stop with the limo. He had just unstoppered the decanter when the car gave a jolt.

"Fuck!" he cried.

"Jackson?" Richard Plante said.

"Sorry, sir," said the driver. "A dog ran in front of us."

"Shit." F. X. was writhing under his seat belt.

"You okay?" said Lynn.

"I just spilled ice water all over myself."

"Lucky it was just water," said Chaka.

"It's fucking freezing."

"Language, language," said Richard.

"Here we are, sir," said the driver.

Lynn looked out the blackened window and saw that they were in front of her house. "At least you'll be home soon," she said to F. X.

"Yeah, after driving forty-five minutes in the freezing cold, sopping wet. My top's broken. I still can't put it up."

Lynn had been in F. X.'s BMW. She didn't remember it being a convertible.

"Still?" said Richard. "That shouldn't be happening. Did you talk to my guy?"

"Yeah, he said he couldn't take me for a week. I haven't even owned the thing one week!" F. X.'s voice was bitter. Not just bitter—petulant. He was staring down at himself, plucking his pleated dress shirt away from his body. Lynn glanced across at Chaka, who was just sitting there, swinging her leg and smiling faintly.

"I'll call the Maserati guy myself tomorrow," Richard said firmly. "He'll see you. And Lynn?" He peered doubtfully out at her little stucco house. "Uh, do you have a dryer?"

"A hair dryer?"

"I was thinking a clothes dryer. If you have one."

"Yes, of course I do," she said, stung.

"Then perhaps you wouldn't mind sticking F. X.'s clothes in for a few minutes? I'm sure that'll do the trick." Richard Plante turned his wrist to look at his watch.

"That's okay," F. X. said. "It's mainly just my front. I think a dryer would wreck this shirt." He had shrugged out of his tuxedo jacket.

Lynn threw a grateful look his way.

"You know, though," he said, the old light in his eyes, "I wouldn't mind if you'd throw my undershirt in. It wouldn't take long and I could just drive home in that with my jacket over it."

"Great!" said Richard, reaching for his door handle even though he was on the street side. F. X. got the message and opened his own door, and he and Lynn climbed out.

"Thanks so much," she called back into the car.

"Night, kids," came Richard's voice as the car door

slammed, and without waiting for them to even step to the sidewalk the black limousine pulled away.

Cute place, Lynnie," F. X. said, looking around, already unbuttoning his shirt. He seemed more relaxed now that they were out of the car. And his undershirt really did look soaked. He stripped that off, too, then looked at her and grinned. "Still vain as ever." He turned this way and that to give her the full view. "I work out."

Lynn gave a flat, cursory smile.

"Is Jamie in good shape?"

"He is." She scooped the sopping undershirt from his hand. "Sit. I'll be right back." The stacked washer/dryer was in a closet down the hall toward their bedroom. Lynn waited for F. X. to sit. She didn't want him following her.

"Look," he said, "I know you're mad I was there tonight. Believe me, it wasn't my choice. It wasn't exactly fun for me, either."

It was true, Richard Plante *had* had the air of the conqueror. "Does Richard know?" She couldn't help asking. "About you and Chaka?"

"I don't know what the hell she told him. She says she didn't, but she'll say or do whatever suits her purposes."

"Well," said Lynn, "good riddance, right?"

"Yeah. Right." His voice was glum.

Had he really liked her that much? Poetic justice. But as pleasant as it was to see F. X. upset over a woman, Lynn also felt bad for him. It was probably the first time he'd met his match. She moved to leave the room with his shirt.

"Hey," F. X. said plaintively, "would you do something for me?"

"Sure." She turned back.

"Do you mind sticking my socks in as well? They're soaked. I think the water spilled down my pants." Then his face changed—eyebrows, corners of the mouth lifting. "My boxers are wet, too."

"I'm *not* drying those." But she grinned and put out a hand for the socks.

"You're a good sport," he said. "Really."

The washer/dryer was hidden behind folding doors in the hallway. Lynn put the clothes in, felt the *ribbity-crank* of the setting dial as she turned it. She was in no hurry to get back to F. X. "I'm just going to check my messages," she called over the sound of the dryer.

In the office-bedroom, she glanced at the clock that sat next to the phone on the desk—but the little Tiffany clock, engraved as a closing gift from one of Jamie's deals, wasn't where it usually was. It had to be after one in the morning. Which meant four A.M. New York time.

Lynn picked up the phone, sat down, and punched in their code. There were three messages. The first was from Jamie. She smiled at the sound of his voice. "Hello, darling wife, I'm trying to get on an earlier flight home. I'm so sorry about everything, I miss you. Okay, then, I'll let you know."

Earlier? What about the breakfast he had with Les Hatchett? She'd thought he already was on the earliest possible flight, considering. Lynn kicked off her high heels under the desk.

The next message was from her mother, and she saved it without listening to the whole thing. She wanted to hear the third to see if Jamie had called again. But when had these messages come in? This time she listened for the time/date voice. "Five forty-five P.M." But how could that be? She'd been home. Or was that when she'd been in the shower? "Listen," came Jamie's voice, rushed and excited, "I've got to run, they're boarding, I got on a nine o'clock flight."

Lynn turned her head at the sound of a familiar noise from the front of the house—the jangling of keys against the lock. She raced to the living room, the rest of the message trailing after her. "Hopefully I'll be home by one."

Jamie himself was on the threshold, overnight bag in hand. He moved his head to look at her, with an expression she did not understand. Where was F. X.? No longer on the sofa. She swung round to look where Jamie had been facing. And there was F. X., standing in the kitchen in front of the open refrigerator, a glass of water in his hand. His chest was bare. If anything, his pale feet sticking out from his tuxedo pants looked even more naked. Everyone was silent for a long moment.

"Jamie," she said.

He raised a hand. "Don't." And stepped back out the door, pulling it carefully shut after him.

Lynn turned back to F. X. He looked as stunned as she felt, but then he shrugged and she had a sense of him *smiling*.

As if released, she rushed to the door.

"Jamie? Jamie," she called softly, sticking her head outside. She moved onto the front steps. He was already at his car. His green Audi was right in front of the house, right behind a flashy, low-slung, red sports car. The thought flashed through her mind: Thank God he doesn't know it's F. X.'s.

Jamie had his car door open. "Wait," she cried. He looked up at the sound of her voice, and relief flowed through her. But he gave a single, furious shake of his head and got in. The car door slammed, and to her utter disbelief he drove away.

Twelve

H ey."
  Lynn whirled around. F. X. was in the doorway, right behind her, his still-damp undershirt on, his jacket and dress shirt over his arm.

"He's gone?" As if the fun had been cut short.

"Just go," she said. To think that for a moment she'd felt sorry for him.

"Hey, is there anything I can—"

"Seriously. Now." She slipped past him into the house, allowing herself a shove that left him on the other side when she shut the door.

She watched from the living room, through the big bay window, as he, too, got into his car and drove off. She was left alone. Everything was so still. Lynn stood there at the window like a ghostly widow waiting for her man's return, the stiff black voile of her skirt swaying against her bare ankles as she stared into the night. She stood there for a long time, it seemed. At last she turned away. What to do, what to do? She paced, then headed for the bedroom.

But what was there to do in that room but stare down helplessly at the bed, their cloudlike white bed that seemed to call to her. Should she throw herself down on it and sob? Did she even feel like sobbing? If she *had* thrown herself down—and somewhere deep down Lynn must have known this—the chances were good that she would have fallen asleep that way, fully dressed, her face buried in the soft pillows, worn out by the long hours of opera and dinner, the emotional turmoil of the evening. It was a weeknight, after all, hours later than she usually went to sleep. The bed called to her, but no, she turned away.

How had this happened? It didn't make sense, there was no reason for it. Jamie shouldn't have run off like that. He must have known there was a good explanation. He couldn't really think . . . And was she supposed to just sit here and wait for him to come back? What if he made her wait two days again?

Once, when she was eight or nine, Lynn had told her mother that she was running away and had slammed out of the house. But once outside she'd looked up and down the street and hadn't known what to do. There was her mother's car in the driveway, unlocked. She'd climbed into the backseat and before she knew it had fallen asleep, worn out by all the fighting. Ella had been frantic, calling the police, her older sisters canvassing the neighborhood on bikes, her father on his way to the Oakland airport. Lynn had slept in the car for three hours.

Now she flung herself into motion, swooping here, there, catching up items—a fresh pair of underwear, a comfortable pair of shoes, her toothbrush from the bathroom. All of them she shoved into the black leather hobo bag she occasionally used for work. If Jamie wasn't going to stay, neither would she. She'd go to her mother's, at least for the night. Lynn hurried back to the living room and emptied the evening clutch she'd used for the opera into the larger purse as well. But she hesitated there, slightly disgusted with herself for this forethought—for having the presence of mind to gather what she needed for more comfortable husband-fleeing. She thought about flinging the clean underwear and toothbrush from her purse for a somehow purer flight, but in the end left them.

She took Melrose west, then Santa Monica, switching to Wilshire Boulevard where it crossed Santa Monica, speeding toward the house where she'd grown up—stately and white at the top of a steeply sloped lawn, the two-story, circa 1930s Monterey Colonial on one of the hilly, professor-laden streets of Westwood. Lynn's parents had acquired it early in their careers thanks to a generous university loan program. (Philippa's lips had gone thin when she realized that the fairly modest house was probably worth more than her own, far grander one.) Lynn was about to switch lanes for a right turn onto her mother's street when it struck her: What was she doing, it was two in the morning. She took a deep breath, closed her eyes for the quick second that's all you can spare when driving, and got into the left lane to make a U-turn instead at the next possible corner. It was so late that there was hardly any traffic. Lynn was back home barely forty-five minutes after she'd set out—but just a minute or two too late to see the dark green Audi pulling away from the curb in front of the house.

Thirteen

Glynnis Bastien strode into their office Monday morning, a newspaper flapping in her hand. "Nice pic," she said.

"What?" Lynn looked up distractedly. She would never, ever be able to explain how she had made it through the weekend. On Friday morning she had tried Jamie's office—his cell phone was no help, he kept it so that it went directly to his office voice mail. His secretary, surprised to hear from her, had reminded her that Jamie wasn't even supposed to be back in town until early afternoon. They weren't expecting him in at all that day. Lynn ended up calling in sick herself, which only made the ordeal worse—an extra, interminable, lonely day going crazy alone in her house. Thank God for her mother, thank God for her sisters. Thank God for call waiting so she could stay on the phone with them without worrying about missing Jamie's nonexistent calls. Her mother had told her to come right over, but Lynn hadn't wanted to leave the house in case he came back—although she hadn't told her mother that. She had to be careful; she didn't want her family to hold too much against him later. *Where was he?*

"Look, it's your husband." Glynnis flattened the newspaper on Lynn's desk. "Who's the babe?" The paper was folded open to an inner page, and a picture of Jamie stared up at her. Leaning into him was an attractive young woman. "It's a nightclub opening," Glynnis said. "This past weekend. In New York."

The newspaper was *Women's Wear Daily*. There were four party pictures on the page, with the headline *N.Y. Aerie Gets Heiress Crowd*. Lynn took a deep breath and peered closer. The caption read, "Barbara Hatchett and friend." In the photo, Jamie looked startled. The dark-haired girl, however—you could tell her lipstick was dark red even though the photo was black-and-white—was smiling like the cat that got the canary. Lynn disliked her on sight. "Oh, that's just the daughter of this architect Jamie's doing some work for."

Glynnis eyed Lynn, her finger still tap-tapping the newspaper.

To the far left in one of the other pictures, a crowd shot, Lynn thought she recognized Annika's profile. "Mind if I look at this for a minute?"

"Be my guest. I'm done with it." To demonstrate her lack of interest, Glynnis took her seat at her own desk.

Sure enough, Annika's name was in the accompanying text about the new nightclub's opening. So were the names of several young Hearsts, some Gettys, and a Greek princess or two. No mention of Jamie or his brother, although one presumed that was how Jamie came to be at a New York nightclub with Annika and her good friend, the famous architect's daughter. Whom she so dearly wanted to introduce to Jamie. The party had taken place Saturday night.

Even before this, it had occurred to Lynn that Jamie might have flown back to New York. He had to be there Monday anyway—he usually flew out Sunday afternoon. And wouldn't that explain so much: How he had gotten through the painful crawl of time without calling? It wouldn't have crawled for him—he'd have been busy, making last-minute reservations, traveling. Lynn had been sitting, agonizingly powerless, in their home office by the phone when this thought occurred to her on Saturday morning, and immediately she'd scrabbled around on the desk for the scrap of paper with the number of the hotel where Jamie always stayed. In her eager, weary haste she couldn't find it and had ended up dialing information—the sort of waste Jamie hated. But within a minute she was on the phone with the hotel front desk: "Could you please connect me with Jamie Prosper's room?" Wifely righteousness in her voice.

She was put on hold. The concierge came back. "I'm sorry, madam, there is no one staying in the hotel under that name."

Lynn's eyes had flitted to the place on the desk where the little clock usually was. She remembered that it was missing. Where had it gone? Had Jamie moved it? Taken it? When? It was still early, even in New York. Perhaps he just hadn't checked in yet. Usually check-in wasn't until two or three.

"He'll be checking in shortly," she said. "Why don't I just leave a message for him."

"I'm sorry, madam, we cannot take messages for persons who are not guests of the hotel."

"But he'll be checking in."

"I am sorry, madam," the man repeated, with finality this time.

"Okay then, I'll just call back."

"Very well," he said, but Lynn heard his skepticism.

She'd sat there at the cheap, laminate Parsons table they used for a desk, her hand still on the phone, her mind a sluggish muddle. She tried Jamie's cell phone yet again, knowing it would be to no avail. She had already left a long message explaining exactly what had happened with F. X. Two messages, actually, since her first had gone on so long she'd been cut off. Should she try other hotels? It was then that Lynn thought of Andy. Of course. Jamie would call his sibling. It's what Lynn had done, wasn't it? (The time change, to both Hawaii and New York, had been a particular blessing in the late and early hours.) Maybe Jamie had even gone to stay with Andy. Andy was currently in Philadelphia with Annika, an easy train ride from New York.

A woman answered when Lynn tried the number Andy had given them. "Annika?"

"Yes?" was the cool reply.

"Hi, it's Lynn. Listen, is Andy there?"

"I'm afraid he's not," said Annika, sounding no less formal.

"You wouldn't happen to know where he is?"

"Can I ask why you're asking?"

"Sorry." Lynn realized how odd she must sound. "I didn't mean to be abrupt. I'm just trying to track down Jamie in New York. I was wondering if Andy was planning to see him. Do you know if Jamie called?"

There was silence on the line—for too long. "You know, Lynn, perhaps it's best if you talk to Andy. Unfortunately, he's not here at the moment. Shall I have him ring you back?"

"Is he going to be long?"

"I'll certainly give him the message when he returns."

"Look," said Lynn, "I'm just trying to reach Jamie. Maybe you could give me Andy's cell. It's important, so if you—"

"Oh, I understand the situation fully. I repeat, I will pass your message on to Andy."

"Did Andy go to New York?"

"I'm hanging up now, Lynn. Good-bye."

Lynn had shoved that call to the back of her mind, but now she could just see it—the whole thing arranged between

Annika and "Barb," the trip into the city for a big nightclub opening, "to cheer Jamie up." The infuriating thing, now that it was Monday, was that Lynn had known exactly where she could reach Jamie from the moment she'd woken up—at his office in New York. But she had resolved, rather virtuously she thought, not to try to call him again before he called her. She'd left messages, had explained everything. Dee and Sasha had both pointed out Jamie's pattern of wanting time alone when upset, and Lynn had agreed that this made sense. But there was also a sense of aggrievedness behind her decision to wait for him to call, even once she knew where to reach him. "It's in his court now," she'd said to her mother. "He's the one who should apologize. It's like when someone hangs up on you—they're the one responsible for calling back." Lynn had felt a little frustrated by her mother's failure to clamor her agreement to this. "The main thing," Ella Kovak had cautioned, "is to communicate. You can't have a marriage without that." "You're the one," Lynn had snapped, "who always told me that women have to expect and demand to be treated respectfully."

But all strategizing and argument went by the wayside with Barbara Hatchett grinning up at her in newsprint. Lynn's fingers flew through the law firm's New York office's 800 number.

"So, was the party fun?" said Glynnis behind her. "Oops, sorry, didn't realize you were on the phone."

"That's okay." Lynn dropped the receiver back down on its base. "I wasn't there."

"Of course you weren't. I mean, did Jamie say it was fun? It's supposed to be the hot new place."

"Do you always read *Women's Wear*?" Lynn asked instead.

"Yeah, it's great. The museum gets it, didn't you know? Down in publicity. You should read it. You can keep up on things—art parties, museum openings, stuff like that. Especially since you're doing more and more of that liaison stuff," she added, her tone curdling. She turned back to her own desk and started moving things around. There was no way Lynn was going to make that phone call to Jamie with Glynnis sitting there.

Finally, about twenty minutes later, Glynnis got up and left the office. Lynn quickly picked up the phone and dialed. She listened through the toll-free number's recording and punched in the four-digit extension number Jamie had given her when he first started going to New York. Some weeks he was at that extension; others he ended up bumped to a different office. He picked up on the very first ring. "Jamie Prosper." It always threw Lynn, hearing his gruff work voice like that, a tone that said, "I'm busy, what do you want?"

"It's me, Lynn."

There was a pause, then he said, "I can't talk now, I'll call you later." And hung up.

Lynn stared at the phone in her hand.

Glynnis came sauntering back in. She gave Lynn a curious look. "You okay?"

"Sure." Lynn looked up at her from her seat. "Why?"

Glynnis shrugged and sashayed to her chair. She looked as though she were about to say something, but Lynn's phone rang. Lynn lunged for it.

"Lynn?" It was a woman's voice. "It's Kerry. Kerry Scoville. I just had to call. We saw the picture of Jamie."

"You did? In *Women's Wear*?" Lynn glanced over at Glynnis. She was listening unabashedly. She gave Lynn an encouraging nod.

"It was so fun to open the page and see him. Like knowing a celebrity. Did he have a blast?"

This made a second person who assumed she'd talked to

Jamie. Lynn felt intensely grateful that at least she knew about the picture this time.

"It sure sounds like he did," Kerry said.

"What?" Lynn said stupidly.

"When George talked to him, it sounded like he had a blast."

Jamie talked to George Jacquemet but not his own wife?

Kerry said, "When I told Libbet, George called him right away. You know, to give him a hard time about getting his picture in the paper."

"This morning?"

"Sure, when else? I just saw it this morning."

"What did Jamie say?"

"What? Oh, you know. But here's why I'm really calling. We wanted to invite you guys for dinner. Maybe with Libbet and George? I would have called much earlier, but with the baby and everything . . ."

"That's right," said Lynn. "How's the—"

"So we were wondering if you're free Friday."

"Uh." Lynn's gaze skittered across her desk. "I'm not sure if Jamie—"

"Saturday would work, too. Or the following Tuesday. And we can talk about Tahoe."

Lynn felt as though her brain were about to explode. Why did Kerry get *Women's Wear*? It was a fashion trade journal. Why was everyone reading it suddenly? "Jamie's usually in New York during the week."

"Every week?"

"Well, just right now."

Kerry gave a cackling little laugh. "No wonder you two have such a good marriage."

Fourteen

He hung up on you?"

Thank God Lynn had been able to reach Dee at work. "Can you believe it?"

"What did he say about the photograph?"

"I didn't even have the chance to ask."

Her sister's speechlessness gave Lynn pause all over again.

"What do you think I should do?" she said. "Call back?"

"Well," said Dee, carefully.

"This is ridiculous!" Lynn cried. "What do you think is going on? On one hand, you can see it from his point of view. I mean, he did come home and find a half-naked man in his kitchen."

"You're apologizing for his behavior? He disappears for five days, you have no idea where he is, and then he hangs up on you?"

"Not five days. Friday, Saturday, Sunday. It's just Monday morning now."

Dee sighed.

"What are you saying?" said Lynn. She had a sickening sensation in her stomach.

"You know where everything is, right?"

"What do you mean?"

"Papers. Financial stuff."

"You're kidding. Wait, you think he's leaving me? That's why he's not returning my calls?" Lynn's voice rose. "You think he's having an affair with that girl?"

"Not at all," Dee said hurriedly. "Maybe it's just . . . a way to get back at you."

"I didn't do anything!"

"Of course you didn't. And I'm sure it will all turn out to be nothing—a misunderstanding. But as your older sister . . . Anyway, this is stuff you should know no matter what. Bank accounts, the mortgage, all that. I know you, Lynn—I bet you don't know any of that, do you? And not just you. All women should."

"Now you're sounding like Mom."

"I know you're not going to like this, Lynn, but I want you to call this friend of mine. Georgia. She's an old friend from college. In fact, I don't know why I didn't introduce you guys ages ago. She's in L.A. You'll love her, she's great, a real ball-buster. She sued one of those men-only golf clubs to make them let her in."

"Really?"

"She knows all about this stuff. She'll basically give you a checklist. Really, Lynn, what if Jamie were in an accident and you didn't know where anything was? I bet you guys don't even have a will."

"She's a financial advisor?"

"Now don't get defensive, she's a lawyer. Like the top, uh, family-law lawyer in Los Angeles. She's always written up in magazines. Georgia Vaughan. But I know she'd be happy to talk to you—as my little sister, not a client or anything."

"Jamie was probably just in a meeting. You know he's always brusque when he's at work."

"It's not like he's missing anymore," Dee said, as if she agreed. "You know exactly where he's staying in New York, you have all his numbers at the office. Or you can always call his cell phone."

"Right," said Lynn.

"Call Georgia. I think it will make you feel better. It's always better to operate from strength and knowledge, in any relationship."

After hanging up with Dee, Lynn sat staring blankly above her desk. She had no intention of calling her sister's friend. Maybe she should run out for a coffee. She could stand getting out of the office for a minute or two. She looked around for her bag. Glynnis was out and had taken her purse with her. Lynn glanced at the clock. Somehow, it was practically lunchtime. The corridor was empty, too. Lynn reached for the phone—and dialed Jamie's hotel, the one he hadn't checked into yet the last time she'd tried. Of course, he'd be at work now, not in his room, but she could at least leave a message. She was transferred to reception where a man answered. Could it possibly be the same awful one from the weekend?

"Jamie Prosper, please."

There was hardly a pause before the man chirped, "I'm sorry, ma'am, we have no guests by that name."

She insisted on spelling the name, had him check again, had him look under both the firm's name and Les Hatchett's, then hung up on the man midsentence.

In one of their conversations over the weekend, Sasha had said, "Don't you think it's interesting how Jamie's always running away?"

Lynn had been reminded of how annoying, how self-righteous her middle sister could be. "What do you mean, always?"

"You're the one who told me about that time at the movies in Santa Monica."

"That wasn't running away."

It was, in fact, an old joke that Lynn couldn't let Jamie out of her sight. The time Sasha was referring to, Lynn and Jamie had each been coming from work from different directions and had planned to meet at the ticket booth. But they'd almost missed the movie because, instead, Jamie had been waiting outside the parking structure half a block away. Lynn still didn't understand how he could have possibly thought they'd agreed to meet there. What if for once she'd parked somewhere else, found a spot on the street? In the end it hadn't mattered because they'd found each other in time.

Another time, Jamie had dropped Lynn at a bookstore while he went to park the car. She wanted a new book to read, then the plan was to go down the block for ice cream. Half an hour went by and he hadn't come back. Finally, without her book, worried and annoyed, she ran down the street to the ice cream place. He was sitting at one of the tables.

"Are you saying Jamie's looking for an excuse to get away from me?" Lynn demanded of Sasha.

"Calm down. You always make it seem like I'm attacking you. I hope you're not like that with Jamie."

Dee had insisted on giving Lynn Georgia Vaughan's number, and Lynn had pretended to write it down but hadn't. She did, however, remember the name of the firm. She reached for one of the phone books under her desk.

"Law offices."

She asked for Georgia Vaughan and was passed along to another woman, this one with a British accent. Lynn smiled at the thought of ball-busting feminist Georgia Vaughan with a snooty British secretary. She explained who she was and was put through instantly.

Georgia Vaughan had a low, hoarse voice with a slight Southern accent. "Dee's little sister! I've heard so much about you. What can I do for you? I sincerely hope this isn't a business call."

"Not at all," said Lynn. "I was just talking to Dee and she was saying how we should meet. She raves about you. You've been in L.A. since the two of you were in college together?"

"Since after law school. I just love it here. I'm a hedonist at heart—the weather, you can play golf year round." Georgia gave a laugh. "Did Dee tell you? She gets a kick out of that—me, in saddle shoes. The world is full of surprises, right?"

"I think Dee also wanted you to give me a lecture," Lynn said. "She thinks I don't know enough about our finances, my husband's and mine. She wanted me to ask you what I should know: tax stuff, wills, community property, that sort of thing."

"Your sister's right, every woman should ask those questions. We don't like to, do we? The same way we don't want to bring up prenups. People think it means you must have a bad marriage. That's just ignorant."

"That's what Dee says."

"Well, I'm glad that's all this is because Dee always says both her sisters married lovely men. So, shoot, Lynn Kovak. What exactly can I tell you?"

"Actually," Lynn said with a nervous laugh—after all, Georgia had sued a club for being sexist, "I did change my name. It's Prosper now."

"Prosper?" An odd note entered Georgia's voice.

"I know it's sort of retrograde . . ."

"Tell me your husband's name?"

"Jamie. Jamie Prosper."

"Lynn, may I put you on hold for a second?"

"Sure."

It was only a minute or two before Georgia came back on the line. "Lynn," she said, all trace of joviality gone, "I am very, very sorry. I can't talk to you anymore. I have already been approached by the other side."

Fifteen

L ynn gripped the steering wheel tighter at the memory of those words. "I'm so very sorry, Lynn," Georgia Vaughan had said, "my hands are tied. It would be completely unethical for me to talk to you anymore. I'm going to give you a name . . ."

Georgia's name had done the trick. C. Bradford Froemming III took Lynn's call right away. He couldn't meet with her until Wednesday, two days away, but ordered her to gather immediately all pertinent financial information to bring to the meeting.

Lynn had protested. "Jamie keeps most of that at his office, I think."

"You think? From now on, you need to know. Is it at his office, or maybe somewhere in some little love nest?"

"There's nothing like that. That's not what this is about."

"How do you know? From now on you have to assume the worst. It's the only way to protect yourself. You didn't think he was filing for divorce behind your back, either, did you? As soon as we hang up I want you in your car on the way to his office."

Lynn had to check the huge directory in the lobby of the building where Jamie worked to remind herself which floor his firm was on. She hadn't actually been up to his office that often. If she was meeting Jamie she usually waited for him in the lobby. When she got off the elevator on his floor, however, she remembered a back exit near the restrooms. Jamie had taken her that way once when they'd stopped by after hours on the way home from a movie so he could pick up some file. "I'll go out the front way," Lynn whispered to the empty corridor, as if this promise made aloud proved she wasn't trying to sneak in like a criminal.

Jamie's office was the second closest to the back door, and Lynn didn't run into anyone she knew. People were probably still out to lunch. Jamie, she knew, usually ate at his desk. Then Lynn remembered her new lawyer: Jamie *claimed* he ate lunch at his desk. No, he did; she knew he did. She'd always thought it was part of why he wasn't that happy at work—he didn't socialize much with his co-workers. He said he just wanted to keep his head down, get his work done, and come home to her as soon as possible. Lynn's eyes filled. She'd wanted to call Jamie right away, to confront him with her knowledge of Georgia Vaughan, but C. Bradford told her not to. "Wait until you've gathered all the information you need. There will be plenty of time for confrontation."

Lynn closed Jamie's office door softly behind her, then rethought, and opened it, leaving it just barely ajar. A closed door implied secrecy and might incite curiosity, especially with Jamie out of town. He'd left a suit jacket, dark blue, hanging on the back of the door. Lynn had the feeling it had been there for ages, forgotten in all the back-and-forth to New York. She couldn't believe it, she simply couldn't. Did Jamie really want a divorce? When had he called a lawyer? And why Georgia Vaughan? Lynn would have imagined he'd call a man, a conservative, white-shoe-firm sort of lawyer—more the way C. Bradford "Call me Bradford" sounded. She tore her gaze from the empty jacket, forced herself to think about where Jamie might keep their personal files.

On the desk was a file organizer filled with thick sheaves of paper—current deals, probably. As Lynn came around to his side of the desk she noticed the large blotter, the kind where construction paper is inserted into a leather frame, and a matching cognac-colored leather penholder filled with a single type of pen, like an accountant's bouquet. The blotter— which must have come with the office, she couldn't imagine Jamie buying something like that—was pristine. He hadn't doodled on it at all, which struck her as poignant. Or perhaps it was simply changed regularly. He had a picture of her in a burl-wood frame—taken by the wedding chapel clerk right after they were married, with Lynn grinning a little crazily. Next to it sat a small Tiffany clock. The one missing from their office at home? Had he brought it to work? She read the name on the plaque at the top—the name of the company in some deal he'd worked on—but didn't recognize it, not that she'd ever made note of the name engraved on the one at home. Glancing at the door, she slid the clock off the desk and into her purse. It belonged at home.

A row of low, horizontal file drawers lined the back wall, but Lynn started with the small two-drawer file cabinet tucked under the desk. It seemed the intuitive choice for personal files. She found it right away, a file marked "Family Finances." Everything seemed to be there: bank statements, income stubs, mortgage payments. Jamie was organized in a way that made organization look easy. He didn't handle all the finances; Lynn paid the household bills. She could have found any piece of paper needed from her own files, but it probably would have entailed a messy search through a bulging, haphazard collection of receipts and bills.

"Xerox if you can and leave them where you found them, but if not, take everything with you," the lawyer had instructed. But Lynn couldn't bear the idea of looking for the copy machine, trying to figure out how to use it. That seemed like stealing from Jamie's firm. The whole thing was wrong—it felt wrong. She couldn't imagine Jamie instigating a divorce behind her back. She should just sit down and pick up the phone right now to call him.

She looked up. Jamie's secretary, an older woman named Ruthie, was outside the door. Their eyes met through the narrow gap, then Ruthie opened the door and stepped in.

"Hi," said Lynn, jumping up. "I'm just getting some files for Jamie."

"Can I help you find something?"

"That's okay, he told me where to find them."

"Does he need me to FedEx anything to him in New York?"

"Actually, it's just our personal files." Lynn stood there, gripping the file.

"You've found everything, then?"

"Yes." It was clear that Ruthie was going to stand over her if she continued to look.

"I didn't see you come in," Ruthie said.

"You didn't?"

Ruthie smiled gently. "Maybe you came in while I was still at lunch."

"I should probably get going." Lynn leaned over to pick up her purse and felt the guilty weight of the clock inside the soft black leather. "It's so nice to see you, Ruthie. All's well?"

"Oh, yes. We miss Jamie, though. Mr. Answurth was

saying"—Mr. Answurth being the managing partner—"that it's almost as if Les Hatchett is drumming up more business just to keep your husband busy. Anyway, it's wonderful for the firm, right?"

"That reminds me, Ruthie, do you happen to know the number of Jamie's hotel offhand? Just so I don't have to look it up?"

"The new one, you mean? I was just livid with the old one. We were supposed to be guaranteed a room there." She rattled off a name and number, then looked quizzically at Lynn. "Don't you want to write it down? Wait." She reached into a pocket in her pleated skirt, pulled out a small pad and pencil, and jotted it down for Lynn. "There," she said, handing it to her with a smile. "I'll probably see you next at the Christmas party, won't I?"

"Oh," said Lynn, "right."

Ruthie held the door open for her, pressing back against it to let Lynn slip by. File and scrap of paper in hand, Lynn headed down the corridor to the rear door. There was no reason now to bother with the front.

What were you doing in my office?"

"That's the first thing you say to me?" Lynn was back in her own office. "After hanging up on me? After—"

"I didn't hang up on you," Jamie said. "I just couldn't talk right then, I've been moving offices. I called back a minute later and they said you were on the phone. Then they said you were out."

"You didn't leave a message?"

"No." He sounded sheepish, and Lynn had to smile. He hated leaving messages, especially at work. She'd always seen this as part and parcel of his quietness.

Abruptly, though, she recalled their new circumstances. "How did you know I was at your office, anyway? Your little spy Ruthie? Does she know?"

"Know what? She said you told her I'd asked you to pick up some files."

"You talk to everyone. You talk to Ruthie, you talk to your good friend George Jacquemet. But you can't be bothered to call your wife. Maybe I should have asked Ruthie what you were doing at a nightclub opening with your rich client's daughter."

There was a pause. "You saw the picture? Look, I'm sorry about that."

"So sorry you called a divorce lawyer?"

"What?" Jamie sounded genuinely confused.

"I know you called Georgia Vaughan."

"Who?"

"Oh, come off it. Just the toughest divorce lawyer in Los Angeles." C. Bradford had told her that.

"I have no idea what you're talking about. What makes you think I called this person?"

C. Bradford had also warned her that if she was foolish enough to talk directly to her husband, she should not be inclined to believe a word he said. "Men lie," was C. Bradford Froemming III's succinct wisdom. "What makes me think it," she said, "is that she told me. She said she couldn't talk to me because you had already contacted her."

"She said that? She knew my name?"

"You must not have realized when you hired her that she went to Princeton with Dee."

"I didn't hire anyone. I don't know what you're up to, Lynn."

"What *I'm* up to?"

"What were you doing calling a lawyer in the first place?"

Even through her anger and sorrow, Lynn felt a certain pride in Jamie's sharp mind. He always cut straight to the critical point. "You run off, I have no idea where you are for five days—"

"It wasn't five. Maybe you were planning this all along— you and your new lover?"

"Lover?" Lynn couldn't believe he'd said that—they both hated the word. "Didn't you get my messages?" she said.

"You think it'll give you some kind of advantage? To get in first and pretend I'm the one at fault? Guess what, Lynn, we live in a no-fault community property state."

"No-fault community property? Obviously you're the one thinking about divorce."

"No, I'm not!" he practically yelled, and at that moment Lynn's heart misgave her. In the cautionary tale of Jamie's parents' divorce, it was Philippa—the person who didn't want one—who'd unleashed that dangerous word. Out of pique. At which point Jamie's father had just sighed and said, "If that's what you wish."

"Although most people would say," Jamie said, lowering his voice—which made Lynn wonder where he was, what his office in New York was like, "that considering what happened, I *should* be thinking about it."

"Nothing happened," Lynn said. "Nothing happened and you know it."

"Really? How would you feel if you'd walked in and found me undressed with someone else?"

"We weren't undressed!"

"With a Maserati. That was his car, right?"

"How would I know?" she lied. "Look, did you listen to my messages or didn't you?"

"I listened."

"And?"

"And?"

This was infuriating. Did he really not believe her? "How about me?" she cried. "Spending the weekend half crazed because I had no idea where you were? Imagine my relief to learn you'd passed the time hanging all over some woman in a nightclub?"

"My boss's daughter!"

"Oh, that makes it okay? And I was with *my* boss's benefactor's assistant. Look," she said, "I'm not saying mine didn't look bad, but you don't really believe I'd do something like that?"

Jamie was silent.

"Maybe for a second," she said, "in the heat of the moment, you might think it."

Still nothing.

"You can't really think I'd do something like that! Oh, I hate you, say something!"

"Don't raise your voice to me."

"Oh, right, my loud Jewish voice—what an embarrassment. Just like at Thanksgiving. No wonder you're dying to leave me."

"What are you talking about now?"

"Nothing. Your mother. You and your hateful family. The whole awful spread of it at Thanksgiving—it just summed everything up."

"Are you talking about the food?" He sounded confused. "I *told* you, you did a great job."

"Not the food, although your mother was nasty enough about that, too. I mean the families, the marriages. The differences. Your mother—"

"No, Lynn, this is *your* chip, on *your* shoulder."

"It's how she sees it."

"I'm sick of you blaming my mother for— Oh."

"What?"

"Just wait. I don't believe . . ." Lynn heard phone sounds, the beeps of a number being punched in. "I'm calling my mother on conference call," he said. "Don't say anything."

"No, I don't want—"

"Shhh!"

A phone rang. Jamie's mother answered.

"Mom," Jamie said, "I'm at work but have a quick question. You didn't happen to call some lawyer in L.A., did you?"

"No, of course not."

"A woman?"

"Oh." There was a pause. "She didn't call you, did she? I distinctly remember not giving you her number. Those female lawyers are so aggressive."

"Mother, what did you do?"

"Nothing." Jamie's voice had been stern; still, Lynn was surprised to hear Philippa quail before it. "Just, after you told me what Lynn had done, I happened to . . . You remember when we talked on Friday, I told you I was leaving for that golf tournament in Arizona? Well, one of the women in my foursome happened to mention that she was a lawyer specializing in divorce, so I told her a little about the circumstances, but I don't think I mentioned your name."

"She knew your name?"

"Well, of course, we played together all day."

"And you told her I wanted to hire her?"

"Of course not, I just told her a bit about my concerns. You know, about the extent of the family holdings, if Lynn should try to get her hands on that."

Lynn gave an audible gasp.

"I'll talk to you later, Mom, I've got to run." Jamie broke the connection with her.

After the click, there were a few seconds where nothing

was said. "I can't believe you told your mother," Lynn said at last. "What did you tell her? She already hates me."

"I barely told her anything. This isn't about her."

"Yes, but she . . ." Lynn broke off. Jamie sounded so different, stern and direct, so unlike the husband who'd run off the other night.

"I'm tired of this," he said. "It doesn't matter, I'm done."

"Done?"

"Why do you think I was calling earlier? When I couldn't talk and then called you back? You think I haven't been thinking about you all weekend?" Lynn held her tongue, did not say, *While living it up in nightclubs?* "I was calling to apologize."

"Oh," she said in a small voice. "Okay."

"Oh, never mind."

"No," she said, "tell me. Please." She was sure that this was important, that this was the moment that would turn everything around.

"Fine," he said, but in a hard voice. "I realized that I hated being apart from you. That I didn't care about anything else, we'd figure it out somehow. But when you called, there were people around. I was in an open office. I wanted a little privacy to talk. Look, I was going to beg you to move to New York, okay?" He gave a laugh.

"You were?"

"Les has been on me about it for weeks. It would just be temporary. If that's what we wanted. That's what dinner was about."

"Dinner?"

Jamie made an exasperated sound. "That's why I was home early. Les had to switch our breakfast and we grabbed an early dinner the night before at the airport instead. He had to fly out suddenly, and I was able to switch flights. Because

I couldn't wait to see you. That's why I was moving offices. Les wants me at least to be working out of his building when I'm here. And, you know, in my blind stupidity I started to think maybe it wouldn't be such a bad thing, for us to be in a different city for a while. A fresh start. So, yeah, I was getting up my courage to ask you if you could possibly think of moving here for six months. Then I find out what you've been doing. Calling divorce lawyers."

"Jamie, listen."

"No, you listen. You listen for once. You always want to talk everything to death but you never listen. I'm done. I'm tired. I'm tired of feeling this way, tired of your explanations."

"That's not fair. What am I supposed to do, not tell you what happened?"

"Go ahead, I heard your messages, but maybe you left something out. Last chance, anything else you want to tell me?"

"Last chance?" She stopped herself. "I don't know what you're talking about," she said. "I love you, that's all."

"You say you hate me."

"Look, I'm sorry," she said. It was almost a relief to be back to this familiar territory. "We've talked about this. You know I don't mean it."

"That's right, we *have* talked about it and I've told you how much it bothers me, and you ignore that. That's what I mean."

"I'm sorry," she said. "I'm sorry."

"How could you think that of me? That I'd go behind your back and get a lawyer? Without saying anything to you? You say it doesn't mean anything when you say you hate me, but you say it and you say it. You must hate me. You've convinced yourself I'm the sort of person who'd do something like that."

"But you did the same thing! You thought I'd . . . Look," Lynn said, her voice trembling, "when you think about it, this whole thing's based on a little mistake. I should have told you earlier, you should have known me better. Nothing between us has changed."

"Really? Do you really feel that?"

"Yes." But somehow it didn't sound convincing. Lynn heard a rustling behind her and realized that Glynnis was back in the office. Even before Jamie spoke again she felt her throat close. She shut her eyes, the phone digging into her cheek.

"I just don't know where we go from here," he said.

"What are you saying?"

"Maybe it's best that I'm in New York right now."

Lynn was aware of Glynnis behind her. "That's it?"

Jamie hesitated, as if waiting for her to say something else. "I guess so," he said. "As far as I'm concerned."

Lynn hung up the phone—gently.

Sixteen

Lynn knocked on the rickety wood frame of Jessica Klein's screen door even though it was clear from the noise and the outline of the crowd filling the dim room inside that she didn't need to. As she reached for the handle, one of the shadowy figures inside thrust the door open.

"You!" the man exclaimed. "I was hoping I'd see you here." There was something familiar about him. Lynn peered into the gloom—and recognized Peter Fairhaven, the movie director from Mona's dinner. He grinned a toothy English grin. "Surprised?" He ushered her inside.

It wasn't at all what Lynn expected. Jessica's invitation had been a formal one: *Please Join Me for a New Year's Day Open House*, engraved in elegant maroon script. But there was nothing elegant or formal about this party. The room was crowded and dark—surprisingly so considering that it was early afternoon. People were standing all over the place holding plastic cups and cigarettes, and practically every surface was littered with bottles of cheap champagne, plastic orange juice containers, platters of guacamole and chips. There was a row of windows behind the long kitchen counter at the back of the room, but the shades had been pulled down—cheap vinyl roll-up blinds, but each painted with an imaginary, Giorgionesque landscape. By Jessica, Lynn assumed; they were beautiful. Clamp-on lights, the kind you see on construction sites, had been placed sideways on the counter, pointing up to illuminate each one.

"Jessica told me she'd invited you," the director said.

Lynn already regretted having come. The invitation had arrived weeks ago addressed (handwritten calligraphy) to both her and Jamie. It must have come before they separated because this fact hadn't struck her as tragic at the time. If they'd still been together, she doubted they would have ended up coming. They probably wouldn't have been back in time from Christmas. Lynn hadn't intended to show up herself. It was just that without work to go to over the holidays, and basically no one she could bear to talk to but family members, the days and nights had crawled by. Pretty much the only thing that got her through all those endless hours was . . . Trollope. In her agonized distraction, Lynn had happened to pluck an old Anthony Trollope novel, one she'd read before, from the living room shelves. First she'd sunk onto the floor with it, then moved to the sofa, the long one she and Jamie used to share. She'd finished the one book, then had gone back to the same place on the shelves for another. Trollope was comfort food. She was already well into his six-book so-called political series, the Palliser novels. How grateful she was that he was so prolific. Forty-seven novels should keep her going for a while.

Lynn realized that the director was waiting. What was he doing at this party, anyway? Lynn had just read an article about a movie of his newly out—a romantic comedy. She'd been startled by how big the female lead was, although supposedly she'd done it for scale. "You know Jessica Klein?" she said.

"You're choosing to ignore my declaration, I see."

Lynn gave him a blank look.

"That I was hoping to see you?"

"Oh. Well." She thought for a moment, or tried to. Her brain was like treacle these days. "I'm sure you say that to all the women you find at the door." But that made her think of F. X., who'd been leaving messages for her, both at work and at home. Was he here? She wanted to look around to see, but Peter Fairhaven held her eyes as he shook his head deliberately.

"I've watched every woman come and go for the last hour," he said. "I've been waiting for you."

Lynn felt a funny flutter in her stomach.

He was dressed in black tie, or the remnants of it. Tie and jacket were gone, the top buttons of his dress shirt unbuttoned. His hair was a mess. Everyone else was in casual clothes— jeans, little cotton skirts, and T-shirts. There was even one girl in pink velour sweats with a red flannel heart appliquéd across her bottom.

"You do remember me, right? We met at that dinner for Hugo Stanhope."

"Of course I do. You're Peter Fairhaven."

"So you know who I am now? Hang on, are you blushing? That's the most charming thing I've seen in some time." His eyes crinkled up at the corners—nice brown eyes, but light ones, with golden flecks, so different from Jamie's dark velvety eyes. "How long did it take you to figure out?"

"My husband told me right after," Lynn said, and looked down at her feet.

Oddly enough Peter Fairhaven looked down, too. "Er, might I get you a mimosa?" he said, suddenly polite British schoolboy.

"Yes, please." Equally polite and a bit too British sounding herself. Yes, go away for a minute, she thought. Stop looking at me like that.

He was back almost instantly with one of those precarious plastic champagne goblets filled to the brim. She had to take it from him carefully, slowly and carefully bring it to her lips. Their eyes met over the rim. She was aware of the shape of her lips on the plastic, the slight suction needed to lower the level of champagne.

"You don't have any comment?"

She glanced down at her champagne. "It's very good, thank you."

"Once again I'm referring to my stalking you at the door."

Lynn had taken another sip, and it took her a second to swallow it down. "It looked like you were just standing having a conversation with some people."

"You were watching me?"

She almost laughed. "Don't flatter yourself. I saw your anonymous back through the screen door."

But he was grinning, which sharpened his features. There was no denying that he had a nice profile. *Aquiline* was the word that came to mind. Since the day she'd laid eyes on Jamie, Lynn had never found herself attracted to anyone else. She fought the impulse to grin back.

"I spent Boxing Day with your sister-in-law," he said.

The impulse vanished.

"We were all at the same house party, in Surrey. Remember, I know Piers? How at that dinner I asked what she was like? She's quite nice. I shouldn't have been such an arse about it."

"Oh?"

"Lynn," he said. "I know."

"I beg your pardon?" She mustered every ounce of dignified chill that she could.

"Your marriage. I . . . heard."

"What did Julie say?"

His eyebrows went up.

"My sister-in-law, what did she say? About Jamie and me?" Lynn knew she shouldn't be asking.

"She just said—look, this is completely inappropriate of me, isn't it, bringing this up?"

Lynn wanted to shake him: *Tell me what she said*.

Christmas with Jamie's sister. Not that Jamie had been there. No, he'd been in St. Louis, probably with Andy and Annika as well—that had been the plan. Lynn and Jamie took turns for Thanksgiving, but they always went to St. Louis for Christmas. Her family, being Jewish, had no claim on the holiday. Lynn imagined everyone gathered as usual around the big fireplace in the Prosper living room. The room, with its bank of French doors to a back terrace and acre of lawn, had originally been the conservatory. The original living room of the three-story house Jamie's great-great-grandfather had built in what was now a suburb of St. Louis was so vast that it was currently only used as a sort of grand hall for parties. Christmas dinner was in the elegant, formal dining room with its hand-blocked antique wallpaper, every bit of the meal cooked by Philippa, although she had two women who came in to serve and clean up afterward. And then there was the sweet children's service when all the carols were sung. The first time Lynn had attended with Jamie's family she'd been surprised to find she knew all the words. She'd always thought of "Silent Night, Holy Night" as a Jewish song. Ridiculous when you thought about it, but it had been on a holiday album she'd listened to as a child by a Jewish folksinger who was a friend of her parents.

Lynn should have been there, too. She and Jamie had made their reservations ages ago, including the flights to Tahoe afterward. Had he gone to Tahoe by himself? Or worse, with the Jacquemet-Scovilles?

As the day scheduled for their departure had grown nearer, Lynn kept expecting to hear from Jamie, at least regarding the airline tickets. The date for his office Christmas party passed, then hers, and no word. She did get one message—from Jamie's secretary, Ruthie. It had made Lynn's blood boil, the tears of frustration flowing hot. Ruthie said that Jamie had asked her to pick up some things he'd be needing in New York, that he'd FedExed Ruthie the house key so Lynn didn't need to be there; she only needed to call if the specified day, during work hours, was not satisfactory. After that, Lynn resolved not to call Jamie, something she'd been debating on and off since their last awful phone call.

Twenty-four hours before their original departure date, Lynn finally called the airline to cancel her reservation. She had imagined it would be a total loss of a prepaid ticket and had taken a certain pleasure in this. But the person on the phone gaily informed her that if she booked a new ticket within twelve months to any destination so long as it was from the same departure city, she could use the credit. A different departure city would mean a hundred-dollar surcharge. Lynn left Jamie's reservation in place, partly out of spite since she knew he wouldn't be using it. As far as she knew, he hadn't returned to Los Angeles. Let him cancel it himself, or switch to a flight out of New York, which would mean paying the fee—unless he bought a brand-new ticket from New York to St. Louis for Christmas and saved the one out of Los Angeles for later, for when he had to come home to deal with his things. She'd wondered if he'd think of it—this way to save the hundred dollars. But it wasn't her problem anymore.

"I should just back off and leave you alone, shouldn't I?" Peter said. "I wasn't going to call or anything, not for a while. Of course you need time. My behavior is inexcusable."

Lynn felt frozen, as if he was talking to someone else and

she was just watching. Blindly at first, her eyes moved around the room. People were talking, laughing, all around them in convivial clumps. The party was so different from the ones Lynn usually went to—for the museum, mainly. It wasn't stiff or slick. It certainly wasn't beautifully done. It was hard to fathom but people actually seemed to be having fun. There was a looseness to this party that Lynn felt she'd almost forgotten about. The efforts she had gone to in her own home for Thanksgiving! Jessica Klein and her friends would have laughed at her. Just as, for very different reasons, Jamie's mother had. Inexcusable.

"I'm sorry," she said. "I should go."

"But you just arrived."

Her eyes were roaming the room again. She hadn't seen Jessica. She'd call tomorrow and apologize. Or not. Lynn backed away from the director toward the door. She'd barely made it five feet into the house. "I'm actually not feeling very well," she said, and realized this was true. She felt queasy. She held out the plastic champagne cup. He took it from her. Their fingers brushed. She quickly looked away.

"Can I call you, though?" he called after her, but quietly so no one else would hear.

She pretended she hadn't, either, and pushed the screen door open.

"Lynn Prosper! Where are you going?"

It was Jessica. Lynn was caught, she hadn't been quick enough. She turned to see her hostess elbowing Peter in the ribs. "What did you say to chase her away?"

Peter stared helplessly at Lynn.

"And where's that handsome husband I've heard so much about? You should hear Mona and F. X. going on about him. Not that I don't adore you, Lynn, but I was dying to meet him."

"Jess," said Peter, putting out a restraining hand.

"Jamie couldn't make it," Lynn said with a glance at him. "Actually, we're separated."

"No!" Jessica looked genuinely shocked—almost, Lynn thought, as if she'd known them as a couple. "I'm so sorry, that's dreadful news. It wasn't F. X., was it? He loves to be a troublemaker. Oh, I could kill him. Does he know? Have you seen him? I think he's back east. Something with his son again."

"F. X.?" said Peter.

"Oh, you poor dear," said Jessica. "I was a complete mess when I got divorced, and I wasn't even sure I loved him."

"You were married?" Lynn was dumbfounded.

"Oh, you should have seen my wedding hat, it was gorgeous. Literally a work of art, hundreds of layers of this amazing Japanese paper I tore into shape by hand." She made tearing motions in the air in front of her face. "Wait, you did see it—it was part of my installation for Mona. It was right at the entrance on a Plexiglas pedestal. The Oakland Museum has it now. They're thinking of buying it for their permanent collection."

"When were you married? How long ago did you get divorced?" Lynn was dimly aware of Peter still there, but really, he receded in the midst of all this new information.

"Oh, years ago," said Jessica. "I'm completely over it now. Let's see, it was two years ago. They say it takes you twice as long to get over it as the time the marriage lasted. But I don't think that's always true, it can't be. We were married nine months, and I've been fine for a while. No wait, that's wrong. It's half the time you were married. How long were you two married?"

To her horror, Lynn's eyes filled. She quickly tilted her chin to let the tears drain back. This reminded her of a fraternity boy in college who could open his throat to swallow practically an entire half gallon of soda from the bottle—also handy for alcoholic beverages. One of F. X.'s fraternity brothers, she remembered.

"Oh, honey." Jessica leaned forward and tapped Lynn's wrist. Her hand was paint-flecked, the pale yellow splotches across her nails looking like badly applied polish. "I shouldn't have asked. I reminded you of your wedding, didn't I? That's the hardest thing, all those people coming across the country to witness your vows—to bear witness. That's when you realize that a marriage isn't just about two people, it's much bigger than an expensive party. That standing up before friends and family, before an entire community—"

"Actually," Lynn said, "Jamie and I eloped."

"Oh!" said Jessica. "Right. That's so romantic! So personal. The spontaneity, it shows . . ."

"Jessica," the director pleaded. And hadn't he had a fiancée at that dinner?

"You poor dear," Jessica said. "I'm sure it's temporary."

"No." Unconsciously Lynn squared her shoulders. "We're getting a divorce."

That, finally, had been Jamie's holiday message to her. Two days after Christmas there'd been a knock on the front door—a man holding a manila envelope out to her, and a clipboard for her to sign. Lynn had even thanked him profusely; she must have seemed crazy because he'd smiled uncertainly as he backed away.

She roused herself. "I should probably get going." She couldn't look at Peter. "I hope you don't mind," she said to Jessica. "It's a great party—really. I thought I was up for it, but. . . ."

Jessica patted her arm in sisterly fashion.

"I'll walk you to your car," Peter said.

"No!"

Jessica looked up at this.

"No, that's okay," Lynn said, more calmly. "Please don't leave the party, I'm fine. My car's just over there." She pointed vaguely, edging to the door.

Jessica stepped forward, in front of the director, and gave Lynn a hug. "Call me," she said. "I understand." And to Lynn's relief, she escorted her out the door.

Seventeen

L ynn and Jamie had vacillated between being proud of the story of their wedding—it was romantic—and embarrassed by it—they had been cowards.

The whole thing had started with Jamie's sister's wedding. The date had already been set when Lynn and Jamie first met, and Lynn hadn't expected to be asked to be a bridesmaid—of course she hadn't, not back then. Julie would have already asked her friends, and she and Jamie were so new—although everyone could tell from the start how serious they were. That Christmas however, Lynn's first with the Prospers, there was a crisis in England and Julie came home to St. Louis alone. The wedding was soon on again, though with the date pushed back. By then, Lynn and Jamie were engaged themselves. They purposely set a date way after Jamie's sister's new date, but Julie and Piers ended up pushing their wedding back yet again, to just a few months before Lynn and Jamie's.

It wasn't hard to see why Philippa was beside herself. Still, Lynn thought it completely out of line for her to suggest that Lynn and Jamie were being selfish and stealing Julie's limelight.

"We had ours planned ages before she changed hers," Lynn had protested to her own mother. At no point during all this did anyone suggest that Lynn, by then Jamie's betrothed, be added to the bevy of bridesmaids, not even when Lynn shyly asked Julie, whom she genuinely liked, to be one of hers.

Julie's wedding, when it came, was predictably lavish. "Everything about it was perfect," Lynn reported to Sasha, whose own wedding had been a modest backyard affair. "It was the event equivalent of her dress." All three sisters indulged in some snide laughter over that one. Julie's dress had been a giant, over-the-top bouffant of satin duchesse, rosettes, and diamante. Her "something old" had been the eighteenth-century lace veil originally made for the very first viscountess. It trailed seven feet behind as Julie glided down the cathedral aisle followed by the large wedding party in which the groomsmen—a final, galling detail—turned out to outnumber the bridesmaids.

Less than a month after Julie's nuptials, seven weeks before their own, Lynn and Jamie headed to Tahoe after Christmas for some skiing. As always, they flew into Reno, where they rented a car. This time, however, they decided to go into town for something to eat, and it was thus that they passed the large neon sign blinking WEDDING CHAPEL. Lynn had had no idea that Reno was just like Las Vegas, a place where you could get married on the spur of the moment.

And now . . . Jamie hadn't called over Christmas, he hadn't called to tell her he was filing for divorce, nor had he called the day after she was served with the papers—their anniversary.

When Lynn fumbled for the phone half asleep and heard Philippa's voice, she instinctively turned on her side toward Jamie—who wasn't there. Of course he wasn't, just the flat, white expanse of duvet. Lynn pushed herself up against the pillows, took a firmer grip on the phone. She could hear the light long-distance crackle in the background.

"Lynn?"

She tried to clear her throat noiselessly. "Yes?"

"I hope I didn't wake you. I thought you'd surely be up by now. Don't you have to get to the office for that job of yours?"

"Is there something I can do for you, Philippa?"

"Yes, there is." Briskly, as though Lynn had been remiss. "Several years ago I lent you a pair of earrings, a lovely pair, gold, rather Ottoman looking, with the emeralds? You remember?"

"You mean the ones you gave me right before the reception?"

"I don't think it was *right* before, as you put it."

Philippa had insisted on throwing a post-elopement reception, but Lynn knew it had been a bitter second-best for her. As if to punish the newlyweds, she'd chosen a particularly inconvenient date for them to have to fly to St. Louis.

"Yes, we flew in and you handed the box to me right before the party." Lynn had had to change them for the earrings she'd brought with her and had been afraid that they didn't really go with what she was wearing, beautiful as they were.

"For that occasion, yes, I did want you to have them. I was happy for you to wear them. I hope you didn't think they were an outright gift? In fact, I was a little surprised when I went looking for them and realized you'd never returned them. They are quite valuable, and of even greater sentimental value, of course, having been in the family for generations."

"Philippa," Lynn said with a sigh, "do you want me to send them back to you?"

"I think that would be best, yes. Make sure you use FedEx

or someone with a tracking number and all that, not the post office. And perhaps you should insure them."

Lynn sank back against the pillows. "For how much?"

Her mother-in-law hesitated, and Lynn realized that she didn't want to say, even though she'd already announced that the earrings were valuable. "Perhaps you'd better not mail them after all. Why don't you just put them aside for Jamie? He'll have to come to Los Angeles again, won't he? You still have so many of his possessions."

When Lynn didn't respond, Philippa said, as if innocently, "Will you be seeing Jamie? When he comes?"

Was Jamie coming? Was Philippa saying that he'd already made plans? He must be back in New York again by now, but he probably told his mother everything. No doubt it was being under her sole influence over Christmas that had led to his filing for divorce when he did. If only—if only!—he hadn't been on that deal in New York, this never would have happened. But immediately Lynn chastised herself: It was time she accepted that this was Jamie's choice; it was how he thought of her and what he wanted, otherwise it wouldn't be happening. He'd said himself that she shouldn't blame his mother for everything.

But how could he do it without even talking to her? Because he didn't want to be talked out of it, that's why.

"If Jamie wants to come during the day," she said to Philippa, "I'll probably be at work." Was he even planning on telling her? She certainly wasn't going to force him to see her if he didn't want to.

"Perhaps that nice Barbara Hatchett will help him," Philippa said.

"I'm afraid I don't know anything about that."

"No? I just thought she might. Such a dear girl. A friend of Annika's, you know."

Lynn couldn't stop herself. "I didn't know she lived in Los Angeles."

"She's one of those fun, lively girls who seems to be everywhere at once! I'm sure if she is in town she'd be delighted to help Jamie."

Lynn didn't comment.

"It really is too bad that house of yours isn't in a better neighborhood," said Philippa. "I've always said that."

Indeed she had. And what was her point this time? That she regretted that Barbara Hatchett might witness the extent of Jamie's slumming? After they'd bought the house, Lynn had overheard Philippa on the phone describing it to one of her friends. "Hancock Park," she'd said crisply, although in fact the neighborhood was only, in real-estate-agent-speak, Hancock Park adjacent. "No, they didn't want to be in Bel Air. Yes, more of a starter house. I'm sure when they buy their next one . . ." To be fair, Lynn's mother had hardly been enamored of the location, either. "Hancock Park?" she'd said. "It's so conservative. They didn't used to let Jews buy houses there, you know."

"Do you know what you're going to do about it?" Philippa now asked.

"About what?"

"The house, dear. Isn't that what we're talking about? I'm sure Jamie wouldn't want you to feel rushed."

Lynn recalled Jamie's bitterness about the mortgage. Had there been something in the divorce papers about the house? Lynn hadn't been able to bear reading them through. She'd have to call C. Bradford. Had he been sent the papers as well? How could he have been? She'd never mentioned his name to Jamie. And Jamie hadn't used Georgia after all. There'd been a different firm on the letterhead.

"I hope you know, Lynn dear"—Philippa's parting shot—"I certainly never wanted things to end like this."

Lynn switched off her alarm clock, which would have gone off the next minute anyway, and trudged to the bathroom. With a glance at the mirror—she didn't look as bad as she would have thought, almost rosy-skinned—she crouched down to open the cupboard underneath the sink where she kept her jewelry box. Jamie always said how foolish this was, that one day she was going to drop something down the drain. But it was generally while standing in front of the bathroom mirror brushing her hair or putting on makeup that Lynn remembered to put on earrings. Not Philippa's. She'd tried those on only once or twice after the party Philippa had thrown for them. They were too long, too heavy, too valuable. Lynn hadn't so much as thought about them in more than a year.

Her jewelry box was pink and white, shaped like a miniature armoire. Lynn had owned it since she was twelve. She kept it under the counter for safety, but also because she'd be embarrassed for anyone to see it. She didn't know why she didn't get rid of it and get something else. She opened the jewelry box's bottom drawer—its tiny drawer pull had been missing for years. She kept Philippa's earrings tucked way in the back in the little white cardboard box they'd been in. But when she pulled out the box it was empty. Lynn stared for a moment, uncomprehending. She began pulling apart the cotton inside even though it was clear that the earrings weren't there.

Calm down, she told herself. She must not have put them back in the box.

She rifled through the rest of the jewelry—she didn't have that much. Kicking aside the bath mat, whose shag left wormy indentations in her knees, Lynn knelt on the cool tile floor and pulled everything else from under the sink. Reaching in, she swept her hands around the dusty interior in case the earrings were lodged in a dark corner. But she knew they weren't. She was running out of time; she had to get dressed for work. She pawed through the jewelry box one more time, then shoved it and everything else back under the sink, forcing the doors closed on the jumbled mess.

"I must have already given them back," she muttered to herself. Philippa had implied that even she'd had the impression Lynn had done so. Lynn gave a nod, as if that dismissed the problem, and felt a wave of vertigo. She just had time to spin around to the toilet to throw up.

She hunched there in shock. She must have stood too quickly. She'd been bent over for a long time in an awkward position, her head inside the airless cabinet. Was she coming down with something? Food poisoning? No, that didn't make sense, it would have hit her earlier. What had she eaten last night? Just a piece of bread, she realized, with butter and honey. She'd meant to get something else, but she'd started reading and the evening had just passed. It was funny, Trollope's Palliser novels were supposed to be about the political world, but what they really seemed like they were about were the transgressions of women. Even the title of the first in the series: *Can You Forgive Her?* And the one she was in the middle of now, *The Eustace Diamonds*, was about a young widow trying to make off with the family jewels. Oh, Lynn would have loved to tell Jamie about that—he would have appreciated the irony.

Lynn's desk at work was covered with little pink message slips, some of them weeks old. She really did need to get her act together. The top one was from Sasha, left, according to the scribbled time, just fifteen minutes before Lynn got in. *Call*, it said. *Tried at home but already gone.* There were multiple messages from her lawyer, from F. X., from Peter Fairhaven.

"Miss Prosper?"

Lynn looked up. Earl Smithson was standing in the doorway. "You look lost in thought," he said. "Thinking about the proposal?"

Lynn must have looked blank.

"For the budget meeting. Richard Plante."

"Oh," she said, jumping up. "Yes. Yes."

"I just received a call from him. He'd like to meet with us. He says he'll be messengering over some information for you to look at. Some ideas he has, I gather." Earl made a face, and Lynn attempted a companionable grimace. Her face felt stiff.

"I'll take care of it," she assured him.

"Good. I know it's in good hands." He paused, and for the first time since Lynn had known him he looked ill at ease. "And how were your holidays, Miss Prosper?"

"Actually, I have something to tell you. Jamie and I, we're, um, getting a divorce." She was pretty sure he knew already— Glynnis? "I just wanted you to know."

"Miss Prosper! I'm so very sorry. So very sorry to hear that."

"Thank you," she said.

"It seems quite sudden."

"Yes, it is."

"I don't suppose there's any possibility—any possibility of a reconciliation?"

"I don't think so, no." *Since we don't talk.*

"I beg your pardon for intruding on such personal matters. I know it's out of line but, Miss Prosper, I want you to know it is your well-being we have at heart here."

"Thank you, Mr. Smithson, that means a lot to me."

He glanced at her officemate's empty chair. "Miss Bastien doesn't seem to be in the office much."

"I believe she's at the printer's this morning."

"You know, she's shown a decided interest in this project of yours, with Mr. Plante. I was a little surprised. I'd been thinking perhaps development would be a better fit for her." He was speaking briskly now but managed to convey an air of saying these things for Lynn's sake. "She's very on the up-and-up, that young lady. Perhaps you should pull her in? Get her involved? That's the way you stroke a man like Richard Plante—he wants a team, not just one person."

"Should I mention it to her?"

"Perhaps, perhaps." And he strolled off, back down the hall.

Lynn had given absolutely no thought to the proposal for Richard Plante. She realized how much she had let things slip. Was that why Earl wanted to bring Glynnis in? Or was it simply punishment for having lost Jamie? She opened the file cabinet under her desk to get out the files of old ideas and proposals there had been no money for.

When everything was laid out on the desk, it made an imposing pile. Lynn's spirits rose rather than sank as she flipped through it. There was a lot there, a lot to go over, a lot to be done. It was, in fact, just what she needed—some hard work. Once she looked over everything, she knew she'd be able to churn out a good proposal in no time. Tapping the mass of papers into a neat pile, she had a flash of insight. This was what Jamie had been doing all this time, burying himself in work. She found the thought comforting in an odd way. One of the hardest and strangest parts of the whole thing for her had been not knowing what Jamie was thinking or doing—how time was passing for him.

The same thing had happened, or sort of, the day after

they met. They'd had that instant connection, leaning together against the jukebox in that noisy, dingy bar, but Lynn had felt nervous the next morning at work, waiting for Jamie to call. And she'd waited and waited. People came by her desk and asked if she wanted to go to lunch with them, and she turned them down, saying she had some work to finish, knowing she was being an idiot. As the hours passed, she tried to fight the growing feeling of dismay. She had felt in her bones that something important had happened the night before, but of course that kind of feeling can be an illusion. How often did women—and men—get that feeling in a bar and then nothing comes of it?

Later, Jamie told Lynn that he'd been meaning to call at ten sharp. He'd gotten in to the office before eight but figured, correctly, that people in the arts came in later. He, too, had spent his first couple of hours in the office watching the clock, but just when he was finally about to pick up the phone, he was pulled into a conference. It lasted more than three hours, and then everyone went straight to lunch together. There was nothing he could do. "You poor thing," Lynn had laughed when he'd finally called and all was well. "It must have seemed interminable." But the truth was—and this was one of the things Lynn really did love about Jamie, even when it told against her—he really hadn't thought about her at all while in the conference, so focused was he on the rather thorny legal issues at hand. He'd impressed his superiors greatly that day with his incisive comments.

Lynn was halfway through the folders on her desk when the phone rang. She froze. Jamie?

"Hullo?" It was an English voice.

"Oh," she said. "Hi."

"You have the loveliest voice, you know. It's a pleasure to hear."

"Um, thank you."

"This is Peter, by the way. Peter Fairhaven."

"Yes, I know."

"Oh. Good. I'm only calling because—you didn't by any chance get any of my messages, did you?"

"I did."

"So . . . you chose not to respond?"

"I guess not."

The director gave a bark of laughter. "If you weren't breaking my heart it would be rather humorous."

"Comments like that don't help your suit at all," Lynn snapped.

"Suit!" he said. "What a lovely, funny word. If you were trying to put me off, you just . . . That's exactly why I like you. Who else would use a word like that? And one that's perfectly apt. Like I'm a lovesick suitor out of Trollope."

Lynn stiffened at Trollope. She had liked the word *apt*, had even smiled into the phone at it, but Trollope—Trollope was too close. Could she have mentioned that she was reading him at Jessica's party? She was pretty sure she hadn't.

"*Le mot juste*," Peter said.

That was better. "I hate Flaubert."

"You hate Flaubert?" He sounded astounded. "The man's a god of literature. How can you hate him?"

"Fine, not hate. That's too strong an emotion."

"Ah," he said. "That's very damning indeed."

"I have to go. I have a proposal to get out."

It was just one word, *proposal*, but suddenly Lynn felt uncomfortable, as if the air had become charged. She was pretty sure he'd noticed, too. "Very well," he said after a moment. "Have dinner with me, then?"

"I can't have dinner, thank you." Now she just wanted to get off the phone.

"I'm going to keep trying, you know. Tell me one good reason you won't have dinner with me."

"I'm busy?"

"In general is what I mean. I take it your no is a general one?"

"Don't you have a fiancée?"

"Is that what you think of me? That I'm the sort of man who'd be engaged and still ask you out?"

"Yes. I mean, I don't know you at all."

"Poppycock."

"What?"

"I know it's too soon, but can you honestly say you don't wonder? About the possibility? Yes, the timing's wrong, I know that."

"Good-bye," said Lynn, and hung up. She turned from her desk—and gave a start when she saw F. X. standing there.

"Flirting on the telephone? How come you never flirt with me?" he said. "You never even call me back."

"What are you doing here?"

"I hope that was Jamie you were talking to."

She blinked at him. "You haven't talked to Jessica?"

"Jessica?" He frowned. "No, not lately. Why? I've been pretty caught up with . . . In fact, that's why I keep calling. Didn't you get all my messages? Look, I know you probably think I'm not the best father, but that's only because that psycho bitch won't give me a chance. And now that she might be about to give me one . . ."

It had never occurred to Lynn that F. X. had been calling to talk about anything other than what had happened with Jamie. Well. He might be solipsistic, but she was just as bad.

F. X. came all the way into the room, pulled Glynnis's chair around, and dropped into it. "You don't know what it's been like," he said, and to be fair he did look hollow-eyed. "She's been holding this over me for months. First he's supposed to come for Christmas, then she promises right after."

"You didn't get to see your son for Christmas?"

"Yeah, but I had to fly there at the last minute. It's like a game for her. Cost me a bloody fortune, two layovers. Have you ever tried to make reservations for Christmas at the last minute?"

It was, of course, a rhetorical question, but Lynn thought of Jamie.

"Finally—finally!—she buys Michael Joseph a ticket to come out next month. I still don't believe her, but anyway, she wants me to give her a fucking itinerary! He's coming for two weeks. I don't believe *that*, either, because she won't tell me the return flight. She'll probably snatch him away the next day if she lets him come at all. So I need your help to put together a good itinerary."

"F. X.," Lynn said, but he wasn't listening.

"You know, all the fun things we'll be doing. If I screw this up she'll probably use it as an excuse not to send him at all. It needs to be really good."

"F. X., I really can't help you with this."

"Sure you can. I know you don't have kids yet, but you grew up here. We don't have to do it right this minute. I don't need to get it to her until sometime tomorrow. Oh," he said, "you mean you won't help me at all." For a minute it looked like his face was going to harden into some new cruelty, then his cheeks sagged. "It's Jamie, isn't it? Goddamn bad luck! He'd be mad if he even saw you talking to me, right? I get it. But don't you think, just this once, if you told him what it was about, he'd understand? I mean, my kid! Jamie's a good guy, he'd understand."

"Jamie and I are getting divorced."

F. X.'s mouth fell open, which in its own way was gratifying. "Not because of me?"

Lynn lifted her chin. "Why, don't you like that power?"

"Of course not!" His expression of shocked innocence had so many layers of irony that they almost canceled each other out and made it true. "I wouldn't want a responsibility like that."

Lynn laughed.

"What's happening to you, Lynnie? You've gotten hard. This isn't like you."

Not hard, she thought. That was before, when she was encased in that pearly, nail-hard coat of complacent love. Nothing got through to her then.

"Seriously," F. X. said, "is there anything I can do? Call Jamie? You can tell him Chaka came over to my place later that night. She'd probably even talk to him, but he'd have to promise to keep it quiet."

Whatever hard composure of Lynn's F. X. thought he saw finally cracked. "Are you saying I should tell Jamie that? Or that it actually happened?"

"What?" F. X. looked confused.

"That Chaka came over. That same night."

"Of course she did—she saw I was upset. Why would I say it otherwise? She told Richard she was tired, he dropped her off, she called me while I was driving home and met me at my place."

"You say all sorts of things. You say you're visiting your girlfriend in Venezuela for the weekend—but wait, she's from Brazil. And you weren't there after all, you were on the East coast visiting your supposed son."

"Supposed?"

"No, I mean . . . I believe that part."

F. X. was staring at her. "Boy, I guess we really aren't the friends I thought we were."

"I never know what's true with you, F. X."

He looked at her as if he couldn't believe what he was hearing. "Those are just details. Why do you care where she's from? I told you, anyway—her parents are living in Venezuela now, but they're from Brazil. And I had to be careful about Chaka—I mean even before Richard, because of all the custody stuff."

"And then you leave that voice mail. What were you hoping would happen with that?"

"God, Lynn, it's not like I think these things through." He stood. "I was just trying to be funny. You can't make me responsible for all your problems."

"No," she said. "You're right."

"I mean, I don't see how it could be about me." He began pacing around the small office. "That would be crazy. Nothing happened."

Lynn didn't respond.

"It's true, I've broken up relationships before."

"You have?"

"Not marriages. Well, I don't think so. Not good ones, anyway."

And there, thought Lynn, was his rationalization for Chaka and Richard.

"I never would have teased you like that if I thought it would matter. You guys seemed solid."

Lynn didn't think she could bear this conversation any longer. "You're right," she said, rising now, too. "You wouldn't have been able to do any harm if it hadn't been meant to happen."

He looked at her. "You believe that?"

In a strange way, it was the only circumstance under which she could stand this outcome.

"If there's anything I can do," he said.

"You've done enough! I mean, no, I don't think there's anything *to* do."

"Ah, Lynnie." F. X. was at the door. He hesitated, then took a step back toward her and pulled her into a bear hug. At first Lynn just stood there, staring blankly over his shoulder. But his hold on her felt warm and human, and suddenly she felt so tired. She closed her eyes and rested her forehead on his shoulder for a minute, taking deep breaths. He had on a wool crewneck sweater and it felt scratchy but not uncomfortable against her cheek. "Don't worry," he murmured in her ear. "We can talk about Michael Joseph later."

Lynn's eyes flew open, only to see, through the glass wall of the office, Glynnis striding down the hallway toward them. F. X. turned to look, too, and his face took on its old devilish cast. She was all motion, wearing a pair of wide gauchos and high, dark brown lace-up boots, her arms swinging. Yet Lynn had the impression that she had been standing and watching before taking up her stride.

"Oh, hello," said Glynnis, in the doorway. "I'm sorry, Lynn, I didn't know you were with someone." She looked from Lynn to F. X. expectantly.

"Glynnis, this is F. X. Donahue. He's an old friend of mine from college."

"Oh?"

"And he's also Richard Plante's . . ." She drifted off, at a loss.

"Gofer," said F. X. "Minion."

Glynnis moved closer, hand extended. "I doubt that very much."

To Lynn's dismay, F. X. held Glynnis's hand too long. But why was she surprised? "Well," she said, "thanks for coming by." When he didn't move, Lynn said, "I don't want to keep you."

F. X. slapped his forehead—unforgivably stagily. "I almost forgot. Why I came to begin with. Richard asked me to drop off these files for you, Lynn." It was Glynnis he was locked in on. "Just some clippings and things he'd come across that he thought might interest the museum. Sometimes he even walks around, dispensing jewels of wisdom, and I jot them down. No pressure to use them. He says to tell you he's just trying to be helpful and is excited about being involved." Finally, reluctantly, turning back to Lynn, he pulled an envelope out of the inner pocket of his jacket—now that she thought of it, she'd felt a papery rustling when they hugged. The envelope was fat and appeared to be full of lots of pieces of paper. F. X. winked at Glynnis. "Told you I'm the errand boy."

Glynnis grinned back at him with a wide, horsey smile.

F. X. stepped back with a mock salute. "I know you two lovely ladies need to get back to work."

"Well!" said Glynnis, after he'd disappeared.

"Look, Glynnis . . ." When her officemate turned to her, Lynn realized she actually needed to come up with something to say. "I'm getting really swamped with all this Richard Plante stuff. Would you have any interest in helping out with it?"

"Trying to get me to do your work for you?" But she met Lynn's eye and a look passed between them. "Okay," said Glynnis, "let me see that." She held a hand out for the envelope.

Lynn watched as Glynnis rifled through the little scraps of paper inside. "God, what rot. What are we supposed to do with this? I'll tell you what," she said. "I'm going to go Xerox all of this on normal-sized pieces of paper, and then we can sit down and go through it."

After Glynnis left, Lynn sat down at her desk and rubbed the back of her neck. *Oh, Jamie.* More than anything she wished she could tell him all this. How had they gotten to this place where she couldn't?

On one hand, she could understand it—the quick filing of divorce papers. He'd said more than once that it would be over if she ever slept with anyone. He'd feel bound to stick by his word, to show that he was sticking by his word. He believed there'd been something going on with F. X., so he left. But how could he believe that? Why did it not occur to him that she might be completely innocent? She did blame him for that. How could he not have known that she'd never do something like that? The whole point of everything, of their marriage, of *them*, was that he knew her and she knew him. But apparently she'd been wrong, and F. X. was right: He couldn't have wrecked things if there hadn't been other problems between them. It was almost as if their happiness—*her* happiness, she guessed she should say—had been on borrowed time. And now Jamie might be coming to Los Angeles and she didn't even know about it. It was silly, this not talking. It was childish. Lynn suddenly felt older. Older and wiser. She reached for the phone, only to realize that she didn't even know the number at Jamie's new office. It had come to that. Did he not even think about her at all? She dialed his cell phone, expecting to be forwarded to his new office voice mail.

"Hello?" Jamie sounded annoyed, and Lynn realized that it was the second time he'd said it.

"Sorry. It's Lynn."

"I know."

"You never answer this phone. I just meant to leave a message."

"Oh. Do you want me to hang up so you can call back? If you don't want to talk to me."

"No—no, it's fine. I was just saying why I didn't say anything right away."

"Oh. Um, well, I was expecting you to call."

"Yes, I got the papers."

"I know. Look, I—"

"Your mother called this morning."

"God, what did she want?"

Lynn felt encouraged by this. "Basically, to show me up as a slattern for not being awake when she called at the crack of dawn."

Jamie snorted, and Lynn had the oddest sensation of a loosening and a tightening in her chest at the same time. "Look," he said, "I really am sorry."

"You want to sell the house, right?"

"What?" he said. "Well, I guess. Eventually. We don't need to worry about that now."

"No, we should sell. Right away. The market's only going to go down. The house is a huge burden for you. It has been all this time."

"That's not true. I shouldn't have said . . . I just felt like a failure for not being able to afford anything better."

"That's ridiculous."

"You thought it was too small."

"I did not."

"You were always apologizing for it—how it was 'the nicest of its kind.'"

"It is. *You* always said how small it was, and how the neighborhood was dodgy. I'd much rather have it than the Jacquemet-Scovilles'—you know that! I said things like that because of how *you* felt."

"And you wonder why I have a hard time believing anything you say?"

"That's totally different! Why am I always the one in the wrong? Look at *you*. Our marriage has fallen apart and all your grasping, social-climbing mother cares about is getting her stupid earrings back!"

"What are you talking about?" His voice was cold.

"Those earrings she gave me after we got married! At that awful reception she made us go to in St. Louis." Lynn could hear how childish and pointless this was, but she couldn't help it, it was a relief to be back on a subject where she bore no fault and in fact was the wronged party. "I don't even like them!"

"Oh," said Jamie. "Well, if you don't like them, who cares?"

"I *don't* care. She can have them. Even though she did give them to me. They were clearly a gift at the time."

"Lynn, you should keep them if you want them." She could hear Jamie trying to be reasonable.

"I don't want them! I just couldn't find them."

"You lost them?"

"No, I didn't lose anything. I never wore them. I know exactly where I kept them and they just weren't there. I must have given them back to your mother ages ago. When she asked about them, she even said she thought she had them but then she couldn't find them."

"No," he said, just like that, "we must have them. I'd remember if you'd sent them back."

"Right," she cried, "like you're ever around! Tell your mother to search her own house first."

"You have to admit, it sounds pretty strange, Lynn. I wasn't going to make a big deal of it, but Ruthie says you took the clock from my office, the one—"

Lynn slammed down the phone.

She was just passing the department secretary's desk with some vague plan of going to track down Glynnis about the Xeroxing, when the young woman looked up and saw her. "Oh Lynn, I just put a call for you through to your office. It's your mother, I think."

Lynn ran back to her office and snatched up the ringing phone. "Oh, Mommy," she said, "you're not going to believe—"

"I know!" came her mother's exultant voice. "Isn't it exciting? Sasha, pregnant!"

Eighteen

It wasn't until Lynn threw up again the next morning that she even thought about the possibility.

She couldn't be pregnant. She always used her diaphragm—although of course there was a small failure rate. But she'd had her period since the last time she and Jamie had slept together, which had been right before that last business trip, the one that made him miss the opera. It had been a very light period, Lynn recalled, lasting just—had it been two days? But she'd been right on time. She was actually due for her next period soon. Maybe that's what this was, some sort of PMS side effect, not that she'd ever had any before, not even bloating. It was as if her sister's pregnancy had somehow, subconsciously maybe, seeped into her own life. Sasha was pregnant, but Lynn was the one throwing up. Or did Sasha have morning sickness, too? Lynn realized that when she'd talked to her sister she hadn't asked nearly enough questions.

On the phone the night before, she'd tried hard to stick to the subject of how excited she was for her sister, but Sasha, annoyingly, kept stopping to say, "Oh, Lynn, is this too hard for you?" to the point where, when Sasha mused, "Maybe we'll have to find a bigger place," it was almost to appease her that Lynn blurted, "I'm putting the house on the market."

"I can't believe this is happening to you," Sasha had said.

Evidently she believed it enough to alert their mother, who was soon on the phone to Lynn as well. "Just because Jamie wants to sell the house," Ella said, "doesn't mean you have to. Have you talked to the lawyer?"

"I'm happy to sell," said Lynn. "What's the point? The last thing I want to do is stay in this house by myself." But when she started talking wildly about letting Jamie have any profits since money was so important to him, Ella was appalled.

"The house is community property!"

"But his salary paid more of the mortgage."

"Oh, Lynn, this is exactly why community property laws are so important, they're to protect . . ."

Lynn got off the phone as soon as she could—which only freed it up for Sasha's renewed assault, clearly at their mother's behest. Lynn was pretty sure the only reason Dee hadn't been dragged into it was the time change, although Dee was also more inclined to side with Lynn. It would have been interesting to see how the scales tilted: family dynamics versus Dee's firm beliefs about women's place and role in the world.

"If you're even thinking about this," Sasha had said, "you at least have to talk to Robin." Robin was an old friend of hers from high school. "Did I tell you she went into real estate? You need to have someone there looking out for you."

Sasha had insisted on calling Robin as soon as they hung up, and Robin had been able to squeeze Lynn in the very next morning—for breakfast, before Lynn had to be at work. The appointment was presented to Lynn fait accompli. Now, with less than an hour before she had to meet Robin, Lynn cursed her sister. Without the breakfast date she could have crawled back in bed for a while.

Robin was already at the table when Lynn got to the Marie Callender's a block or two from the museum. She slid into the semicircular banquette with its olive-green Naugahyde and felt a wave of nostalgia—mixed with revulsion. The restaurant had been Robin's choice, a rather odd one. The chain, originally famous for its pies, had been popular in the 1970s; Lynn's father had often taken the girls, back when he still lived with them. They always used to order the same thing: shepherd's pie, the famous Marie Callender's cornbread, lemon meringue pie. But although there was one so close to work, Lynn hadn't been inside a Marie Callender's since. Maybe Robin was just trying to be accommodating.

Lynn had seen her sister's friend once or twice over the years when Sasha was in town, and recognized her easily. But she looked different now. The words *fiercely groomed* came to mind. Robin's dark, sculpted eyebrows in particular stood out as works of art. She had short, spiky hair and was wearing an expensive-looking ribbed tank top, the designer version of a wife-beater, a name Lynn hated so much she had never worn one herself. Robin's arms were muscled, like taut rubber bands. Back in high school she'd been on the plump side. She was poking at, but not really eating, the large, crumbly square of cornbread on her bread plate.

"You okay?" Robin asked, looking at Lynn. "You look a little green around the gills."

A waitress came over with a coffeepot, and the thick, dark liquid burbled into Lynn's cup. "Actually," said Lynn, the memory coming back all too vividly, "I threw up this morning."

"Oh, are you preggers, too?"

Lynn froze. "No, I—"

"Sasha told me. Exciting, right?"

"Very."

"Oh my God," Robin said, "I'm so sorry. I forgot for a minute . . . I mean, it's just that Sasha always talks about you as so happily . . . and here I'm . . ."

"It's okay." Despite everything, Lynn was amused to see this new Robin thrown off her stride like that.

Robin reached over and patted Lynn's hand. "Of all people, I know how hard it is. Geez, I'm sorry. Of course you're not pregnant. I'm an idiot. Do you think stomach flu? Because, Lynn, if you want to reschedule, all you had to do was call and tell me. You can reach me 24/7 on my cell. I'm here for your convenience, you know that." Although she'd grown up in Los Angeles, Robin spoke with what sounded like a New York accent. Lynn realized she was hearing the cadences of a real estate agent. A file folder lay on the table. Robin followed her eyes. "Right," she said. "Let's get started, then." She tapped the file. "I already have some interest."

Lynn laughed. She had talked to Robin for the first time only the night before. "The house isn't even on the market yet. You haven't even seen it."

"Don't worry, we'll take care of that. You don't have any time this afternoon, do you? The point is, it's a very desirable location. Believe it or not, there's not much on the market there and starter houses are the only thing moving."

"But how could there already be interest?" Lynn asked.

Robin looked at her pityingly. "I happened to mention it. You know, to another agent in my office. One of our top guys, after me. I mentioned I was having breakfast with an old friend who might, just might, blah blah blah. The next thing I know, he's coming by my desk before I leave to meet you—"

It was only eight thirty in the morning. Robin had already been to the office?

"—and he says can he bring someone by this afternoon."

Lynn opened her mouth to protest.

"Don't worry," said Robin. "I told him hold your horses. But when he heard that you work at an art museum and everything, you could just see him thinking, *chic, artsy.* The poor guy was practically salivating. Now's the perfect time, before prices really start to drop, if we price it right."

"But I don't even know if—"

Robin put a hand on her arm. "Don't worry."

"How quickly can these things happen? I mean, if we do decide to sell. And someone makes an offer right away."

"We're not just going to take the first offer that comes along. I want to have at least one open house. But once you accept an offer, it depends. Sixty days, thirty days? If you need longer, you put that in your counter, or we let the buyer's agent know ahead of time. Were you thinking of buying something else, or do you want to rent maybe for a while?"

"I—"

"Because my own personal advice would be to rent. I say personal because professionally, of course, I want you to buy." She laughed merrily but was also regarding Lynn closely. Lynn had the feeling Robin was waiting for her to say something.

"You know, right?" Robin said.

"Uh . . ."

"About my own divorce?"

Now Lynn remembered. Sasha had said something, but that had been a while ago, before mention of other people's marital woes riveted Lynn's attention. "Yes, Sasha told me," she said.

Robin nodded approvingly but still seemed to expect more.

Lynn didn't want to ask how long it had been or why it had happened. Robin probably assumed that Sasha had told her the whole story, and would be insulted at the paucity of Lynn's knowledge. "So, how are you doing?" she asked.

Robin flicked out her hands in a self-mocking, *Chorus Line* gesture. "How does it look like I'm doing?"

"Great," stammered Lynn. "You look absolutely fantastic."

"Yeah, it kind of made me realize, okay, girl, no more fooling around. Time to get your act together. People always say marriage makes you grow up, but that's a crock. We both know that, right? It's divorce that makes you grow up."

"What happened exactly?" Lynn saw that it was okay to ask.

"Crap, who knows? Tony was a piece of shit. No, seriously, you wanna know what happened?"

Crock, crap, shit. Lynn didn't remember Robin talking this way. Was that the real-estate influence, too?

"What happened," said Robin, "was that little by little, for no reason—oh ho, so I thought—my darling ex turned jealous. He was a nightmare, always wanting to know where I was, demanding I be home by a certain time to make his dinner, for crap's sake. Like I was his chattel or something. And God forbid I should ask where he'd been when he crawled in at one in the morning. He said I wasn't giving him any freedom. The schmuck. It turned out he'd been having an affair the whole time he'd been on me. That's what he was talking about—freedom to fuck eighteen-year-olds."

"Eighteen?" said Lynn.

Robin turned weary eyes on her. "Does it matter? But," she added more cheerfully, "it was the best thing that ever happened to me. You'll see. I know it's hard now, but in the end you're going to say, 'Thank God my life took that turn.' And you tell Sasha that Robin is going to be right there for you. I'm going to make it a breeze, plus get you lots of money for your new life." Robin frowned. "Do you have to split with the jerk? Sash says he was the jealous type, too."

Robin's jacket, a serious-looking suit jacket, light gray glen plaid with thin lines of lavender and a slight sheen, was draped over the banquette next to Lynn. The lapels looked wide, the buttons large. The padded shoulders seemed to hold their shape aggressively, even folded like that. "Robin is an incredibly loyal friend—for me that counts for something," Sasha had said, her warning tone anticipating her sister's reaction. Lynn could imagine the agent suiting up, covering up those tan, ropy arms and looking even stronger. No, Robin wasn't ridiculous, she was formidable. Lynn was glad to have her on her side.

"So, are you?" Robin said.

"Sorry?"

"Free this afternoon. Make it after work. I have an idea for you—something you might like. It wasn't what I was thinking for you at first, but, yeah, I think it'll cheer you up."

"Do you mean a house? I don't think—"

"Apartment. Just to look at, get your feet wet."

This was too fast, but Lynn didn't feel capable of turning Robin down outright. "Where is it?"

Sasha's friend shook her head. "I'm going to surprise you. I'll pick you up. That way we'll kill two birds. I can check out your place."

On the way home from work that day, Lynn stopped at the drugstore. As she scanned the shelves for home pregnancy tests she told herself it was crazy, that she probably wouldn't even bother using it. But when she got home she went straight to the bathroom, brown paper bag in hand. She tore the package open with clumsy fingers, unfurled the onion-skinned information packet. Sitting on the toilet, she pored over the tiny print: how to take the test, how long to wait for the blue line that meant you were pregnant to show up, about the reliability of the test. A negative result didn't necessarily mean you weren't pregnant; it might just be too early for the test to tell. Then Lynn came to the part about testing the first urine of the day for the surest results. She stared at the wand, imagining how she would have to hold it gingerly under her. She wanted to take the test, get it over with. But she knew she should wait. If it came out negative, she wouldn't be convinced and would only have to go out to buy another one for tomorrow. Reluctantly she shoved everything back in the box. Robin would be there any minute to pick her up.

Lynn still had to go to the bathroom. She pulled everything out again and checked to see if her watch had a second hand.

Hey," said Robin, "forget I was coming?"

It had taken Lynn a while to get to the door. "No, I—"

Robin pushed past and gave a low whistle. "Nice. Very nice. You mind?" She took in the wet bar (created by the previous owner from an unmissed coat closet), knocked on the rather charming decorative columns that divided living from dining area, made her way through the kitchen. Lynn caught up with her in the hallway in time to see her merely poke her head into the two bedrooms. The real estate agent did, however, open the bi-fold doors hiding the stackable washer/dryer, and even checked inside the machines. "Nice," she repeated. "This is going to be a cinch. A pleasure."

"Do you need to see . . ."

"Nope. Got it. For now at least. We should get going. I'll drive."

"I'd better follow in my own car," Lynn said. She had thought this through. "I need to pick something up at the market on the way home."

"I don't mind, I'll take you on our way back." Robin jangled her keys.

Lynn dismissed that as a possibility and scooped up her purse.

"Where are we going?" she asked when the two were in the car. Robin drove a jaunty yellow Honda Civic. Lynn had been expecting the requisite real-estate-agent BMW or even a baby Mercedes.

"I want to surprise you." Robin gave her an encouraging glance. "I think you'll get a kick out of it."

They drove a while in silence, Robin heading west on Melrose and then north on Doheny, humming to herself. Lynn was grateful for not having to make conversation. She wasn't paying much attention when they pulled up at the elaborate entrance to what appeared to be a large apartment building. They had come in under a covered area, so she couldn't really see where they were or how tall the building was. A valet opened the car door for her. Another man stood at the revolving door, ready to give it a push.

"So?" Robin said with pleasure. "What do you think?"

"Nice," Lynn said.

Robin looked disappointed.

"Very nice," she amended, trying to sound more enthusiastic. A glitzy high-rise wasn't what she'd had in mind, not that she had anything in mind.

The lobby was large—two, perhaps three stories high—and lined with shimmering, heavily veined, golden-brown marble. It was like being in an enormous agate cave, and there was even a stream of sorts, a narrow reflecting pool along the wall opposite the reception desk. A mere inch or so of water ran over smooth black stones set into cement, creating the visual paradox of rippling imperturbability. The elevators, a bank of four of them, had doors of polished brass.

Robin stopped to consult with a doorman, one of three at the front desk, then joined Lynn at the elevators, keys in hand.

When the elevator came, its particular chime seemed familiar, and Lynn had the sinking feeling that this place was her destiny.

She didn't even register what floor they got off on. Robin was fiddling with a set of double doors, throwing one of them open to reveal a generous entryway. Its marble floor led to a good-sized living room that seemed even larger thanks to an entire wall of glass. They must have been pretty high up. Lynn went over to the windows and looked out over a sparkling city panorama.

The test hadn't been conclusive. There hadn't been a clear blue line. But she was pretty sure there'd been something. When she'd held the test up to the light, trying to figure out what she was seeing, there'd been something faint and bluish. When you thought about it, there had to be a blue line already there either way—waiting to come out when enough of the right hormones hit it, like invisible ink or at least lemon juice, which, as Lynn remembered it from childhood, could be seen while supposedly still invisible if you peered at the page just so, with the light shining through. Was that all she'd been seeing? She would have to wait until tomorrow morning to know for sure.

"And down here are the bedrooms," came Robin's voice. The real estate agent had been talking this entire time.

Even through Lynn's shoes, the deep, chocolate carpeting felt luxurious underfoot. It ran throughout the apartment— wall-to-wall in the living room, down the long hallway. "Maybe we can get them to replace it with something lighter," said Robin. But it made Lynn think of an animal's pelt with its silky, not quite organic sheen, and she could imagine it as furniture enough in this apartment, with all that glass and the views. She wanted to just lie down on it, like that heart-breakingly still painting by Rousseau of a man lying horizon-

tal under a night sky, but with a headdress that she always
mistook at first glance for a woman's long hair. *The Sleeping
Gypsy.* Lynn had always thought of him as listening, if only
to his own dream. Wasn't there a mandolin in the painting?
It was in the Museum of Modern Art. In New York.

Jamie. She'd have to call and tell him, of course.

"Look at this," called Robin. "This is fabulous, I can see
you here."

Lynn followed her to the master bedroom. Pale walls,
chocolate carpet, another spread of windows. In this room,
however, the glass started two and a half feet off the ground, not
flush with the wall but pushed out about eight inches so that
a small ledge was formed, running all the way across that side
of the room. You could use it as a bookshelf. There was,
inexplicably, a bottle of moisturizer left on the ledge, and a
Princess phone sitting on the floor. Otherwise the room was
empty.

What would he say? Would he be happy? Or would it be
a burden, a disaster, another shackle? Maybe she shouldn't
tell him. But a protest rose in her chest. Anyhow, he'd find
out eventually, no matter what happened between them. Of
course he had to know. She'd have to call him again. She
shouldn't have hung up on him like that.

"Are you imagining where all your stuff will go?" Robin
asked. "I'd put the bed there. Then you could just turn your
head and get that fabulous view."

"Mmm," said Lynn. She turned from the bedroom, peering into but barely registering the bathroom, then on to the
closed door of a second bedroom, which turned out to be not
a bedroom at all, but a small utility or laundry room—
although there didn't appear to be a hookup. Perhaps a very
large closet? It was strange, but Lynn felt a rush of pleasure
as she looked into this blank, useful space, and she finally

allowed herself to recognize the emptiness she'd been feeling since taking the pregnancy test. It was the absence of dread.

Lynn found Robin waiting for her in the up-to-date kitchenette. The real estate agent had clearly decided to leave her alone to take her time. If only Lynn hadn't let Sasha call her friend. With any other agent she could have simply dropped the matter. "This place must be a fortune," she said politely.

"You'd be surprised." Robin named a figure that did surprise Lynn—in its reasonableness. Just one third of their monthly mortgage payment. Robin ticked off on her fingers: "Number one, it's a sublet; two, believe it or not, this building's not an easy sell. It's always been an older crowd here, but now they want to be in those newer buildings along the Wilshire corridor. Young people don't think about a building like this, but the way I see it, it's just what you could use—comforting, easy, with the doormen and everything taking care of you. There's a pool, a gym, parking. And it would just be temporary. Everyone says stay in the market, but I tell you, in your situation, you make a mistake—real estate rebound, right?—and if it goes down again, you can end up really stuck. I shouldn't say this, but you see it all the time."

"I think I need to mull it over a bit." Lynn was edging toward the double doors, which seemed flimsy compared to the rest of the apartment—cheap hollow core stained to look like walnut.

Robin followed her. "You take all the time you need. Absolutely no rush. But can I give you a bit of advice?"

"Of course." Lynn was distracted, still thinking about how the conversation with Jamie would go.

"Don't do that with your forehead, hon, it's all lines across. You don't want that, especially now that you're single again."

Nineteen

As soon as Robin drove off, Lynn got in her car and raced to the drugstore. She bought three pregnancy tests—just in case there's another unclear one, she told herself, keeping up the pretense that this time she'd wait until morning.

Within ten minutes of arriving home, Lynn had another inconclusive test: the appearance of what was perhaps a blue shadow, but no obvious line. It was her own fault, she really should have followed directions and waited. It was almost midnight in New York. Even if she wanted to call Jamie—and why should she, she had nothing concrete to tell yet—it was too late. He liked to get to sleep early on weeknights.

Lynn changed into a nightgown and got into bed, pulling the comforter around her. Could she really be pregnant? Those darn tests. She should buy stock in the company that made them. The little pamphlet had said something about implantation bleeding—which could explain everything. What she'd assumed was her period had really been too short and light. What would it mean, if she really was pregnant?

If it was true, she'd been pregnant the whole time—including when Jamie disappeared to New York. What if they'd known then? Wouldn't that have changed everything? It struck Lynn how quickly things had happened—no time for reflection, no time for discussion. Maybe they should have been going to couples therapy. If only they'd recognized the problems before that awful night. She'd done things wrong—she absolutely saw that now. And why had she hung up on Jamie? That was just rude. She would have been furious if he'd done that to her, and would have expected him to be the one to call back. If only they hadn't been separated like that—because of New York, that stupid job. Lynn just knew it wouldn't have come to this otherwise. She wasn't saying it was the only reason. (But wasn't it?) To say that the detail of being physically apart shouldn't have made that big a difference—well, she and Jamie wouldn't have met in the first place if it hadn't been for the *detail* of them both being brought to the same birthday celebration. No matter what the pregnancy test said in the morning, she was going to call him. It was the right thing to do, especially because of hanging up on him. It wasn't that she thought calling would fix everything, but they should at least be able to talk. Was she crazy for thinking that if he knew she was pregnant, he'd be happy—maybe even despite himself? She still thought she knew Jamie, at least a little.

Lynn shifted in her comfy cocoon of bedding. It was too early to fall asleep. With a sigh, she kicked her way out. She'd been so preoccupied she'd forgotten to check messages when she got home.

She caught her breath when she heard Jamie's voice. "I just wanted to let you know," he said, "I'm sorry about my mom, and I didn't mean to fight about the earrings. I agree with you. I thought she gave them as a present, too. So if you find them, you should keep them. About the desk clock, I didn't mean to make a fuss. I know it's dumb but they're sort of sentimental—workwise, I mean. I had no idea you cared about them." Lynn hit speakerphone and dashed back to the bedroom for the slouchy hobo she'd been carrying the day she took the clock from his office what seemed like ages ago. It wasn't really her style and she hadn't worn it since. The clock was still in the purse.

"Uh, okay," she heard as she hurried back to the room. But Jamie had stopped speaking and there was only the hiss of open line. Then he said, "I really do want to talk to you, though."

Lynn placed the little clock back on its old spot on the desk next to the phone. Jamie had sounded different—wistful. Lynn sat down and pulled the calendar toward her and counted the intervening weeks yet again. It didn't change: five and a half. At first it had sounded like the pregnancy test should be conclusive by five weeks, but the instructions were a little hard to interpret. They kept referring to ovulation and missed periods as starting dates, as opposed to when you had sex. And, yes, the days she'd circled when she thought she had her period were exactly when implantation would have happened.

Lynn was dying to call someone—her mother, Sasha. It was too late to call Dee; she was in New York, too. But Lynn knew she couldn't call any of them. If she was pregnant— if!—Jamie was the one who should know first.

If, if, if.

Lynn snatched up the phone. He had called her, hadn't he? Sounding as though there were something he wanted to say to her. It was a sign. She'd apologize if she woke him. It seemed wrong to wait until morning, too calm and cold-blooded. Thankfully, she remembered which hotel Ruthie had mentioned. As Lynn waited to be connected to Jamie's room, it occurred to her that she should have given more thought to how she was going to introduce the topic. Should she wait to hear what he had to say first? Just tell him, she told herself. Tell him as much as she knew. The phone rang and rang, and then she was shunted to a message center. She hung up.

Lynn glanced again at the clock—the replacement clock. Yes, after midnight there. Had Jamie slept through the call? He was usually such a light sleeper. Where else could he be at that hour? On a work night. In Manhattan.

Lynn had to admit, she'd been heartened by how few of Jamie's things Ruthie had taken. When she'd arrived home that night she'd glanced into his closet—the one in the office, the bedroom closet was all hers—and it hadn't looked depleted at all. In the old days of happiness Jamie was always up before she was, and she loved to lie in bed in the morning listening to his footsteps go back and forth down the hall as he got dressed. He'd pop back into their room to check on her, maybe ask what she thought of a certain tie even though he was as good a judge as she. Jamie was one of those men who enjoys wearing a suit. He even liked putting on black tie.

With a frown, Lynn pushed herself away from the desk (already imagining herself swollen, unwieldy) and stood. She moved (waddled?) to the closet. Had Jamie asked for his tuxedo? Had that been one of the things he saw himself as needing in New York? She rifled through the closet, dry-cleaning plastic grabbing at her hands. No tuxedo. Not anymore.

Despite everything, she fell asleep easily after that—and woke early the next morning feeling refreshed. It was as if her body, newly important in the scheme of things, was taking care of itself. She'd heard about that—that you should trust your body, follow cravings and the like. Once again, the pregnancy test remained inconclusive. Or was she just reading it wrong? She could swear there was a shadow of a blue line. She definitely felt different, her breasts fuller than usual. No false positives, only false negatives. She wouldn't even ask

Jamie where he'd been the night before. He was free as far as he knew. He was allowed to go out at night in New York if he wanted. It had probably been something for work, anyway.

The woman Lynn was put through to when she called Les Hatchett's office and asked for Jamie sounded so friendly. "Why, Lynn, hello," she said, liltingly introducing herself as Sita. (Indian? Pakistani?) She seemed to know exactly who Lynn was, and sounded happy and not at all surprised to hear from her. "You've just missed him," she said apologetically. "He's off-site today with Mr. Hatchett."

Lynn felt encouraged enough to venture, "Will he be calling in for messages?"

"Oh dear, they're out in the middle of nowhere on a construction site all day. I don't know if there's even cell phone coverage. And you know he needs to go straight to the airport from there. He was worried he'd miss you and instructed me to ask whether he can come by tomorrow at, say, five thirty? He said to let you know he'd call in to confirm whether that time worked for you."

Jamie was going to be in L.A.? Tomorrow? Lynn felt a wave of warmth toward this Sita woman who seemed to be on her side—on her and Jamie's side. Old Ruthie had never been so forthcoming. Lynn didn't want to disappoint Sita by revealing how little she knew of Jamie's plans. But what did it mean that she assumed Lynn knew? What had Jamie communicated to her about Lynn? "That's great," she said to the assistant. "Very helpful, thanks." And being out all day on a site—that sounded more like architecture than law. Lynn was glad for Jamie. "If you do happen to speak with him before I do," she said, "could you please tell him that I got his message and that five thirty is just fine, that I'm, um, looking forward to seeing him."

"I'll do that!" said Sita, and Lynn hung up, smiling.

*   *   *

Lynn had agreed to meet Jessica Klein for an early-morning exercise class before work. They'd made this plan before the morning sickness started, which to Lynn's relief was not in evidence that morning. In fact, she felt great. She'd been a little surprised when Jessica suggested an exercise class. You can spend your entire adult life in the art world, get to know hundreds of artists, and still fall victim to the cliché of the solitary, tormented genius—as opposed to the perky girl artist who grew up in L.A. and did frenzied aerobics.

When Lynn arrived at the address Jessica had given her, she wasn't there yet, but the exercise studio was filling up. There was a calm to the place that made Lynn wonder if frenzied aerobics were not in store for her after all. All Jessica had said was that the class was pretty challenging. The room was carpeted, with a barre running around three sides, and mirrors on all four. Lynn slipped off her athletic shoes and socks. All the other women were barefoot, their ankles trim in footless tights. Most wore oversized T-shirts instead of the more body-conscious workout clothes you usually saw. It wasn't a particularly young group, either, although there were two or three very fit-looking women who looked to be in their early twenties. Lynn pushed her shoes into a corner and took a place on the main barre just as Jessica hurried in. The minute hand on the large wall clock clicked, audibly, to the eight o' clock position, and a remarkable-looking woman floated to the front of the room.

Floated wasn't the right word. There was nothing ethereal about her. She looked like a solid Polish peasant girl: broad Slavic cheekbones, upturned nose, wide mouth, and stick-straight blond hair chopped off in a bob. But she seemed to move without locomotion. She was wearing black footless

tights and a loose, black, long-sleeved leotard—and looked
about seven months pregnant. Her cheeks were rosy and she
had a placid, determined look in her china blue eyes that said,
I'll pop this child out and be back to work the next day.

"Hello," she said, smiling at Lynn. "I'm Martha. First time?"

"Yes, I'm with Jessica."

Jessica had squeezed in next to her at the barre, forcing
the next two women to reposition themselves. Martha smiled
as if Jessica were her absolutely favorite person in the room.
"Don't worry if you can't do everything right away," the
instructor said. "Just do your best." Then, with a stern "Okay,
ladies," she dropped into the classic knees-bent-legs-shoulder-
distance-apart, center-of-gravity stance, and raised her arms,
bent at a ninety-degree angle, in front of her face. Every other
woman in the room did the same, with Lynn glancing around
to see what to do next.

After mere minutes of tiny little lifts, Lynn's biceps and triceps
were burning. A few more minutes into the session, after a series
of scoop-lower-and-tucks at the barre, her legs were shaking.
Panting, she glanced at Jessica, who winked back at her.

When they were all seated on the gray industrial carpet for
a butt-firming exercise known for good reason as "the pretzel,"
Martha called out, "Stacy's getting married next weekend!"

There were oohs and aahs, and heads turned toward one
of the younger women in the room, a pretty blonde in the
front row who, Lynn had noticed, did the exercises with almost
as much ease as the instructor.

Two older women, clearly friends, were directly behind
the bride-to-be. The girl looked over her shoulder at them.
"So, what's the secret?" she asked. "You've both been married
a long time, right?"

"Almost forty-five years," said the silvery-haired one.

"Twenty-seven," said the other, to whom earlier, during

deep squats, Martha had called out, "Keep going, Christine, and the slopes will be a breeze this year!"

The silver-haired woman smiled—or maybe it was a grimace as they were still doing the painful lift, lift, lift of the pretzel. "I'd say the secret is . . . just staying. That's really all there is to it—just sticking with your marriage. Well, and choosing wisely."

In the mirror, Lynn saw Martha touch her big taut belly complacently.

The one named Christine was nodding. "Sylvie's right. There really is no secret, just weathering the bad years. Every long marriage has its ups and downs."

The bride-to-be did not look enthralled with this answer, and Lynn could understand why. Bad *years*? She imagined Sasha making a face at that sort of marriage—or perhaps not. Sasha had been married more than a decade already.

In the mirror, staggered rows of pretzeling women were reflected back at Lynn. Rows of women, rows of wives, soon-to-be-wives, hoping-to-be-wives. Yes, it was terrible to admit, but she had seen the avid curiosity with which each and every woman in the room had looked up to hear the veteran marrieds' words of wisdom. Lynn saw the intent expression on her own face as she worked to twist and lift the leg.

Was that the problem—that she hadn't worked hard enough? Had she given up too easily? Lynn had taken her marriage—no, not just her marriage, the love she and Jamie had—for granted, had assumed that everything would be fine simply because of their love. She'd paid lip service to the idea that marriage was hard work, searching in her own marriage for what she could possibly call hard: cooking dinner (or more often, heating it up) when she didn't feel like it, being the one responsible for picking up the cleaning and doing the taxes, putting up with tacit insults from his mother. Of course Jamie had made mistakes, too—he hadn't told her enough, he'd jumped to crazy conclusions. Why hadn't she worked harder to straighten things out? Lift, lift, lift.

"Switch sides," the instructor sang out, gracefully shifting her bulk.

And now she was pregnant. Maybe. She *felt* pregnant. At any rate, it was a wake-up call—about what she really wanted, about what was important. And say she *was* pregnant. What about those nice messages Jamie had left? Hadn't he been waiting for her to say something in that first, awful phone conversation? Why, oh why, had Glynnis come in? And even the second time, he'd sounded tentative. Why had she jumped to talk about the house? She'd let Philippa get the better of her. There wasn't any real reason she couldn't move to New York, was there? Which was what Jamie had been about to ask her to do, before this all started. He'd wanted her to move. There were lots of museums in New York, and anyway, if she was pregnant she'd probably want to take time off.

"Do you have time to grab a coffee before work?" Jessica asked as she and Lynn sat putting their shoes back on after class. Jamie was incommunicado all day, and then would be on a plane—coming here. She would see him tomorrow. Lynn felt as though she had all the time in the world. The beautiful day stretched out before her. There actually was a big opening at the museum that night, but Lynn didn't really have anything to do for that—just show up.

When they were settled at an outdoor table at a coffee place half a block down from the studio, Lynn said, a little to her own surprise, "I've been thinking about your work."

"Really?" Jessica's face lit up, but there was also a hint of wariness.

Lynn was acutely aware of her position in Jessica's eyes as a representative of an important museum. She plowed on anyway. "You're so good. Your work is so beautiful."

Jessica smiled in relief and gratification.

"I was thinking. . . . well, the notebook." Lynn faltered for a moment, unsure if she shouldn't stop right there. "It really is interesting," she said, "reading it. I mean, I loved it. I kept going back between it and the paintings." Jessica was clearly trying to keep an open, interested look on her face. Lynn noticed the residue of the red lipstick the artist must have applied before class on her lips. "I'm just not sure you need it."

"But how will people know what the pictures are about? You just said . . . and the whole point is the story."

Lynn put a hand on Jessica's arm. She could feel the butterfly beat of the artist's pulse, the beating fear of being misunderstood, of wanting—no, needing to explain. Lynn felt transformed, suddenly calm and sure of herself. "The whole point is your paintings. Everything is in them, I promise you. You should have confidence that they're enough."

"You mean"—tentatively—"that with the notebook it's almost like I don't think the work itself is good enough?"

"Exactly!" Lynn was pleased with how quickly she had understood. That boded well. "Don't you believe," she said, feeling giddy, "that the whole story—the whole meaning— eventually comes out? I think it always does. If something's important, people search for it, they make the effort. Anyway," she said with a grin, "you can always go back and tell the story of the notebook when they interview you for *Art in America*."

The two women laughed together, but almost immediately Jessica went back to staring into space, her coffee cup raised partway to the remnants of red on her lips. The cup, too, had a trace of red. Now there was an image for her to paint, Lynn thought. She picked up her own cup—chamomile tea, just in case. "Do it," she urged—unnecessarily now, she could see. Jessica's mind was clearly working. "I think it'll be a big, big leap for you."

Twenty

"U h-oh," said Glynnis, "look who's here."

Lynn stiffened and looked up. An endless stream of young men and women in black trousers and crisp white shirts crisscrossed the museum atrium with their trays of champagne glasses, although guests were still relatively few. There was even a special treat that evening: "caviar shooters." A pretty server stood near the entrance, her tray held in place by a strap around her neck so that she could demonstrate to suitably impressed guests how to put a dollop of caviar on the back of your hand, shoot it back, then swig down the proffered shot glass of a new brand of premium Finnish vodka, one of the evening's underwriters.

Lynn didn't even need to follow the angle of Glynnis's lifted chin, so unerringly did her eyes find the person in question, as if she'd known he'd be there all along. Jamie was standing at one of the bars set up around the periphery, his profile to them as if he were about to take his drink and move away.

"Were you expecting him?"

Lynn regarded her officemate. "You knew he was coming."

Glynnis shrugged. "He was on the list. I figured you knew. I didn't want to upset you," she added, undermining her first excuse.

"What's he doing here?" Lynn was talking more to herself.

"Well, he was listed under 'Les Hatchett plus three.'" Glynnis frowned. "There's something going on with that, I think. So Jamie didn't mention he was going to be in town? What are you going to do?" She was clearly relishing the situation.

If Lynn had been alone she might have tried to make a dash for it, to the ladies' room or her office upstairs, for a temporary reprieve at least, not to mention a glance in the mirror. But under Glynnis's watchful eye there was nothing for it but courage. "I'm going to go say hello."

She was about two thirds of the way across the atrium when Jamie saw her. His eyes lit up, but he made no effort to come toward her. He waited—why did he always wait like that?—smiling, at the bar. Still, something in Lynn shifted, and she felt a smile starting on her face, too.

He spun his back to her. She drew up short in astonishment. No, he was back, holding two champagne glasses.

"What are you doing here?" she said. He held one of the glasses out to her. "Isn't that for someone else?"

"Nope, just you."

She was dying to look around—for Les Hatchett, or worse, Les-Hatchett-plus-three's daughter. Jamie kept smiling at her. "How did you know I'd be here?" she asked.

"Uh, it's your job? Do you not want it?" He looked around for somewhere to put the glass down.

Her hand shot out. "I'll take it. Thanks." They both took care that their fingers did not touch as the champagne flute exchanged hands. "Why didn't you tell me you were coming?"

He frowned. "Didn't Sita reach you?"

"Yes, but about tomorrow."

"Five thirty's okay? You can get home that early? If not, it's fine, I can start without you. Unless, I mean, you don't want me in the house when you're not there."

"Start what?"

He stared at her. "You said you wanted to put the house on the market. I figured you'd want me to get my things out of there."

"Oh. Right." What else could she say? Nothing, not yet. The strangeness of it swept over her, the two of them standing there, so formally, everyone in cocktail attire and the bright daylight still streaming through the massive skylights.

Important museum openings operate on a backward principle: The earlier you get there, the greater your social clout. Trustees and the most generous donors might arrive as early as four thirty or five for a special viewing and sometimes even a ceremonial board meeting. At six, the doors open to donors the next level or two down, and an hour later comes another surge. By then the caviar will have disappeared and the earliest arrivals will be thinking of moving on to the private dinner held somewhere else with an important artist or two thrown in. At any rate, the VIPs are long gone by the time the sushi, raw oyster, and lobster quesadilla food stations are cleared from the floor so that the DJ can set up and the last stage of the evening, the "young art lovers" party, can begin.

"I didn't know I was coming," Jamie said. "I mean tonight. I flew out with Les. On his plane. He sprung it on me. I was just supposed to take a normal flight. I didn't think I'd be here until midnight or so."

"He has his own plane?"

"Well, the corporate jet."

Lynn knew full well that most architects do not have corporate jets. If they did, Philippa would have been thrilled about Jamie going into architecture. "So he's here, too?" she said.

"Somewhere. Er, just so you know," said Jamie, "his daughter decided to come, too. At the last minute. I really did think I was going to be flying commercial."

"It's fine, Jamie. You look good," she added.

"So do you."

Lynn lifted the narrow champagne glass to her lips to take a tiny sip, but didn't, and lowered it again. "Are you liking work?"

"I am—much more. Actually, I want to talk to you about that. I—"

"There you are!"

Lynn recognized Barbara Hatchett right away—the shoulder-length waves, pale skin and dark lips from the newspaper photographs, even her slouch of privileged elegance. She was clearly going for a 1940s starlet look and had on baggy, pleated trousers and a white silk blouse à la Katharine Hepburn. Her eyes moved from Jamie to Lynn, and then she turned to Lynn, lips stretched in a smile. "It's Lynn, right? I'd recognize you anywhere from Jamie's descriptions."

"This is Barb Hatchett," said Jamie. "The daughter of my boss in New York."

"Oh, Jamie," said Barb, "aren't you funny."

"It's so nice to finally meet you," Lynn said.

"Oh, you, too." She eyed Lynn up and down and seemed to derive some satisfaction from what she saw. "Ooh, is that champagne?" she said, turning to Jamie. "Yummy, did you get one for me?"

"Here," said Lynn, holding out the champagne glass from which she had yet to drink. "I think this one's yours."

Barb looked startled, but, evidently deciding to make the

most of the moment, she took the champagne. "Thanks so much for holding it for me, Lynn. I guess it's fitting. Did Jamie tell you? That we have reason to celebrate? And you, too, Lynn, because you work here, right?" She turned back to Jamie. "Daddy's going to do it!"

Jamie's eyes met Lynn's, and they seemed to be desperately trying to tell her that he had nothing to do with this.

"I don't know if you're senior enough to have heard, but there's going to be an announcement," Barb said to Lynn. "It's been a big secret but now it's official. My father has agreed to do the redesign!"

"He has?" said Jamie.

"Redesign?" said Lynn. Although the non-original sections of the museum had been added fifteen years ago, Lynn, like anyone who had grown up in the city, still thought of them as new.

"Isn't that exciting? It seems you guys here did such a great job at fund-raising that there's a movement to pull the whole thing together a little better, make the museum more cohesive, I guess. Not such a muddle. Of course, you know how that goes. Usually when you try to do a remodel you're better off pulling the whole thing down and starting from scratch. Especially when you have a visionary like Daddy involved."

Jamie turned to Lynn. "I didn't know."

"Of course you did, silly," said Barb.

"I mean," he said, "I knew we were in talks, that's why I'm out here, but . . ."

"Congratulations," said Lynn.

The architect's daughter parted her matte red lips and showed the tips of her perfect teeth. Lynn half expected a snake tongue to dart out. She sensed Jamie trying to catch her eye but ignored him. "So nice to meet you," she said, "but now, if the two of you will excuse me, I have some things I really should see to." She gave an apologetic grimace, one she knew Jamie would see right through. "I'm afraid this is work for me."

Lynn still had the idea of disappearing upstairs for a breather, but Earl Smithson flagged her down. He was with Richard Plante, Mona Frumpke, and another man who looked familiar. "Ah, Lynn," Earl said, "Richard was just asking after you. And you know Les Hatchett?"

"Only by reputation." She managed a gracious and admiring smile. "Congratulations, by the way. I understand we'll be seeing a lot of you here. Or perhaps we're the ones who should be congratulated."

Earl eyed Lynn assessingly—respectfully, even. "Can't keep our brightest in the dark, can we?" Lynn could tell he was wondering where she got her information. "Lynn is one of ours," he explained to the architect. Lynn realized that Earl hadn't mentioned her last name. He tended to drop the "Miss Prosper" thing in what he considered grown-up company. "We were just telling Les of your department's windfall thanks to Richard here."

"Aw," said the billionaire to the multimillionaire, "Earl's just trying to get us into a pissing contest, so you'll pony up, too. Maybe do the new wing pro bono." Les Hatchett's eyebrows shot up. "Seriously," said Richard, "I've been wanting to do something like this for a long time. People just don't understand how important art is in making the world a better place. And Earl was telling me what a big percentage of the museum's paintings are in storage. Now that just seems like a crime to me."

"Indeed."

"You and I need to get together to figure something out," Richard said to Les Hatchett. "Lynn's been really helpful. We should have her in on the discussions, too."

"Oh, Lynn's a wonder," Mona agreed, eyeing her. She hadn't changed her hair. It was still raven-hued.

An elderly woman swept up to the group, a longtime trustee whose mother, the only child of one of the old Hollywood studio heads, had been one of the museum's founders. "Mona," she exclaimed in a quavering voice, then did a double take. "And dear Lynn. Just the person I was hoping to find."

Earl murmured something to the architect, who had absolutely turned away from Richard at his mention of collaboration, and the two drifted a few feet from the rest.

"Doris darling," said Mona, "first I'd like you to meet one of our newer patrons, Richard Plante."

The grande dame squinted at him, as if through a monocle. "Ah, Mr. Plante, a pleasure. An absolute pleasure. Yes, we've heard all about you and your interest in our little museum." She had taken his hand and was clasping it warmly in her own crepey, spotted one, whose thick blue veins seemed to do the job of bones. It was a regal hand, though, and heavy with a number of the largest diamond rings Lynn had ever seen. Doris Shoemaker nodded at Richard Plante like a Mandarin, her thin, flat hair looped and coiled about her head, and Lynn realized that she was witnessing a carefully orchestrated scene, one going exactly according to plan. Richard Plante was looking upon the older woman with eyes filled with awe. "I was just saying to dear Smitty, we've got to figure out how to get the young people as concerned about the future of art as we are. We old fuddy-duddies aren't going to be the ones to take the museum into the twenty-first century."

It was Mona's turn to draw Lynn smoothly back. Richard gave no sign of noticing any of the departures.

"Can I get you a drink, Mona?" Lynn offered. Mona just patted her on the shoulder and sailed away. Lynn had done her job, had played her role well in this intricate dance. She had linked hands with rich Richard Plante, guiding him through the steps to land him in place for his next partner to take over. What did it matter that she hadn't known that this, specifically, was her task? What did it matter that the whole thing suddenly made her sick? She had reaped too much benefit lately to call herself innocent.

Lynn had come to rest on the edges of the atrium, under a red neon exit sign next to the corridor leading to the men's restroom. The skylights were dark, it was finally night, but the space remained bright—the sharp, bright white of modern architecture—and was now crowded enough so that you didn't really distinguish individuals, just a mass of people.

Then the crowd parted. Lynn straightened as she saw Jamie coming toward her, once more with two champagne glasses in his hands.

"I think I owe you this," he said, holding one out.

Lynn took it, this time without hesitation. "Thank you. I can use it."

"Tired?"

The corners of her mouth lifted.

"I really am sorry," he said.

"For what?"

This seemed to disconcert him.

"She seems nice," Lynn said.

"Look, Lynn—"

"It's fine, Jamie, I don't care."

"Is F. X. here?"

"How would I know?"

"Honestly, Lynn, I don't want to fight."

"Neither do I." A frustrated jerk of her hand sent champagne sloshing from the narrow glass. "I don't know why we do keep fighting."

He had settled alongside her against the curved wall. Neither said anything for a moment. It felt comfortable to be standing there next to him. But there was also the sense that they didn't have much time. If only there were something Lynn could tell him right then. It was as if he were waiting, waiting once again for her to say something.

It's true what they say, that sneaky behavior draws the eye. A flushed Glynnis stepped from the shadows of the corridor at Lynn's right and looked warily right and left before moving off into the throng, her usually smooth ponytail ratted in the back. Instinctively Lynn glanced Jamie's way, which had the effect of alerting him. So they were both watching when, a moment later, F. X. strolled from the same corridor with far more nonchalance but tugging his jacket into place, tucking his shirt more securely in. Perhaps he felt their eyes on him. He turned his head. Lynn quickly looked away, but he saw this and waved. Her terse shake of the head only elicited a wide grin. When Lynn glanced at Jamie she saw that not only had he taken in the whole thing, he looked amused.

"There you are, Lynnie," F. X. said. "I've been looking all over for you." He glanced at Jamie, who looked right back, smiling pleasantly. "Might as well make it official," F. X. said. "Considering." He stuck out his hand. "F. X. Donahue, pleased to meet you." Jamie nodded as the two men shook hands. "Hey, you haven't seen Chaka here tonight, have you?" F. X. asked Lynn, with a hint of agitation that struck her as either masterful misdirection or . . . she didn't know what. "Lynn knows this, but most people don't realize," he said to Jamie, "I have terrible luck with women. That's probably why I never got anywhere with your wife."

Jamie raised a polite eyebrow. "You don't say?"

"Nah, come on, none of it meant anything. Lynn here is pure as the driven snow, you should know that."

"F. X.!" Lynn said.

"You won't believe this, Jamie, but when your wife first met me, way back in college, I was pretty studly. Hah. You wouldn't know it now." His tone was suddenly bitter. "First, my son's mother dumps me, now this Brazilian guttersnipe—and believe me, she really is one. All the best to Richard when he finds out. Although that guy's either dumber or cannier than he seems. Tell your husband, Lynn, I'm not usually like this. But Lynn's been a huge help, with my son, with everything."

"Really?" said Jamie. "How so?"

For the first time F. X. looked caught out. "Well, she hasn't done anything—yet. But she's been great moral support. To be honest, I think she was worried you'd mind."

"Really?" said Jamie. "Still?" He was looking at Lynn. "I really must have been a jerk."

"Aren't we all, man?" said F. X., shaking his head. "Aren't we all." He slipped in between them and flung an arm around each. "You two! I'm glad this is all out in the open. You really are great kids."

"Lynn?"

Lynn looked up and there was Peter Fairhaven. Hurriedly, she disentangled herself. "Peter. Hi." She glanced back at Jamie and F. X. They were watching attentively. "Peter, I'd like you to meet some friends of mine. I mean, my husband—ex-husband. Jamie."

"Not quite ex yet," Jamie said amiably. "It takes six months. But I guess Lynn can't wait."

"Peter Fairhaven," Peter said, advancing, hand outstretched.

"Not the director?" said F. X. "F. X. Donahue. Big fan." He shook Peter's hand vigorously.

"Thank you," said Peter, taken aback.

"I know, they're chick flicks, right? But you gotta watch 'em. To see how the ladies think."

"Exactly," said Jamie. "I used to read Lynn's ladies' magazines for just that reason."

"No you didn't," said Lynn.

"How would you know?" said Jamie.

"We lived together!"

"Maybe I sneaked them. I would have done anything to figure you out."

In fact, F. X. had once told Lynn that *he* used to read women's magazines for that reason, and Lynn had passed this along to Jamie in one of her early attempts to explain just how ridiculous and harmless F. X. was.

F. X. was grinning when Peter turned to him, brow furrowed. "Did you say your name was F. X.?"

"Francis Xavier!" he said cheerfully.

"No, I mean . . ." The director looked at Lynn. "Didn't Jessica say . . ."

"Jessica Klein?" said F. X. He nudged Jamie. "*Artiste. Muy caliente!*" To Lynn's utter surprise, Jamie laughed. It was as if the two men were ranged against her and Peter, and Jamie was enjoying it. "Oops," said F. X. to Peter, "you're not seeing her or anything, are you?"

"No. I . . ." Again, he glanced Lynn's way.

Enlightenment dawned in F. X.'s gray eyes. "Oh, you must be the guy Lynn was flirting with on the phone the other day."

In a million years, Lynn would never have thought she'd be so glad to see the Jacquemet-Scovilles bearing down on them.

"Look!" said Bruce Scoville. "I told you she'd be here. Right? Lynn works here! Hey, Jamie." He wound down to a confused stop. "You here, too?"

"Look at you two," said Kerry Scoville. "You two are amazing."

"I didn't know you guys were coming," said Lynn. "What a nice surprise. Did Jamie mention it to you?" She surveyed the foursome: Bruce with his hands on his hips like the Pillsbury doughboy, snake-hipped George Jacquemet with a smirk on his lips, the two women looking as if they wanted to start whispering to each other.

"I kept thinking about what you said at the shower," said Bruce. "About art? I thought maybe I'd been too hasty, we should come down and see for ourselves. So we joined the museum and here we are!"

To the tune of twenty-five hundred dollars if you're here this early, Lynn thought, with a surreptitious glance at her watch. "I'm so glad. And how's the baby?" she said to Kerry, who looked as trim as ever.

"Hey, Jamie," said George, "sorry Tahoe didn't work out. We should try again."

"Seriously," said Kerry, "you guys are so civilized, you should be, like, role models for divorce."

"Don't get any ideas, wife!" said Bruce, and everyone—the foursome, that is—cracked up. When the hilarity died down, there was nothing for it but to introduce everyone. The Jacquemet-Scovilles didn't seem to register Peter Fairhaven's name, but Libbet was definitely eyeing F. X. appraisingly, looking from him to Lynn, to whom he was standing quite close.

"Do you work here, too?" she asked him.

"Me? No, I'm just an old buddy of Lynn's from college. My boss brought me tonight. In fact, he's over there, and I think it's me he's looking around for. I better run. Life as a flunky." Everyone smiled. F. X. started to move off. But when George Jacquemet leaned in toward Jamie and said, "I think

I saw a little friend of *yours* over there," F. X. turned back, locked eyes with Jamie, and said, "Hey, thanks for putting up with me. Now that we've met, I'm sure you'll forgive that one little kiss with your wife. Just the pressure I've been under. Not that Lynn"—he gave her an appraising and frankly lascivious look—"doesn't look amazing." He gave Lynn a quick squeeze on the shoulder, cocked a finger at Peter, and said, "Lucky man, love your films," and walked away.

"Old friend?" said Libbet. "Sounds like!"

Jamie, to Lynn's bafflement, continued to look amused. He leaned forward and kissed Lynn on the cheek. "I probably need to find my boss, too. I'll see you tomorrow."

"Um, will Barb be coming?"

Jamie drew back, as if disappointed in her. "No, why?" He nodded to Peter and the rest and was gone.

Libbet turned to Peter, as if noticing him for the first time. "Films?"

Twenty-one

The next morning, the morning of the day on which Jamie would be coming to pack up his things, Lynn sat on the edge of the toilet in the bathroom of the house they wouldn't be living in together anymore. She extended a weary finger and pushed the unused pregnancy test she'd just opened into the trash can. She reached for the brown paper bag with its two more tests and tossed that in the trash, too. Then she leaned forward to reach into the cabinet under the sink for the box of tampons.

She kept her head down at work that day, letting messages pile up—but none from Jamie. She hadn't seen him again at the party—she'd left shortly after, herself—but she would have thought he'd call. Peter had called. A message from him was on her desk when she got in, like in the old days when men sent bouquets or their calling cards after a ball to show their interest. Or just to be polite. Lynn could imagine herself accusing Jamie, "You didn't call!" To which he'd respond, the small crease between his eyes pointing out how unreasonable, how demanding she was being, "But I knew I'd be seeing you this afternoon."

Lynn also hadn't been looking forward to facing Glynnis that morning, and sure enough she came into the office with a bright-eyed, expectant look. "Your friend F. X. is fun," she said.

"He's really bad news," Lynn said. "As far as going out with, I mean."

Glynnis laughed. "What do you think, I was born yesterday?"

Lynn was home in plenty of time for Jamie's arrival. Too early, in fact. She went from room to room, opening closets—pulling out a suitcase here, a garment bag there. What an idiot she'd been. She even traipsed out to the garage (leaving the door open in case Jamie came when she was back there—although why she was always thinking and worrying about him was beyond her). She found two more suitcases out there, as well as some old, flattened boxes she'd forgotten they'd saved. Back and forth she went, with as many boxes as she could carry at once. She was soon hot and sweaty and dusty, breathing hard as she dropped another cobwebby load on the living room floor. But who cared how she looked? What did it matter? And even if it had been true, what heights of brilliance: to think an unplanned child was just the thing to save a troubled marriage. Lynn kicked one of the dirty old suitcases out of her way and it skittered across the floor, knocking into the stack of equally dusty boxes, which toppled and made a mess across the rug— the quite good Oriental rug, an old one given to them by Philippa.

Practically everything of value in the room, including the old mahogany dining table and eight chairs, came from Jamie's mother, from the seemingly endless series of third-story attics in the St. Louis house. Lynn remembered the first time she'd walked and sometimes practically crawled through those rooms behind Philippa. Her heart had grown grasping little fingers at the sight of all those dust-covered treasures that were not hers. Old trunks. Spindly pie-crust tables, a wingback chair with a spring popping out, a whole room of old silver.

Lynn's family had never owned even one Oriental rug, and here were dozens, rolled up and dusty, stored away for being too threadbare or simply not as good as others.

"Take what you like," Philippa had said. "Jamie's the oldest."

"What about Julie?" Lynn had asked.

"The oldest boy, I mean. Anyway, with Piers's family, Julie will hardly need any of these old things." Philippa had flicked her hand dismissively. Minutes later, though, she stood in the middle of the largest attic room, turning slowly to survey all that lay there. "When you look upon this," she'd said, "you can see who the Prospers have been."

"What are you doing?" Jamie asked. He was standing just inside the front door. "Sorry," he said, "the door was open."

"It's your house, too." Briskly, Lynn brushed her dusty hands off against each other, then on her pants.

Jamie took a step into the room. "Oh," he said, "boxes." Clearly, it hadn't occurred to him to bring any himself. Of course not. "So, we're going to do this?" he said.

"Guess so."

He just stood there, looking around.

"Most of the furniture's yours," she said. "Your family's."

"We should just split everything."

"No!"

Jamie looked up.

"Pretty much the only thing we bought together is the sofa," Lynn said, in better control. They both looked at it, long and inviting in front of the window.

"You should have it," said Jamie.

"You don't want it?"

"I just don't know where I'd . . ."

It was of course a trick question—their first piece of furniture together, so many happy hours. But why torment him now? "What are you going to do?" she asked. "Have everything shipped back to St. Louis? Since you're in a hotel."

"Uh . . . I guess."

"If you set up the movers and everything, I can be here for them. You don't need to come back for that. Unless, of course, your mother doesn't trust me."

"Lynn," Jamie said.

"That reminds me." She turned on her heel and marched, without looking back, down the hallway to the second bedroom. She grabbed up the little clock from the desk—the inexpensive laminate table. He probably wouldn't want that, either. When she turned around, Jamie was right there behind her. She thrust the clock at him. This time, their fingers did touch. "Here," she said, stopping herself from jumping back—or brushing up against him like a cat. "I don't know why you thought I wanted it."

"Well, you took it from my office."

"Only because you moved it there from here."

"No I didn't."

"Then what happened to this one?"

"I don't know. You must have moved it."

"I didn't!" There they went again. But when had the little clock disappeared? Before Jamie went to New York? Lynn couldn't remember. All she knew was that she'd been angry because she'd assumed he'd moved it even before she found out he wanted a divorce. Thought she'd found out. At any rate, the missing clock had been one of the factors that seemed, at the time, to add up.

"It doesn't matter," Jamie said. "It'll turn up somewhere."

"Like your mother's earrings? I told you, I didn't take any of it. Oh, it's pointless."

"Lynn," he said as she flounced away from him. "Lynn." He followed her back out to the living room. "I believe you."

"About what?"

"I don't know. I don't know anything anymore. Don't you want to talk about it?"

She gave a laugh.

"Look," he said, "I apologize. I believe you, that you didn't sleep with F. X."

"*Now* you believe me? What made you change your mind?"

His mouth twitched, and she had the sudden vision of herself backed into a corner at the museum party by Jamie, F. X., and Peter Fairhaven. Her mouth twitched, too. She could tell, Jamie had seen it all—what it had been like for her with F. X. "That's what made me so mad," she said, trying to hang on to her righteous anger. "That you didn't believe me. You should have known me better than that."

He pushed at one of the dusty cardboard boxes with his foot. "Do we really have to do this now?"

"When else are we going to do it?"

"I don't know."

Never! "We need to do it," she said. "We're going to have to be showing the house."

"Already?"

Lynn felt a spike of annoyance. "Robin has people coming every day next week. It could sell very quickly."

"Really? Do you think we'll get much over asking?" Now the eagerness in his voice made Lynn turn away. "Where will you live?" he asked.

"I think I found an apartment I like."

"Already? I didn't know you were looking."

She shrugged. The obvious answer was that there was a lot he didn't know.

"Can I see it?"

"I haven't definitely taken it. I've only seen it once."

"Why don't we go look at it?"

"What are you doing, Jamie?" If he thought they'd made a mistake, why didn't he just say so? Was it because of Peter now?

He nudged the box again, pushing it away. The room really looked a mess—dust, disarray—and they hadn't even started packing yet. Somehow everything already looked used up, abandoned. "I just don't want to do this right this minute," he said. "Do you?"

In the car on the way to the apartment, Lynn kept thinking about telling Jamie how she'd thought she was pregnant. Even though it turned out she wasn't, it felt strange that he didn't know. She wondered what he'd say. She'd get an honest reaction, probably, since she wasn't pregnant after all: an expression of horror, then relief. But she had to stop thinking of these things as signs. Whether she was pregnant or not, what reaction he had or didn't, these weren't hints the cosmos were trying to throw out for her.

"You're so quiet," Jamie said, glancing sideways to look at her. They'd taken his car, the green Audi, which was how he'd gotten to the house. Part of her wanted to ask him about the logistics of *that*—had it been waiting at the airport all this time, in long-term parking perhaps, and how much had that cost? Or had he arranged for someone to pick it up from the airport, where he'd left it when he fled? And kept it where? In his office parking structure? Is that something Ruthie would have arranged for him? And why didn't Lynn just ask? That's what she'd normally do, wanting to get it all straight in her head.

Jamie seemed different, too. Happier. More carefree. Lynn realized how long it had been since she'd seen him like this. Maybe that was why she'd agreed to go with him.

"Can I just ask you one more question?" he said.

"Sure," she said, thinking he meant about the apartment.

"When I came back to the house, where were you?"

"What? When?"

"After I found you with F. X."

He hadn't *found* her with F. X. "Wait," she said, "what are you talking about? When did you come back? You didn't. Did you? Was I asleep?"

"Evidently not—not there at least."

It was then that Lynn remembered the aborted drive to her mother's. "You came back?"

"I drove around and then I parked one block over for half an hour. Remember," he said, "how on the phone afterward I begged you to let me know if you had anything else to tell me?"

"I drove to my mother's. I was upset, too, you know."

"So if I call your mother . . ."

Lynn couldn't believe this. "You *don't* believe me! Why do you say you believe me when you don't?"

"I don't know what you want from me, Lynn. Anyone would have thought the same thing in that position. Don't I at least get points for not asking about that kiss F. X. mentioned? I thought *that* was pretty good of me." He was clearly trying to lighten the mood.

"That was completely innocent. F. X. was doing that on purpose."

"So you did kiss? Kidding!" he said, seeing her face.

"Pull in here," she said. "Here's the building."

Robin had been thrilled that Lynn was looking at the apartment again. She'd apologized for not being able to meet her there, but no problem, the key would be with the doorman. And she was delighted to inform Lynn that the owner had dropped the rent once more. "It's a sign," Robin said. "You're meant to have it. I'm glad you ignored me about snapping it up earlier."

The double doors shook as Lynn struggled with the key. The doors felt so flimsy, as if Lynn could put a foot through and kick her way in. This made her worry about what lay behind them. Was it much worse than she remembered? Would Sasha's good friend let her make a mistake like that? Finally she got the door open and was fiddling to get the key back out of the lock. Jamie stepped around her. She followed him to the middle of the living room, which was bigger than she remembered. And the view really was remarkable.

"I don't know why we're doing this," she said.

"This is really nice."

"It's a little tacky."

"No, I like it. It's so different from the house, it's . . . liberating. I can see why you didn't want all that furniture—it's great empty like this." He turned back to her. "It would have been weird not to be able to imagine where you were living."

"What's your hotel like?" she asked.

His face became alert in a way that made her skin tingle. "I'm not exactly staying in a hotel anymore," he said. "Don't be mad. You see, Barb—"

"You're living with her!"

"What? No! It's just her old apartment—it's furnished, one of Les's buildings. It ends up costing a lot less than the hotel, and he's the one paying—"

"Where's *she* living?"

"She moved to the penthouse. She's incredibly spoiled. She's only twenty-two."

The idea of Barb Hatchett's youth did not make Lynn feel better.

"But that's not what I wanted to tell you—it's connected, but . . ."

But what? Could it get any worse? Just spit it out, she wanted to say.

"I quit the law firm."

This was not what Lynn was expecting.

"Les offered me a job—again. This time I accepted."

"In New York?"

"With his architecture firm."

"As his in-house lawyer?"

"Not exactly—although I'll be looking over some of that stuff, too. It's a huge pay cut," he said quickly.

She stared at him for what felt like a long time. "Why? Why didn't you just tell me if you wanted to stop being a lawyer? You know it would have been fine with me. I would have been thrilled."

His chin went up at this.

"Why couldn't you do it before?" she cried. "When we were together?"

"I don't know." He was just standing there, arms down by his sides, and there was a tough, stubborn set to his jaw, although he lowered his head again. "I just couldn't, I guess. I felt responsible."

"Responsible? I begged you to quit!"

"I thought maybe," he said, "you'd be glad for me. That I finally got up the nerve."

Lynn stared at him, her mouth working. He sighed deeply and turned away, as if to give her a moment alone. He took a few steps toward the hallway, toward the rest of the apartment.

"Don't go there!"

He turned back, surprised.

Lynn's lashes were wet, to her fury. She never ever wanted him to see that little utility room. "Let's go," she said.

"Can't I see?"

"No. I really want to go now. I have to get back. We have a lot to do."

"Are you mad?"

"Jamie," she said, "I want to leave. Now."

It was hard to believe, hard to fathom how the two of them had gotten to this point, yet the reality of their current situation was undeniable. All along, she'd been reading his tone, trying to interpret, second-guess, but none of that really mattered, did it? What mattered was where they'd ended up.

She took one last look at the city lights. That night on Mulholland, Jamie hadn't said "I love you" until she'd pushed him to. What would have happened if she hadn't?

Back in the car, as Jamie was concentrating on making a left turn out of the building's circular driveway into traffic, Lynn said, "It was pretty convenient for you, then."

"What do you mean?" He tried to glance at her but had to keep his eyes on the road.

"F. X. that night. Our fight. Funny how it allowed you to make exactly the decisions you obviously wanted to make. Without having to consult or consider me."

"You're right," he said at last. "It did. It made it easier."

"What exactly is it that you want from me now?" She knew, she just knew that he wouldn't say, *Nothing.*

"You seem sad," he said. "What are you thinking?"

"I *am* sad." As if at the suggestion, her eyes swam again. Jamie turned his head to try to see her face, and she saw that his eyes were moist, too. That somehow made things crystal clear. "You know," she said, "I never used to believe what people said, about timing being important."

"Oh, Lynn."

"You don't really want to go back, do you?"

"To the house?" His voice cracked.

"To the way things were before."

It was a moment before he answered. "No," he said. "I guess I don't. But can't we . . ."

"Jamie, look. It's fine."

"This isn't what I wanted."

"Obviously, there were a lot of things wrong."

He turned his head. "Did *you* think so?"

"We couldn't even have a conversation without it turning into a fight."

She was glad they were driving. He had to keep focusing back on the road. There was something soothing about being in a car, too. *I don't know where we go from here.* Lynn remembered how angrily Jamie had said those words. Now, they merely seemed prophetic. But that's how things happened sometimes. "Would you mind," she said, "when we get back— if you just got your clothes from the house today. I don't think I can . . ."

"Of course," he said, "if that's what you want. Yes, of course."

"You don't have to worry," she said. "I'll take care of everything else. Or if you want to do it yourself, maybe I could be out when you come—you could come tomorrow if you want, if you're still here. Or I think I might just get in my car and go to my mom's for a bit, and then you could take your time now, getting what you need."

"Whatever you want," said Jamie. "I can do whatever you want."

Except, of course, coming back to L.A. and erasing everything that had happened. But no, Lynn couldn't honestly say she thought that would be a good idea, or that she even wanted it anymore.

Twenty-two

No one said to Lynn, "In the meeting with Richard Plante, make sure to micromanage the billionaire a bit." Oh, and throw in a tantalizing reference or two to the New Millennium Campaign (as they were calling the upcoming push for a huge new endowment that would also be funding the remodel). But that was exactly, instinctively, what Lynn did—drawing a hidden smile from Glynnis when she prefaced yet another series of specifics by saying, "These are small details, Richard, but I know you said you wanted to be hands-on."

They were in one of the smaller boardrooms, arranged around the table informally, with Richard Plante at the head and Lynn and Earl Smithson on either side of him. Glynnis had surrounded herself with an array of folders and papers as if to explain her distancing of herself by an empty seat. To Lynn's relief—more for Glynnis's sake than her own, although her officemate hadn't said another word about him—F. X. was not at the meeting.

"Great, great," said Richard, "it all sounds great. Just what I had in mind." But he pushed himself up from the table and began pacing back and forth. He was wearing another of his baggy linen suits, this one oatmeal colored and coarse, like jute. He shoved his hands into his pockets, gravely distorting the shape of the trousers, and took a defiant stance over the museum director, who looked up at him mildly. "About this New Millennium endowment," Richard said.

Because the billionaire was looking directly at him, Earl Smithson did not let the light of triumph flash in his eyes; Glynnis lowered her head over her papers, as if searching for something important.

After walking Richard Plante out with her boss—Earl had silently made it clear that she was to accompany them, that a retinue was in order—Lynn made her way back to her office. Only then, through the glass wall, did she notice the change: a stark Josef Albers work on paper, squares superimposed on each other, red, black, and white, where the verdant Corot had hung for so long.

Glynnis had gotten back to the office first. "Oh, you," she said without looking up. "You just got a call from Peter Fairhaven."

Lynn made a noncommittal sound and dropped her papers on her desk.

Glynnis spun her chair around to face Lynn. "So, is he going to be another of your donors? Really, Lynn, you should just move to development and be done with it. The pay's better there."

Lynn smiled weakly, again about to turn back to her desk.

"How do you know Peter Fairhaven, anyway?"

Glynnis rarely initiated conversation, as if it were beneath her. But here she was, waiting, a sharp, defensive look on her face. She wasn't really pretty but there was something compelling about her. She had strong features—a long, square face, wide mouth, straight nose with flared nostrils that looked like

Picasso had drawn it. She was tall, too, about five foot nine, and that day she was wearing wide-legged flannel trousers. She sat cross-legged like a man, the open triangle of ankle on knee, waiting for Lynn's answer. Everything about her demeanor looked aggressive, but Lynn sensed that now, now was the time to tell her some small thing. "I was seated next to him at a dinner party," she said. "The whole time I didn't know who he was. I kept asking questions like, 'So, how are you enjoying Los Angeles?' I thought he was just some English guy visiting."

Glynnis sat there, her gaze impenetrable. Lynn's first thought was that she was simply going to turn back around, back to her desk. She felt a funny catch in her throat.

Glynnis's laughter rang out. "Oh, Lynn, Lynn. I can just see it—so earnest and curious and sweet. That's your trick with all these men."

"Some trick," Lynn said, forcing a smile, "getting divorced."

"Being married and divorced is much more attractive to men than just being single. It really is unfair. And Earl said I should be nice to *you*."

"He did?"

"Haven't you noticed how nice I've been? He's devastated, Earl is, like he's lost a son. He said Jamie was by far the best of the spouses."

"He said that to you?"

"We have lunch together every now and then."

"Wow. I've only had lunch with him once." As reward for Richard Plante's check.

"Yeah, but you've never slept with him. Oh, close your mouth, Little Miss Wide-Eyes, it was ages ago, when I first started here. I put an end to it when I realized it wasn't going to help my career at all, but we're still friends about it." Glynnis was watching for Lynn's reaction.

"Did you know his father was a dentist?" Lynn said.

"Yep, Earl had this love-hate relationship with him. How'd *you* know? Jamie?"

She nodded.

"So," said Glynnis, "what happened with Jamie? At the party."

"Oh, he came over the next day." She felt compelled to add, "I knew he was coming into town, he just got in early. I wasn't expecting him at the party."

"He came early to surprise you?"

The eagerness in her voice bothered Lynn. "Glynnis," she said, "he was coming to go through his stuff."

"Oh. Then you guys are really going through with it?"

Lynn just looked at her.

Glynnis shrugged. "I just thought, maybe now that he could be back here, with the remodel and all. Isn't he going to be working on that?"

"I really don't know."

"Maybe F. X. could say something to Richard Plante, and . . ." She trailed off when she saw Lynn's expression. "I know it can't be fun," she said, "me always overhearing stuff. It's not your fault you have to share an office."

"I'm glad we do. But I really do think things are final with Jamie."

Glynnis gave a curt nod. "So, do you mind if I ask? What's the deal with Peter Fairhaven? He sounded very keen. Very interested."

"You talked to him?" Lynn remembered the receptionist sticking her head down the hallway to call, "Your mother's on the phone," and imagined her doing the same for a Hollywood director whose call she might have assumed Lynn would want to take.

"Does he know how recent the split is?"

Lynn realized that what she was hearing in Glynnis's voice was disapproval. "Actually," she said, "he's friends with Jamie's sister's husband from school in England."

"Oh. So you're *not* going out with him?"

"No. Why?"

"No reason. It's none of my business. It just seemed . . . I mean, it's pretty soon, isn't it?"

"Do you know," said Lynn, "you are the last person I would have expected to say that. I would have thought you'd have the opposite advice: 'Get out there.' 'What's good for the goose . . .'"

"You should call Peter Fairhaven back, then." It was a challenge.

"I'm going to."

"Good."

They sat there, knees almost touching in their rolling office chairs, as if at an impasse. Suddenly Glynnis thrust herself to her feet, her chair rolling back to hit her desk. "Or perhaps you want some privacy!"

Lynn realized that Glynnis had been waiting for her to pick up the phone right then. "No," she said, starting up herself, "that's not . . ."

"No, be my guest!" And she strode from the room.

Lynn sank back into her chair, pulled herself in to her desk. She moved around the little pink message slips until she found one with Peter's phone number. Just as she was reaching for the phone, it rang.

"Hullo, Lynn?" The mild British accent.

"Peter. I was just going to call you."

"Were you?"

They were both silent, then the director cleared his throat. "Were you, um, going to call for any particular reason?"

Lynn smiled on her end. "Well, it's rude not to return phone calls."

"I never thought you were being rude," he said in a low voice. When she didn't respond to this either, he said, "This is just a polite call, then?"

"What else would it be?"

"I was always taught that politeness at its best boils down to simple kindness."

"I agree," said Lynn, thinking of Philippa, who imagined herself the last word in manners.

"Well, then," said Peter, "it would be terribly impolite of you not to agree to have dinner with me."

It took Lynn a moment to untangle his meaning. Oh God, she thought. Then: Why not? Wasn't that why she'd been about to call him? What did it matter anymore, anyway?

"Lynn?"

"Yes?"

"Might I have the privilege? Of taking you to dinner? Is next week too early?"

"You overestimate my popularity."

"What? Oh."

She was amused and not displeased to hear Peter Fairhaven's discombobulation.

"Are you saying you're available sooner? Tonight, perhaps?"

"Not tonight!" Jamie was still in town. Lynn knew he wasn't leaving until tomorrow morning. Not that she was going to see him again. "You're not free tomorrow night, are you?"

"Saturday? I'll cancel any and all plans for you."

"Oh, don't do that."

"Just kidding," he said. "I wouldn't."

Lynn didn't mind that, though; it seemed to even things

out. After she hung up with Peter she sat for a minute, staring at the phone. Why not just get everything over with? She picked up the handset again and dialed Robin's office number. Robin wasn't in—Lynn hadn't really expected her to be—but she left a voice mail saying that she would definitely take the apartment and wanted to talk further about getting the house officially on the market as soon as possible. Then she looked around the office, trying to think of all the things she needed to take home with her for the weekend, and got ready to go to her mother's house for a good cry.

Twenty-three

Lynn woke up in her old bed in her old room in the house of her childhood. She did not wonder with a start where she was. She knew exactly. What seemed hard to grasp was that she had ever lived anywhere else. She let herself hang half off the bed, as though that were part of the waking process, staring down at the apple-green carpeting. It was plush wall-to-wall carpeting and ran all through the house, upstairs and downstairs, even in the master bathroom, which had seemed the height of luxury to Lynn growing up. Several years earlier, when the carpeting was finally worn beyond reach of even one more cleaning, Lynn and her sisters had begged their mother to look into whether, as they suspected, there were hardwood floors underneath, but Ella said she couldn't be bothered with refinishing and all that mess. She'd replaced the carpeting with the same cheerful green.

Now, though, Lynn was glad. She had come to be comforted and had ended up staying over. She had fallen asleep early, which must have frustrated her mother. They'd barely talked. Lynn had curled up in a big old chair with saggy springs and, finally, had been able to sob and sob to her heart's content. Ella made soup for the two of them for dinner. That is, she'd opened a can of Campbell's Hearty Chicken Noodle, which had actually been perfect, and afterward Lynn had crawled upstairs to her old bedroom.

When she came downstairs, her mother was already at the table in the breakfast nook, reading the morning paper. Everything looked as it always had, the breakfast room and connecting kitchen still papered in the sunny citrus wallpaper that had been there when her parents bought the house. The smallish dining room table and six chairs were only a slightly tight fit. The actual dining room, much larger, had always been her mother's study.

Ella looked up from her morning paper and peered at her daughter over her reading glasses with an encouraging smile. She wasn't dressed yet. Throughout Lynn's childhood her mother had had a series of floral-patterned quilted robes that zipped up the front, which were her customary breakfast attire. "Good morning, darling," she said. "I've been thinking."

Lynn slid into her old seat.

"Are you feeling all right?" Ella's voice was both warm and lecturesome.

"Fine." Lynn drew a section of the paper toward her with one finger.

Her mother put a hand over Lynn's. "I can't help thinking that you and Jamie haven't really resolved anything."

"Resolved? We've resolved to get a divorce. What more can we resolve?" Just like that, she was a sullen teenager again in her mother's house.

"But what are Jamie's thoughts in all this? I still don't have a sense of that."

"You think if you knew, you'd be able to talk him into changing his mind?"

"It's not a matter of changing his mind," Ella said. "It's knowing what's in his mind. Communication is so important in a marriage—"

"Like in your marriage? More important than actually living together?"

"Lynn," her mother said warningly.

"What?" she fired back. "What?"

"Your father and I communicate very well, and you know that. If other people don't have the insight to understand our marriage, well, that is their limitation."

"Obviously I have lots of limitations! Ask Jamie! No wonder he thought being married to me was such a burden."

"He said that?"

"God, why are you tormenting me?"

"Oh, darling," her mother said, "I'm sorry. You know I only want you to be happy. I'm just trying to understand."

"Maybe we only thought it was a good marriage because everything was easy. But the second we ran into problems . . ."

"That's what I mean," Ella said, eager again, as discussion always made her eager. "About sitting down and talking."

"We did talk, Mom. We talked and talked, and the more we talked the more it was clear that this was what Jamie wanted."

"What about what you want?"

"I don't know what I want," Lynn cried out. "Why? Are you saying I should beg Jamie to stay married? Is that what you're saying? *That's* a nice marriage! That I should have ignored all the things he thought about me? Have you actually thought this through, Mom? You think I should have up and moved to New York—quit my job to follow him, where I have no friends, no money, nothing to do all day except follow my man who can't even be bothered to consult me about the decision? Is that what you're saying?"

"You didn't mention that Jamie wanted you to move."

Lynn thrust back her chair in disgust. "Are you honestly saying you would have advised me to do something like that? You of all people?" She stood over her mother, breathing hard.

"No," Ella said at last. "I'm not saying that."

"It's over, Mom. I finally accept that, and if you want to help me, you will, too. In fact," she said, "I'm going out with someone else tonight." Lynn took in her mother's expression with perverse satisfaction. Up until that moment she'd been set on canceling.

"Do you really think you're ready for that?"

"Please. What is this, *Gone With the Wind*, where Scarlett's supposed to wear a black mourning hat for a year? Jamie's out at parties and nightclubs with other women." Lynn turned away as if to storm out through the kitchen. With a sigh Ella rose, too, to take her cup of tea to the sink.

"Mommy?" said Lynn in a different voice altogether. "Can I stay here for a few days? Just until I get the apartment thing figured out?"

Ella enfolded her daughter in her quilted robe. "Whatever you want, darling. Take your time."

I liked that, meeting your mother," Peter Fairhaven said as they walked down the front path toward his car. "Like being a teenager again."

"How old are you, by the way?" asked Lynn.

"Thirty-eight."

"I'm almost thirty."

"Ah yes, a critical piece of information, but I didn't like to come out and ask a woman of your mature years." Grinning, Peter held the car door open for her.

"I asked," she said, trying to get into the car as gracefully as possible—he was standing right over her—"because I don't really know anything about you. I mean aside from the fact that you're a famous movie director."

"Not famous. Not yet. And that's because you didn't bother to know. If you'd wanted to, you could have found out all sorts of things about me. That's what I would have done, Googled you, read everything I could find. But you didn't think you'd be going out with me." He swung the car door shut and made his way around the front of the car to his side. "Did you?" he said, as he got in.

"Maybe this isn't such a good idea after all," Lynn said, her hand back on the door handle. "It's all going too fast."

Peter glanced wryly around him, as if to say, *We haven't gone anywhere, it's only a car, we're not having sex*—and Lynn blushed at the very intimation, or imagined intimation, and because she felt like a baby. "You're making everything so weighted," she said. "You know you are. I thought this would just be, you know, dinner."

"I don't believe you really thought that," he said with an intensity that startled her.

"This is clearly a mistake," she said. "I think I should just go home." She'd been counting so much on his light urbanity.

But now he had a funny half smile on his face and was tilting his head toward her window in a way that made her turn and look, and there just outside the car window was, of course, her mother's house, the reassuring white clapboard with dark green trim rising above them atop a steep front lawn—a surprisingly small lawn, as the lots in this hilly, desirable neighborhood weren't as generous as the houses seemed to merit. When Lynn turned back to him, the tension was somehow gone.

"I like your mum," he said, truly smiling. "She's smart. She's concerned about you."

"You got that from, 'Hello, I'm Ella Kovak, nice to meet you, I'll call Lynn'?"

"Pretty much."

"What can you possibly like when you don't know anything about a person?"

"You're kidding, right?"

"No." Lynn frowned.

"What do you like about anyone? You respond to a person or you don't."

"You just know?"

"Right."

"And you're never wrong?" said Lynn.

"Certainly I'm wrong sometimes. Listen, I'm going to change the subject. I like you. I think I like you. I don't really know you yet, but as you now know, I'm thirty-eight. I have a bit of life experience. I'm feeling very, very confident in my own judgment."

"That's changing the subject? Wait a minute, you just broke off an engagement."

"Yes?"

"Well, your judgment must not have been the best there."

"On the contrary, I'm confident I did the right thing. You saw her."

"That's awful, I hate that sort of thing! You thought enough of her to propose. And now you're mocking her to someone you barely know? Is that your idea of flirting?"

"Sorry. You're right. You're absolutely right. That was terrible of me."

"I mean, you proposed to her to begin with."

"Actually, no."

"She proposed to you?" That was interesting.

"It just sort of happened. She did keep hinting about rings, so I bought one for her. It didn't seem like that big a deal and it made her happy. I was never thinking I'd actually marry her."

"That's even worse!"

"Yes, it was bad, very bad. I'm bad. Hollywood's bad." He caught himself. "Not that I'm trying to pawn off my own bad, careless behavior on the movie industry. You'd scold me for that, too. Look, I don't know how to explain this to you, but you're just very, very different from most of the women I meet."

Lynn rolled her eyes.

"Seriously. That's why I broke off my engagement. Not because I was planning to go after you," he said quickly, seeing her face. "You were married then. That was the whole point. Look, I saw you at that blasted dinner of Mona's, sitting across the table from your husband. I saw how the two of you looked at each other, almost secretly, as if you were trying to spare the rest of us poor mugs the sight of your sheer happiness. I watched you, and I saw this whole life. There it was in front of my eyes, and I wanted it. I looked at you and it was as if everything just went quiet. You were in this bubble. I wanted that."

"But you were obviously wrong about that," Lynn said, unsteadily. "Your questionable judgment again." The little laugh she gave sounded false. "Anyway, you're saying it wasn't me that interested you, but this illusion you had of my marriage."

"Illusion? No, it was you, too. I just thought you were unattainable. So instead I decided to strive for what you had."

Lynn looked down at her hands in her lap.

"You won't believe me," he said, "but I broke it off with Joan that night when we got home. I don't know if I'm saying this in my defense or as a confession, but I was drunk a lot of the time back then. It just seemed . . . easier. But then I decided to stop, and I found myself thinking of you every now and then. And can I tell you, when I did, I'd always smile."

Lynn was suddenly aware that they were still in front of her mother's house. If her mother happened to pass one of the living room windows and glance out, she'd wonder why they hadn't driven away, what they were talking about sitting there in the car, he half-turned in the driver's seat to her, she staring out the windshield.

"And then, when I heard—I'm sorry, but I was happy. I thought, Well, that's it, that's fate."

"Fate!" she said.

"I congratulated myself—that your husband was such a patent idiot, or going through some crisis of his own. Whatever. Who cared? My good fortune. And perhaps now you, you're trying to get revenge or drowning your sorrows or on the rebound. It doesn't matter, I'm happy you're here. I'll take my opportunities as I find them." He faced forward again and turned the key in the ignition. The car, which Lynn had paid little attention to when she got in—a bit boxy, angular, an old Nissan?—roared to life with unexpected vigor. She glanced over and noticed the winged insignia on the steering wheel. Not a Nissan. An Aston Martin. If Jamie saw that, she thought, it would just kill him.

"Shall we move on?" Peter said cheerily.

One thing about Peter, Lynn quickly learned, he didn't mind talking. He relished it, in fact, endlessly, every nuance explored. Almost as soon as their plates were set down in front of them in the little Italian place he'd picked (Lynn had despised herself for the pang of disappointment she'd felt, even though she recognized that the restaurant had been carefully chosen with the opposite intent of impressing), he said, "So, what exactly happened between you and Jamie?"

Lynn made a face.

"Too personal?"

"I thought you said you didn't care, you were just happy it happened."

"I admit I'm curious. Weren't people surprised?"

"Yes."

"Besides, I want to make sure I don't make the same mistake."

She looked across the tiny table at him, and he looked back at her and smiled. And just like that, just when it shouldn't have, the whole tenor of the evening changed. It became lighter, more casual—exactly what Lynn had said she wanted. She wondered if Peter had somehow engineered it that way. He seemed capable of that kind of control. Moreover, there was something appealing in the thought. Jamie had never been like that. He and Lynn had always been equals. In fact, Lynn was always in charge of making plans and reservations. It was nice to leave all that in someone else's hands, and she thought she understood for the first time why women often marry men who are at least a little older.

It was a relief to tell him—to tell someone—the whole story all at once, beginning to end. He asked for it, didn't he? She started with that first dinner with F. X., ending with Jamie coming home to find F. X. half naked helping himself from the refrigerator. "It was just so frustrating," she said, caught up in her story. "So pointless."

"That's hardly flattering to me," Peter said dryly. "I like to think that one day you'll look more happily upon the cause and effect."

Lynn laughed, covering her eyes—and heard Peter say, "That does explain it, though."

She dropped her hands. "Explain what?"

"Your husband's behavior."

"But nothing happened."

"Yes, but if he hadn't come in just then?"

Hadn't he been listening? "Nothing still would have happened—what do you think?"

"*Une femme est une femme.*"

"Excuse me?"

"Nothing, just a Godard film." Lynn wanted to say that she knew very well it was the name of a Godard film. "It's not that I don't believe you," he said. "The point is, you don't know. Jamie did come home."

"What do you mean, I don't know?"

"You don't know what would have happened."

"Of course I know. Nothing." What was it with men? "I know myself. That absolutely wasn't a possibility."

"But you can't fault Jamie for not knowing that."

She could and did fault Jamie. "Why, would you have done the same?"

He reached across the laminated red-checked tablecloth and tapped her hand lightly. His touch almost made her jump. He was watching her closely; she was pretty sure he saw it. "Well, I wouldn't now," he said. "I'd know better. That's all you broke up over?"

"No. No, of course there were other things—basic differences."

After dinner, Peter drove her back to her mother's house. He came around and opened the car door for her. He smiled down at her, and Lynn had the impression that he was very pleased with himself—with the evening in general. She felt a tremor of nervousness as he walked her up the front path. She wished she hadn't let him walk her to the door. He stayed on the step below the top one, which was a little disconcerting—

she was getting used to his height, his looking down on her. He took her hand, the one not holding the key to her mother's front door. But he didn't try to kiss her. It was she who broke eye contact first. He squeezed her hand affectionately.

"Can I call you?" he said.

"Sure."

"Good, then." He smiled very kindly at her, then was down the steps. Partway down the path, he turned—to make sure she had the door open—and gave a parting wave. The satisfied look in his eye just as he turned away made her wonder if this weren't some trick of his, not to kiss, a ploy to make the woman acutely aware of what was being withheld.

Twenty-four

For their next date, a full two weeks later—another ploy, to stretch it out like that?—Peter chose the newest, hardest-to-get-into restaurant in town. Was he satisfied that he'd made his point? Or was he rewarding Lynn? This time, he talked more about himself—and his movies.

"Have you seen my new one?" he asked, making a face, but he didn't take his eyes from her.

"Yes."

Lynn had dragged her mother to the movie the morning after their first date, making them practically sneak into the earliest show as if in danger of being caught in the act. To Lynn's surprise, her mother had volubly proclaimed her enjoyment. "So sweet," she'd said. "Romantic. And funny." Lynn herself had been relieved that the movie was intelligent and quite charming, but her mother's response, for some reason, had made her surly.

"Well?" he said. "Did you like it?"

"Very much."

"You're not going to say any more, are you?" he said.

"Nope. Not right now."

She still had the sense of his being in control, of his having planned it this way. Perhaps he was even somehow responsible for this new unperturbed air of hers—as if this were a formal ceremony, a Chinese opera in which they were playing their roles, smiling at each other from behind the masks. Or else, Lynn told herself, she was being crazy and reading too much into everything. "Actually," she said, "I will say one more thing about your movie. It seemed . . . sweeter than you seem."

"Would you believe me if I told you that there's more of me in that movie than right here at this table?"

"I'd assume it was a line."

He grinned. But Lynn remembered reading how Anthony Trollope had once dismayed a woman seated next to him at a dinner, who'd read and admired his books, by being the prototypical gruff English gentleman, concerned with his roast beef and hunting. It had seemed so at odds with his insightful, complex handling of his characters, particularly the women in his novels.

There was one unsettling moment as she and Peter were leaving the restaurant. The hostess must have been away from her station when they came in, but on their way out Lynn recognized her as the same one from the restaurant she'd gone to with F. X. The girl probably jumped from restaurant to hot new restaurant. "Good night, Mr. Fairhaven," she called suggestively after them, but Peter, unlike F. X., gave absolutely no indication of knowing her.

That evening, when he took her home—she was still staying at her mother's—Peter joined Lynn on the top step, right in front of the door, nowhere for her to go, and he leaned forward to kiss her. Lynn felt almost relieved, and turned her head so that the kiss would land harmlessly at the corner of her mouth.

He pulled back. "Don't turn away from me like that, as if the thought of kissing me disgusts you."

"It—it doesn't," Lynn stammered.

"If you're not ready to kiss me, fine, I can understand that. But I'm not some child, I'm a grown man. I can wait. You don't have to feel pressured." Some flicker of stubbornness, of disbelief, must have crossed Lynn's face. "Don't worry," he said dryly, "I don't plan on being a monk. Grown-ups have sex, Lynn. It's okay."

"You're saying—"

"There are women I sleep with, yes." He looked down at her. "Do you think women don't find me attractive? Women find me attractive." His mouthed tweaked, as if at the memory of one such moment.

"So you just . . ."

"Go to bed with starlets? Is that where your mind's going? Like the hostess at the restaurant? I saw you giving her the fish-eye. No, I don't indulge in that sort of behavior because I believe it's cruel, and I really do try not to be cruel when I can avoid it. I actually prefer intelligent women—you're not as much of a fluke for me as you think you are."

"Who do you sleep with, then?" She couldn't help asking.

"Several old friends. When we want the same thing."

"When you were engaged, too?"

For the first time he looked uncomfortable. "I wasn't a perfect angel where Joan was concerned. That should have been a sign to me."

"So you assume that with the right woman you'll be faithful?"

He put his hands on her shoulders so that she was forced to tilt her head upward to him. "You can't expect to know everything ahead of time." He bent his head over her once more—his choice, this time, to place the kiss in the corner of her mouth.

Twenty-five

L ynn closed her eyes. The sun felt warm on her face and she could feel the slats of the bench against her back. It had been years since she had been to Roxbury Park in Beverly Hills, but F. X. had begged her to come along.

Lynn hadn't heard from him after the museum party. Occupied with Glynnis, she'd imagined. She'd wondered idly if he was still seeing Chaka as well, and whether Glynnis knew about her. Richard hadn't mentioned Chaka in their meeting, either—but why would he? All around, it was better not to ask. And then F. X. *had* called. He'd reiterated his old plea for advice on what to do with his son in such a way as to imply that he'd been asking and asking, waiting desperately for Lynn's answer all this time. But he was clearly nervous about his son, and Lynn had come up with the idea of the playground there. She and her sisters had gone practically every weekend when they were little, taken by their father to give their mother a few free hours to write. The park had seemed vast to Lynn back then. Her strongest memory of the place was of running long and hard after her two older sisters, across lawns and through bushes and trees that at the time had seemed junglelike. They were running to catch the ice cream truck. Lynn remembered the clenched anticipation as they dashed to the back parking lot, afraid each time that the truck would no longer be there. It hadn't occurred to them as children that, this being Southern California, the truck sat on the same spot all day long, year round.

"You don't know a good real estate agent, do you?" F. X. said.

Lynn's head jerked up. How long had she been sitting there, not speaking? She glanced at her watch: almost three o'clock. Soon it would be time to take F. X.'s little boy over to buy an ice cream. Lynn had already peeked—the truck was where it had always been. Of course it was. Although February, it was in the seventies. "A real estate agent?"

F. X. kept his eyes straight ahead, on his boy on the jungle gym. "I'm thinking of getting a bigger place."

"Because of Michael?" F. X. called him Michael some of the time, but more often referred to him as Michael Joseph. It was just a matter of time, Lynn thought, before he became "M. J." "But he's only here for two weeks, right? Or do you think he'll be coming out more often?"

Melissa, the boy's mother, had finally agreed to the visit, F. X.'s longest yet with his son and the first time she'd allowed him to have the child to himself. F. X. hadn't believed it would happen and kept expecting her to cancel at the last minute. Lynn could see why—it was quite a leap from visitations of an hour or two at her house in Connecticut or at F. X.'s parents' house, to a full two weeks in Los Angeles on his own. Michael's nanny had flown out with him, then had turned around and taken the next flight back to New York. Melissa's stance was that she couldn't bear to see F. X. for even as long as the handover took, but it had also come out that she was going to Greece during those two weeks, which of course meant a long flight in the other direction.

They both watched as the little boy skidded down the slide with a war cry for the hundredth time. The bigger slide on the other side of the park, the one Lynn remembered going on with her sisters, was shaped like an enormous robot, probably two stories tall, with the slide coming out of its mouth. F. X., behaving with a degree of paternal carefulness that seemed quite unlike him, had deemed it too fast and high for Michael, who now stood triumphant at the bottom of his slide. He turned to wave to them once more before plowing back to the stairs in a way that reminded Lynn exactly of F. X. in college when he used to play rugby. Lynn touched a hand to her stomach. There was a pervasive sadness, as if she'd lost the baby, as if she'd been pregnant in the first place.

"I think Melissa's setting me up," F. X. said. "She's up to something. She never even let me have one week with Michael Joseph before. I think she's planning on using something I might do while he's here against me later."

In profile, F. X.'s blunt nose and the flattened cleft of his chin were like small slips of the sculptor's knife made the best of in that leonine head. He seemed both distracted and focused in a way Lynn had never seen in him before. It was this that had made her finally take pity on him and agree to join him at the park. With the help of her mother's endless resource of graduate students, she had even scared up a tag team of babysitters. F. X. had taken two weeks' vacation from work but still had to show up at the occasional meeting or dinner—so he said. Lynn did wonder whether he didn't make use of the babysitters to slip out now and then to see one of his various women. It was difficult to imagine that F. X. had changed so completely.

"She called yesterday from Santorini. She was cagey about when Michael Joseph was going back."

"Doesn't he have a plane ticket?"

"Yeah, but when I mentioned it she said, 'Oh, we'll talk about that later.'" F. X. turned to Lynn. "Do you think she's just trying to get my hopes up? Or is she planning on letting him stay longer because I haven't done anything wrong yet?"

The look of naked yearning on his face unsettled her. "Doesn't Michael have to be back for school or something?"

F. X. gave her a look. "He's not even four yet. He's in preschool."

Lynn wanted to remind him that the idea for this age-appropriate and highly successful outing had been hers.

"I should get a new place, anyway," he said. "I should buy something. The place I'm renting is a dive."

It was actually a perfectly nice apartment in Santa Monica, Lynn knew, a large if ordinary one-bedroom. She had even gone with F. X. to buy a bed for Michael, a child's bed, blue and shaped like a car, currently set up in what had been the dining room with Thomas the Tank Engine sheets. It was amazing how much extra time she seemed to have now, without a husband to go home to.

"I should probably get a different car, too," he said, then perked up. "How about you? Don't you move soon? Do you need help? Or is new boyfriend going to be there?" F. X. was smiling now, his attention fully on her. "Peter Fairhaven, right? Don't worry, I'm not stalking you, Glynnis told me all about it."

"You're seeing her?"

He shrugged. "She's a good kid. Kind of wild."

"Please," said Lynn, "I don't want to know."

"Yeah, Chaka didn't like it. She put her foot down."

Chaka? "But she's engaged. How can she complain?" Now

that she thought of it, the last time a call from F. X. had come in for Lynn, Glynnis had stalked out of the office.

"I tell you, Lynnie, I've got to get out from under that woman's thumb. I need a good woman." Up went the lecherous eyebrow. "Why not you?"

She just looked at him.

"I know, I know, I missed my opportunity. You're taken again. So? Tell papa everything. We really are friends, now, aren't we?"

"I'm not taken. There's nothing to tell." Were they friends? Here they were, sitting together on a park bench on a Saturday afternoon, watching his child play. Lynn had the feeling F. X. wouldn't have allowed any of the women he was sleeping with along on an afternoon like this. Or was she kidding herself? Again. But she definitely couldn't imagine Chaka here. And she felt at ease there on the bench next to him, she had to admit that. It felt peaceful. It felt like a choice. This was her life now.

"What does Jamie think?" said F. X. "Does he know?"

Lynn straightened. "Jamie and I don't really talk. He's probably moving back east for good."

"You think?"

"He took a new job there."

"Oh."

"Why?" F. X. had sounded uncharacteristically nonplussed by this news. Lynn remembered something Glynnis had said, and had a sudden suspicion . . . "You didn't say anything to Richard Plante, did you?" she said. "About asking for Jamie to be on the museum job?"

F. X. looked at her as though she'd lost her mind. "What, you think I spend all my time plotting about you two? Sorry, I have my own problems to worry about."

"No, I know, I mean . . ." She was spluttering.

"So? What's he like—Peter Fairhaven?"

"Fine. Nice, I guess." She was trying to retrieve a modicum of dignity.

"Yeah, it must be a real trial, dating a famous Hollywood director. Is he taking you to Squaw?"

"We've only been out to dinner once or twice. Wait, what?"

"To be honest, I wouldn't have guessed you'd appeal to someone like that."

"Gee, thanks."

"Just saying, he must be more mature than I am." F. X. was chuckling.

"Keep going," said Lynn, "because I'm not insulted enough yet."

"Seriously, whatever's going on, you seem happier. I'm happy for you, Lynnie. You deserve it."

Lynn thought, *I seem happier*? She leaned her head back against the bench. She hadn't seen Peter for a couple of weeks—some promotional things, he'd said, plus a stop in England to see his family. In some ways, she'd been relieved when he'd left town. Her sisters had been frustrated by her reticence about him, too. Lynn had said, "Please, I just don't want to talk about it right now"—reminding herself uncomfortably of Jamie. Before he'd left, Peter had asked her out for the first Saturday he was back—booking her way in advance. She'd rather liked the old-fashioned ritual of it. He *was* nice. But Squaw? Had F. X. read somewhere that he skied? Had Glynnis? Yes, this was her life now. It didn't feel bad, the yelps and screams of young children floating on the air, muted by sunlight. Insects buzzing in the bushes behind her.

"About your real estate agent? You happy with her?"

Lynn's eyes blinked open. "What? Oh, yeah, she's good. Actually, she's a friend of my sister's. She did a great job. We had multiple offers." ("Jamie must really trust you," C. Bradford had said wonderingly, when he heard that Jamie had given her power of attorney. Lynn had been secretly disappointed. She'd been imagining other meetings—sad ones, of course, to sign papers, go over last details.)

F. X. peered at her. "You okay?"

"I'm fine. Just a little sad—the house and everything."

"I meant what I said about being friends." He leaned back against the slats of the bench and sighed. "Sometimes things just don't end up the way you thought they would. I wish I *could* do something."

Lynn had a vision of asking F. X. to track down and seduce Barb Hatchett, to make her anathema to Jamie. She smiled faintly. She and F. X. watched Michael Joseph circling and climbing some more.

"You have her number?"

"Who?" For a crazy instant Lynn thought he meant Barb.

"Your agent." F. X. sounded exasperated.

She turned to him. "You're really thinking of buying something?"

"Why do I get the feeling you're stalling? Are you just against giving me *any* woman's phone number? On principle? Afraid I'll ask her out?"

Lynn thought of Robin and had to smile. "No," she said, "Not at all."

Twenty-six

Lynn's third Saturday night date with Peter, the one set up so far in advance, was a departure from their usual (as Lynn already thought of their tête-à-tête dinners). Peter had called the evening before, mainly to say hello now that he was back, but also to ask if she minded going to a screening with his longtime producer and the producer's model-actress date for the evening. "He wants to meet you," Peter said, which gave Lynn a nervous thrill: Peter had talked about her? He warned that it wasn't a fancy red-carpet screening or premiere, just a utilitarian industry screening at the Director's Guild. The film turned out to be utilitarian, too—neither terrible nor great. Peter's producer seemed perfectly nice but was exactly what Lynn would have expected from a Hollywood producer; likewise the model-actress. Lynn and Peter barely had a chance to exchange a private word all evening—they'd all driven together, in the producer's car. Yet somehow on this, their third date, they took on the role in the foursome of the comfortable, long-standing couple.

After the screening, the model-actress suggested the Bel

Air for a nightcap. Lynn had always heard that the hotel bar was a renowned pickup spot for high-priced call girls. Nothing she saw led her to believe otherwise. With Peter and his producer gossiping about the director of the movie they'd just seen and his contretemps with one of the studio executives, and with women who looked like former Las Vegas showgirls coming and going behind them, Lynn's thoughts strayed to what Peter had said about sleeping with other women. Was that why he only asked her out for these ritualistic, Saturday night dates? Across the men, the producer's date gave her a smile, and she smiled back. Lynn couldn't say she was happy about the sleeping-with-others thing. (Dee would be outraged, which was why she hadn't mentioned it to her.) She was appreciative, though, of the wiggle room it gave her.

At the end of the evening, Lynn was dropped off first. As the producer swung his enormous black Mercedes into the circular driveway, she leaned over to give Peter a good-night peck on the cheek. He accepted it with a smile. So she was confused, and felt a flash of alarm, when he slid out after her. He leaned back into the car. "Just be a minute," he said, to her relief.

It was the first time he'd been to her new building. There were lots of different doormen, two or three per shift, and it appeared to be part of their job to know Lynn by sight already even though she'd just moved in. Now, as she and Peter ran the gauntlet of the front desk, one of them called out, "'Night, Miss Kovak." Lynn wanted to say good-bye to Peter at the elevators but found it impossible to pull off under the doormen's watchful eyes.

"Kovak?" Peter said when the elevator doors closed them in.

"My maiden name."

"I'm aware of that. I simply wasn't under the impression that your divorce was final yet."

"It's not. But I . . ."

He grinned. "You don't have to explain to me."

"I'm not."

"Shh, don't worry." He touched a finger to her lips, which did worry her. She had the impression of a small electric shock. Or maybe it actually was a shock. Had Peter felt it, too? He was busy looking around the elevator. "Nice," he said, reaching out to touch the smooth back wall, now running his finger along the line of brass separating the perfectly matched panels. "They don't make them like this anymore." Lynn could feel his attention leave her as he filed away the look of this elevator, perhaps for a future scene in a movie.

Lynn struggled with the locks, as she always had to, the doors to her apartment shuddering embarrassingly. When she turned back to Peter, it was to find him watching her. Now he cocked his head and leaned closer, as if in slow motion. She became aware of the mechanical hum of the building. The irony was that if it had been another of their intimate dinners, just the two of them all evening, Lynn probably would have lost her nerve. Or not felt compelled. Just before his face came so close that it went out of focus and she closed her eyes, she saw his lips curve in a knowing smile. But it was too late, her chin was already lifting on its own accord.

He drew back. "I want to ask you something."

"What?" Was this another trick? He was standing so close.

"Well, it seems . . . I'm to be a judge at this film festival. At Squaw Valley. I was wondering if you'd be interested in coming. As my date." Her mouth opened in protest, and he said, "They're giving me a suite, and if it doesn't have two bedrooms, we can exchange it."

So that's what F. X. had been talking about when he'd mentioned Squaw.

"Does that interest you at all?" Peter said.

"When is it?"

"A couple of weeks. I don't want you to feel rushed. I just thought I'd like you to be there with me."

"Wow. I'm flattered."

"Don't be ridiculous," he said sharply. "You know that's how I feel." Then he did lean over her for the kiss.

When she was finally safe inside, the door shut on his well-pleased grin, she told herself, *No, it can't be.*

Twenty-seven

I've been getting the strangest calls from the little lordling."

"What are you talking about, Daddy?"

Lynn and her father were having brunch at the Bel Air Hotel, at one of the prime outside tables overlooking the famous swan lagoon. The Bel Air wasn't the sort of place they usually went when Harold was in town, but he'd mumbled something about "doing something special," so Lynn suspected the idea was to cheer her up. Her father had also pointed out, perhaps to forestall argument, that the place was very convenient to her mother's house, where he was staying. Lynn had acquiesced gracefully to the gesture and didn't mention to either parent that she'd been there the night before.

"Do you mean Julie's husband?" she said. "Piers?"

"That's the one."

"And don't call him lordling," she said, as if it still mattered. "Why is he calling?"

"It seems he's fallen in love with me."

Harold Kovak chuckled at the expression on his daughter's face, which to do her justice transformed immediately into forbearance of the eye-rolling kind. For as long as Lynn could remember, her father had had a certain type of student, usually male, mooning around him, hoping for enlightenment.

"He wants to come to Berkeley for two weeks, sometime in March. He proposes it as 'independent study.' Says very earnestly that he does not expect to receive any university credit or a grade. It seems he has to be in the States, anyway."

"When in March? It's March now." A thought occurred to Lynn. "It must be for Andy's wedding. He's probably trying to put the two trips together." Lynn hadn't given Andy and his upcoming nuptials any thought in all the turmoil, but it was unsettling not to know anything about them. She'd never even seen an invitation. She couldn't have been kept out of it more completely. Would Jamie be Andy's best man? Would that be hard for him, on top of the divorce? And of course Annika and Barb were friends—would Barb be in the wedding? How convenient, with Jamie single, too.

"Isn't the girl he's marrying in graduate school?" said her father. "They're doing this in the middle of the school year?"

"You said no to Piers, of course."

Harold looked uncomfortable. "Of course."

"Good."

"He has absolutely no skills or expertise, does he? I'm not running a drop-in ethnobotany commune. Although the truth is I am a little low on lab workers this quarter. These kids, they think they're too good for grunt work."

"Daddy! You're not thinking about letting him come, are you? When is he supposed to show up? You can't do this to me."

"Sweetheart, it has nothing to do with you." Harold smoothed crumbs from the heavy pink linen tablecloth, which caused a busboy to rush over with one of those little crumb-sweeping gadgets. He didn't leave until he had swept the whole table.

"It's just that," her father resumed, "I'm getting this sense of . . . desperation from him. He's seeking something, clearly."

"Oh God."

"You remember how he was at Thanksgiving?"

"Vividly. One of the good things that was supposed to come out of this divorce was not having these people in our lives anymore."

Her father looked up at her from his waffle.

"I'm sure they see it the same way," Lynn said. "Philippa's probably thrilled to be rid of me. I know she is. And just in time not to invite me to Andy's wedding and have to introduce me to the cardboard Peales! Remember how I wasn't even a bridesmaid at Julie's wedding?"

Harold Kovak frowned at this apparent non sequitur.

"But no, we weren't engaged when she asked them. At least, that's the excuse Jamie's mother gave. Everyone knew we'd be getting married! It wasn't like there was a question." Lynn was pretty sure that if Jamie had been dating someone like rich Barb Hatchett at the time, Philippa would have seen to it that she was a bridesmaid. "There was one big table for the wedding party, and I was stuck with some cousins." What had rankled most was that Lynn had thought that Julie, unlike Philippa, liked her. If Lynn had been a bridesmaid, would she and Jamie have ended up eloping? She had known at the time it would be one more thing Philippa would hold against her.

"Rites of passage are important," said Harold.

Lynn stared at her father in dismay. "You think the fact that we didn't have a real wedding mattered?"

"Hmm? Oh, no, it's that you reminded me again about the English lad."

"Daddy, you know full well his name is Piers. Call him Piers, for God's sake."

Harold was eyeing her intently now, his deep-set eyes nearly black. He looked exactly like what he was, a Jewish Berkeley professor in his late fifties, probably of Eastern European heritage. But there was also something elegant, almost Renaissance about him. You could imagine him in a velvet doublet and hose, amusing the Virgin Queen as a foreign envoy to the court. "Sweetheart, please tell me it wasn't about the families. That's not what was behind it, was it? Because your mother and I always thought—"

"I know, I know! That Jamie and I were too different, the backgrounds, I know! You should have heard the lawyer when I told him about the families: the religion, the money stuff, even our personal styles are so different." C. Bradford had nodded and said, "Yep, you're right, those sure are a lot of strikes against you. To be honest, we see a lot of it, people who thought they'd be the ones to overcome the differences."

"Remember Thanksgiving?" Lynn said. "It was like *Mansfield Park*."

Her father looked confused.

"You know, the novel. How one sister married what's-his-name, the rich one who owns Mansfield Park? But the other sister married a sailor, and they live in squalor. The spread of the one family by marriage." This was what Lynn had wanted to tell Jamie, but he'd cut her off. She'd been proud of the analogy, unflattering to her family as it was. She still couldn't get over the idea that there would be thoughts she'd never get to tell Jamie about. Thoughts she'd had while they were still together!

Her father was looking at her with a concerned expression. "That's not at all what I meant," he said. "Background, schmackground, it's you your mother and I are worried about. I tell you, if I'd worried about Grandma and Grandpa Bernstein approving of me, you wouldn't be here today. Those German

Jews were worse than any WASPs. Your mother's mother thought my family was a bunch of Russian peasants." His eyes danced at the memory. "And we Kovaks gave as good as we got. We thought the Bernsteins were bourgeois know-nothings. Which they were, by the way. Your mother and I didn't care about any of it."

"But you were all Jewish. You had that in common."

"Pfft, if anything that made it worse. Now, I can't say I fully understand what went wrong between you and Jamie. Perhaps I'm not so good a judge as I prided myself on being. But you and Jamie seemed alike in the important things. Not alike, that isn't the right word. *Simpatico*. I don't understand why people persist in thinking that marriage is something different from friendship."

"Why don't you and Mommy live together?"

Harold stopped, the strawberry speared on his fork halfway to his mouth. He looked from Lynn to the strawberry with its jaunty beret of whipped cream, then gently laid the fork on the rim of his plate. "Why do you ask that now?"

"It was always, if outsiders didn't understand your marriage, then that was their lack—they were to be pitied for closed-mindedness. And I know it's real and it works for you and Mommy. But what sort of example was that for us—for three daughters? I could never have imagined living apart from Jamie. It's exactly because we were apart that everything went wrong. But the fact that something like that could wreck things—I mean, if our marriage had been solid. . . Grandma and Grandpa Kovak were separated for years during World War II, weren't they?" And what example did Jamie have? A father who left because life was too short?

Harold Kovak leaned back in his chair, and Lynn was suddenly aware of how grizzled he was; she became aware of his age in a new way. "Your mother and I certainly never meant to make you feel foolish for not understanding. We just . . . fell into it, I suppose. It worked for us. It does for a select few—no, not select, that's not the impression I mean to give." He sighed.

"How do you ever really know?" Lynn said. "I thought we were so happy."

"Ah, sweetheart."

"I was happy we eloped! I wasn't sorry. It was the two of us. But now everything seems like a sign."

"Ignore the signs!" Harold looked surprised to hear these words coming out of his mouth. An early, much-acclaimed paper of his had been titled *Recognizing the Signposts: A Uxtlapotl Shaman's Journey.* "The one thing you shouldn't lose sight of is why Jamie chose you."

"Oh, Daddy, it's done. I wish everyone would just accept that."

Ignore the signs, her father said. But last night there'd been a sign Lynn couldn't ignore. Peter Fairhaven's kiss had been a shock, so perfect was it, like a movie kiss, everything in languorous slow motion. When he'd lowered his lips to hers (he was a good bit taller than Jamie) she had felt as though she were falling—falling backward, or rather being lowered gently onto the most luxurious and flowing of beds. When he'd raised a hand to the back of her head, she'd felt that her hair must be like silk under his touch. The first time Lynn and Jamie kissed, they'd bumped foreheads, not quite in sync. They'd laughed, and had to start over.

"I did use to think it meant something, that Jamie chose to be with someone like me, that it was sort of a way of saying he did want something different. But we were young, it was probably just a rebellion for him, and now he's reverted back." Like Andy, she thought.

"Here's what I'm thinking," Harold said, "and I say this

as your father who loves you and wants to see you happy, and who maybe has accumulated a little wisdom in his longer time on earth. So please take what I'm about to say in that spirit—for yourself and your future, whatever and whomever that holds. You talk about all these differences, but what strikes me, as a not quite impartial observer, is that you're doing the same thing you complain about in Philippa. You're categorizing and then agreeing that the differences between you and Jamie are undesirable. You wanted Jamie to be exactly the way you wanted him to be. So, sweetheart, maybe you need to stop focusing on how opposite you are from Philippa and give a little thought to the ways in which you haven't been so different as you think."

Lynn followed Sunset Boulevard's rolling curves eastward, toward her apartment. She was almost unaware of the act of driving. It was like being on an amusement park ride where the car automatically follows its rail. She had all the windows open, and with the warm breeze blowing in her face it was almost like being in a convertible. I should get a convertible, she thought. She'd never seen herself as the convertible type. Was she? It had been so long since she'd thought of herself as anything not in conjunction with Jamie. Well, not that long. They'd been married three years, together a year and a half before that. Four and a half years in total. Not so long in the grand scheme of things. One day it would seem like a blip. Lynn didn't much like that idea.

Three years of marriage. Did you stop counting when you separated, or when the divorce was final? Lynn and her sisters had always seen Philippa as having brought on her divorce herself, but for the first time it occurred to Lynn to wonder how Jamie's mother had felt at the time. Dismayed when her husband acquiesced so easily to her demands? Lynn had a sudden image of Philippa standing in her chilly, stone-walled entry hall in St. Louis, one Ferragamo toe pointed out on the checkerboard marble at an almost strained angle, her expression unreadable as the light streamed in and her husband placidly walked out the door with his suitcases.

Lynn's car slid into the circular drive in front of her new building, and one of the men opened the car door for her. She smiled at the guys at the desk, aware of their watchful presence behind her as she waited for the notoriously slow elevators. When an elevator finally opened, Lynn gave the man emerging from it a polite smile, too—then took in the handsome, dissipated face. "George?" It felt odd to say the single name since she never thought of him that way. George Jacquemet.

"Why, Lynn Prosper, what are you doing here?"

"I live here." She took a better look at him. It was Sunday afternoon, yet George had on dark suit pants and a rumpled white shirt, his jacket crushed over his arm. He looked a little green even in the elevator light, which Lynn had noticed before was remarkably flattering. His jaw looked dirty with stubble. He had clearly been out all night. She wasn't at all surprised by the thought of George Jacquemet having an affair. He seemed unabashed at being caught.

"Visiting someone?" she said.

He shook a finger at her. "Dirty mind. I'm coming from a poker game. It went a bit late." His hand was in his pocket, jingling coins.

"I hope you won, at least."

"Hah." A bleak look skittered across his face, but then he sniggered. "Yeah, except for the forty thou." Lynn's mouth fell open, which made him really laugh. Lynn imagined the disapproving eye of the doorman upon them. "Didn't you know that about me, Lynn? I thought everyone knew. But how about you, you sneaky thing? Miss Butter Won't Melt in Her Mouth."

Lynn stared at him, not quite understanding.

"Can't blame you, though." He grinned.

Lynn knew that the best thing was to ignore George Jacquemet, not to enter into his thinking at all. "What do you mean?" she said.

"I guess it's okay to say now, but we saw it coming. You and Jamie never were right for each other, were you? I mean, I get why you stuck it out—basically good guy, good family. That's a pretty sweet setup in Tahoe, sounds like. Not community property, though, huh? Since it's from Jamie's family. Shit," said George—Lynn realized she was positively gaping at him. "That was pretty insensitive of me."

"No, sorry," she said, "it's fine. Yes, it's all his. It's all very amicable."

"Kidding aside, it would be much more fun if you were going to be there."

This confused Lynn for a minute. "Oh," she said. "You're going? With Jamie?"

"Yep, the whole crew in a couple weeks. It's not our weekend for the time-share so we'll be staying with you—with Jamie, I mean. Since it didn't work out over Christmas. Although now, of course, we understand why." George drew closer—Lynn could smell the alcohol exuding from his pores. "Got to tell you, Lynn, this new girl of Jamie's may be rich, but you're much hotter."

Lynn quashed the impulse to kick him in the balls. Was Jamie really going to be friends with these people now? She pushed the button for the elevator, which to her relief hadn't gone anywhere and opened right away. But maybe he'd really liked them all along, and only her disapproval had stopped him. He'd invited them to Tahoe, had clearly told them the truth about the house. Jamie wouldn't have wanted to let that sort of misapprehension slide—not with friends.

"Anyway," said George, his hand shooting out at the last minute to hold the elevator door, "I know you can't be all that upset. Things hot and heavy with that director guy? Ha, got ya!" Lynn's cheeks had grown warm at the memory of that kiss. "Guess you didn't see me last night, but I was here when you guys came in. Hey, you know what, we should set something up. I know Lib would love to—maybe dinner, the six of us, you, your new friend, the Scovilles? No reason to choose sides, right?"

Lynn made herself smile. "No reason at all. Well, I really should get going."

"Oh! Sorry." George stepped back, dropping his arm. "Boyfriend stashed away up there?" he called as the doors slid shut between them. Lynn leaned back in her agate box, then remembered to push the button for her floor. The last thing she wanted was for the doors to open again on George Jacquemet's leer.

The phone began to ring inside the apartment as Lynn fumbled with the stupid doors yet again. She'd never had to fight like this with their old door. There were actually two different locks, and the two keys looked almost identical. Lynn hadn't gotten to the point where she could tell them apart by feel or some tiny visual clue. She counted four rings and sighed. Voice mail had picked up. But when she got inside, there was no flashing light on the phone signaling a message.

The phone came jangling to life again. Same person? Lynn snatched it up.

"Hello, Lynn?"

"Julie?" She was shocked.

Jamie's sister gave an embarrassed laugh. "I hope you don't mind. When I called the old number it gave me this one. How are you?

"Are you calling from London?"

"Where else would I be?" Julie's voice had a pleasing, silver-bell quality.

"This is so funny," said Lynn. "My father was just—"

"Lynn," said Julie, "we weren't really sure how to tell you. Or if to tell you. I mean, who should call and all that, and Jamie didn't want—"

He's marrying Barb Hatchett!

"The wedding's off," Julie said.

"What?" Lynn felt thoroughly confused.

"Andy and Annika. The wedding's off."

"Oh, Julie."

"I know, I know. Oh, Lynn, I know you're not officially going to be part of the family soon. Andy wanted to tell you, but Jamie said it wasn't appropriate anymore. But he didn't specifically tell me not to call. It just seemed too strange, your not knowing. But maybe you don't want to?"

"No, I'm thrilled! I mean, I'm so glad you called to tell me. But Andy . . . what happened?"

"I don't know when I'm going to stop feeling like you're my sister."

This brought Lynn up short. It wasn't something she would have thought of saying about Julie. But she didn't doubt Julie's warmth, not at all. Julie had never been anything to her *but* warm and sweet. Lynn suddenly felt very, very petty. "I'm sure it will work out," she said. "And I really am glad you called to tell me. It makes me feel . . . The strangest thing, I was just talking to my father . . ."

"Oh, and Piers," Julie said.

"What?" Lynn was startled, because of course she was thinking of Piers, too.

"No, you. What were you going to say?"

"About Piers?"

"Oh, I wish you were going to be there, we could talk in person," Julie said. "It won't seem the same without you. Everything's just terrible."

"Wait," said Lynn, "are you coming to California, too?"

"Yes, yes, of course," Julie said distractedly. "You didn't like her, did you?"

"I—" Lynn hesitated, remembering the ups and downs of Julie's own wedding plans. "Julie, isn't there a chance things can still work out? Between Andy and Annika?"

"*Annika?*" Julie said. "No, that bitch is already engaged to someone else."

Twenty-eight

It had been a blessing in a way, to hear the story from Julie, with all the details Lynn would have had to query and press out of Jamie if they'd still been together, feeling sordidly avid all the while.

Apparently the evil Annika had met this guy, the son of a Belgian billionaire industrialist, in some nightclub in the meat-packing district of Manhattan. Andy had been there that night. So had Jamie. And night-clubbing, jet-setting, Jamie-chasing Barb Hatchett? If so, this was a detail Julie left out. As best as they could reconstruct it, Annika must have slipped him her number when she was supposed to be on her way to the restrooms, and she'd met up with him again the next day. It was, Julie said, a *coup de foudre*. When Lynn repeated back this phrase questioningly, Jamie's sister had exclaimed in disgust, "That's how she put it to Andy! As if that excused her behavior, the ball-busting, money-grubbing, social-climbing bitch." Lynn didn't think she'd ever before heard Julie swear.

The very next day after breaking the news, Annika and

her Eurotrash boyfriend—or rather, fiancé, if such a thing were truly possible—left for Brussels, where Annika claimed they intended to be married as soon as possible. Lynn couldn't help wondering, had she taken her wedding dress with her? Another question she didn't feel comfortable asking, but she had a horrible vision of Barb Hatchett standing at the altar with Jamie in Annika's cast-off, fur-trimmed Queen of Winter gown, as if the whole thing had been planned between the two friends.

Needless to say, Lynn called her two sisters as soon as she got off the phone with Julie, just as she had called them to report Jamie's brother's engagement. There was a difference though, this time. In the past—that is, when she was with Jamie—Lynn had always felt vaguely guilty to be running to her family with gossip. Now, she felt justified. Who else did she have?

"What was Andy doing in Philadelphia all this time, anyway?" Dee asked. "Had he gotten a job?"

"I think so," Lynn said. "Something about a bank there. But it sounded sort of like a temporary thing, just while Annika was there."

"If it was just some random bank job in Philadelphia, Annika probably saw it as second-rate," said Dee, who clearly saw a job like that as second-rate herself.

"Julie said he'd applied to business school for next year. At Wharton."

"Oh, poor Andy," said Dee. "Well, let's hope that's over with now. That would just be tragic, Andy in business school. I wonder what he actually wants to do?"

Sasha, when this part of her sisters' conversation was relayed to her, said, "He once told me he'd love to do something on the Internet with the native crafts he'd seen. I could see that, couldn't you? And actually, maybe business school wouldn't be bad for that. Hey," she said, "I wonder if Piers will go to Daddy now?"

"Why wouldn't he?" said Lynn. "My getting divorced clearly didn't stop him—or Daddy."

Sasha responded to Lynn's sarcasm the way she always did, with infuriating reasonableness. "It was you who said he was tagging it on to the trip for the wedding. But I guess you're right, it sounds like seeing Daddy is the more important part of it to him. Like he's missing something in life. Really, you can't begrudge him that."

Why was it, Lynn wondered, that when Julie's husband was missing something in his life he only needed to go off for a couple of weeks and wanted to work things out within the constraints of his marriage?

All three sisters, however, were united in relishing the sweet irony of Philippa, forever looking down her nose at the Kovaks, being rejected by someone richer and more social.

"Poor Andy," said Lynn. "I should call." According to Julie, Andy was in New York now, with Jamie.

"Don't you think you should talk to Jamie first?" said Dee. "It's a little weird to be talking to both of his siblings but not him. Especially since Andy's staying with him." Andy hadn't felt right remaining in Annika's Philadelphia apartment after her departure, particularly since she left no information about what she intended to do about the lease. ("Wait, Andy's in New York indefinitely?" Dee had asked. "Is he commuting to his job? Did he quit?") But this was a detail no one, at least no one in Lynn's family, knew.

Should Lynn call Jamie, or should she not?

Finally Dee had said, "The question to ask yourself is, what do you want out of the call?"

It was a sobering question. Hadn't Jamie told his brother and sister that he didn't think it was appropriate for them to call her? And he hadn't called himself. And now he was going to Tahoe with the Jacquemets and the Scovilles. And who else? George had called Barb "his new girl." These were the people he was choosing to spend his time with now.

"I don't know," she told Dee. "Just to show my sympathy for Andy, I guess."

"Then you should call," said Dee.

"Peter asked me to go away with him for the weekend," said Lynn, and the subject of Andy, or calling Jamie, was forgotten.

Twenty-nine

S orry," said Peter. "I couldn't bring myself to ask for separate rooms."

"It's okay," Lynn said. "Really."

The two of them surveyed the bedroom. It was classic
English country: cabbage roses on the wallpaper, swags on
the curtains, even bad oil paintings of dogs. Exactly the sort
of room Lynn could imagine in one of Peter's aristocratic
friends' country houses, except that this one was in the middle of a Lake Tahoe ski resort. A few days before they were
to leave, Peter had called—Lynn had immediately picked up
the hesitation in his voice—to say that some friends of his
from England, she'd met some of them already, were planning
on coming over for the festival. Apparently the opportunity
to heckle him was too great to resist. Oh, and they had rented
a house.

Lynn had to wonder if they had chosen this particular one
on the basis of its bedroom decor? Some xenophobic, home-
away-from-home impulse? The bed itself looked far too authen-
tically shabby Brit. It was large and puffy-looking, but in a

misshapen way, like a bad soufflé that might collapse at any moment, and it was topped by an unappetizing crocheted coverlet of avocado and mustard. Lynn approached and gave it a tentative poke. Her fingers left a lumpy depression. Peter dropped their bags and they went back downstairs.

Hugo Stanhope and his friends were all in the living room with its soaring, knotty-pine ceiling. Aside from the bedrooms—or perhaps just that one bedroom—the rest of the house appeared to be done up in ersatz Swiss ski chalet. There were old, crisscrossed snowshoes on the walls, red-and-white Swiss flag needlepoint pillows, a cuckoo clock, heart cutouts in the flat slats of the staircase banister. Tea was being served. The young furniture-making lord himself was manning the teapot in baggy cords and a fisherman's sweater. His younger brother, Nicholas, who had greeted them when they arrived, was lounging on a velvet sofa, flanked by two women who had been introduced simply as Vanessa and Clary. They were, Lynn gathered, Hugo and Nick's girlfriends. One had red ringlets, the other brunette. Nick, who looked very much like his older brother but with a more pleasant face, jumped up, took Lynn by the elbow, and led her over to a deep wing chair next to the fire.

"Milk, sugar?" Hugo asked with a mock bow.

"Both, please," said Lynn, who never took tea that way.

Hugo, manipulating the creamer and tongs, not bothering to ask how many lumps, nodded approvingly. A uniformed maid came in with a fresh teapot, then slipped back out again, disappearing into the bowels of the house. Could they possibly have brought servants with them from England? "Petey says I've met you," said Hugo, "and I can't say that I see why he'd lie about something like that."

"I suppose there are any number of reasons."

The future marquess looked at Lynn sharply. "Such as?"

Lynn hadn't meant it; it had just come out.

"Come on, Huge-o," said Nick.

"There are always reasons for lying. The *Gaslight* motive being my personal favorite." This from a man Lynn hadn't noticed before, reading at a table at the far end of the room.

"The what?" said Hugo.

"It's an American film," said Peter, still leaning against the doorway. "A man's trying to convince his wife she's going crazy."

"Have you met Simon? Simon Funnelston?" said Nick, as the reading man unfolded himself from his chair and came forward.

"Our tame journalist," said Hugo.

Lynn recognized him—the rabbity one with the bad British teeth from Mona's dinner in Los Angeles. "What sort of things do you write about?" she asked.

"Not *my* work," said Hugo. "No, he restricts himself to the real arts. Daubs and dykes lately, hasn't it been, Si?"

"I don't care for that dyke comment," said the redhead with a frown.

"She is one. That's not my fault."

"Hugo's talking about the last artist I profiled," the journalist said to Lynn. "Ilona Rostov, and she is indeed a lesbian. The sad thing is, it's overwhelming her art, which is exceedingly fine. But she does female nudes, so you see, it is a little charged."

"But that's her choice, isn't it?" said Lynn.

"Exactly!" said Hugo.

"If you met her you'd see it's more complicated than that. Her work, it just seems to pour out of her. Perhaps I'm an absolute PR dupe, but I don't think she's trying to publicize or politicize anything. Really, her drawings are like Rembrandt, Rubens. They're exquisite."

"I haven't heard of her," said Lynn.

"You should meet her! She just moved to Los Angeles—I saw her when I was out last, for Hugo's thing. Would you like to meet her? I could arrange it. I have her number, we could call . . ."

"Perhaps I could read your piece about her?" Lynn said, with a glance toward Peter, whose face gave no clue as to the reliability of this person.

"Sure, sure, absolutely," said Simon, looking crestfallen.

It occurred to Lynn that so many of her conversations about art ended up disappointing someone. "Are there any pictures with the article?"

He brightened. "Actually, I have some slides of her work with me. But only if you really want to see them."

Hugo Stanhope was visibly bored. "I hear your brother-in-law had a superb time in the land of nuts, sprouts, and lotus-eaters," he said to Lynn. "Nicky, who knows about such things, tells me Harold Kovak is your father."

Who knows about such things. Was that sneering comment supposed to mean that his brother did drugs? "That's right," she said, "I forgot that you know Piers."

The future marquess chuckled disconcertingly.

"Brother-in-law?" said Brunette Ringlets. "Are you Julie Monkham's sister?"

"Sister-in-law," said Lynn. "Former sister-in-law. I used to be married to her brother. I mean, officially I still am, but just for a little longer."

All eyes flicked to Peter.

"It will be like a family reunion, then," said Hugo.

"Didn't Hugo mention?" said Nick, looking concerned. "That Piers and Julie are coming to lunch tomorrow?"

"No," said Peter. "Hugo did not mention."

So Andy's canceled wedding hadn't caused them to skip

their trip to the United States after all. Lynn hadn't called either Andy or Jamie. Instead, she had finally written a letter to Andy, which, for lack of a better alternative, she'd enclosed in a note to Jamie ("Do you mind giving this to Andy? I was so sorry to hear. Thanks.") addressed to him at Les Hatchett's New York office. The address had been easy to find.

Nick shot his brother a look. "Julie has a place about half an hour away," he explained to the others.

"These Americans do come in handy," Hugo murmured. "The family connection completely slipped my mind."

"That's understandable," said Lynn, "since you say you don't remember meeting me in the first place."

Hugo gazed at her appraisingly. "I hope it's not a problem."

"Not at all."

"Well, kiddies," said Peter, pushing off from the wall, "I've got to dash over to festival headquarters. There's some sort of meeting—a rehearsal, I think, for the awards ceremony. I should only be an hour or two. If you don't mind dropping me," he said to Lynn, "you can have the car to go explore for a bit."

"There are some lovely shops at the top," the red-ringleted girlfriend said, swinging her legs up onto the sofa, onto the younger Stanhope's lap, which meant, Lynn supposed, that she was Nick's girlfriend—although the English were so odd, you never knew.

After dropping Peter off, Lynn continued down the mountain—the wrong direction, the wrong thing to do, but she couldn't help herself. It was an old, familiar drive. Although it was barely past five thirty, the sky was so overcast with heavy, potent clouds that it was almost dark out. The streetlights hadn't come on yet, and, peering through the windshield, Lynn felt like one of those characters in a movie who has to drive and drive, on the lam from something, heading toward who knows what. She made good time—it was late enough so that most of the ski traffic was over. When she reached the Y in the road just before Tahoe City, she made the right, which switchbacked her toward the West Shore.

What was she doing? The house would be dark, deserted. Julie and Piers weren't in Tahoe yet—their plane, Nick had said, came in later that evening. Not that Lynn cared about the house itself. She'd purposefully taken the keys off her key ring before she left L.A. And the second she got there she'd just have to turn around to go back and pick up Peter.

The house, when Lynn finally drew abreast, was ablaze with light. Her heart pounding, she kept driving until she was five or six houses past, then turned around in a driveway. The road ran around the lake; she had to go past again to get back. She rolled by the house once more, drifting to a stop on the shoulder one house beyond. There were two cars in the driveway—rental cars, they looked. Had Piers and Julie gotten here early?

Who was Lynn trying to fool? She had felt sure, ever since hearing that Julie and Piers were coming—and she'd had an inkling even before that—that this was the same weekend Jamie would be here with the Jacquemet-Scovilles. She sat watching from inside the dark car. Inside the house a figure crossed one of the living room windows. Carefully, as silently as possible, Lynn opened the car door and inched out. But at her first step away from the car she slipped and had to grab for the door handle to steady herself. The road was treacherous—black ice. This, she told herself, was not going to end well.

Although the house wasn't as large as many along the lake, it was hardly a simple fishing cabin, either. It still had the same old wooden plaque over the door—*Trout Lodge*—that Jamie's father had joked clinched the deal for him. Most houses in Tahoe had similar hand-tooled plaques, usually bearing the owners' name. These were given as purchase gifts by the lucky real estate agent and were exactly the type of thing that allowed a family like Lynn's to look down on people who had "places" in Tahoe or anywhere, really, when it came down to it. But Lynn had to admit, it was a very nice house—two stories, the first built of stone, not merely faced with it the way newer ones were. It had the kind of setup common in houses on the lake, with the entrance and the living areas on the top floor, the bedrooms on the lower ones, closer to the water. A wood deck led, bridgelike, to the front door (Lynn and Jamie had had the deck refinished the summer before, in a burst of homeownership pride), and beneath it the slope— a huge snowdrift now—fell away so that if you were standing at the bottom you'd be next to a bathroom window on the lower level.

Lynn crept a little ways down the slope, the better to see into the living room without being seen. As she got closer, she could hear music, voices—then a loud rattling and grinding. She froze, but it was just a snowplow passing behind her. Someone inside had also heard and turned to the window. Lynn recognized Libbet Jacquemet. Instinctively she ducked—even though it was light inside and dark out, and Libbet probably wouldn't have seen her.

But the damage was done. Lynn's foot slid, her heel hitting ice, and suddenly she was sliding down the snowy slope. It probably would have been fine—it all happened quietly—but Lynn tried to catch herself on a shrub, digging her heels in to stop. The shrub gave, her heels again met ice—and she careened forward until she hit the side of the house. With a thud.

"What was that?" said a woman's voice above her. Lynn

froze, hands up against the side of the house—rough redwood siding down there.

"Probably just a clump of snow from a tree," she heard Jamie say. One of the windows in the living room must have been cracked open—the heating in the house had always been hard to regulate.

"Pretty big bang," said another male voice. George Jacquemet?

Then came the voice Lynn had been waiting for and dreading—she recognized it right away. "Ooh, maybe it's a bear. I've heard they've been really bad this year. They can tear a door off its hinges!"

"I'm sure it's not a bear," Jamie said. But the front door opened, and Lynn ducked her head as more light poured out.

"Jamie, be careful," Barb called.

"Should we all come?" said Bruce Scoville.

Lynn huddled against the wall, making herself as small as possible, but the clouds had suddenly cleared and her shiny silver ski jacket seemed to glow in the moonlight. (Her newer, black ski clothes were in the very house she was now skulking outside.) There were footsteps on the deck above, then silence for what seemed like a long time.

"It's not a bear," Jamie said. "Just a big branch that I guess fell. I'm just going to try to—"

"Need help, guy?"

"No, I'll be right back. Actually, George, do you mind closing the window? It was getting a little cold inside." Lynn heard the front door close, and a minute later a window snapped shut above her head.

By the time Jamie got down to her, half sliding, half climbing, she'd edged almost all the way under the entry deck where she wouldn't be visible from the house. But when she saw him standing there in the snow, hands on his hips, she straightened as much as she could, brushing herself off with what she hoped was aplomb. "Sorry to bother you," she said in a whisper, "I was just hoping to get my ski stuff. I'd forgotten I'd left it all here." She plucked at her jacket. "I had to get this from my mom's. It's Sasha's old one, from college, I think."

"What are you doing here—spying?"

"No! Don't flatter yourself. I just happen to be here for a film festival, and I wanted my jacket."

"That's right—Peter Fairhaven. Does he know you're here?"

"I didn't know *you'd* be here with your new friends. Never mind, I don't want to interrupt." She took a step away and immediately slipped again, this time falling hard on her back.

"Oh God, are you okay?" He pulled her up, staring horrified at her midsection.

She looked down: there was a large, rust-colored smudge where she'd crashed into the house. "I'm fine."

"But from before, when you hit the house?"

"Maybe just a splinter." She held up her hand.

"You hit really hard. Shouldn't you get checked?"

"I'm fine. Really."

"Look," he said, "I know you're—"

"Jamie? Is everything all right?" Lynn and Jamie both froze at the sound of Barb's sharp voice; neither of them had heard the front door open.

"Yep," he called. "Be right there. Just trying to get some branches away from the house." He started moving around, making scraping noises.

"Why?" said Barb.

"Um . . . they're a fire hazard."

"In the snow?"

Jamie looked at Lynn helplessly. "Chimney," she mouthed. "Sparks."

"I don't want some sparks from the chimney to . . ."

"Well, hurry up," said Barb. "You have guests." The door slammed.

"Oh, Jamie," said Lynn, unable to control her face anymore. "The boss's daughter? She's a *bossy* little thing, isn't she?"

"Just how pregnant are you?" he said, and Lynn was shocked to see how furious he looked. "I saw the tests. In the trash. Nice, to leave them around for me to see."

It took a moment for her to catch up. "What were you doing snooping in the bathroom?"

"It was my bathroom, too, once."

"Whose fault is that?"

"Look, if you don't want to tell me . . ."

"I'm not pregnant, you idiot."

"Then why . . ."

"I thought I was. But I'm not." Did she *look* pregnant?

"Oh," he said. "Sorry. Um, does Peter know?"

"Peter?" She realized what he must be thinking. "It wasn't Peter!"

"Shh!"

"You idiot," she hissed, "It was you. I mean, it wasn't, but . . ."

"That's impossible."

"Oh, we never had sex?"

"That was ages ago."

"Right after Thanksgiving. I counted the weeks."

"Oh my God," he said. "Oh my God. Why didn't you tell me?"

"Because I wasn't pregnant!" This was all taking place in lowered voices, hushed exclamations. "You left. What was I supposed to do, call you up and say, hey, congratulations, guess what bullet you just dodged?"

"That's not how I would have thought of it."

This was what she could not bear to hear now. "You better go in," she said. "Your friends are waiting."

"They're not my friends."

"You invited them here. It sure sounds like you've been hanging out with them. George had a lot to say about *Barb*."

"Yeah, well I got nice reports about you and Peter Fairhaven, too."

"Look, you better go. Your new little girlfriend is going to come looking for you again."

"Will you stop . . ." But the sound of the door opening above them stopped them both.

"Jamie?" Barb called.

"Be right up. Just this last branch." He reached for a large branch that actually had fallen at some point and began shaking it, making as much noise as possible. Mercifully the door banged shut again.

Lynn cracked up silently.

"Oh, shut up," he muttered.

"I should probably get out of here," she said, giggling. She took a step away from him and fell again—hard. Jamie was instantly at her side. "Are you okay?" He pulled her up by both hands so briskly that she half fell into him. They stayed like that, him holding her there, for a moment.

"You should go in," she said, stepping back. "I'm fine." She turned away from him and began to edge up the slope, hugging the deck to stay out of sight, although it wasn't the easiest route. Jamie followed close behind in case she fell again. He dragged the branch behind him, rustling it as loudly as possible. There was one last step and she'd be back on the road. He put a steadying hand on her elbow, and she took the giant step, then turned from the road to look back down at him.

"I'm sorry," he whispered.

She nodded, and made her way carefully to her car.

The bed in that ridiculous chintz English Tahoe bedroom was as bad as it looked—lumpy, and hot and cold at the same time, the coverlets too heavy, the sheets clammy. But Lynn didn't care. She was just glad to be alone for a minute. Peter was still downstairs. She'd probably been rude, but she didn't care about that, either.

Peter had been in high spirits from his meetings, and they'd ended up grabbing a bite to eat at the hotel. He'd kept up a light patter about all the Hollywood types but had looked Lynn's way searchingly once or twice in the car on the way back to the house. Everyone was still at the dinner table when they came in, although the men rose when they saw Lynn. "Come, join us," Nick said, and Peter had already moved toward them before he realized that Lynn wasn't following. When she saw from his face that it would be difficult to extricate himself gracefully at that point, she was glad. She excused herself, begging tiredness, the long day. "I'll be up soon," Peter called after her, as she climbed the staircase to the landing where the bedrooms were—more pine slats with cutout hearts. This house had a burnt-wood plaque of its own over the front door: *Lovebirds' Nest*.

Closing the door to their room behind her, Lynn massaged some of the tension from her neck. A floorboard creaked in the hall. She froze. Seconds passed, but no Peter. Should she read a little? It was only then that she noticed the hot-water bottle at the foot of the bed, in a thick cable-knit cashmere cover, no less. When she reached for it she wasn't sure if she was surprised or not to find it warm—filled with hot water.

How could anyone have known she'd be coming up to bed this much earlier than everyone else? If she hadn't, would some mysterious upstairs servant have come in an hour or so later to refill it? Lynn remembered what Jamie had told her about the time he stayed at the Peninsula Hotel in Hong Kong for work. There was a butler on every floor and they left tiny pieces of wood against the door to keep track of whether guests had come or gone from their rooms. And Lynn herself, when Philippa had stayed with them over Thanksgiving, had woken early the next morning to make sure a pot of hot coffee was ready for her mother-in-law. When Philippa hadn't emerged for another hour, Lynn had thrown it out and started a fresh one—and heated extra water in case she wanted tea instead.

Feeling foolish, Lynn tucked the hot-water bottle down near her feet under the sheets. The effect was instantaneous. The bed was transformed into a more welcoming place, the clamminess banished. Perhaps the British had the right idea after all. The air in the room was chilly, almost breezy, but the bed now felt cozy, a haven in the big piney house. She reached for her book—she was still working her way through Trollope. The door creaked open and Peter came in.

"Already in bed?"

Lynn threw back the covers.

"Ah. Fully dressed."

"Have you seen this?" She pulled out the hot-water bottle. "It's great. They really work."

"So I've heard."

"You've never actually used one? A hot-water bottle?" She was uncomfortably aware of the false animation in her voice.

"You mean those things we natives pull out for the tourists? Actually," he said, taking it from her and turning it over in his hands, "you'd never find anything so twee in England."

He tossed the hot-water bottle back on the bed and sat down next to her. "Tired?"

"Port after dinner? Is that how it works?"

He brushed a stray strand from her forehead. "Is that why you put up with me? To satisfy your insatiable curiosity about the habits of the British ruling class?"

"Pretty much." But she had to drop her eyes.

"Mmm," he said.

There was nowhere for her to go, backed against the pillows—but no, that wasn't how she felt about it. To prove it, she leaned forward determinedly to meet his lips. They kissed for a while—a long while—and it was the same as before. Smooth and perfect.

There had been lots of these picture-perfect kisses since that first one at her door. In the two weeks in between they'd started seeing each other more often—every other day, then almost every day. They had progressed to more than kisses, but not much more. Peter had asked, as if amused by the situation, how long Lynn had waited before sleeping with Jamie. She had been able to say, in complete honesty, "Until he said he loved me." This had temporarily silenced Peter, and she had not been required to clarify that this watershed event had taken place a mere four nights after she and Jamie first laid eyes on each other.

"May I?" said Peter, lifting a hand to her breast. Why did he have to ask? But it felt good, his hand on top of her soft sweater—a cashmere sweater she rarely got to wear in Los Angeles. His hand moved under the sweater, working that Peter magic so that her skin felt silky, alabaster, perfect.

"Wait!" she cried, not immediately, not by any means. Several items of clothing—of both of theirs—had slipped away.

"You're beautiful." He gazed down at her.

"I'm not." She turned her head away. She didn't doubt his sincerity.

"Lynn?"

She shook her head.

A lot of time seemed to pass before he said, "Ever?"

In one of the volumes Lynn had read during her blind march through Trollope, the heroine falls in love with a handsome bounder. She realizes her mistake soon enough, and there is a much nicer young man on the scene who begs her to be his wife. But she turns him away, operating under the unfortunate conviction that a girl can only give her love once. Other characters in the book, even the stiffest and most upright, beg her to reconsider, to allow herself and the worthy young man happiness. Lynn had stayed up until two in the morning to finish the book, sure that Trollope must give in at the last minute with some sort of happy reversal. But no, he remained true to his tale of a girl who let herself go too far with the wrong man (just kisses!), who crossed a line, if only in her own mind, that could not be uncrossed.

Lynn didn't know anymore what theories of love or fate she believed in. Hadn't she taken it for granted that she and Jamie were meant to be together forever, and that everyone else saw it that way, too? But no, the Jacquemet-Scovilles had never thought they belonged together. And that's who Jamie was with now. Although he'd said . . .

"Uh-oh," said Peter, "you're back to the way you were at the beginning, falling silent like that. I don't think I want to know what you're thinking."

Lynn lay still, eyes averted. How was it that Peter saw everything so clearly? Lynn had always thought that Jamie understood her so well—that had been the basis of everything, she'd thought. But he hadn't understood, and it had all turned into such a mess. And here was Peter, who seemed to see her so clearly, if in a completely different way. Didn't that mean something? But why had he asked? *May I? Ever?* If only he hadn't asked, if he'd just *done* it, wasn't there a chance she'd have gone through with it? Eventually? She half wished it had happened that way. That would have been better, easier. If he'd just waited, bided his time, nudging her a little further along each time. To say you know in advance how something's going to turn out is plain crazy. Anyway, Jamie had assumed she'd slept with him long ago.

Lynn realized that Peter was waiting. She flung an arm over her eyes. "I'm sorry," she said.

She heard his exhale. "Exhausted?" he said. After all that, he took pity on her.

She nodded, arm still covering her face.

"Shall I sleep on the floor?"

"That's all right," she said. If she could have known that Peter would find this most painful of all, her small, unconcerned smile at his offer of chivalry, she certainly would have spared him. She really was exhausted, and she settled back into the depression her body had made, facing away from him but close enough to feel the warmth of his presence. Men were warm. Almost immediately, she felt herself falling into sleep.

As she drifted off, she heard him laugh—a little spitefully?— "You're sure your husband won't mind your spending the night in bed with me?"

Thirty

Lynn kept waiting for Peter to make some reference to the night before, especially once they were away from the others, in the car on the way to the hotel for the morning's slate of screenings. But he didn't, so she didn't either. Instead he chatted away entertainingly about the filmmakers they'd be seeing that day, particularly a new young one he saw as quite promising. He somehow managed this without any obvious air of avoidance, although now and then Lynn did feel, just a tiny bit, like a convalescent left temporarily in his care. People came up to him all morning, and Peter introduced Lynn to them all, as if she were still someone significant in his life. As they left the last screening—there had been three shorts and one full-length feature, all before noon—a grandmotherly little woman hurried up to him. "Mr. Fairhaven?" she said.

He smiled politely, but when she kept nodding and beaming, he finally said, "Can I help you?"

"Oh, you already have! Your movie *Reunion*, it gave me new hope about love."

"Really?" said Peter.

"Now I may not look it, but I'm a pretty cynical old lady. But your movie! And it wasn't just that they ended up together again in the end—you made it clear there was still a pretty big 'if' there. But I thought, yes, that's what people should want—the risk is worth it!" She turned to Lynn. "Have you seen the movie?"

Peter turned to her, too.

"Yes," she said, hoping it just felt like she was blushing. "I liked it very much."

The woman gave Peter a birdlike nod with her chin. "I just wanted to tell you."

"Thank you," he called after her.

Piers and Julie were already there when Peter and Lynn got back to the house. Piers jumped up from the sofa and made his way straight to Lynn. He pulled her in for a too-lengthy hug, then held her away from him, beaming. "Your father changed my life!" He looked better than she remembered, ruddy-cheeked and brighter-eyed. "Harold, he's like . . . Words can't describe."

"Surely they can," said Hugo Stanhope. "That's what they're there for."

It was Lynn who initiated the embrace with Julie. "It's so good to see you," she said.

"Really?" said Julie. "I'm so glad. I was afraid I'd never get to see you again. Although I suppose that now that you and Peter . . ."

"How's Andy?" Lynn said quickly. "I've been thinking about him." Which was utterly untrue. Up until that moment she'd completely forgotten about Andy. She should have said something to Jamie.

Julie made a face but was interrupted by Piers. "You won't believe what I've been through," he said to Peter, who was standing behind Lynn, his hand on her shoulder, just like a couple. "You've met Lynn's father, right? No? You must! Two weeks, just two weeks with the man. Julie was an angel about it, weren't you, love? I feel like I finally know how to live my life. You should make a movie about it. I'm like an apostle now. It's my mission to spread the word."

"Well, save your testimony for the table, please," said Hugo. "Luncheon is on, and I'm famished. Piers, why don't you take in Lynn, offspring of the good prophet's loins?"

While their host dispatched everyone to their seats, Piers said to Lynn, "Julie told you about Andy? Tragic. I think he's making a big mistake. It's a fool's errand."

"What is?" said Lynn.

"He's on his way to Bruxelles." Piers pronounced it the French way, impeccably. "Didn't Julie tell you? He's going after Annika."

"Who are we talking about here?" said Hugo. Suddenly everyone at the table was listening.

"Julie's poor brother. His fiancée—well, she ran off with this other bloke. Met him in a disco, if you can believe that."

"Your brother-in-law's already engaged?" Hugo said with a glance toward Lynn.

"Well, it *was* pretty fast," said Piers. "But he thought he knew. Love at first sight." He shook his head. "Although that's what she says *she* has now with her little Eurotrash piece of shit. Love at first sight of his daddy's bank account, I'd say."

Hugo exchanged a look with Simon, the nice journalist with bad teeth, whose eyes went from Lynn to Peter. Lynn suddenly understood. "This is Julie's other brother," she said. "The younger one. Not my ex-husband."

"Jamie?" said Piers. "No, course not. He's a sensible bloke. He's the one we're staying with here."

Now it was Peter's turn to look up sharply. He was across

the table from Lynn, and his eyes rested on her, then moved away.

"Well, good riddance," said Nick. "Right? She must have been a tart."

"Sounds like your brother's well rid of her," kind Simon said to Julie.

"I know," said Piers. "Right? But try convincing Andy of that. He's gone after her. It turns out she's not married yet. She said it was happening right away, but I guess not. Hah! Still, he's only hurting himself."

"I disagree," said Julie in a clear, high voice.

"You disagree that it's a hopeless errand for Andy? Look, I know your mum's egging him on, all that Mayflower business. When actually, those blokes on the Mayflower weren't so . . . But I shouldn't complain, it's why she likes me, right? Poor Andy, though. His only reward will be a hard chuck between the ears. He'll come drooping back to us like Jonny on a bad day."

"Jonny?" said Lynn.

"Piers's favorite hound," said Julie. "Did I tell you he's taken up hunting, he's— But, anyway," she said, checking herself, as Andy's woes took precedence over her husband's sporting enthusiasms, "Piers is right about my mother, she's awful about that sort of thing." Another glance Lynn's way. "But my point is that Andy still loves Annika. He thinks he still loves her—although now we all know she's different than he thought. But he hasn't accepted that yet. So of course I'm not happy he's going to Europe after her. Of course I hope he doesn't succeed in getting her back. But I understand why he has to go. He needs to know he's done everything in his power to try to get her back. That's the sort of person he is. He doesn't take love lightly, he's an idealist, and I wouldn't want that part of him to change."

"But what if he does get her back?" said Nick.

"Exactly!" said Piers.

Julie shook her head. "How could he live with himself if he didn't try?"

"God help him," said Piers.

"Well," Julie said heatedly, "I wouldn't respect a person who loves someone one day and doesn't love them the next! Even if he's making a mistake, these are Andy's feelings now."

"But just to follow what you're saying through logically," said Hugo, "wouldn't you say that no matter how long it takes a person to get over someone, there does come a time when, one day, one wouldn't feel it anymore. We all know love doesn't always last forever. So to say that to admit to a demarcation is a character flaw . . . I'm sorry, but one day, or even say one minute, love is there; the next, it's not."

The dark-ringleted girl stirred in her seat.

"That's so English," cried Julie. "Your debate club sophistry! You know what I mean. I'm not saying I want my brother to succeed. He's better off without her. He'll realize that eventually—he'll see her for what she really is. It's not like I think this will break his heart forever. He's just out of college, practically! But I love and respect him for going after her. I wouldn't call that weak at all." She glared down the table, particularly at the men, then down at her plate.

Lynn had never seen Julie like this. She'd always thought of Jamie's sister as an untroubled little thing. Now she wondered what Julie had thought of her and Jamie's breakup, although she seemed to be speaking with no awareness that her words might easily have applied to them as well.

Julie looked up again, with an abashed smile. "But tell us," she said to Peter, "how's the film festival? Have you seen anything good?"

*   *   *

Lynn wished she could run away, but instead she just slipped upstairs—to the powder room, everyone would assume. She shut the bedroom door behind her. Maybe she could pretend not to feel well. That would solve everyone's problems. They were one ticket short for the best screening that afternoon. Simon was offering to skip it so that both Julie and Piers could go, and now everyone was calling around trying to scrounge another ticket. Even Peter was having difficulties finding one.

Lynn knew it was wrong, but she lay down on the lumpy bed. It had been made since morning, no sign of the hot-water bottle. She'd give herself a minute, maybe five. She reached for her book (which wasn't that good; she was getting to the bottom of the Trollope barrel). But before she could find her page, she heard a soft tapping. She sat up. Was it a knock? Then another, louder. When Lynn opened the door she found Julie there, arm raised as if about to throw a baseball, girl-style.

"I was just . . ." Julie said.

"Oh, is everyone ready to go?" Lynn had almost forgotten her new plan. She winced and hunched over a little.

"Are you okay?" Julie said.

"Oh, I'm fine. Just feeling a little—"

Julie nodded matter-of-factly. Which was odd. Usually she was so sweet and caring. "Can we talk?" she said.

"Of course." Lynn stepped back to let her into the room. "I really am so sorry about everything with Andy. I didn't get to tell Jamie . . ."

But Julie was rummaging in her shoulder bag. She thrust out a closed fist. Without thinking, Lynn put out her hands, and into them Julie dropped—Philippa's missing earrings.

"*You* had them?"

"Don't think badly of him!"

"Jamie?"

"No. Piers."

Lynn and Julie stared at each other for a long, confused moment. *Light-fingered Larry.*

"Why would Jamie have them?" said Julie. "Please don't blame him for my mother's bad behavior." Lynn sank down on the bed. Julie primly sat down next to her. "It's my fault," she said. "I should have told you. We came up after Thanksgiving, and that's when I found them."

"The earrings were here? In Tahoe?"

Julie shook her head. "In Piers's things. He took a clock, too—a gold thing. It had Jamie's name on it, a business thing, so I didn't think you'd care about that. I left the earrings here, in the dresser drawer in the room you guys use, because you always come after Christmas and then you'd find them."

"But Julie, I would have known I hadn't left them here. I never bring them to Tahoe. I never even wear them."

Jamie's sister shrugged wearily, and Lynn wondered how many found objects she'd had to replace as best she could.

Lynn held the earrings back out to Julie. She'd barely looked at them. "You should give them back to your mother. They're not mine."

"Yes, they are. I know the whole story. We've treated you horribly!"

A thought occurred to Lynn. "Julie? Does your mother know? About Piers?"

Julie made a face. "She figured it out right away. The first time Piers visited. He can't help himself—really he can't."

"What did she say?"

"My mother? Oh, you know—the funny, eccentric English. Really, Lynn, you can't hold her against all of us. And she knows you were good for Jamie, really she does. She just . . . she just can't bring herself to admit it. But you should hear her talking to her friends, about how cultured you are. 'A true bohemian spirit,' I once heard her say to her friends."

Lynn laughed. "I'm hardly bohemian."

"And she loved that you appreciated that Hermès belt. She always mentions that, that you have flair. I didn't want you to know about Piers. You guys have such high standards—I didn't want you to think less of him."

"Oh, Julie," said Lynn, feeling truly awful.

"I hate that girl," Julie cried. "I can't believe Jamie likes her. I *don't* believe it."

Lynn was aware of her own breathing as they sat there together on the lumpy bed, her own heartbeat. She was curious about Julie's train of thought, how one comment led to the next. Lynn wished she would burst out with more information. But she drew back from this thought—and physically, a tiny bit, from Julie. Any eagerness to hear more would be unseemly, and wouldn't do either of them justice. "Did Jamie tell you we saw each other?" she said.

"No! When?"

"Here. Yesterday. I went by the house."

"Why?"

Lynn looked down. "I don't know. It was stupid." What did it mean, that Jamie hadn't mentioned it to Julie? "Does Jamie know you're here now?"

"Of course." Julie looked confused. "We had to tell him where we were going for lunch."

"Does he know about . . ."

Julie tossed her head in disgust. "Why do you think he let her get her claws into him? Oh, Lynn!"

Julie thought she'd been asking about Peter, Lynn realized. All she'd meant was whether Jamie knew about the earrings.

"I'll be glad when he goes back to school," Julie said.

"School?"

"You know, graduate school. Architecture."

She meant Jamie. For a moment Lynn had thought they were back to Piers—that perhaps he was going back to her father. "Since when?" said Lynn.

"Well, he's always wanted to." Julie looked at Lynn—surely she knew that. "I don't know why he never did. My mother, probably."

And maybe me, too, thought Lynn.

"Oh," Julie said, her face easing, "you mean when did he decide to apply. So he didn't mention it? It's funny, he hadn't said a word about it to us, either, but it was practically the first thing he said last night when we got in. I was hoping it was to get away from that girl. Oh, Lynn, are things really serious with Peter? No, sorry," she said, jumping up from the bed. "It's none of my business. Of course you should do whatever you want. I've already said too much." In one step, she was at the door. "We should probably get back downstairs."

"Julie, wait."

Jamie's sister turned back to her reluctantly. "I shouldn't have said so much about Barb."

"Would you do me a really big favor?" Lynn said, standing, too. "I was going to tell everyone I'm not feeling great, but the truth is, I just don't feel like being with everyone and going to the screenings."

Julie stared at her for a moment, her eyes going back and forth across Lynn's face, then she nodded slowly. "Do you want me to tell them for you? I can do that. You can just stay up here."

"I'll come down, but if you said something first . . ."

Julie was nodding, eagerly now. "I know, that makes it easier. You sure you don't want to go . . . with Peter?"

"I saw so many this morning," Lynn said, almost plaintively. "And this way Simon can go."

"You don't have to explain. Not to me." Julie had a funny, pleased expression. "But will you call me? Sometime? Jamie's leaving for New York tomorrow, but we're staying the rest of the week."

"I'm leaving tomorrow, too," Lynn said. "My sisters are coming into town."

"Oh, please say hello from me. I was always so envious of your sisters. And Lynn," she said as she slipped through the door. "Please don't think too badly of him."

This time, Lynn knew Julie meant Piers. But she wasn't thinking of Piers at all.

Thirty-one

H e's a thief?" Sasha's voice rose above the low hum in the dark, somewhat dingy coffeehouse on Abbot Kinney Boulevard, causing a head or two to swivel.

"More like a kleptomaniac," Lynn said, lowering her own voice in hopes that her sister would follow.

"And Jamie didn't know?"

"He's only a kleptomaniac," said Dee, "if he doesn't know what he's doing."

"I think we know what kleptomaniac means, Dee," Sasha said. The sisters, when together for any length of time ("any length of time" encompassing as short a slice as ten minutes), reverted back to their adolescent selves, at least intermittently.

Their visit was a last-minute one. Shortly after hearing about Lynn's impending weekend with the director, her sisters had announced that they'd both be in Los Angeles the following week, getting in on Monday. Sasha's story was that she wanted one last visit before she was too pregnant to fly, and Kam would be out for a week anyway with some longtime customers. Dee, who still had that deal in San Diego, figured she'd pop up to see Sasha. Lynn had smiled to herself at their concern. Now she gazed fondly at them across the small, scarred table, crowded with glasses and foam-rimmed latte cups. "I've missed you guys so much," she said. "I'm so happy you're here."

"I can't believe you didn't sleep with him," Dee said. "I never thought he was it, but weren't you curious?" Lynn had finally told her sisters about the perfect movie kisses. "You're so old-fashioned, Lynn."

"I'm not old-fashioned." They also knew about her Trollope obsession. "I just didn't want to. Why did you think he wasn't it?"

Dee shrugged.

"I would have slept with him," said Sasha. "Although actually, you never know. Someone's who's that good a kisser, it almost makes you suspicious what they're making up for." Sasha styled herself a wild child and a woman of the world, but in fact her husband, Kam, was the only man she'd ever had sex with.

"I'm sure he's quite good in bed," Lynn said.

"So strange," said Dee, "going through the whole next day like that, no talking about it. I don't think even Jamie would be that bad."

"He was probably relieved I stayed at the house that afternoon," Lynn said. "And then he had to sit up on the stage at the award ceremony that night, and I left for the airport first thing in the morning. I was able to change my flight."

"What did his friends say?" said Dee.

"We acted as though that had been the plan all along, because of you guys coming."

"So, what are you going to do about the earrings?" asked Sasha.

"I'll return them, of course."

"Why? To whom?"

Lynn shrugged. "I guess I'll mail them back to Philippa. Well insured."

"It's so funny that Philippa knew about Piers," Dee said. "You can just see it—in her mind it probably made him even more aristocratic. Just one of those foibles the nobility pick up at public school."

"At least no one in our lowly peasant family steals," said Sasha. "It's just what Little Miss Perfect Garden Club Milquetoast deserves."

"No, Julie's nice," said Lynn.

Sasha turned to her sharply.

"Piers is, too." Lynn was going to stop there, but then she added, "He's funny, and he has a good heart. They seem really happy together. They clearly adore each other."

Sasha and Dee exchanged a glance.

Sasha pushed her empty cup away from her. "Do you have them with you?" she said. "The earrings?"

Lynn was about to deny it. But she reached for her purse. She had found a small Chinese silk pouch when she got home, and for reasons not quite clear to herself she was carrying the earrings around in it, zippered into a side compartment of her purse. She extracted the little bag and without untying the drawstring pushed it across the table to Sasha. Sasha shook out an earring and held it first to her ear, then to Lynn's. "They really are pretty," she said. "They suit you."

"No, they don't."

"You know who they really don't seem like?" said Dee. "Philippa."

"She got them from *her* mother-in-law," said Lynn. "Whom she hated. You're lucky," she said to Sasha, "Kam's mother is so sweet."

"Yeah, but she's driving me crazy about the baby."

Dee pushed the earrings along the table toward Lynn. "Put them on, why don't you."

"Yes, let's see them," said Sasha. "Just for a minute."

Reluctantly Lynn picked them up. They had old-fashioned looped catches that went through the ear.

"Here, let me," said Sasha, and deftly slipped in the earrings, first one, then the other. She sat back to look, giving her head a coquettish little shake, as if she were the one with them on.

"They're perfect," said Dee. "You never wear things like that."

"They're not me."

"Yes, they are," said Sasha. "Just a different you. Wear them to your appointment. They make you look, I don't know, important."

The reason the three sisters were meeting in Venice was that Lynn had an appointment for work nearby. Mona had called before Lynn left town for the weekend and had asked if she could meet her at a Santa Monica address at eleven A.M. on Monday. This request had been quite clearly, purposefully, cloaked in Mona-mystery, and Lynn had refrained from pushing for details.

"How is work, anyway?" said Dee. "Are you still worried?"

"Not really. Just . . . I don't know. There's so much I haven't even told you yet—about this other English guy I met there, the arts editor at this big paper in London, although you'd never know it, he's so nice. It was embarrassing. I assumed he was just some lowly hack. But he told me about this most amazing artist who just moved here and says I should meet her. And—"

"We'll be seeing you again, though, today," said Dee. "For dinner, right?"

Sasha laughed, stroked her stomach. "We're going to be eating the entire day. Seriously. We already had breakfast this morning with Mom, now this—she wanted to come, but we wouldn't let her, she gets you all the time. And we're meeting Robin for lunch."

"Both of you?" Dee was no more friends with Robin than Lynn had been.

"Robin hasn't seen Dee for ages," said Sasha. "She thinks she has this guy she wants to set her up with."

"In New York?"

"I think now that she's so happy and settled, she wants everyone else to be. Robin always was the *Hello, Dolly* type."

Lynn thought of Robin's taut-as-a-rubber-band arms. "Robin's met someone?"

Sasha looked at her.

"What?" said Lynn.

"Uh, your friend?"

"Who? What are you talking about?"

"Your friend F. X."

"With Robin? No, she's just his real estate agent." Then Lynn remembered a voice mail from F. X. that she hadn't bothered to answer: *Thanks so much for introducing me to Robin. She's amazing—changed my life—and M. J.'s, too. She found us a great place.* She now even remembered the sardonic chuckle. *I think I'm in love.* And right before Lynn had left for Tahoe, Glynnis had surprised her by saying something breezy about F. X., how there was no competing with true love. Lynn had assumed she meant Chaka.

"You didn't hear that the mother is giving him custody?" said Sasha. "Full custody. Can you imagine?" She shook her head. "It sounds like she met some guy with a yacht and wants to go off . . ."

"Wait a minute," said Dee, "the mother's *saying* F. X. can have full custody, or legally he's getting custody? Does F. X. have a good lawyer?"

Both sisters turned to her in disbelief.

Sasha resumed. "Robin adores the little boy, too. She always was good with children. Before she went into real estate, she thought about being a kindergarten teacher."

Lynn tried to imagine this, to envision the whole domestic scene, and found to her surprise that she could. She remembered F. X. saying he wanted to trade in his sports car, and thought of Robin's unexpectedly rinky-dink car. He'd probably want her to get something more substantial, too. A Volvo? Lynn could see Robin happily driving the family Volvo, little M. J. in the backseat.

"Speaking of which," said Dee, "what are *you* going to do? Finally?"

"Do?" said Lynn. "No, I think it's great."

"I mean about Jamie."

"What am I supposed to do? It's done."

"That's not how it sounded," said Dee. "From your description, it doesn't sound done at all. Where's he going to be? Which architecture school? Has he already applied?"

"Do you want it to be done?" said Sasha.

"You're forgetting that he's seeing someone else now," said Lynn.

"You said Julie said you basically pushed him into her arms. Not that I think Julie knows anything," Sasha added, almost defiantly.

"If he wanted—"

Dee smacked her hand down on the table; cups and saucers rattled. "Please tell me this isn't about waiting for the man to call. Ella Kovak's daughter? If Mom were dead she'd be rolling in her grave."

"Of course, I'm not waiting for him to call," said Lynn.

"What then?"

"Seriously, Lynn," said Sasha, "what do you want?"

Lynn rose abruptly. The table tottered, the cups and saucers jounced again.

"Where are you going?" said Dee. "Oh, your appointment. Do you need to go already?"

"I don't know," she said wildly. She glanced down at her watch. She really did have to go. "I have to think."

"Don't think," said Sasha, who had been watching her sister closely all this time. "*Do.*"

When Lynn continued to stand there, next to the cluttered table, Sasha waved a hand at her. "Go, go," she said. "Don't worry, we'll take care of the check."

Look at you!" Mona Frumpke held out both hands to Lynn, her squared-off nails as deeply shellacked as a Porsche. "What fabulous earrings." She took Lynn's chin in her scary forefinger and thumb to turn her head from one side to the other. Lynn had the not wholly comforting feeling that she had impressed beyond expectation.

"So here's what I wanted to talk to you about," Mona said, guiding Lynn to a chair in front of a large, glass-topped desk before resuming her seat on the other side.

Lynn hadn't known that Mona had an actual office, and certainly never imagined so businesslike an arrangement. The office was sleek and vivid, with bright yellow walls and white leather upholstery. Every piece of furniture was a Modernist icon. Lynn was steered to an Arne Jacobsen Swan chair; the desk was a huge sheet of glass balanced on two Warren Platner wire bases; the sofa near the door, Florence Knoll.

"I'm sure you already heard the murmurs and bruits around town, about our little project?" Mona raised an arched eyebrow, reddish-brown today, delicate as an insect's antennae. Lynn merely smiled and inclined her head, hoping this would be interpreted as knowledge. To her frustration, Mona seemed to abandon the subject. "Have you seen any work you like lately?" she said. "Young artists?"

"Actually, it's funny you ask. I just heard this past weekend of someone who sounds really interesting. I'm supposed to meet her next week. Ilona Rostov."

"Russian? Like in *War and Peace*? Sounds old-fashioned. No, I haven't heard of her."

"She's English but recently moved here. And there is something old-fashioned about her work. I think you'd like it, at least from the pictures I've seen. It reminds me of Jessica Klein."

Mona tossed her head. "I don't like to do the same thing twice."

"It's not that her work is similar." Inexplicably, Lynn felt her confidence grow. "I'd say it's more that there might be something similar brewing underneath." *Part of the same movement*, Lynn wanted to say—but that seemed too grandiose. "She does these incredibly beautiful, detailed nude drawings—and yes, I did think of Jessica when I saw them. Don't you think there's something heartbreaking in Jessica's work? Just the sheer beauty of it? Maybe that it's about love. Or the desire for love? And then when I saw Ilona's work, I had the urge to write a paper or article about it, discussing the two, or . . . or"—her neck and chest felt hot—"put together an exhibit or something. Although for that, of course, you'd need at least one more artist, they're so young and unknown."

Mona narrowed her eyes. "How did you come across this girl?"

"A British arts writer named Simon Funnelston. He was really the one who found her. He just did an article for—"

"I am very aware of Simon Funnelston and for whom he writes," said Mona. "Simon Funnelston," she repeated. "Impressive. This was through Peter Fairhaven?"

"Yes." Lynn hesitated, wondering if it would be held against her. "But I'm not seeing him anymore."

"Really?" Mona looked interested.

Lynn maintained a steady gaze although she was dying to look away. There must have been some movement, some tremble; the elaborate golden earrings swayed against her neck. Mona pushed herself up from behind the desk and came around to Lynn's side. Lynn stood, too, wondering if this was her dismissal. But Mona walked over to the sofa and patted the cushion next to her.

"I wasn't going to tell you this," she said, "but Smitty showed me that memo you sent him, about Jessica. He was amused. I, however, was impressed. It was so beyond your scope of responsibility, and so impassioned. And once I'd met you, I realized it was your light touch behind all those fabulously witty attribution labels next to all those—I'm sorry, dear—but dreary paintings on the museum's walls. 'The gift of a grateful Board of Trustees in thanks to Mrs. Quentin L. Leib, née Heller, who leaves us,' et cetera, et cetera. Grateful to have finally been able to shove her off the board! And she made you put in that 'née Heller' part, didn't she? Fabulous! I laughed out loud. Like reading an entire history of the museum's rocky board meetings in code." Lynn opened her mouth to protest, but Mona raised a hand. "Don't say a word. Smitty's going to shoot me for doing this, but that's exactly the touch—the tone, I should say—we're looking for. You're wasted in education, my dear, and I don't think Smitty's right to be guiding you toward development, although it's certainly a quicker way to the top, and you've been very lucky there. Of course, with a smaller institution, everyone has to be more a jack-of-all-trades."

Lynn tried to keep an intelligent, inquisitive look on her face.

"There's a place at the new museum for you if you want it. It's going to be very small at first—the museum, not your place in it! But it's a different beast altogether, so you need to think about what you're looking for and if this is really the right thing for you. I can't be more specific at the moment, but I'd love to have you on board from the start. It's a risky move, I'll tell you, although I can assure you that the funding, the initial funding, is all in place. It's all contemporary art, though—does that interest you?" Mona asked this last question with a smile, as if she already knew the answer. "The site's here, in Venice, but it's not going to be provincial, not if I can help it. There will be some travel—probably just New York at first. Does that bother you?"

"No . . . no," floundered Lynn.

"In fact, if you could manage it, I'd love for you to take a trip to New York. Soon. Sort of a test run, to be frank. Do you think you could come up with some excuse to take a day or two off? There are some people I want you to be introduced to, and actually an artist whose work will interest you. This week would be ideal. Things are happening quickly now."

"Sure," Lynn said, staring at Mona in something like wonderment, "I can do that."

"Fabulous. I love that, turning on a dime. Hah! This is a good sign indeed!"

"I'm not usually like that," Lynn felt compelled to say.

"No, but when the time is right." Mona leaned forward—the two women were sitting quite close—and put her hands over Lynn's. Lynn thought she was about to say something profound or congratulatory, but what she said was, "Those really are extraordinary earrings. Wherever did you find them?"

"These?" Lynn raised a hand to them. "They were my mother-in-law's."

"And she gave them to you?"

Lynn nodded.

"Lucky girl, she must like you." Mona sighed. "I've given my daughter-in-law jewelry. Several lovely things, if I do say so myself. She never wears them. I never can seem to please her."

This was so odd. Lynn had thought the meeting was over. It had felt like an end. "I didn't know you had a daughter-in-law," she said.

Again Mona sighed. "I have one son. They got married four years ago. She's a darling girl, really. I don't have a thing to say against her. Except that I've tried my hardest and she doesn't seem to like me."

"I can't believe that's true, Mona."

"Oh, it is."

"Why do you say she doesn't seem to like you?" Lynn said carefully.

"She's cool to me—very cool. Whenever I try to make an offer, she says, no, no, don't go to the trouble. My son says she can tell I don't approve of her, but that's not true at all. Maybe I don't agree with her taste all the time—to be honest, it's very pedestrian, but not bad. She just needs a little educating."

"I was probably the same way to my mother-in-law," Lynn said, thinking of how stiff and unbending and defensive she'd been. "She probably says the same things about me."

"I doubt that. You're a doll."

Lynn had to laugh. "Mona, I'm always on my best behavior with you. The sad thing is, if we end up working together, you'll come to see all my flaws."

"There's nothing sad about that," Mona said crisply, back to her usual self, standing and extending her hand. "I look forward to it."

Thirty-two

The elevator doors slid open. The architect's New York offices were big and white, with white desks and cubicles and an overflowing clutter of books and papers—not unlike the museum offices. Les Hatchett even had some good art up on the walls, including, Lynn noticed, a series of Josef Albers lithographs hung in a row next to the elevators.

"Can I help you?" said the receptionist, whose desk was placed to one side at the front of the loftlike space. Les Hatchett had the two upper floors in a nondescript midtown building and clearly did not believe in impressing clients with the money spent on his own workplace.

"That's okay, I'm Jamie Prosper's wife. I know where to find him." This was a lie, but Lynn marched self-confidently past the desk, past the woman's startled expression. Fortunately, several phone lines began to ring at once, and the receptionist, who looked very young, turned to them instead.

Around the periphery of the offices, near the windows, stood a line of drafting tables where the architects presumably worked. Lynn scanned the row but did not see Jamie. She tapped the shoulder of a young woman working at one of the near tables. "Excuse me, I'm looking for Jamie Prosper."

"Oh, Jamie, he's upstairs, I think. They should just be finishing their meeting." She gestured to a white wrought-iron spiral staircase, belle époque style, that Lynn had failed to notice in the middle of the open space.

"I'm his wife," Lynn said over her shoulder, smiling to herself as she made her way up the narrow stairs.

Lynn couldn't quite believe she was doing this. Yet that thought wasn't accompanied by any sense of nervousness or unease. If she'd had to describe herself at that moment—to her sisters, say—she would have pronounced, *She sailed on imperturbably*. She could have further analyzed her own choice of phrase by pointing out that her use of third person indicated the sense of detachment she was feeling from her own actions. All these thoughts flew around Lynn's brain, and underneath, like the thrum of a ship's motor, "Jamie, Jamie, Jamie."

Then there he was, coming out of a conference room carved from the raw, industrial space by pressboard and a tall, pale wood door. She was almost to the top of the staircase when he saw her.

"Lynn! What are you doing here?"

"Oh, I just dropped in." She felt as though she should be wearing a cunning hat with a feather in it. Jamie looked astounded. She was not displeased to see Les Hatchett follow Jamie out of the room, engrossed in conversation with another, younger man.

"Why, Mr. Hatchett," she said, moving smoothly forward with her hand extended. "You probably don't remember me, but we met at the museum in Los Angeles. Lynn Prosper, Jamie's wife."

The architect looked surprised, but recovered himself and shook her hand warmly.

"You're not by any chance breaking for lunch?" she said, clasping his hand with both of hers as she imagined Mona might. "I was hoping to steal Jamie away for a bit." She winked broadly at Les Hatchett. "Some unfinished business. Ready?" she said, turning to Jamie. She took him by the arm, practically dragging him down the clattery staircase. Halfway down she turned to look back at Les Hatchett, who was watching them with an air of indecision. "I really appreciate this," she called up to him. "Just a little longer, and I'll have no more claim on him."

"Just what do you think you're doing?" Jamie hissed when they were safely out of sight at the bottom.

"Let's get out of here. You know you want to escape."

"That's my boss!"

"Do you want to go back?" She was herding him toward the elevators. "Is there a coat or anything you need to get?"

"No!" Then, "You're crazy."

Lynn smiled. She'd won—this part, at least.

"Jamie!" It was a woman's caw.

"There's something we need to talk about," Lynn whispered hastily to Jamie. "I really don't want to do it here." Then she turned to confront Barb Hatchett. Jamie, she noted, did not.

"Jamie!" repeated Barb, her whole posture a stamped foot, and Jamie had to turn. "Where are you going? What about lunch?"

"Oh," said Lynn, "did the two of you have plans? I should have called ahead. Now Barbara, you don't mind if I steal Jamie? Just for an hour or two. We have some last details to go over. I'm sure you want everything to move forward smoothly with the divorce."

"Of course—I mean, no, I don't, that's between the two of you." Barb drew herself up while shooting Jamie a look, but a confused one. "Why didn't you mention that Lynn was in New York? You told me *we'd* have lunch."

"I didn't know," he said.

"It was a last-minute trip," said Lynn. "And I don't have much time." She reached for the elevator button.

The receptionist was watching, rapt. The architect's daughter must have realized this, too. She stepped back. "Well," she said, "I'm glad I saw you, Jamie. It would have been rude to just stand me up."

"You should see what he does when he's married to you!" Lynn said gaily. The elevator door opened and she stepped in, taking Jamie with her.

Jamie strode down the street. Lynn, so surprisingly in control moments ago, hurried to keep up with him. What should she say now? The simple yet inarguable *Please, I don't want to get divorced*?

"How's Andy?" she said. "I heard . . ."

"He's home again."

"And, um, Annika?"

"Still in Brussels."

Lynn thought that was all she was going to get out of him, but after a few more steps he said, "They're not married yet, even though she said they would be. But I guess she's planning on staying there with him."

"Oh," said Lynn. Once again she saw Barb with Annika's wedding dress, stroking the fur trim every night.

"You lied," Jamie said. "You had the earrings all along."

She slowed at this. Julie hadn't told him? That was funny—as though she'd decided to leave it to Lynn.

But Jamie was still marching along.

"I didn't have them," she called after him, hurrying again to catch up. "I can—" She'd been about to say, "I can explain."

She said, "I'll tell you the whole story if we can stop walking for a minute. Is there somewhere we can go?"

"Here," he said, coming to a halt in front of a doorway. "We can go up."

Lynn looked up at the bland brick building. "Is this where you live?"

He gave her a look as if despairing of her intelligence.

In the small elevator she tried again. "You seem so angry with me."

He made an exasperated sound and reached into his jacket. He handed her a slim paper folder.

"What is it?" But she could see for herself. It was an airline ticket. Jamie Prosper, it said. JFK to LAX. And the date on it was the following day's.

The elevator doors opened. "You spoiled my plan," he said, and they stepped out. In the long, drab hallway, Lynn threw herself into his arms. "Really?" she said.

He looked down at her, and his face relaxed—her old Jamie. She smiled back at him, waiting. Now was the time for him to bring his lips to hers. "I'm sorry I spoiled your plan," she said. And could have kicked herself. Why couldn't she shut up and wait? But now he *was* lowering his face toward her, and at the same time—she couldn't help herself—she sort of flung herself up at him. They overbalanced and Jamie's head hit the wall. Lynn's mouth opened in concern—and he kissed her. He turned her in his arms, and now she was against the hideous brown wallpaper, now he was. When they came up for air she noticed that the hallway smelled like cabbage. Lynn literally turned up her nose at Les Hatchett, at Barb Hatchett, and all their wealth and fame. So much for bloodless movie kisses, too.

"Come on," Jamie said, digging his keys out of his pocket. There were three different locks he had to open with three different keys. He, too, struggled with his new door. Inside, he emptied his pockets onto a small entry table, just the way he used to at the wet bar counter in their house. She took in the swooping shapes of two overstuffed, burgundy velvet sofas, the ornate marble fireplace they flanked, the zebra-striped rug they stood on. Lynn had never liked Barb, but still, she was shocked by the decor. An Art Deco mirror hung over the fireplace, with églomisé glass sconces on either side. Jamie came over and pulled her down on one of the sofas. They sank back into it, thrown off balance. It was too deep.

"I know, I know," he said.

"I don't know how you've been living here." They both sighed happily. Lynn tried to get comfortable on the sofa in his arms, but it was difficult. It was almost as if the puffy cushions were trying to throw them apart. It didn't matter.

Eventually, though, Jamie did try to right himself. "I do need to explain," he said.

"No. You don't."

"When I got here, and was suddenly doing work I really liked, it's true, part of me didn't want to go back."

"If I hadn't been so mad," she said, sitting up now, too, "I would have told you that I didn't mind moving to New York—no problem."

"Really? You would have done that for me?"

"Happily."

"I . . . I was going to ask, but then . . ."

"Shh." But then she said, "Don't you worry that we're going to have the same problems all over again?"

"No." He was studying her eyes, looking first into one, then the other.

"Really?"

"We'll probably have the same fights, but we'll know better than to break up over them."

"And I'll never say I hate you again."

He grinned.

"Okay, but I'll try."

"I know you don't mean it," he said.

"It's an awful thing to say—you're right. I shouldn't say it to anyone."

"I was the awful one. I filed for divorce."

"You thought I'd cheated on you."

"What was I thinking?"

"Actually, there is one lie I told you. Not the earrings, something else."

A very slight furrow appeared on Jamie's forehead.

"It's not really anything," she said quickly. "I just want to clear the air, start fresh. And it was so stupid."

For a moment he looked as though he didn't want to know. "Fine," he said. "What is it?"

"You asked about it—when F. X., in front of the Jacquemet-Scovilles, apologized for having kissed me?"

The furrow deepened, but Lynn saw Jamie will it smooth again. "Yes?"

It was like exhaling, to get to tell him everything—about F. X. pulling her into the bizarre room with all the gilded chairs at Mona's art party, how he had showed up at Mona's, and even what he had said about *épater le bourgeois*. "Oh, and I lied about driving myself to the restaurant, that first night we had dinner. I didn't want to go with him in his car! I just didn't know how to get out of it."

"That's it?" Jamie said. "I can't believe you were worried about *that*. And I have no right to be jealous about Peter Fairhaven. We both slept with other people."

Lynn went still.

"Just so you know," he went on, "I wasn't, not all along. Just after . . . but neither of us did anything wrong. We were separated, getting a divorce. I think we got unhinged without each other. In a way it probably made us realize what we'd lost."

Lynn managed to keep her face steady—even made the effort to soften her eyes more. Oh, the irony of it. She couldn't tell him the truth right then. She had no interest in having any superiority over Jamie—not sexual, not moral, nothing. He was right, they were even. They'd been equally foolish, equally quick tempered, had equally fallen victim to pride.

"I didn't feel like myself without you," she said, and while she was aware of how happy she felt, how relieved, there was something bittersweet there, too. She'd been given a frightening intimation of what life would be like—of how lonely and *wrong* it would be—without Jamie. What if, when they were old, he died before she did? She wrapped herself in his arms on the ridiculous velvet sofa. The time would come when she'd tell him the whole truth about Peter, and he'd probably even be happy about it then. There was so much to tell, about her possible new job, and Robin and F. X., and how even Sasha's sweet mother-in-law could be annoying, and that her own mother had been on his side. And was he really going to go back to graduate school? If so, it was doubly good that they'd sold the house and the new apartment was so cheap—and he hadn't even seen the tiny spare room yet!

But if there was one thing Lynn had learned from all this, it was that there was plenty of time for everything to come out. Especially if you were going to spend your lives together.

Jamie stroked her cheek, making an earring bob.

"Hey," he said, "aren't you going to tell me about these?"

Lynn turned her face to him, eager to begin.

Acknowledgments

I cannot thank Lisa Michel and Susan Kandel enough for their help with this book—for their excellent, thoughtful advice and also their long forbearance. Thanks, too, to Jean Hanff Korelitz, whose generosity as a writer is outweighed only by her generosity as a friend; to Brian Morton, for helping me turn the corner; to "civilians" Susie Huang and Lynn Johnson Kidder for giving me hope; and to Caryn Karmatz Rudy and Jackie Cantor, for their astute and exceedingly kind shepherding. I'm grateful to Tom Rosch for many reasons, not least for showing me the awful truth; and I want to thank Catherine and Amelia for their understanding when I had to turn my attention to this less perfect, less beautiful third child. I took too long for my grandparents, Rose and Milt Forman, and my mother, Vicki Michel, to be able to read my thanks here, but my debt to them is immense.